FRANKIE GOSLING

An intriguing and touching life story inspired by true events

FRANKIE GOSLING

An intriguing and touching life story inspired by true events

Fiction based on real events, by
NOLWEN JONES

Copyright © 2025 Nolwen Jones

The moral right of the author has been asserted.

Apart from any fair dealing for the purposes of research or private study, or criticism or review, as permitted under the Copyright, Designs and Patents Act 1988, this publication may only be reproduced, stored or transmitted, in any form or by any means, with the prior permission in writing of the publishers, or in the case of reprographic reproduction in accordance with the terms of licences issued by the Copyright Licensing Agency. Enquiries concerning reproduction outside those terms should be sent to the publishers.

The manufacturer's authorised representative in the EU for product safety is Authorised Rep Compliance Ltd,
71 Lower Baggot Street, Dublin D02 P593 Ireland (www.arccompliance.com)

All people and events in this publication are fictitious and any resemblance to real persons living or dead is purely coincidental

Troubador Publishing Ltd
Unit E2 Airfield Business Park
Harrison Road, Market Harborough
Leicestershire LE16 7UL
Tel: 0116 279 2299
Email: books@troubador.co.uk
Web: www.troubador.co.uk

ISBN 978 1 83628 074 3

British Library Cataloguing in Publication Data.
A catalogue record for this book is available from the British Library.

Printed and bound in Great Britain by 4edge Limited
Typeset in 11pt Minion Pro by Troubador Publishing Ltd, Leicester, UK

Cover illustration by Dave Hill

This book is dedicated to my brother, his children and his grandchildren, with the hope that it is passed down the generations to provide an insight into the historical roots of our family and that my nieces and nephew, their children and their children's children will think of me when I am gone!

Prologue

My Parents

My father, who would, through exasperation, often become cross with my mother, was – if she had only realised it – a great family man. He was never tactile with his children, either lovingly or otherwise, but did have a strict approach to our upbringing and instilled honesty, good behaviour and good manners in us. A promise was a promise and there was no manipulation of the truth.

Outside of keeping promises and being honest, it was particularly important to my father that my brother Steffan and I learned the importance of being loyal, punctual and reliable at an early age. Laziness was not tolerated; we were encouraged as brother and sister to compromise and share. We were also reminded, repeatedly, to be respectful, polite and considerate of others.

Jobs were scarce in the remote area of Wales where we lived. Most men worked in farming or had businesses that supported the tourist industry. The coast was a few miles away from our home and was dotted with picturesque villages and attractive traditional ports. Our little local town was often overwhelmed by visiting families from England during the summer months. Steffan and I welcomed the children of those families, but – like other children in the area – we were rather cautious with that welcome, feeling a little intimidated by anyone with an English accent or whose parents owned caravans and posh cars. My father – like other local Welshmen – was grateful for his job, which allowed him to "only just" support his family. Working for the government, as an electrician's assistant, offered little in the way of promotion and there was no real career path for people like him. With no means of transport to get to colleges in the nearest big town to attend training courses, and insufficient funds for accommodation, career progression was almost impossible, even for those who were well motivated.

I remember one autumn, at the end of British Summer Time, my father forgot to put the clocks back. He did not own a watch. This act of forgetfulness meant he missed the bus to work, so he had to walk fifteen miles to ensure he did not let his colleagues down. Tea breaks were allowed twice a day and the men could purchase tea or coffee in the work canteen. My father would often continue working instead of taking a break. He was too proud to let his fellow workers see that he didn't have the money to buy a cup of tea every day and, even worse, be considered "tight". The exact opposite was true; he would have given his last penny to anyone in need and was a generous, kind and very agreeable man.

My father's priority, outside of his work, was his family. He had been one of eight children and his young life had been hard. He was often bullied by his elder brothers and his parents had little time to spare to address the needs of each child. At the age of ten, after falling into a stream and fearing the wrath of his mother, he attempted to dry his wet clothes around a campfire. It was thought that putting on damp clothes before going home led to him developing rheumatic fever, the consequences of which, although not apparent at the time, were to influence the rest of his life and, ultimately, ours.

His mother (Grandma Jones), although strict, did her best to keep her children well fed. She was a superb cook and thought that dinner-table etiquette and table manners were imperative. This table discipline was replicated in our own home. As a family, we always sat down for meals together. We ate what was given or went without. Serving dishes, serving spoons, side plates and cups on saucers were the order of the day, even though none of our crockery matched and most of the vegetables came out of a tin.

Grandad Jones, often watched by my father, was a skilled carpenter, whose eyesight was so poor that he needed his face to be just a few inches from his wood, which necessitated hunching his back to use his tools for ten hours or so each working day. After a hard day's work, aching and bent over, his only pleasures were his cigarettes, a drop of whisky and an evening in front of the coal fire. Outside of sharing his skills at carpentry when the children ventured into his workshop, there was little interaction with his children.

Following in his father's footsteps, my father was very gifted practically, making furniture for the house and toys for me and my brother. One Christmas, we woke up to find a wonderful handcrafted doll's house for me and a huge wooden fort for my brother under the Christmas tree. These gifts were followed in later years by homemade go-karts, kites, hamster cages and a hand-carved huge wooden "key of the door", which, as I no longer lived at home when I received it, was sent through the post to me on my eighteenth birthday. I don't remember my mother or father receiving gifts from each other.

My father – as was the case with many fathers during the 1960s, but which likely wouldn't have been the case today – wanted to ensure that whatever the "tendencies" of my brother, he was going to do everything in his power to ensure that Steffan would grow up to be a man with no feminine inclinations. My brother put in a request for an Action Man in his letter to Santa one Christmas, but this was scribbled over emphatically by my father, who insisted my brother was never going to be allowed to play with dolls. Although I loved my father's home-made toys, the best gift he ever gave to me was the one that lasted the longest – the benefit of his advice.

He instilled in me the importance of being ladylike, advising me that while men whistled, ladies sang, and that women sat properly with their legs crossed or knees together, did not slouch, and that they walked gracefully, with their toes pointing forwards. Following this latter advice, I checked my feet while walking and realised that my stride was like that of a boy. I took rather large steps and my feet were splayed. For the next few months, I focused on my feet when I walked, keeping my toes pointing forwards. Today, I notice how many women walk with splayed feet. My father was correct in his view; it is not very flattering. Later in life, I considered myself to be an elegant and very feminine woman, improved by the fact that I had feet that pointed in the right direction of travel! The credit for all of this went to my father. I never told him how much I appreciated his advice.

When he reached his early twenties, all my father desired was to escape from his elder brothers, have a job, a good wife and a comfortable albeit rented home. He wanted children who could benefit from an upbringing that, in many ways, would be different to his own. Often, though, his parental guidance conflicted with the example set by my mother, whose opinions, values and standards were often different to those of my father.

My mother was English and moved to Wales with her family in her adult years. She was an illegitimate baby and never knew her father. Her upbringing was shared between her grandmother and her own God-fearing, forbidding and austere mother (known by everyone as Granny Lane) and my grandmother's brothers, who were remembered by my mother as being gentle and kind uncles. All my grandmother's siblings grew up to be professionals in different fields. The description of my mother that follows may seem harsh and I harbour a tiny feeling of guilt. This is offset, though, by a strong conviction that what I say is true, and the satisfaction that I fully supported her practically when I became an adult, even if this was more out of a sense of duty than love.

Although often dissatisfied with her lot, my mother

was not an ambitious woman and was not particularly good at anything beyond looking after the house. Although she could be aggressive when on familiar ground, she was generally under-confident, blamed everyone other than herself for her misfortunes and hated a challenge. She was very slap-dash when it came to practical matters. As for her hobbies and interests; well, these are difficult to describe as outside of bringing up her children, housework and, as we grew older, her shop work, the only "hobby" that springs to mind, which certainly brought her pleasure and joy, was eating cakes, biscuits and sweets – or anything sugary for that matter. Her cupboards were always full of a great selection of bought goodies and her idea of a shopping trip was a dash around the shops, then a cup of tea and a "big" cake. It had to be a "big" cake; there was no such thing as just a cake. There were times in my life when I was fond of her and would look forward to her company, particularly after my father passed away, when the character that so often forced me to walk on eggshells to avoid her disapproval was somewhat subdued.

Taking the lead from her own mother, my mother was a religious lady, always referring to God as "Him upstairs" accompanied with a thumbs-up gesture pointing towards heaven. Whenever she asked for God's help, which was often, she apparently always preceded the request with "If you are not too busy...". She was convinced God always delivered, even when it came to a win on the pools or, later in her life, premium bonds. She used the term "*when* Ernie comes" not "*if* Ernie comes". Ernie never came with a big prize win. She was also very tough. She was widowed twice. Her first husband died within a year of their marriage and my father also died before she did. She pulled through both periods with the support of her family and her unerring belief in God. She showed Steffan and I no physical love or affection, but I do believe she loved us in her own way.

Although she was basically honest, proudly paying all her bills and instilling integrity in her children, despite her God-fearing beliefs, I am unable to describe her as being a totally truthful or genuinely nice person. She wasn't naturally nice, but could *be* nice. I never questioned anything she ever told me when I was a child and believed all her accusative stories about people she was envious of, and her tales about her pre-marriage praiseworthy achievements. I believed and trusted everything she told me. I was to find out later in my life, though, that she didn't always deserve this trust, as she could be inventive and "fibs" came easily to her. She also had a gift for twisting context to support her arguments, playing psychological games and inventing conversations that had never taken place, especially conversations with my father. She would run people down, particularly other mothers, to raise her standing in my eyes and once described herself to me as being devious – believing this to be a character strength.

That said, she was a protective and reasonably good mother in her younger years, ensuring we were warm and well-fed. She was much more easy-going than my father and would tolerate a lot of cheekiness from her children. She prided herself on allowing us to have our say, which, according to her, was not the practice of other mothers. Her tolerance, though, was to change when I reached my teenage years, when just having a say turned to demonstrations of my character strength, strong reasoning and the challenging of her parenting skills. This concerned my mother, as she realised that I was growing up and what she really wanted more than anything was to retain control of me for the whole of my life.

The life story that follows was written in 2024.

Part One

A tale of Sadness, Resilience, Triumph and Intrigue.
(Fiction based on real events).

CHAPTER ONE

West Wales, 1960–1963
Shame, Fear, Loneliness and Guilt

I was five years old and was sitting in the sunshine on a kerb on the edge of the playground with my new best friend, Gwen. Lots of other very small children were running around and chasing either each other or balls or leaves that blew in the breeze. I liked Gwen. Sitting with her meant I wasn't alone during playtime. While waiting for Miss Jay, our impatient but kindly schoolteacher, to ring the bell signifying the end of playtime, we played with the kerb gravel, forming shapes and patterns with it, talking and laughing until something quite routine for me took place. I wet my knickers. This wasn't unusual, so I continued playing, saying nothing about what I had done and not moving from my position on the kerb. My knickers, as usual, were soaked and a dark stain had developed on my dress. The ground around me became damp. Gwen noticed the dampness spreading towards her along the white concrete of the kerb and stood up in horror.

'I am telling Miss Jay what you've done,' she shouted and ran off in the direction of our classrooms.

I sat in my wet state for a while, not feeling particularly uncomfortable, I was used to wetting myself, but I dreaded the thought of hearing the high-pitched voice of Miss Jay screeching out my name, Nolwen, across the schoolyard. This didn't happen and, at the sound of the school bell, I made my way to the classroom in my wet knickers, feeling sheepish and mentally preparing myself for a reprimand. Nothing happened and our lesson continued as normal. I was relieved once I realised that I had escaped the shame. Gwen never sat with me again, but fortunately I made other friends. The knicker-wetting continued for a few years.

I clearly remember a warm and sunny spring day, when it was time for the six-year-olds in Miss Jay's class to practise something similar to "The Green Cross Code". A make-believe zebra crossing with flashing amber Belisha beacons was set up in the square, fenced-off, tarmacked school playground. The young children whispered excitedly to each other while standing in a queue, waiting for their turn to cross the zebra crossing as they had been taught. I remember that I was about twelfth in the queue. I stopped my whispering when I felt a familiar sensation. I crouched and pressed my hand against my crotch, tears welling up in my eyes. I put my hand up for attention.

'Miss, Miss,' I called out. 'Please, Miss.'

Neither Miss Jay nor the other teachers noticed my desperation. I clenched my fists, screwed up my face determinedly and bounced up and down on the spot, hoping that the urge would go away, but, to my dismay, it became steadily stronger and stronger. My turn to demonstrate that I knew how to cross a road came, and in my haste to relieve my straining bladder and scamper off to the toilet, I cut the corner of the zebra crossing off and skipped over the last two white painted stripes. This was the perfect scenario for Miss Jay as it gave her the first and perfect opportunity to show everyone how *not* to cross a road.

'Nolwen,' she squawked, 'that's not how to cross the road safely, is it? Start again.' Obediently, I carried out her instructions with embarrassing consequences. I felt ashamed, so very ashamed. I wish Mam had warned Miss Jay about my knicker-wetting. Perhaps then I would have been first in the queue to cross the road and would have been able to get to the toilet in time.

My time at Trehywel Infants School came to an end and I have no other memories of it. However, I clearly remember my home life at that time and the few years that followed. I lived in a remote countryside area of West Wales with my parents, Annie and Ben, and my younger brother, Steffan. We lived in a terrace of tiny, rented, two-up, two-down cottages. None of the cottages had bathrooms or central heating, but did have flushing toilets located in corrugated iron sheds in the garden. My father, Ben, worked as a poorly paid electrician's "mate" in a government department fifteen miles from our home. As we could not afford a car, he caught two local buses to get to and back from work daily. My mother, we called her "Mam", was a typical housewife of the era, who spent her days looking after us children and the home, usually managing to fit in forty winks at some point in the afternoon.

A family of four, two adults and two boys, lived in one of the cottages adjoining ours. Occupants of the house on the other side changed regularly as it was rented out to the military on short-term let contracts.

Rushing indoors one afternoon during the school holidays, I shouted, 'Mam! Mam! The Wilsons have moved out from next door! Do you think the new people will have a little girl I can play with?' I had set my heart on having a girlfriend to play with when I wasn't at school – someone who would want to be with me at weekends and during the holidays to share my dreams. My brother climbed trees, made dens and kicked footballs around with the boys next door, but I was left out unless they needed a goalie or a skivvy to carry their den-making materials from one point to another.

'I'm not sure,' my mother replied. 'You might be lucky this time, Nolwen, but don't build your hopes up. Meanwhile, go and collect some sticks for the fire and make sure they are dry,' she ordered.

I set off with her shopping basket, searching for sticks. Once in the woods, I chatted away about the possibility of having a new girlfriend who lived next door to my imaginary friend, Ninan. Ninan had been my imaginary friend for years.

'Oh, Ninan, it would be lovely to have another friend, wouldn't it?' I suggested.

She didn't reply, but I knew she agreed with me. We

conjured up a picture together of what the new girlfriend would be called and what she would look like.

'I think she will be older than us, Ninan, so she can help me with my reading and read stories to me before I go to sleep. Mam and Dad never have time to read to me and when I asked my dad the meaning of the word "sod" yesterday, he said, "Look it up in the dictionary, Nolwen, that's what it's there for." I couldn't be bothered to go and find our children's dictionary, so didn't get to know the meaning of the word sod.'

My father always replied to my questions about English comprehension in that evasive way. Looking back, I presume he didn't know the answers, being a practically skilled man as opposed to having great academic capabilities. He was far more inclined to educate my brother on "boy/man" skills than tolerate my curiosity with words. Ninan left my life some years later. I felt lonely without her.

I spent most of my school holidays wandering around in the local countryside alone, but with my imagination for company. Even at a young age, I had an appreciation of beautiful countryside, the sounds of the birds, the colourful flowers – bluebells, daisies, buttercups or foxgloves – and the green of the trees against the blue sky. I had picked this appreciation up from my father, who took me and my brother for long countryside walks, pointing out trees, plants and wonderful views. When alone, I stayed fairly close to home but wandered through woods and fields, listening to the birds, watching the cows and sheep, paddling in streams and picking flowers for my mother. When it was bad weather, I read my Enid Blyton books indoors, but wasn't allowed to read these out loud as it annoyed my father. I was permitted to join him and my brother when they played card games and draughts together, but my concentration levels were so low that my father would lose his patience with me.

'Nolwen, if you take your time and think things through, you might win a game for once in your life,' he said repeatedly.

I don't ever remember winning a game.

'Mam,' I called one day, after losing yet another game to my brother, 'I've finished playing draughts. Can you teach me how to bake a cake?'

My mother didn't know how to bake a cake. In fact, despite often "blowing her own trumpet" to her family, especially me, she had very few skills. This meant that – provided I could get his attention – I relied on the mentoring of my father as I grew up.

The weeks during the summer holidays passed slowly for me, so I looked forward to school in September. Meanwhile, I had my thoughts, dreams and books.

As it happened, a family did move in next door. I rushed indoors with an excited voice, late one evening, shouting, 'Mam! Mam! Someone has moved in next door.'

'Calm down, Nolwen,' she replied. 'Don't go knocking at their door. Give them chance to settle in.'

I busied myself in front of my new neighbour's house

for the next few days by skipping over my frayed skipping rope, playing hopscotch against myself and reading my book on their garden step. The next day, I decided that I had waited long enough, and even though I knew I would probably get a telling-off from my mother, this didn't worry me enough to curb my impatience. I had convinced myself that a little girl called Gaynor had moved in, so I knocked on our neighbour's door. It was answered by a young couple, whose names were Dougi and Jane.

'Hello, I am Nolwen,' I announced. 'I live next door. Does your little girl want to come out and play?'

Dougi and Jane looked at each other, smiled kindly and invited me in.

'This is Janet,' Jane replied. 'She can't come out to play with you, but you can stay here and play with her for a while if you like.'

Janet, not Gaynor, was only three months old. With disappointment written across my face, I said, 'Thank you, but I must go home now. My mother will wonder where I have got to. Goodbye!' and with that, I returned home.

I woke up the next morning, thought briefly about the loss of my friend, Gaynor, but then was distracted by the sound of raised voices. My stomach clenched and my body stiffened. My parents were arguing. Their arguments always revolved around money. My mother was, to her credit, responsible for paying the bills and buying the family's food and clothing. That said, she seldom bought clothes for herself and never wore make-up, jewellery or perfume. Likewise, my father never went for a pint with his friends or workmates. The money he earned just about covered our rent and other essentials. We were never cold nor hungry and, as children, had sweet treats, memorable birthdays and exciting deliveries on Christmas morning.

'You're holding back too much money from your pay packet,' my mother yelled nastily at my father. Followed by, 'How much pocket money have you kept for yourself this week?'

I had no idea what my father needed pocket money for as he rarely went anywhere to spend any money. When he did make the journey into the local town, it was only to visit his parents, or to buy basic tools or wood to make furniture for the home and toys for me and my brother. He never wasted his wood and stored spare pieces away until he found a use for it. However, when the need arose and following a good search for a piece of wood he knew he had, he would find out that it had been repurposed by my mother for firewood, when her children had failed to find the obligatory dry sticks.

During these arguments, which my brother and I hated, we comforted each other, listening to the heated words and willing them to stop. That particular day, my mother continued with her accusations, blaming my honest, hard-working father for her extreme financial difficulties, which didn't really exist.

'You're selfish,' she shouted with a pointed finger. 'You don't care about me and the kids.' Her admonishments were unrelenting.

I sat on my bed, concerned about the screaming and shouting, while Steffan stayed huddled under his blankets, trying not to listen to the harsh words. Eventually, I plucked up the courage to leave my room and I walked gingerly to the top of the stairs. I stopped and listened, waiting and hoping that my mother would stop her allegations. I walked down a few stairs, then sat down, chewing my knuckles. The argument became yet more heated, then stopped suddenly. At first, I was relieved that the house had become silent, but then an unfamiliar sense of panic and urgency spurred me into rushing down the rest of the stairs, which led me into our small dark hallway. My parents were standing close together in the little hallway when I arrived at the bottom of the stairs, hoping desperately to distract them from their quarrel. I stopped and stood perfectly still, afraid and shocked at the scene in front of me. My father had my mother pinned against a wall with a hand on each of her shoulders.

I screamed and screamed. 'Stop! Stop it! Dad, stop!'

He looked at me, then let go of my mother and moved away. I was not sure whether he intended to harm her or not – I guessed probably not. I knew he loved her, despite those occasions when she threw disparaging remarks in his direction or found fault with something he had or hadn't done. Although my mother had the ability to goad, provoke and push my father to the limit of his patience, his reaction that day was unusual for him. In my young mind, my mother was the guilty party. My father could do no wrong. Later in life, I found out that he bitterly regretted his actions and had promised and vowed never to behave like that again, which he never did. As it happened, it was my mother who resorted to anger and rage as life went on.

With the situation calmed, I went back upstairs to my room and all remained quiet in the rooms below me. I was not comforted by my parents after that unhappy experience and no one referred to the scene I had witnessed during the following day. My life and, surprisingly, theirs resumed normality within a few hours. With hindsight, I later concluded that my mother was just seeking attention and only needed appreciation and a cuddle to keep her from these angry displays of discontentment.

Mam came to wake me the next morning.

'Come on, Nolwen. Get up!' she encouraged with a smiling face. 'It's your birthday today!'

I guessed that my parents had completely made up their differences and I felt relieved. I should have jumped out of my bed with happiness and excitement, but a feeling of guilt overpowered these emotions. I knew that I would soon be found out. I had wet the bed.

'Oh no, Nolwen, not again,' my mother complained crossly as I got out of bed and she pulled at the sheets and blankets.

I felt ashamed, so deeply ashamed.

The bed-wetting mishap could not be put down to my being shocked and upset from my experience in the hallway the previous day, as my crime was a regular occurrence. Although I was never physically punished for wetting the bed, my mother had a gift for making me feel bad about it. I wonder now why she didn't wake me up a few times in the night, so that I could have emptied an obviously weak bladder. The answer is clear; the toilet was in the garden and she needed her own sleep.

I was eight years old that day. My latest bed-wetting incident forgotten, I counted down the hours, knowing that my father would bring home a present for me after work that evening. I presumed it would be a book, something educational like a metal globe of the world or some additional items for my pencil case. However, to my absolute delight, it was a small, second-hand, two-wheeled blue bicycle, with a basket on the front and thick rubber tyres. I could not believe my eyes.

'Go on!' my father ordered. 'Get your coat. We're going for a ride.'

I sat on the seat with my feet on the pedals. The bike was the perfect size for me. My father strapped a length of rope to the seat and ran alongside the bike keeping me steady and the bike upright. After an hour or two, I had just about mastered the technique. Stopping and starting regularly, with the rope still attached, I rode and he ran the two miles to Grandma Jones's house to get some birthday money and show off my new skills.

When I got off the bike, though, my father noticed a wet telltale stain on my dress. Tutting and shaking his head, he said, 'Oh, Nolwen,' in an exasperated tone. 'Why didn't you tell me you wanted to go to the toilet?'

'I don't always know when I want to go, Dad,' I replied. Once again, I felt guilty and contrite.

The routine of our summer school holidays continued until the day my father woke up with a stiff neck. He could not look ahead without screwing his face up in pain.

'I'm going to have to visit the doctor,' I overheard him telling my mother.

'What will the doctor do?' I asked with concern.

'He will cut my head off,' my father replied.

I wandered off, with a vivid picture of my father trying to walk around with no head attached to his shoulders. This image concerned me for days and I worried about how our family would manage if my father could not see to go to work.

Chapter Two

West Wales, 1963–1964
Poor Eyesight, Embarrassment,
Low Self-Esteem and Guilt

Keeping a promise and being honest, traits instilled in me by my father, proved a challenge even before I had reached the age of eight.

To my dismay, my parents were arguing again and I was unsettled.

'But where can it be?' my mother exclaimed as she pulled out cabinet drawers and opened and slammed cupboard doors. 'I know I left a pound note on the hall table after paying the milkman. I don't have enough money to pay the bills as it is, without a pound going missing.'

'I earn enough money to provide for you and the kids,' my father shouted back. 'Stop your moaning. It will turn up.'

'But the insurance man is due this afternoon,' my mother replied with more concern than anger in her voice this time. 'You'll have to pay him out of your pocket money. You must have a good stash put away somewhere.'

My father glared at her, then stormed out into the garden, slamming the door behind him. The insurance man didn't get paid that afternoon. We all hid quietly in the hallway when he knocked at the door. He knocked three times, then turned to walk down the garden path.

'He's gone,' my father said, peering behind the living room curtains.

We all sighed with relief.

The following day after hours of searching by my mother, my brother and I were called in from playing to face some serious questions about the missing pound. We knew nothing about it and convinced our parents of such, by following our answers to their interrogation with the phrase, "Honest, Mam. Honest, Dad". Our use of the word honest bound us to the truth and was the family's way of ensuring we believed one another. The pound was never found and I have no idea how my parents survived without it, until my father's wage arrived the following week.

The pound note was not the only item that went missing over the following few weeks. Dad's old working boots were taken from outside the front door, milk was stolen every Saturday from the doorstep and, even more strangely, bundles of newspapers that my mother stored away and used to light the fire also disappeared from the unlocked shed that housed our toilet. Our neighbours suffered similar losses; a pint of milk was stolen on different days from each home, eggs were taken from henhouses and apples from trees. The residents in the street decided to set up the equivalent of a neighbourhood watch, but whoever was doing the thieving escaped their surveillance.

The thefts went on, but I continued, unperturbed, to enjoy my outside play even without my imaginary neighbour's little girl, Gaynor. I explored the surrounding area, wandering a little further away from home than usual. On the outskirts of what I called "our woods", I decided to look for what I had heard my parents describe as a partially derelict old drover's cottage. My parents referred to it as "Pat's cottage", having known the old shepherd who had lived there for many years and had since died.

At the time, I was preparing myself to become a homemaker and had various dwellings for my dolls, old saucepans and mud pies in old sheds and in escarpment caves close to our house. I thought the old cottage might become an upmarket home for my possessions. I found the cottage and approached it slowly. Suddenly, it started to pour with rain. I heard the distant clatter of thunder and although the cottage looked rather spooky, I dared myself to go in. *Go on, Nolwen*, I whispered to myself, reasoning that I could shelter from the rain and look inside the old cottage to see what was there. With some trepidation, I pushed at the battered, heavy wooden front door.

The door squeaked but opened readily. I gingerly stepped inside and made my way along the dusty hall to the first doorway. Cobwebs and spiders hung around the door handle and frame, which dissuaded me from entering the room. I looked around and opted to try the door opposite, which, although hanging off its hinges, was clear of cobwebs and was ajar. I opened it slowly and was met by a strong waft of stale smoke, body odour and the smell of cooking. I peered cautiously inside the room. It was dark and damp. I suddenly felt very scared, goose pimples rising all over my body. *Get out of here, Nolwen. Get out of here and run home as fast as you can. The place might be full of ghosts.*

As I turned to leave, I heard a shuffling noise and the clatter of tin. I nearly jumped out of my skin as I saw the shadow of a man coming towards me. I retreated into the room and hid behind an old armchair, which had stuffing coming out of its arms and a visible spring on its underside. I could feel myself trembling. I was terrified. An old man came into the room carrying a metal bowl and was followed by a small black dog. The dog promptly gambolled across the room and poked its head around the armchair. He licked my face and barked. I decided that now would be a good time to stand up and show myself. I got up slowly.

'Hello,' I said bravely. 'My name is Nolwen.' Following some quick thinking, I added, 'My dad is coming to collect me in a minute.'

The man, who seemed very old, pulled a pipe from his mouth, called the dog to heel and asked in a stern gruff voice. 'What are you doing here, Nolwen?'

'I am sorry,' I muttered, staring at the old man in his tatty clothes and shabby cloth hat. 'I was looking for somewhere nice to play.'

'Where do you live?' he asked. I described our row of houses and explained that our home was on the main road to the nearest town. 'Alright,' he said, taking in my thin trousers and sandals. 'It's probably a good idea to wait in here out of the rain for a few minutes, then you had better hurry off home and meet your dad before it gets dark. You shouldn't come back here again, though. Do you understand me?' he added. 'The building is dangerous.'

We sat in silence for a short while. He sat in his chair and sucked at his pipe, while I sat on a rickety stool and stroked the dog, who was apparently called Pip. The old man stood up, walked a few steps away from me and then looked out of a cracked window at the back of the room.

'The rain has stopped,' he said. 'It is time to go straight home now, Nolwen. Do you want to take an apple with you?'

I shook my head. 'No, thank you,' I replied warily, remembering my parents' advice about not taking things from strangers. I glanced at a small sack with apples pouring out of its opening on an old scratched table.

We both made our way to the door.

'Bye, Nolwen. Please don't tell anyone I am here or I will have to find another place to live for myself and Pip.'

I shook my head convincingly. 'I won't say anything to anyone, Mr,' I said. 'Honest I won't.'

'Thank you,' he replied kindly. 'Make haste before it rains again.'

I walked as fast as I dared out of the room and into the hallway. On my way out, my mouth dropped open and I started to lift my arm to point, then quickly changed my mind. I could see my dad's old work boots stored tidily away behind the front door.

I turned back to glance at the old man, but thought it better to say nothing about the boots. He had a kindly smile on his face and wrinkles around sparkling blue eyes. I walked out through the front door and, as quickly as I could without running, made my way up the garden path. Once out of sight of the cottage, I tore home as fast as my legs could carry me. Having promised the old man that I wouldn't tell anyone about him, followed by the word "honest", I knew that I could never breathe a word about my visit to Pat's cottage. I never went anywhere near the place again.

When my father came home from work that night, I heard him saying to my mother, 'I saw an old tramp with a black dog through the bus window on my way home from work. He was walking along the road towards Trehywel. I could have sworn he had my old work boots on.'

***

After a long and rather lonely summer with only my imagination as a playmate, it was time to go to junior school. My memories of my junior school years are, as would be expected, more plentiful than those of my infant years and form a mixture of fondness and lament.

Although I was pretty average at sums, I loved to read out loud to my teachers and classmates and enjoyed writing stories. I was therefore looking forward to the new term. I still wet my knickers on occasions, so the bus journeys to and from school were a worrying prospect for me.

After just a few weeks, my handwriting deteriorated and my teacher, Miss Thomas, who was a young, thoughtful and gentle lady, who must have just been starting out on her teaching career, noticed that I was screwing up my eyes to read the blackboard.

'What is the matter, Nolwen?' she asked kindly, one morning. 'Read out to me the words I have underlined on the blackboard, please.'

I was a good reader but was unable to read what Miss Thomas had written. The other children laughed at my poor performance and some raised their hands to show that they could do better. Miss Thomas smiled, then passed me a book to read out loud from, which I did perfectly well. She complimented me and explained to the other children that some children preferred to read from books rather than a blackboard. She gave me a note later that afternoon, which was addressed to my parents. Despite reading well from the book, I still felt concerned about not being able to read the sentences she had written on the board.

'Mam,' I shouted when I arrived home, calculating that it was better to hand a letter about my poor reading abilities to my mother, as opposed to my father. 'I've been given a letter for you from Miss Thomas.'

My mother opened the envelope, took out the letter, then looked at me with a frown on her face. She read the letter slowly.

'What has she said, Mam?' I asked. 'Am I in trouble?'

'No, Nolwen' she replied. 'I need to make you an appointment to see an optician.'

I was only eight and would be the first child in the

small junior school to wear spectacles. Few children of my age had their eyes checked in those days and I dreaded turning up to school wearing the thick round NHS glasses that were prescribed for me, especially as my appointment had been at lunchtime, meaning I would be obliged to walk into the classroom late with my new spectacles on my nose. My face reddened and there was a strange fluttering feeling in my tummy. Despite this, with a brave expression on my face, as if there was nothing different about my appearance at all, I walked into my classroom. I looked across the room at the rows of chairs and desks and saw the faces of small children staring up at me. I noticed that my own desk and chair were empty, waiting for me. My classmates started to chuckle.

'Quiet, everyone,' Miss Thomas said, followed by, 'Oh, Nolwen, what lovely glasses you have chosen. Aren't they great?' she said to the class. 'Who would like to try Nolwen's glasses on?'

To my relief and surprise, the boys and girls got up from their seats and clustered around me, each trying my glasses on and looking into a small mirror that Miss Thomas had taken out of her handbag. By the time my beloved teacher had finished, I felt very proud of my glasses and very special. My spectacles had become the envy of all my classmates, especially the girls. I owe much to the thoughtfulness of Miss Thomas, as I was never teased about my glasses and because of her had no reason to object to wearing them. How my reading and writing improved, though, I will never know, as my glasses were not cleaned from the first day of wearing them to the day I was prescribed a different pair.

***

My first year at junior school passed quickly, with few other events lodged in my memory other than the spectacles. The second year, though, was particularly traumatic for me due to the bullying I endured because of my mother's thoughtlessness. I will never forget it.

I was sitting at our home-made table, concentrating deeply on my homework one evening, when she tried to attract my attention from the kitchen while she was peeling potatoes for our evening meal. My mother wasn't particularly adventurous with her cooking and we had potatoes in some form or other with almost everything.

'Nolwen,' she called out. 'Nolwen,' she repeated. 'Stop whatever it is you are doing and come in here and listen to me.' Once she had my attention, she said, 'I bumped into your friend Janice's mam while I was in town shopping today. She asked me if I thought you might like to stay overnight at Janice's next week to celebrate her birthday.'

I looked up at her and thought about the invitation as I liked Janice. We were both part of a group of girls who played together every playtime. However, realisation soon dawned and I felt a sense of disappointment mixed with dread as I knew I couldn't stay overnight at Janice's house – not only did I wet my knickers, but I also still wet the bed.

'I don't think I want to stay the night, Mam,' I groaned.

'Why not?' she enquired. 'It will be easier for me, as I won't need to get a bus into town to meet you after the birthday party, bring you home and put you on the bus for school the next morning.'

'No, I don't want to stay overnight,' I insisted.

My mother stopped peeling the potatoes, stood next to me and explained, 'You don't need to worry about wetting the bed, Nolwen. I have explained your problem to Janice's mam and told her that you will take your plastic "mac" with you to protect the mattress, just in case you have an accident.'

My "mac," as it was called, was white, oblong and made from a rubbery fabric, which was put on my bed by my mother every time it was made.

'No,' I said firmly. 'I am not going. I don't want Janice to know that I wet the bed.'

It was distressing enough being made to feel guilty by my mother whenever she found my wet mac and sheets; I would feel even worse if someone else found them, on a bed that wasn't mine, and would feel totally ashamed of myself if Janice became aware of my sin. Of course, the inevitable happened and Janice's mam told Janice about my awful secret.

I set off for school at the start of the next week with my satchel on my back, daydreaming as I strolled along as usual, and with little thought about what the day ahead might hold. I had expected the day to start as it normally did and was looking forward to handing over a story to my teacher, which I had written for homework the previous evening. To my horror, though, I was met by a sniggering group of girls, including Janice, at the school gates. They had been waiting for my arrival and started to chant a song which Janice boasted, she had written especially for me.

'Nolwen is a pi-ig, yah yah yah! Nolwen is a pi-ig, yah yah yah! She farts all day, pisses in her bed, Nolwen is a pi-ig, yah yah yah!'

The girls then ran off to their classroom for the first lesson of the day. I was relieved to join them, knowing that the chanting would cease once we were all indoors. Needless to say, I did not go to Janice's birthday party. Every playtime from then on, they taunted me by singing the same words whenever they spotted me. I could just about brave the lyrics "Nolwen is a pi-ig" reverberating around the schoolyard and even the "farts all day" section, but I dreaded hearing the words "pisses in her bed", especially when there were boys in earshot. I felt ashamed and so embarrassed when I heard these words, which did nothing for my self-esteem.

This bullying, which went unnoticed by all of the schoolteachers, became worse and continued well into the next school year. The chanting was supplemented with pinches, slaps and the throwing of stones. I was a brave and proud little girl, so told my parents nothing about my miserable school life.

'Nolwen,' my mother called to me one evening after dinner, when she noticed that I was quieter than usual. 'Is something wrong? Are you upset or worried about anything?'

'No, I am alright,' I assured her, hoping she wouldn't probe any further, as once my mother got a bee in her bonnet, she would be determined to satisfy her curiosity. She would fire out further questions or stern orders to reveal the secret to ensure she knew what was going on. Fortunately, or perhaps unfortunately, she asked no further questions that evening or over the next few days, and an incident in the schoolyard, later that week, resulted in my putting a stop to the bullying all by myself. The solution was not planned or premeditated, but merely an instinctive reaction to events. I was not proud of my actions.

Janice and her group of friends pushed the bullying a little too far one afternoon in the schoolyard. They began their daily provocations, in what was rather a sensitive environment for me. The schoolyard was full of children tearing around, screaming and shouting, playing games and chasing after each other. It seemed to me that there were more boys in the area of the yard where I usually played on that particular day. Possibly because of my relationship with my brother and my being brought up with only boys for neighbours, I liked to pretend that I was tough, portraying myself to the male species as a bit of a tomboy who could look after herself. To be ridiculed in front of the boys was the worst possible way to embarrass me, especially if I was also made to cry.

Using a special stone I had found in a builder's yard close to my grandma's house, I was playing hopscotch with some younger girls, because Janice and her friends had persuaded the other girls of my own age to sever their friendships with me. If I was alone, I was more vulnerable to verbal and physical abuse, so being in the company of anyone was better than no one at all. It was my turn to play.

There were two groups of boys standing close by, watching our game. To my dismay, Janice's group of friends, fronted as usual by their leader, appeared around a corner and sauntered towards me. *Oh no*, I thought to myself. *Please don't sing the bed-wetting song. The boys will hear it.* To my dismay, about six verses were chanted with the same words being repeated louder and louder.

'Nolwen is a pi-ig, yah yah yah! Nolwen is a pi-ig, yah yah yah! She farts all day, pisses in her bed, Nolwen is a pi-ig, yah yah yah.'

I hung my head in shame and I felt embarrassed, profoundly embarrassed.

Not satisfied with her verbal torments, Janice, coming closer to me, thought up another humiliating idea.

'Let's pull Nolwen's dress up and show the boys her knickers,' she shouted. 'Come on, girls, help me.'

The boys, of course, then became particularly interested in the events taking place close to the chalked hopscotch boxes. Sadly, I knew I was about to lose all credibility with those I sought to impress that day.

I stiffened as the girls approached, clenched my teeth, but stood my ground. To run away would have cost me my reputation with the boys. The girls, fired up by the sound of Janice's authoritarian voice, moved in closer, then tugged and tugged at my dress, attempting to reveal all. I held my dress down as best as I could with one hand, as my hopscotch stone was still held firmly in the other. As tears welled up in my eyes with shame, there was little I could do to save myself from both the humiliation of being upset and letting the boys see my knickers.

Janice stopped her shouting and leant towards me to assist her friends with the dress pulling. Suddenly, a great whoosh of adrenalin surged through my veins, preparing my body to fight. With a terror-driven reflex, I lashed out in self-defence, although not at anything or anyone in particular. My special stone, which was about one-inch thick and covered in a shiny tile-like surface, perfect for hopscotch, made contact with Janice's face. The pulling at my clothes stopped, everything went quiet, and after the girls and boys had finished staring at me in horror, they moved away. The boys were cheering and the girls were talking quietly to each other, while putting their supportive arms around Janice, who howled in pain.

'What is the matter with you, Janice? Why are you crying?' Our form teacher asked when we arrived in class after the schoolyard episode.

Janice, with her eyes still brimming with tears, replied, 'Nothing, miss,' and sat down at her desk.

The teacher demanded an explanation about Janice's emotional and physical state from her classmates. Janice's friends gave her a shortened version of the events that had taken place in the school playground. The teacher had not heard my side of the story, but gave some snide advice to her pupils. 'Do not sit next to Nolwen anyone. She is a nasty little girl who hits people with bricks.'

I presume Janice did not tell her parents about our altercation because I heard nothing more about her injury. Like me, she was a proud and tough little girl, who did not tell tales and must have invented some excuse for her injury. To my great relief, neither her parents nor mine ever mentioned the brick incident.

A few days later, spotting me in the schoolyard, Janice tentatively called out my name.

'Nolwen!' I turned towards her with a feeling of trepidation. 'I am sorry about my song and for showing the boys your knickers,' she said. 'Can we be friends again?'

I nodded gratefully. 'I am sorry I hit you with my hopscotch stone, but what about the other girls? I don't think they want to be friends with me.'

She said she would ask them if we could all play together again, then turned and walked away.

Eventually, the other girls came up with the idea that if I turned the skipping rope along with the fattest girl in the class, enabling them to jump over the rope, they would stop singing the Nolwen song and leave me alone. We made a pact and I turned the rope for the rest of the school term. I guess the girls forgot the words of the song, but I never did.

Chapter Three

West Wales, 1964–1965
Abandonment, Shame and More Guilt

It was almost Christmas. I woke up on a Saturday morning, looked through the frosted bedroom window at the wintery scene outside, dressed quickly, then went downstairs to the kitchen to wash my face in cold water in the one and only sink in our home. I didn't clean my teeth, as this wasn't a requirement in our house. Actually, it wasn't even possible, as my mother had only ever bought me one toothbrush and one tin of toothpaste in my life and that was when I went into hospital to have my tonsils removed. My mouth hygiene equipment had been a prerequisite for my hospital stay and was left there when I was discharged. I ran back upstairs, bounced on Steffan's bed to make sure he was awake, then, being the annoying big sister, pulled the bed covers off him.

We heard my father call to us five minutes later, 'Nolwen! Steffan! Come downstairs for your breakfast, please.'

We obediently ran downstairs and sat at the table, where my father had placed two boiled eggs with funny faces drawn on the shells, some bread and butter, and two cups of tea.

'Where's Mam?' I asked, ensuring my mouth was empty of food, as my father had sat opposite us and was drinking a cup of tea. 'She usually makes our breakfast. Where is she?'

'Your mother has gone out,' he replied. 'She has a part-time job now, so I am going to look after both of you myself on Saturdays for a while. The manager of the Woolworths store in Trehywel needs some extra staff to help during the run-up to Christmas.'

Woolworths was the largest store in the little town and sold everything from sweets to buckets and mops.

Oh dear, I thought, glancing over at my brother. He pulled a funny face that clearly expressed his horror at the thought of being under the strict control of my father every Saturday. *Things are going to be a little different around here while Mam is at work.*

My father did a good job of looking after me and Steffan on the Saturdays running up to Christmas. If the days were dry and not too cold, we played outside as normal. On wet, cold days, he played draughts or card games with us. I would lose my concentration after the first couple of games, though, and usually reverted to reading quietly to myself or making clothes for my Sindy doll. I liked her to be dressed in the miniskirts, dresses and checked bell-bottom trousers of the day, which I had seen worn by models on the television. I often pestered my mother to buy me some suitable fabric with which to make similar clothes. I had received my Sindy the previous Christmas, but the factory produced carefully packaged Sindy clothes and accessories, which could be purchased in the local shops, were overpriced and a financial step too far for my parents. Some of the girls at school showed off their manufactured Sindy clothes, Sindy wardrobes, Sindy cars and Sindy horses, but I was very satisfied with my lot and never longed for toys we could not afford. While I could keep myself occupied when at home with my books, my Sindy doll and my thoughts, and pretend that I enjoyed my father's games as much as my brother did, what I still really longed for was my own special friend.

***

One particular Saturday morning, just before my mother set off for work, I knew something was afoot when I heard my mother and father talking instead of arguing for once. I kept very still and listened at the kitchen door, which was ajar. They were discussing my mother's Saturday job, her wages, moving house and, rather strangely, the subject of dogs. As usual, my imagination ran wild. Later that night and over the next few days, I made up stories about my parents giving me a sheepdog for Christmas who would be called Kim and who might be able to replace my longed-for new best friend. We would go to sheepdog trials and dog shows together, I imagined, where we would always come first and be presented with rosettes and silver cups. However, Christmas came and went and though there were lots of Christmas gifts and goodies as usual, to my disappointment, there was no sheepdog for Nolwen.

Time passed uneventfully for some time, although my parents' conversations would turn into arguments every now and again. I would stand guard nearby in case things escalated, feeling tense and apprehensive. On one particular Saturday morning, though, before my mother left for work, they must have reached an agreement on whatever had been triggering the recent arguments, as they were talking and laughing together. I listened in, full of curiosity.

There it is again, I said to myself. I definitely heard my father talk about a new house and, more importantly, use the word "dogs". Perhaps now they've decided not only to buy a sheepdog for me, but one for Steffan, too! I jumped up and down, unable to contain my feelings of anticipation. *Wow! Steffan and I are getting a sheepdog each! Should I tell him?* I considered this, then thought better of it.

Before telling Steffan, I needed to pluck up the courage to ask my father about when the dogs would arrive. I did not have the patience to wait until the end of the day – when my mother would get home from work and would be more likely to spill the beans than my father – but I needed to wait for the right moment. I set the table for our lunch, ate all of it, despite hating the cucumber that had been decoratively made into spiralling curls by my father, and then cleared the seven dishes from the table, which had contained our ham salad and potatoes.

'Dad,' I blurted out when I had piled up all the dishes next to the sink in the kitchen. 'When are we moving house? And when are we getting our sheepdogs?'

My father and Steffan both turned to stare at me with looks of confusion on their faces.

'What sheepdogs, Nolwen?' my father asked me.

'Are we getting sheepdogs?' Steffan shouted, jumping off his chair. 'How many sheepdogs? Will they be like Patch on Blue Peter or will they be puppies?'

My father frowned, then, quickly putting two and two together, concluded that his daughter had been surreptitiously listening to conversations between him and her mother and had, as usual, let her imagination run wild. She had clearly invented a story – this time about sheepdogs – based on pieces of the arguments and conversations she had overheard. To my dismay, he refused to say anything more about sheepdogs or moving house.

A month or so later, my family moved to another rented house, which was on the other side of Trehywel, in a small village called Llancerysmair. Steffan and I changed junior schools and my mother was offered some extra work at Woolworths, which meant she would work some evenings, stocking up shelves and at other times, serve sweets or toys to shoppers during the school holidays when the little town would be inundated with tourists. Our family life changed for the better in that my father's income was supplemented by my mother's extra wages. This meant four big cream cakes every Saturday evening, a second-hand van for my father, and a slightly bigger house with two good-sized bedrooms. My father was able to divide one of the bedrooms into two small box rooms, which served as separate bedrooms for me and Steffan. The new house had a large unkempt garden, surrounded by some fencing and hedges, and, most importantly, two outbuildings.

Sometime after settling into the new house, my father built a wooden bench seat that sat across the inside of his van behind the two front seats. As was the case in those days, there was no need for many health and safety considerations. The bench, with a cushion for Steffan and a cushion for me, and some makeshift handles to hold onto that were attached to the van roof, was comfortable enough. Generally, we only used the van for local trips, but one Saturday, when my mother was at work, my father made a packed lunch and, with Steffan and I balanced on the bench to save arguments about who would sit in the passenger seat, told us we were going on a trip to Cardiff. We set off, with my father making a mental note to make very regular toilet stops for me, even though I was now nine years of age.

The trip to Cardiff was all about my father's determination to better himself and would provide him with an opportunity to earn some extra money to support his family. My assumptions were partly correct. We had moved house and my father explained that we were off to Cardiff to buy a dog. Steffan and I shouted in delight and smiles spread across both our faces as we looked at each other and then up at my father, waiting to hear a little more.

'Right, Nolwen,' my father said. 'Let's get things

perfectly straight in your head. We have an exciting day ahead of us, but we are not going to buy any sheepdogs. Do you understand? Have you heard me? No sheepdogs! We are not even going to look at any sheepdogs.'

I bowed my head in sorrow, then looked up and nodded.

'We are going to buy a twelve-month-old female boxer dog called Jenny,' he continued. 'She will be mine. I am going to train and keep her, then, hopefully, we can organise things so that she will have some puppies during the wintertime when your mother will not be working. I will choose one girl puppy to keep and then, when the others are old enough, they will be sold to good homes.'

'Can I have the new girl puppy?' I enquired hopefully.

'Yes, you can, Nolwen, and when Steffan is a little older, he can choose one for himself too.'

Steffan and I were over the moon and we arrived home later that evening with our first family pet. That day was the start of my father's new venture into the dog-breeding business and eventually he converted the outbuildings into kennels. Puppies were born, bred and sold, and our family unit increased depending on the litter size.

Jenny and any of her very excitable offspring preferred to spend most of their days creating havoc in our house or freely tearing around after each other in the large unkempt garden that wrapped around the house, rather than spending time in their kennels. My mother's wages helped with the dog expenses, but meant she had to work whenever possible – at least until my father's business became more established, she explained to us.

***

The less positive side to my mother working during the school holidays as well as on Saturdays was that Steffan and I had to be looked after by other members of the family when my father was at work. Sometimes it was by my granny and grandfather, but more usually by our Auntie May, my mother's sister, and Uncle Gwyn, who lived not too far away in a remote area of countryside with their three children. My uncle worked some miles away from his home and together they ran a limited smallholding next to their house, which was known as Caegarw. During the holidays, my mother returned home every afternoon and my father returned home every evening after work, but, for some reason, it was decided that Steffan and I would only return home at weekends.

'I like Auntie May and Uncle Gwyn and don't mind staying with them,' I said thoughtfully when my parents told Steffan and me about their plans for us, 'but what about my books and the dog? I don't want to leave them behind.'

'Jenny must stay here, Nolwen, but you can take some of your books with you,' my father advised.

'When do we have to go?' Steffan wailed.

'Tomorrow,' my mother answered firmly.

Steffan and I both felt unhappy about leaving our dog and our favourite possessions behind, but we weren't allowed to challenge the decision with my father present.

We set off in the van to Caegarw the next day with some clothes, my books, my Sindy doll and Steffan's football. My mother carried my rubber mac (which I still needed) and handed it over to her sister who was expecting it.

'Ah, here you all are,' Auntie May said with a welcoming voice. 'Now,' she said, looking at me and Steffan, 'you two, go out and play with your cousins, while your mam and dad have a cup of tea with me.'

When we came in from playing, our parents had left.

We had no choice but to settle in at Caegarw. Fortunately, we both enjoyed the company of our three cousins. I – who no longer had Ninan and was always desperate for friendship – was especially happy to have Mary, the eldest, to play with. She was only a few years younger than me. Steffan enjoyed the companionship of Mary's two brothers, but we often played happily together as a group of five, too. We all got on tremendously well and our cousins generously shared all their dens, toys and treats with us, so our days passed reasonably contentedly. Uncle Gwyn was a kind, fair and gentle man, whereas Auntie May, although never harsh with me or Steffan, made the house rules and was a strict and rather bossy mother. She barked out orders sharply to her children, who, as my mother often reminded me, never dared to answer her back.

Although living in a more disciplined environment, my cousins did have some advantages over Steffan and myself. Gwyn and May were financially a little better off than my parents. May, never to be outdone by any of her siblings, gave her children everything we had and more. If my father made us a garden swing, then Uncle Gwyn, under her instruction, also made his children a garden swing. If I had a pair of roller skates, then Mary had a pair of roller skates and so it went on. When we were all together, though, we were treated equally and everything was shared. Auntie May was generous enough to buy all the fabric Mary and I could possibly need for making clothes for our Sindy dolls. In my adult years, I had fond memories of the two of us comparing our handiwork. Our young cousins also wore better-quality clothes than us and, whether they liked it or not, always went to Trehywel for the weekly shop, beautifully dressed in perfectly matching outfits.

Despite her firmness with her own children, I don't ever remember Auntie May reprimanding me or Steffan for anything. This may have been because we were well behaved or that we just took our cues from our cousins. When it came to my bed-wetting problem, she seemed to be understanding. She never checked the bed in my presence and I never had to admit to my crime. All she did was remove the mac, wash the sheet and then hang that out to dry. Of course, every time I saw the sheet on the washing line, I felt guilty and a sense of shame. To be fair, though, I don't believe Auntie May was making a point or had any intention of making me feel remorseful. The latter came from inside me and not Auntie May. The sheet just had to be washed, dried and placed back on my bed. If my cousins knew about my problem, they were thoughtful enough never to say a word to me about it.

After seeing my sheet on the line for two consecutive days, I felt so guilty that the following night, once Mary had gone to sleep in the bed next to me, I got out of bed and, taking my pillow, curled up and went to sleep on the cold linoleum floor. *You are still a good girl*, I told myself. *Stay here and everything will be alright when Auntie May checks the bed in the morning.* I woke up a few hours later and climbed back into bed feeling stiff and very cold. I was relieved to find that my bed was dry for the next few days.

Towards the middle of the summer holidays, it had been a beautiful summer day and my cousins, Steffan and myself had been climbing a tree that stood above a hedge and bordered the wonderful Welsh rolling hills and countryside. Auntie May called us for dinner and everyone set off quickly except for me. The sun was beginning to set over the golden cornfields in the distance and I stood there, alone and pensive, admiring the beauty. Suddenly, a terrible cloak of sadness descended over my entire body. I couldn't rationalise this feeling at first, then realised that I was desperately missing my parents, the dog and my home. I felt abandoned and very lonely. Emotions of this kind, as well as the shame and guilt I felt when I wet the bed, all experienced so early in my life, left their mark and were to plague me for a good part of my life.

Chapter Four

West Wales, 1965–1969
Diffidence and Disappointment

My memories of my childhood when we lived at Llancerysmair are mixed. I missed my parents and home life very much when my mother worked during the school holidays, but, on the positive side, less financial pressures meant fewer arguments. My body would still stiffen and I would feel very much on edge if I heard my father raise his voice at my mother, fearing an escalation into something like the hallway incident.

Life went on pretty much as usual, though, and after learning to ride my first little bike with thick rubber tyres, which was then passed down to Steffan, there was a gap where I had no bike at all. However, with my mother now earning a wage, my first Christmas in Llancerysmair proved to be especially memorable as I was given my second bike. This was another second-hand bike but was more of a traditional style and in very good condition, which I was absolutely delighted with. In good weather, I would ride my bike and meet up with Janice, who coincidentally lived a mile or so away from my house. We were no longer in the same school, but had long since forgiven each other after the brick incident and become firm friends.

My mother also organised my one and only birthday party when we lived at Llancerysmair. The house was full of excited noisy children, all eager to play the games my parents had organised and to give me the presents they had carefully chosen. I enjoyed the party, but – possibly because it was my turn to be in the limelight – I found the experience of receiving presents from children in front of other children awkward, even though I had often handed over gifts myself at parties. I wasn't sure how to respond once I had opened each gift and didn't know how to encourage the next child in the queue to hand over their carefully wrapped parcel. Do I hold my hand out? Do I just stand patiently and wait? Some children held back, hoping that their gift was going to outshine all other gifts, and I had to pretend that I hadn't noticed that there were more surprises in the offing. I found the whole experience uncomfortable but I delighted in the presents once I had received them all.

Apart from missing Janice's company, I really liked my new school – in fact, my year at Llancerysmair Junior School was the most enjoyable school year of my childhood. There, I met my new best friend, Gem, and together we developed a new passion – music and singing.

My new musical pastime was going rather well and, to my parents' delight, was keeping me occupied outside of my school life. I learned at some point that my grandmother on my mother's side (Granny Lane, as everyone knew her) had been a superb vocalist in her youth. As was usual for me, hearing about something as exciting as this resulted in my imagination firing up on all cylinders. It led me to believe that I had inherited the old lady's musical skills and would follow in her footsteps and become a famous singer.

'Granny,' I proclaimed to her excitedly one day, 'I have started to take some singing lessons with my friend, Gem.'

'What do you do in these lessons?' she enquired sternly.

I explained that I just sang songs, normally on my own in front of my teacher, and usually these were in Welsh. I was disappointed by her reaction, which was to criticise my singing teacher for just listening to my singing.

'Why on earth isn't she teaching you to read music?' she demanded. 'You won't get anywhere unless you can read music,' she added emphatically.

Although she was probably right, her only solution was to buy me a paperback book entitled, *The Rudiments and Theory of Music*. Despite her capability and qualifications, she made no attempt to work through the book with her granddaughter and took no further interest in my latest ambition to become a famous singer.

Sometime later, my singing teacher organised a concert at a day centre for the elderly, where all her pupils sang either solos, duets or musical pieces as part of a small choral group, with the intention of entertaining a rather large audience. My grandmother was in the front row. I sang my solo in Welsh and deliberately watched for her reaction.

She applauded, with no more enthusiasm than anyone else in the audience, and when I saw her next, she said nothing about my performance. I was very disillusioned as I thought the prospect of her granddaughter being a famous singer, who was so eager to follow in her footsteps, would have pleased her tremendously. I was truly desperate for her approval and encouragement, particularly as my parents showed little interest in my new-found pastime. My confidence took a battering. I don't ever remember being praised for anything in my childhood.

A little later, I shared a singing lesson with another child, but suffered another setback to my musical ambitions when, after listening to the other little girl sing, my teacher turned to me and asked, 'Nolwen, why can't you sing your song like Anwen does? Listen to her and try to copy her light, silvery voice.'

My spirits dropped and I felt a mixed sense of hurt, dejection and resentment. I thought I was one of her best pupils. Once again, my confidence took a battering. Gem gave me some reassurance and encouragement, and despite the two musical setbacks and after some persuasion, I agreed with her that we would enter ourselves to sing competitively in some *eisteddfods* that were held every spring in local village chapels all over West Wales. Gem was a Welsh speaker and translated the adjudications for me. We came away winning a few silver cups, but with my confidence levels at a low, the experience for me was very daunting. I felt sick before every competition and physically shook before going onto the stage. Additionally, there was never anyone from our families present to support or listen to us, or to applaud the adjudications and presentations.

Giving up on *eisteddfods*, Gem and I joined local choirs and groups instead, which allowed me to enjoy singing without the pressure of being on stage alone and without the audience's focus being entirely on me as an individual. My singing was consistently picked out from the crowd of choral singers, as I began to develop a unique contralto voice. Unfortunately, although I continued to enjoy choral and group singing, I never agreed to sing solo due to my lack of confidence and what had seemed like disapproval from my grandmother.

***

My school days continued routinely. Mr Mills, the kindly headmaster who ran the junior school at Llancerysmair, also taught our class. His dedication to his pupils was unsurpassed. He was strict enough to command respect, interesting enough to capture our attention during each lesson and gentle enough to be approached whenever we felt upset or unwell. Although we lived in West Wales and he was a Welsh speaker, all our lessons were presented in English, as was the case in other schools in our county. Most of the local families spoke Welsh in the home and it was their first language, so Mr Mills would slip into Welsh when he addressed an individual child on a non-lesson matter. However, when it came to schooling, no Welsh was used in the classroom at junior level. In my case, although my father and his family were Welsh, my mother and her family were English, so we never spoke Welsh in the home and I never learnt the language from my school friends, who could accommodate my shortfall by switching to English very easily. I studied Welsh for my O levels later in my school life.

Mr Mills had a gift for making everyone in his class feel clever and important to him. When I look back at my school years, I think of him with fondness and respect. I wish so many of the other teachers who were employed to give me the best possible start in life and provide me with the initial steps to a successful career could have taken a leaf out of Mr Mills' book. I was only under his direction for one year, but that one year was the most enjoyable year of my schooling life. However, there was yet another blow to my confidence ahead of me, which became apparent when I left the capable and reassuring teachings of Mr Mills and moved up to "big school".

Before moving up to "big school," otherwise known as Trehywel Comprehensive, Gem and I were part of a group of children who were preparing to take the Eleven Plus examinations. There was no secondary school in the town, so the results of the Eleven Plus exams dictated which level class children would be allocated to. The class levels ran from A to E, with class A supposedly being for those with the highest level of academic capability.

'You are bound to be going to class A, Nolwen,' Gem and the other children told me. 'Mr Mills always reads out your English essays and asks you to read books aloud in class.'

'Yes, I hope so,' I replied with a proud, beaming smile across my face.

'We will be able to sit together like we do now,' Gem added, feeling certain she would also pass her exams with flying colours.

Our group of friends drew up a scoreboard, with all our names written on the left-hand side of it. We put a letter from A to E in a column next to each name, indicating the predicted "big school" class level. There was also an expected percentage score column for the subjects of maths and English. No one in our group was allocated to a class at a level below C and no one scored less than ninety per cent in the predicted subject score column.

'How well do you think I will do in maths?' I asked, not needing any reassurance, but enjoying the compliments I was receiving.

'Definitely better than any of the boys,' one of the other girls said.

'Yes, I had one hundred per cent in my last test,' I boasted. 'Much better than Edward.'

Mr Mills had done his best to produce a class of proud self-assured pupils, who would have no reservations about taking their Eleven Plus examinations.

The two scheduled days of examinations came soon enough. Strangely, sitting exams held no fear for me. I relished them, presumably because I was in my own space and not under the spotlight I had endured with singing on stage. I very quickly and confidently completed my maths and English exams and rushed home feeling very happy and proud of myself, having gone through my answers afterwards with Mr Mills.

When I arrived home that evening, I shouted as I came through the front door, 'Dad, I've taken my maths and English exams for my Eleven Plus today. I think I have done well and could do everything on the paper. There's only one other exam left, which I take tomorrow.'

'Nolwen, calm down. Ladies don't shout,' he admonished. 'What exam have you got tomorrow?'

'I think it might be a Welsh exam,' I replied.

My dad looked a little perplexed, but said no more.

I sat the Welsh exam the next day, but hadn't a clue about most of the answers to the questions and was unable to write the short story asked of me about my favourite day spent with my family. I did my best and was not overly concerned, as a score for Welsh had not been listed on the scoreboard my fellow pupils had previously drawn up and we never had any Welsh language lessons at school, so I didn't think the exam was that important.

After the school holidays, the first day of "big school" arrived and I was excited. Proudly dressed in my brand-new comprehensive school uniform, I stood with Gem in the enormous unfamiliar school hall, waiting for my name to be called out followed by a class number.

'Gemma Bowen,' the headmaster called out. 'Year one, class A. Form teacher: Mr Evans.'

Gem was delighted and squeezed my hand. I waited until he ran through some other names in alphabetical order, picking out the names of pupils from my old junior school who had also done well.

'Nolwen Jones,' he finally called out. 'Year one, class D. Form teacher: Mrs Davies.'

I was devastated. 'There must have been a mistake,' I muttered to Gem, who nodded in agreement and put an arm around my shoulders.

We went our separate ways to our classes. I stared down glumly at my new shiny shoes as I walked away, feeling confused, disappointed and isolated without my friend, Gem.

It was many weeks later when I plucked up the courage to query my class level allocation with Mrs Davies. Mrs Davies was an elderly teacher with grey hair drawn back tightly over her head into a small bun at the back of her neck. She had a thin-lipped mouth, which made her look stern and unapproachable.

'Miss,' I called out tentatively before she packed up her briefcase at the end of a lesson. 'Can you tell me why I am in class D, please? I feel sure I passed my Eleven Plus exams and should be in class A.'

Mrs Davies looked at me sternly and said, 'No, Nolwen, you did not pass the exams. You must have had a below-average score to be in my class.' She then continued to explain unsympathetically that I was not clever and would struggle in class levels A, B or C. 'A, B and C are the old grammar school grades,' she said, barely looking up from the papers she was pushing into her briefcase. 'If there was a Secondary School in Trehywel, that is where you would be now. Think yourself lucky that you are where you are. If you concentrate, which seems rather difficult for you, and you work hard enough to get some good marks in your exams at the end of the year, you will have the opportunity to move up to level C.'

With that, she picked up her briefcase and walked out of the room. Unfairly admonished and with her words preoccupying my mind for some time, my confidence once again took a severe battering. I felt demotivated, disillusioned and was still confused about my class grading. It was only many years later, when I thought about which children had been in year one, class D, that I realised some were from families who had English parents, like me, and some belonged to families who moved to Trehywel from England, so did not speak Welsh. I concluded that perhaps our English, maths and Welsh exam results could possibly have been amalgamated unfairly. If Mrs Davies or my parents had made efforts to query the reasons behind my surprising class placing, perhaps my results would have been reassessed alongside the other children and I would not have felt penalised for being unable to speak the Welsh language. I felt very let down.

There was one further blow to my confidence that year, which remains firmly ingrained in my memory. It was my recital of the poem "The Burial of Sir John Moore After Corunna" by Charles Wolfe at the comprehensive school's annual concert later that year, representing class D. The concert was intended for the teachers and pupils of the school and, fortunately for me, not parents or family members. The poem was difficult for a child of my age, but could be read in such an emphatic way that even if it wasn't understood, it would capture the attention of an audience. I learnt the words off by heart and read them out to my class for many days preceding the concert, perfecting my delivery of it as each day passed. Everyone, including Mrs Davies, thought I read it well.

The day of the concert arrived; the concert hall was full of teachers and lots of excited children of all ages. The headmaster and deputy headmaster sat in the front row, waiting for each child to begin their act in turn. My name was called and I got up from my seat at the back of the stage and walked to the centre front. I stood on a pre-marked black spot painted on the floor, which was surrounded by a circle of bright light, and prepared myself to begin.

The room became silent. I looked around at the large number of faces in front of me and started my performance. "The Burial of Sir John…" but as I stood on the stage alone, the anxiety I had experienced during my *eisteddfod* days took over. I remembered every word perfectly, but I read the poem at such speed, the wonderful words were just strung together and came out without impact or passion. I managed to get to the end and walked off the stage, my head bent low and my eyes cast downwards, with the sound of limited applause in my ears. Mrs Davies was in the audience. If she had stood up, given me some reassurance and the opportunity to start again, I feel sure

I would have recited it flawlessly and magnificently the second time around. I was not given that second chance and joined the rest of the children in the audience, feeling sad and disappointed with my rendition of the poem by Charles Wolfe.

Despite the damage to my confidence, my sadness and disappointment – yet more negative emotions I was conscious of at a young age – I eventually settled in at the comprehensive school. I still missed my old Llancerysmair Junior School friends, most of whom were in classes above my level D. Gem and I remained good friends outside of school hours, though, and continued with our singing interests over the next couple of years. The other children from Mr Mills' class had little to do with me, as I had gone down in their estimation. I would not have wanted to go to school at all if it hadn't been for my old friend, Janice, who had also ended up at Trehywel Comprehensive School. Janice sat next to me in class D as she had not done well in her Eleven Plus exams either. Her father was English and, like me and my family, didn't speak Welsh in the home.

Chapter Five

West Wales, 1966
Directional Dyslexia

As well as meeting up with Gem for singing, I met Janice at weekends over the next couple of years. We became like two peas in a pod. With Janice by my side, I felt protected inside and outside of the classroom. Her presence made me feel more self-assured.

One Saturday morning, my father was in charge of us, as usual. I was with Janice doing a jigsaw in my bedroom. Steffan was hiding away, high up in his favourite tree in our garden, and my father was busy with some DIY in the outbuildings, preparing for the arrival of a litter of puppies.

I heard the back door open and my father called up the stairs, 'Nolwen, come here, please. I need you to run an errand for me.'

Always very accommodating when it came to requests from my father, I ran down the stairs with Janice trying to keep up behind me.

'Yes, okay, Dad,' I said. 'What do you want me to do?'

'I want you to take your bike – make sure your basket is on the front – and ride into Trehywel,' he replied. 'I need you to go to the outdoor market for me. You know where it is, just past Grandma Jones's house. You've been there with me and your mother before.'

'But what about Janice? She hasn't got her bike with her.'

My father turned to Janice and said, 'I am sorry Janice, but you will have to go home now, but you can come back tomorrow.'

I waved goodbye to Janice, wishing she could go with me to the outdoor market. I was very uncomfortable doing things on my own, but knew my father wouldn't accept this as an excuse and would insist on his errand being carried out.

'I want a ⅜ inch masonry drill bit from Taff Williams' electrical stall and a packet of 240 grit sheets of sandpaper from the Brogans' DIY stall,' he explained. 'I'll write these items down for you.'

I put my coat on, put my father's list and his money in my pocket, and dragged my bike out of the shed.

Just as I was leaving, my father shouted after me, 'Don't be long, Nolwen. Come straight back as I will need the sandpaper and drill bit after we've all eaten our lunch.'

I glanced at my watch; it was eleven-thirty. We usually had lunch at 1pm.

I peddled furiously, reached the outskirts of the small town, skirted the castle, rode past Grandma Jones's house and headed up the short hill to the field where the outdoor market was held every Saturday. I knew my way there, as I regularly visited my grandma and it wasn't far from where she lived. There was a queue of cars waiting to go through the entrance, so I jumped off my bike and pushed it through the extra-wide double gates, parking it next to a hut, where an old man was taking a shilling off everyone as an entrance fee. I asked him if he would keep an eye on my bike. He nodded and waved me off.

There were, what seemed like, hundreds of stalls in the field, so I wandered around looking for Taff Williams' electrical stall. The stalls were erected on a "first-in, first-set-up" basis and were rarely in the same place week on week. After searching around and asking other stallholders if they knew where Taff's stall was, I eventually found it. His was a busy stall, so I had to queue up behind a line of men waiting to be served. Once at the front of the queue, I checked my list and carefully read out to the man I presumed was Taff exactly what my father had written down.

Next to the name "Taff Williams", he had written the detail describing the drill bit. Taff had hundreds of tool items on his stall, but had no difficulty in finding what I wanted. He wrapped the drill bit in some brown paper and placed it in front of me on the counter. Meanwhile, I dug some money out of my pocket, handed it over and waited for my change. When he leaned over with a handful of coins for me, he knocked over a huge box full of screws, which landed at my feet. I took my father's change, dropped it into my pocket, then – with the help of some men in the queue – gathered up the screws for Taff. Once all the screws had been returned to the box, I set off on my next mission, which was to find the Brogans' stall.

It took me an age to find Brogans and I was quite disorientated by the time I came across the family-owned stall. I bought and paid for the sandpaper, this time with the right money, but then, with a horrible sinking feeling in the pit of my stomach, realised that I hadn't got the drill bit from Taff's stall. My heart started pumping with adrenalin, my hands were trembling and I started to panic. I glanced at a clock hanging above a stall and knew that I had to return to the electrical stall quickly if I was to get home for lunchtime. There were lots of people in the market, making it impossible for me to run back, but I pushed my way through as best and as politely as I could, half walking and half running. I had no idea where I was going, though, and was not even sure that I was heading in the right direction. I stopped and asked for help, but was directed back the way I thought I had just come from. I didn't know which way to go and my head was spinning. I felt as if my brain was full of cotton wool and my heart was pounding. I looked around, totally bewildered, then sat down on the grass, leaning against a stall's table leg. The time was now twelve-thirty. I sat there, not knowing what to do next, looking downwards with my arms wrapped around my knees.

'What's the matter with you, Nolwen?' I heard a kindly voice ask me.

I looked up and couldn't believe my luck. It was my father's brother, Uncle Dan.

'I'm running an errand for Dad and have been looking for Taff Williams' electrical stall,' I explained as I got to my feet, 'but I'm lost.'

He laughed and said, 'Follow me,' then led me straight to the stall.

After thanking Uncle Dan and waving goodbye, I asked Taff for the drill bit. Fortunately, he had put it aside and handed it over to me straightaway. Although relieved, and with my panic subsiding somewhat, I was still a little on edge.

'How do I get to the exit?' I asked Taff.

'Oh, it's dead easy and only a five-minute walk away,' he replied, pointing in the right direction. 'You go down there, then turn RIGHT at the sweet stall and just follow the main thoroughfare to the gate.'

I set off, turned LEFT at the sweet stall and arrived at the exit forty-five minutes later.

I arrived home, not only puffed from my pedalling and exhausted from the whole experience, but late. I handed over my dad's shopping and his change, then tried to explain to him why I was late and how lost I had become when surrounded by so many market stalls. My father could not understand how I had become so disorientated in a square field of straight rows of stalls, which, to him, were set out in a logical way with easily recognisable pathways. I came up with some illogical excuses, then, after pausing for thought, I told him about Taff giving me directions. I asked him how I could tell, for sure, which was my left and which was my right.

My father looked at me with a quizzical expression on his face. 'Which hand do you hold your pen in, Nolwen?' he asked.

'This one,' I said, holding up my right hand.

'That's your right then,' he explained.

I began to question how I could tell which was my left and which was my right if I was referring to a place in which I wasn't currently standing. By the time I explained the logic of my question properly, he had tutted impatiently, given up listening to me and walked away. He had never heard of a condition called directional dyslexia and neither then, had anyone else.

Chapter Six

West Wales, 1968–1969
Sorrow

Sometime after my shopping expedition to the market, there was a blow to our family life. It was a school day and my brother and I arrived home just after 4pm. The school bus dropped us off in front of our house. We walked into the garden, carefully shutting and bolting the garden gate to keep – what was now a small family of dogs – safe, then proceeded up the narrow concrete path towards our house. We still had our boxer dog, Jenny, who by this time had had three litters of puppies. I had been given, as promised by my father, and to my absolute delight, one puppy from her first litter, who I called Kim, and which was, by now, a lively adolescent. There was another puppy from Jenny's most recent litter called Gill, who belonged to Steffan.

We both shouted, 'Mam, we're home!' as we walked through the front door, but, unusually, no one answered and there was no sound of our dogs barking excitedly at our arrival. I opened the living room door, expecting two fully grown boxer dogs and one very excitable three-month-old boxer puppy to come bounding out, with every intention of knocking us over, but nothing happened.

'They must all be in the outhouse,' I said to Steffan.

We dumped our satchels and headed out into the kitchen to be sure our mother wasn't in there cooking. At the same time, our mother came in through the back door and into the kitchen looking extremely worried.

'The dogs have gone,' she told us. 'They are not in the garden. Change your clothes quickly, then we'll all walk around the garden hedges and fences to see if we can find any holes big enough for them to have escaped through.'

We rushed to change our clothes and joined our mother in the garden. We searched and searched until, sure enough, after a while, Steffan came across a scraped-up tunnel in some soil next to a tree that stood adjacent to a wire fence.

'Mam,' I shouted at the top of my voice. 'Come and look here. I think Steffan has found out how the dogs managed to get out.'

My mother hurried over to join us. 'Yes,' she agreed, nodding her head with her lips drawn tight, showing how cross she was. 'I think you must be right.'

Steffan and I climbed up the tree and jumped over the fence, determined to keep searching for our beloved pets.

'Don't go beyond the next field,' my mother ordered. 'Wait for your father to come home. Keep calling the dogs, especially when you get to the far hedge and field gate.'

However, despite our efforts and hoarse voices, we returned home defeated and without our three beautiful friendly dogs.

My father arrived home, just before dark. He agreed that we had probably found the dog escape route.

'You all go indoors now,' he instructed, as he set off on a search with his walking stick and a heavy torch. He arrived home just before we went to bed, followed, to my relief, by Kim, my own weary and wet boxer dog, who had almost found her way back home when he had come across her. I was delighted she was safe. 'There was no sign of the others,' he said in a broken voice that clearly showed how worried he was, but added comfortingly, 'I am sure they will turn up in the morning. Tomorrow is Saturday, so we can all go out looking for them first thing.'

The next morning, there was a knock at our door just as we were eating our breakfast. We were dressed appropriately for another dog search and looked up enquiringly as my mother went to the door. The caller was a local policeman. My mother invited him in, but when he saw me and my brother at the table, he asked my father to step outside. I could tell from my mother's demeanour that the policeman was the bearer of bad news. My father came back into the room some minutes later and, after glancing at my mother, came close to Steffan and me. He pulled up a chair and sat down opposite us, breaking the news very gently but with honesty that there was no need for us to go searching again. I could see the deep sadness in his dark blue-grey eyes and waited apprehensively to hear what had happened to two of our dogs. Distraught and deeply distressed at the news he was about to break to his wife and children, my father put on a brave face and explained quietly that a well-known local farmer had reported to the police yesterday evening that there were three dogs on his land. He raised a hand and shook his head to caution us that the news to follow was not good. What he said next was shocking. He explained carefully that from what he could gather, the farmer, not waiting for the police to respond, had taken up his shotgun and shot our oldest dog, Jenny, and the three-month-old puppy, Gill. My dog, Kim, apparently spooked by the sound of the gun, had run away and luckily escaped being shot by the skin of her teeth.

My father – outwardly composed, yet inwardly angry because he had lost the dogs he had been attached to, witnessed the grief caused to his children and lost out on his new ambitious enterprise – went with the policeman and a local vet to examine the dogs and arrange for the disposal of the bodies. My parents then obtained some legal advice that led to a court case held in Trehywel. I remember sitting with my mother in a room at the back of the courthouse, where she prayed for a good outcome, although I was not sure what that good outcome could possibly be. We were both requested by our solicitor to remain in the room in case we were required to give evidence. We were not called into the court, though my father did give his evidence. My father told us later that from what he understood, the farmer had alleged that the dogs had been chasing his sheep, but the veterinary examination of their mouths did not support this accusation. The farmer had, it seemed to him, just taken some preventative action as he owned sheep that grazed in other adjoining fields. Jenny was very obedient and Steffan's young puppy followed her everywhere.

'It would have been easy for the farmer to secure the dogs until the police arrived, but he chose not to do this,' my father said, voicing his opinion resentfully.

My parents could not afford to continue with any legal proceedings with only a slim hope of compensation. And, by my father's own admission, the dogs were on somebody else's land and he, as a responsible owner, should have ensured that our garden was totally secure with no possible means of escape.

As a family, we were devastated by the loss of our dogs. I heard my father, full of remorse, telling my mother later that day that he thought the oldest dog had been shot right in the middle of her chest, so must have been in the sitting position before the trigger was pulled. I was terribly upset. This was the end of my father's ambitious first little business. He never bought another dog and bred no more puppies. I decided to share my ownership of Kim with Steffan and she became our beloved family pet for many years.

To cheer us all up, my father announced a few days later that he would take us on holiday. We had never had a holiday before. His old van was not up to the trip, so he hired a little Triumph Herald from the local taxi man, who also rented out cars. My mother put a letter together and booked bed and breakfast for three nights in her uncle's guest house in Blackpool.

'We are going for a long weekend to see the famous Blackpool Illuminations,' Steffan and I chanted excitedly, time and time again over the next few days.

We had a wonderful time and there was one special moment I will remember forever. The weather was wet on the Sunday, so our parents took us to the cinema. I don't remember much about the film, but I know that I leant on my father's arm, feeling weary as the excitement of the holiday caught up with me. I could not keep my eyes open. He lifted his arm and wrapped it around his daughter. It felt lovely and wonderfully comforting. I snuggled up, relishing a unique moment of closeness. We had never been a tactile family and I couldn't remember having a cuddle from him before that point. The next time he put his arm around me was after my future husband and I signed the register in church at our wedding.

***

Steffan and I stayed with Auntie May and Uncle Gwyn again for the next set of summer holidays. For the most part, I was happy and loved being with my cousins, but every week I would be overcome by loneliness and longed to be at home with my parents. Other than briefly speaking to Mary about the way I felt, I bottled up my feelings, as it was not encouraged in those days to speak to teachers or parents about emotions, fears or concerns.

My loneliness issue resolved itself later that year as before the Christmas rush, my mother decided to give up her

Woolworths job. After a lot of consideration, my parents had decided to apply to become foster parents. I have no idea what brought this on, but their application was processed successfully and a very young baby girl was placed in their care. She stayed with us for a few months and was visited at weekends by her very young unmarried parents, who loved her dearly. They eventually took her home. Having become too attached to the young baby, we were all very upset when she left us. My parents did not foster any more babies.

My mother later went back to her part-time job and my father continued to look after Steffan and me on Saturdays. He tended to spend more time with my brother as I, being almost two years older than Steffan, became more independent. I would meet up with Janice or Gem whenever possible and now had plenty of friends in Trehywel Comprehensive School.

Having taken the advice of Mrs Davies, I worked hard at all my lessons and concentrated on my homework. I thought I had done well in the exams I had taken during the spring and looked forward to returning to school after Easter. The first thing I did on arrival, like everyone else, was to check the year two noticeboard, where my exam results, details of my form teacher and class level were posted. I had achieved over eighty per cent in all subjects except Welsh and came second in class D overall. *Why am I still in class D?* I asked myself. *Surely if I've come second in the class, I must be good enough to move to level C?*

I registered with my new form teacher Mr Wills, but clearly remembering my conversation with Mrs Davies from the previous year, I said nothing to him about my exam results initially. It was over two weeks later that I formed the opinion that Mr Wills was much more approachable than Mrs Davies and that he wouldn't mind if I posed a question to him about moving up a class to grammar school level. Steeling myself, I asked my question. He rechecked my results, had a word with the headmaster and the following week I moved to join the pupils of year two, class C. It seemed to me that the school system had again let me down and I had had to take matters into my own hands. My results should have automatically triggered a review of my class level and I should have received automatic recognition and praise for my hard work.

Although I wasn't good enough to join Gem in class A, I took my education in class C in my stride and was determined to move up the ladder to class B as soon as I could. I made yet more friends and while I had the company and support of these, I was able to give my teachers the impression that I was a self-assured and well-adjusted young student. My parents slowly became of the same opinion. By the age of thirteen, I was allowed some extra freedom, so every Saturday morning, I would catch the bus outside my house into Trehywel. Once in town, I would spend an hour or so in the library choosing books to read over the following week and then spend the rest of the day with girls of my own age, doing the things that young teenagers do. I still tended to fall into my imaginary world and, one Saturday, while sitting on the bus travelling into town, I studied the other passengers instead of focusing on the journey, imagining where they all lived, what they did as a job and why they were going into town that day. From the expressions on their faces and the way they held themselves, I tried to calculate how many of the ladies were, like me, sitting in wet knickers. *Probably only me*, I concluded.

Chapter Seven

1970
Abandonment and Anxiety

Having lost his small dog-breeding business, my father was still determined to better himself. Following discussions between my parents on his latest venture, it was announced to the family that he was leaving his government job as an electrician's assistant and intended to start his own painting and decorating business.

My father already had his van, plenty of DIY tools and had done lots of painting and decorating at home, so considered that outside of buying a few new paintbrushes, some overalls and some long ladders, he was fully equipped to start a new venture. He had no business plan, little marketing expertise and no financial backing, but with the advice of some other local painters and decorators, who would later become his competitors, together with a timely kick-start offer to paint the outside of a small hotel, his new business was set in motion with immediate effect. He was a man who built quality and craftsmanship into everything he did and he felt sure that word of mouth about his good work in a small town like Trehywel would bring him more contracts further down the line. He dipped into the small pot of money my parents had put away for a rainy day and purchased the additional items he needed.

The small hotel overlooked the sea, not many miles away from our home, and was being renovated inside and out by a family friend. My father's new business started well and the owner of the hotel, pleased with his work, offered him a longer-term contract to also paint all the interior – twelve bedrooms, ten bathrooms, stairs, landing, kitchen and all the reception rooms downstairs. The renovation work was to be carried out slowly, so my father needed no additional help and was gainfully employed as a painter and decorator for many months.

Life went on and work on the hotel eventually finished, but, to my father's relief, other offers of work came his way for a little while. Most of the contracts, which he had no choice but to accept, were for work outdoors, meaning that progress, completion and payment was very weather-dependant. I can remember my father often worriedly staring through the windows at home, willing the rain to stop so that he could get on with his painting. Every delay had consequences. If my father was worried, then so was I. My mother was concerned, but not concerned enough to increase her working hours in Woolworths and retail was the only sector she would consider. Much of the work offered to my father had to be turned down as it needed additional resources that he could not support.

He had survived during the summer months, picking up residential painting and decorating jobs, but was unable to formulate a full long-term schedule whereby future work could be guaranteed. During one particularly wet week in September, when he had spent most of his days in our house with his head in his hands, he checked his work diary, closed it and finally admitted defeat. He decided there and then that his second – very short-lived – business had to come to an end.

Despite the decision to fold the business, my father still enjoyed his painting and decorating, particularly when he worked outside in the fresh air and in fine weather. He could not, though, put his family and home at risk by having no guaranteed regular wage coming in. He applied for jobs with local companies, but soon realised that the best paid and most reliable painting jobs were to be found in South Wales. Here, his skills were in demand, particularly in the industrial area around a town called Porthgranog. With my mother's blessing, he accepted a job close to the town, working for a company who employed a team of thirty painters. He sold his van to top up the family savings and found himself some digs in a village location close to Porthgranog.

With a brief kiss on the cheek for my mother and a wave to Steffan and me, he set off one morning, by foot, with a rucksack on his back, carrying a two-handled canvas bag on a planned lengthy journey to South Wales. I watched him through the window as he walked up the garden path, marched with a sense of urgency along the road and then disappeared into the distance. He didn't look back. I wondered if he would ever come home again and tears welled up in my eyes at the thought of never seeing him in the future. I didn't actually cry, though – Nolwen never "actually" cried. My father was my security blanket and a sense of abandonment flooded my thoughts when he left, but I eventually convinced myself that if his leaving led to a new job and stopped him from worrying about how he was going to feed his family, it was for the best.

My father arrived in South Wales having hitchhiked his way to Swansea, where he picked up a bus to Porthgranog, located his digs and reported to the building where his new company was based. His first job, with six other colleagues, was to paint the railings that surrounded Cardiff Arms Park stadium, a rugby union stadium that had been built a year before his arrival. He boasted about this job for many years to come.

My father returned home at the end of October to visit his family. I was fourteen and Steffan was twelve. We were both old enough to hear about my father's job and to listen to his ambitious plans for the future. We were even allowed to join in the discussions on the options that were available to us as a family. My father wanted us all to move to South Wales.

'But I don't want to go to South Wales,' Steffan declared. 'I've just been picked for the second-year school rugby team. I have Sea Scouts every Saturday and I have lots of friends. I don't want to go,' he said flatly.

I didn't think I wanted to go either and initially sided with my brother, but later announced that I would think about the move. My mother appeared surprisingly indifferent at the time.

The next day, we all sat together around the kitchen table and, as to be expected, the conversation once more turned to South Wales. My father described Porthgranog and told us about the boarding house where he currently lived when he was not at work.

'I live with a lovely elderly couple called Meg and Ifan and their daughter, Sue,' he said. 'They look after me very well. I have a clean bedroom with a sink and Meg is a good cook. She makes me a full breakfast before I go to work and a roast dinner with different home-made fruit pies to follow most evenings.'

I glanced over at my mother who bristled with jealousy, never appreciating compliments about other women. My father then described Porthgranog, explaining that it was not far from the sea.

I didn't like the sound of Porthgranog, as it seemed to be a large industrial town that was not set in the countryside, which I had become used to and loved. As usual though, my imagination took over. Daydreaming, I imagined myself starting a new life, in a brand-new modern school with lots of friends and, more particularly, boys, who, I imagined, would swoon over the "new girl" in school with the blonde hair, trendy glasses and the intriguing West Wales accent. I was brought back down to earth suddenly when my mother, having had time to ponder, produced a series of statements and questions for my father, which she put forward sharply.

'Right, well, we need to be sensible; I can manage here while you work in South Wales, Ben, so do we really need to move? What about long-term job prospects for us both? Do you think your job there is reliable? I can't stand the worry of not having enough money coming in again. Last year was awful, I've had enough of going without.'

She continued relentlessly with her questions and, with nothing positive to say, cleared the table noisily and went into the kitchen. I glanced over at my father who stared into the distance, looking totally dejected. If my father was unhappy, then so was I.

The next morning, it was decided that we were all moving to South Wales. My father had handed over his pay packet to my mother, which didn't contain much money but included a raise as an incentive for him to stay with his new company, so she was reassured. He promised me that once he had bought a new car or van, I would be able to come back and visit my friends, Gem and Janice, in Trehywel. Steffan, being his usual meek and mild self, was railroaded by everyone else into agreement. I was very excited about the prospect of a new life and a new school, imagining all sorts of unrealistic scenarios about a future that would hold the answers to all my dreams.

We waved goodbye to my father, who set off once again later that afternoon for Swansea, feeling confident that some kind soul would give him a lift. It was rare in those days for a driver with an empty car to ignore a hitchhiker. My father's next task was to find us a new home.

A couple of weeks later, we received our weekly letter from my father, who was still enthusiastic about our planned move. He had established, though, that privately rented homes like ours at Llancerysmair were hard to find and those he had found were too expensive. My mother, who was now very keen on the idea of a move, told us that she would write to the Porthgranog council and request an application form for a council house. The form arrived through our letterbox a week later. There was a covering letter with the application, advising her that unless the family resided in the area of Porthgranog, the waiting time would be considerable – probably years.

Undeterred, my parents worked together as a team for once, and by the end of November, my mother had packed up, arranged to store all our furniture in two unused attic bedrooms belonging to her younger sister and organised a lift to Porthgranog for herself, her two children and our boxer dog. Meanwhile, my father had purchased a four-berth caravan for forty pounds, which he had arranged to be sited on a local caravan park. The caravan housed four people at a pinch; it was old and tiny, smelled slightly musty and had probably been used purely as a holiday home for two adults and two small children in its earlier days. The park itself was located on the outskirts of Porthgranog town. Overall, although this relocation was a huge change to our lives, we saw it as providing a fresh start, job stability for my father, the answer to my mother's prayers financially, aspirational dreams for me and the usual quiet acceptance of "life as usual" by Steffan. As it turned out, it met none of these expectations.

***

We met up with my father at our new home in freezing weather at just after 2pm on the first Saturday of December. The caravan site manager had just left, after ensuring that our caravan was successfully hooked up to the nearest electricity point. Willing to help with our family move, my Uncle Gwyn and Auntie May arrived an hour later in a borrowed white transit van. This contained the essentials we needed to survive the coming winter, some groceries and a casserole of Welsh "cawl", which my mother heated up later for our evening meal. Our possessions, including a small paraffin heater, were unloaded and my auntie and uncle set off for their home after accepting only a cup of tea. They glanced at each other with discrete incredulity as they walked away and climbed back into the transit van.

'How on earth can two adults, two children – one, a teenage girl – and a boxer dog survive the winter in that tiny caravan?' Auntie May said to her husband as they waved goodbye and drove off.

We were all very tired, so it was decided that we would just unpack the essential items we needed for that night and the following morning, then have some dinner and work out a plan for the next day. Our dog was put to bed in the kitchen, but, as there were no internal doors in the caravan, she wandered in and out all night wondering what on earth was going on. My parents pulled down a double bed, which was folded up in a compartment against a wall, and my father showed us all how he had ingeniously converted the sofa, which normally adapted into another double bed, into a set of bunk beds for Steffan and myself. A plastic privacy screen divided the caravan in half but, despite this, when I laid on the bottom bunk later that night, I could hear my parents talking. I heard my father say to my mother, 'I hope I've properly supported the top bunk and it holds Steffan's weight. I would hate it to collapse onto Nolwen in the middle of the night.'

'I hope Nolwen doesn't wet the sofa bed,' I heard my mother say.

I stared up at the bed above me. *Dad always does a good job of everything*, I thought. *I am sure Steffan's bed is safely secured*. Nevertheless, it took me ages to fall asleep. The strange thing was that I never wet the bed or my knickers again after that point in my life. I guess my bladder must have finally developed the strength it needed to do its job.

We sorted out our possessions the next day and put everything away in the numerous cupboards and overhead lockers typically found in caravans. Every spare space was used up for storage. Steffan and I had only one overhead locker each to store everything we called our own, apart from our clothes, which were put away in the family wardrobe. There was a tiny kitchen with a sink and a small cooker. There was no fridge, but we had never owned a fridge, so this was of no concern to any of us. The kitchen barely had standing room for two people during the day and a stretched-out boxer dog at night. There were no conveniences at all and we had to either wash ourselves in the kitchen sink or head out in the cold to ablute in the site's communal shower and toilet block. Fortunately, we had electricity to run most of our appliances and lights, although we soon found out that this would automatically cut off if the fifteen-amp allowance was exceeded. The paraffin heater kept us warm.

Steffan and I wandered around the caravan park later in the afternoon and met two families with children who lived on the site permanently. We were quite envious of their huge, luxurious caravans with built-in toilets and showers, and their comfortable lounges, dining areas and multiple bedrooms, thinking they must be very posh and very rich compared to us. We were very impressed.

'Meet us at the bus stop just opposite the park gates any morning you like at half past eight,' the children said, 'and we will show you the way to school.'

My father went to work as usual, but Steffan and I were given a couple of extra days off school to settle ourselves in and walk around Porthgranog with my mother, locating shops, the nearest launderette, the local post office and so on. My mother registered the family at the doctors surgery and dropped into the council offices to ensure that the housing department knew that our family now lived in the area and would need a council house as soon as possible.

The next day, Steffan, myself and my mother, who had decided she needed to introduce the family to the school headmaster herself, caught the bus to the local comprehensive school with our new caravan park friends. We reported to the school secretary, who briefed the headmaster that he had visitors. After waiting in the corridor apprehensively for a few minutes, the headmaster opened his office door and invited us in.

'Good morning, Mrs Jones,' he said pleasantly to my mother, shaking her hand. 'Welcome to Porthgranog Comprehensive School. Please come into my office and everybody take a seat.'

We all sat down and my mother introduced Steffan and myself. The conversation that continued between the head and my mother about our family history, reasons for relocating and so on was so amicable that my mother became very comfortable in the headmaster's presence and her confidence levels took a hike.

'My children's school uniforms are still quite new,' I heard her say, 'but they are grey instead of the stipulated navy for your school.' She paused, hoping the headmaster would interrupt her with an agreement that we could wear the grey uniforms to school. He stayed silent, waiting for her to continue. 'Money is a little tight at the moment as I had to give up my job when we moved house,' she added.

To my relief, she did not mention that we now lived in a caravan.

'I understand,' he replied. The headmaster then nodded kindly and agreed that for the time being grey uniforms would be acceptable. He then enquired about our former class levels, explaining that the levels in his school were standard levels in Wales and ran from A to E in years one to five.

My mother, now feeling very self-assured, answered with no hesitation whatsoever. 'They were both in level B,' she said.

Taking my mother's words at face value and not noticing my look of astonishment, he noted this down and advised us to start school the next morning. He gave us the names of our form teachers and classroom numbers, then stood up, shook hands with us all and we left his office. I was delighted to have moved up a school grade so easily and, for once, was very pleased with my mother's quick but dishonest thinking.

It took us almost two hours to get back to the caravan, as my mother could not find her way out of the school, then we turned left at the school gates instead of right and were unable to find the bus stop where we had been dropped off earlier that day. It was only later in my life that I realised I had inherited my directional and left/right difficulties from her. She eventually allowed Steffan to lead the way and we arrived back to a stone-cold caravan but a very welcoming dog.

Steffan and I set off with our new friends for school the next morning. At the school gates, we all went our separate ways and didn't see each other for the rest of the day. As far as I am aware, Steffan settled in at the new school with no difficulties at all. I sought directions and found my way to my allocated class, again pleased that I had so easily moved up a class level.

However, my pleasure was short-lived. When I stepped through the classroom door, I felt very conspicuous in my grey uniform and knew that it would identify me as the new girl and mean that I would stand out in the crowd. My skin prickled at the stares of my classmates and my cheeks flushed red. I was not confident enough to be the focus of attention and hoped my anxieties and concerns would subside. I made a conscious effort to smile at everyone as I was directed to my seat by the teacher. The girls didn't smile back and I felt snubbed. The boys just stared at me unresponsively. I had no choice but to sit at the desk, which was intended for two, on my own. I predicted that this was a bad start; after a while, with nobody sitting next to me, I would become the girl that no one liked. This was not what I needed or wanted. My dreams, which had included meeting boys who would swoon over the "new girl" in school, with the blonde hair, trendy glasses and the intriguing West Wales accent, were fading fast.

Eventually, the girls in my class became curious about me and excitedly asked questions about where I had come from, what subjects I planned to take and where I lived, etc. I was cagey with some of my answers. I did not want them to look down on me because I lived in a caravan. I tried to mingle with the girls as much as possible and, although they were not hostile to me in any way, I was very much the outsider for a very long time. I knew I needed to bond with at least one or two of the girls for two reasons. The first being to give others, especially the boys, the impression that I had settled into their school and was popular, and the other to build up my own self-confidence and thereby reduce my stress levels. Anxiety was not a familiar term to me, but fuelled by the abandonment I had felt when my father left our home and the other negative emotions I had already experienced as a child, this condition was set to affect my life considerably. I was aware that I became very nervous when I was either alone or conversely in the limelight, or if I found myself in new situations with no support. *Fitting in can take time*, I told myself, and before I had even partially integrated into class 4B, it was time for the Christmas holidays.

Chapter Eight

1970-1971
Low Self-Esteem

Christmas that year had all the hallmarks of being awful.

'I am sorry,' my father said to Steffan and me a few days before the big day, 'but there will only be one small present each this Christmas. Times are hard and once the council allocates us a house, there will be removal costs to pay and items we will need to buy. Things will pick up next year, though, so let's just make the best of it.'

Steffan and I were not unduly perturbed with this news and comforted each other with reminders that we had both saved up our pocket money, which we could use to buy our parents and each other some small gifts. We also graciously advised our parents that our gifts from them could wait, as I wanted a pair of trendy, shiny black patent boots and Steffan wanted an anorak, which could be bought later at the C&A New Year sale in Swansea.

The next day, Steffan and I set off together to do our own Christmas shopping in Porthgranog. We pooled our resources and bought a box of chocolates for my mother and a large tea mug for my father. I spotted a little fluffy toy dog with a bell on its neck on a stall at Porthgranog indoor market, which I really liked and hoped Steffan might buy for me. I looked at the price tag and noted that it was too expensive so I walked away from the stall deciding that I would need to choose something else.

To my surprise, Steffan looked at me and said kindly, 'You can have that dog, Nolwen. I can afford it.' He promptly walked over to the stall, picked it up, handed it to the stallholder and paid for it.

'But I can't afford to pay that much for your present,' I declared.

'It doesn't matter,' Steffan replied. 'Just give me whatever money you have left and I will add it to mine and buy myself an Etch A Sketch.'

Steffan was always better at saving up his pocket money than I was. I will always remember the generosity and unselfishness he showed to his sister that day.

We couldn't wait for Christmas morning to arrive, even if it only meant unwrapping a fluffy dog and an Etch A Sketch.

There was one more Christmas surprise that awaited us. When we arrived back at the caravan with our wares, my father greeted us at the door, smiling.

'Do you remember me telling you about my landlady, Meg, and her husband, Ifan?' he asked. 'Well, I popped around to see them today and they have invited us round for supper on Christmas Eve.'

Meg and Ifan had become very fond of my pleasant,

agreeable father when he had lodged with them, describing him as the perfect tenant. The day he packed up his possessions and vacated their guest house, they had insisted, quite genuinely, that he should bring the family he had told them so much about to meet them as soon as he possibly could.

It was a very cold, icy evening when we walked to Meg and Ifan's house. They gave us a wonderful welcome and a superb supper of home-made pork-and-egg gala pie with all the trimmings, followed by Meg's signature trifle. At the end of the meal, Ifan disappeared into his cellar and struggled back up the steep steps with a large paper sack. The sack was bulging with parcels of varying shapes and sizes, which were very loosely wrapped in colourful Christmas paper. He handed the sack over to me.

'There you are, Nolwen,' he said. 'These are all for you and Steffan. Merry Christmas!'

Steffan and I were incredulous and, when prompted by my father, we reached into the sack, removed and unwrapped a countless number of presents there and then, one after another. We expressed our delight and appreciation with the unwrapping of each package. This kind gesture was so unexpected that my parents were lost for words. They, like us, were beaming with happiness. Once I had opened the last present, I looked up at Meg's face, then shifted my gaze slowly across to Ifan's. What was so clearly obvious to me was that the joy we were experiencing was surpassed by the pleasure Meg and Ifan took from seeing our surprised faces and genuine gratitude. What they didn't know was that they had given a family a Christmas they were never meant to have.

***

Although we became used to living in the caravan, it wasn't by any means easy. We had the bare minimum of possessions and although my father's wage was now reasonable for an employed painter and decorator, he still had a few small debts to pay off from his previous business venture, and my mother was unemployed. We managed to eat reasonably well and the caravan was warm, but there was little money left for treats, new clothes, hairstyles or fancy food. I was at that age when fashion and current trends were important. Sadly, apart from my good-quality school uniform, I was poorly dressed. The only coat I possessed was my navy gabardine old school uniform coat, which I had to wear everywhere. I was painfully aware that the other girls of my age either donned fashionable brightly coloured shiny plastic coats, which were the fashion of the day, or wore their school duffle coats. These duffle coats were in vogue for school wear and if worn over expensive Wrangler jeans were still on-trend outside of school. As I could not even attempt to compete with other girls when it came to fashion, I did my best to keep a low profile outside of school.

Unfortunately, every Saturday morning, my mother insisted that I walked to the local launderette two miles away, dressed in my gabardine coat and carrying a black plastic bin bag full of the family's dirty clothes. I knew that this bin bag, together with my gabardine coat, would do nothing for my dignity or my standing with my school peers if any of them caught sight of me. I was on edge, hoping I would meet no one from school, until I arrived home with my task complete. I hated Saturdays.

The New Year arrived, bringing with it even colder weather. I had heard my father mention to my mother that he wasn't feeling himself and was aware that he was getting short of breath when he climbed the ladders at work. Seemingly not overly concerned, he continued to get up early for work each day and, armed with his lunch box, walked to his work office complex where he stored his tools and where a convoy of transit vans were parked ready to take the workers to their next painting job.

My mother, unlike Steffan and I, who braved the cold once a fortnight and used the campsite's communal shower block, carried out her ablutions in the kitchen. She had never used a shower in her life and had no intention of even trying to use the communal showers in the cold buildings on the caravan park. Every morning, after dressing herself and putting out our clothes, my mother folded up the beds, stored the bedding away in cupboards and then prepared a pot of tea and some cereal or toast for our breakfast. She waved goodbye when Steffan and I left to catch the bus to school. Apart from making her way to the nearest grocery shop for provisions a few times each week, ironing, preparing our evening meals and taking the dog on the shortest of possible walks, I have no idea how my mother kept herself occupied in our little caravan day after day. I suppose even the smallest tasks would have taken her longer than normal to complete with only cold running water, a tiny kitchen, no fridge or freezer, and electricity that would suddenly cut off if the permitted amperes were inadvertently exceeded.

***

With the Christmas break over, I had still not really settled in at my new school and by the end of January, it had somehow become common knowledge that I lived in a caravan on the renowned Delfrynmawr Caravan Park. I had also been spotted, more than once, carrying the black bin bag of clothes to and from the launderette in Porthgranog in my gabardine coat, which invited some teasing. Neither of these things improved my image or the acceptance I yearned for by my fellow pupils. I found the regular launderette activity to be embarrassing and it sparked more and more teasing from the boys in my class. I still sat on my own for my lessons and had not managed to integrate myself into the groups of girls who stood together in the schoolyard during breaktimes. I therefore became isolated and vulnerable. The teasing was temporarily cut short, however, as I was sent home from school one afternoon after complaining of abdominal pain and nausea.

A few days after being sent home, my condition worsened to such an extent that my mother made the decision to ask for a home visit by the family doctor the next morning. Before the doctor arrived, she folded down Steffan's bunk bed so that this, together with my bed, converted back into our daily sofa where she placed my pillows and made me comfortable with sheets and blankets. She sent our boxer dog into the kitchen and blocked her off with our clothes airer.

It wasn't long before we heard the doctor's car pull up outside of our caravan pitch, followed by a sharp knock on the caravan door. My mother opened the door, stepped aside to allow the doctor to enter and quickly closed the door after him to keep the warmth in. The doctor looked around our small home, acknowledged my mother and, probably fearful of being eaten alive, turned towards the kitchen entrance and said cautiously, 'Hello, dog,' to our boxer, who, by then, had pushed her head as far through the rails of the clothes airer as possible to see what was going on. She stared at the stranger with her brown eyes, which were deeply set into her face, creased up by thick folds of soft furry skin that emphasised her expression of curiosity. The doctor turned away from Kim and perched himself on the side of my sofa bed.

'So, your name is Nolwen, is it?' he asked kindly as he scrutinised my face.

'Yes, Doctor,' I replied, nodding my head and feeling sorry for myself.

'Okay, Nolwen,' he continued, 'tell me about your pain and about the way you feel.'

I described my stomach pain, my feelings of fatigue and my sickness.

My mother added, 'And she has no appetite, Doctor, although I am giving her lots of drinks.'

The doctor examined my abdomen, took my temperature, lifted my eyelids and looked into my eyes. He then made himself more comfortable by sitting on the bench seat next to our little dining table and made some notes.

He looked up at my mother and said, 'Nolwen is very poorly. She has yellow jaundice or, to be more exact, has probably contracted a type of hepatitis that has affected her liver.'

To my alarm, I heard my mother ask with concern in her voice, 'Does she need to go into hospital?' Worrying me even further, she added, 'We have little in the way of facilities in the caravan, Doctor, so Nolwen has to go outdoors to access the communal conveniences, which are located in buildings at the end of our road.'

The doctor looked around the caravan and then asked my mother some questions that revolved around our family's circumstances. These included how long we had lived in the caravan; who, apart from the dog, lived with us; how old my brother was; and how long we were likely to stay on the site and so on.

My mother replied with what I thought were pre-calculated answers with an ulterior motive, but they were not too far from the truth.

The doctor said nothing for a while, took another look around our home, deliberated and then, to my great relief, said, 'Mrs Jones, you are here with Nolwen every day to look after her, and she seems to be very comfortable and warm in her bed, so I see no good reason to hospitalise her.' He made some more notes, advised my mother on the best treatment for me and then turned towards me once more. 'Do you think you can wrap up warm and make your way slowly to the toilet and shower blocks when you need them, Nolwen?' he asked. 'With the medication I have prescribed for you, I think you will start to feel a little better soon.'

'Yes,' I said hurriedly, not relishing the thought of going into hospital and remembering that I had my navy gabardine coat to wear over my pyjamas if I went outside.

'Remember to take lots of soap and towels with you, Nolwen, and always wash your hands very well. This rule applies to all the family,' he advised, addressing my mother, 'as this form of hepatitis is contagious and personal hygiene is not easy with the few facilities you have here. Nolwen probably picked up the infection at school or from the communal areas here on-site and could pass it on to others.' He then gave my mother some very welcome news. 'I will write to the local town council with a request for them to put you on a priority list for a council house, as your living conditions here, although adequate, are not suitable on a long-term basis for two teenagers, two adults and that...'

He pointed at the dog, who was now wriggling to get her head out of the clothes airer. This was the reaction my mother was angling for, both when she called the doctor out initially and when she answered his questions. I wondered why she had told a white lie, declaring that we had moved from West Wales twelve months ago.

My form teacher was made aware of the reason for my absence from school and put arrangements in place, through Steffan, for the schoolbooks of one of my fellow pupils, a girl called Diana, who had exceptionally good handwriting and was very conscientious, to be sent to our home. This allowed me to copy up notes from her lessons when I felt better. I was very grateful for my teacher's thoughtfulness and for Diana's willingness to cooperate. I found that when I returned to school, I had little difficulty in catching up on lost time as far as my lessons were concerned. However, once I had returned, fully recovered, but still in my stand-out grey uniform, it soon became apparent to me that, after my six weeks of absence, my situation was now even worse. I had still not established myself as part of the various girl groups and I had not blossomed sufficiently to be swooned over by the boys.

***

The teasing that had started before my illness escalated into bullying by the boys in my class. I was still a loner, which made me an ideal target. Their nasty comments were reminiscent of those of Janice's friends in my junior school years and, once again, the verbal abuse was never in the earshot of my teachers but was kept for the schoolyard or for outside the school gates. The boys, some of whom were fifteen years of age, were intimidating because of their size and the threatening tone of their newly developed deep voices. I was less than five feet tall and very slight, so the boys towered over me whenever they chose to get close. Fortunately, they were content with their derogatory comments about my ugliness, our "gypsy" caravan and my weird accent, and never resorted to any kind of physical abuse. The taunting and goading went on for weeks until I made the decision not to go out into the yard during school breaks, but to hide away in the school library. While sitting there one lunchtime, I formulated a plan, which I hoped would make life more bearable for me.

I had heard that at the end of the next term, another pupil called Ffion was expected to move up to my class as she had done particularly well in her exams that year. I decided that I would approach her and suggest that she might like to sit next to me when in her new class. I felt sure this would help my situation as it would indicate to the boys that at least somebody liked me. I spoke to Ffion the next time I spotted her and, taking a leaf out of my mother's book, concocted some story about my being in an awkward situation where I was causing problems between two other girls, one of whom couldn't make up her mind which of her two friends she wanted to sit with in class. I explained that Ffion choosing to sit with me would resolve the issue. To my delight, Ffion agreed with my idea, but reminded me that my plan could not be put in place until the start of the new school term.

The Easter holidays passed far too quickly for me and although I worried about the prospect of going back to school, I decided to keep the bullying to myself and remain quietly brave, mainly out of self-pride and for the sake of my parents, who I reasoned had enough to worry about with our living conditions and their financial situation. If my parents sensed any kind of unease in their daughter, neither of them enquired as to whether I had properly settled into my new school, whether I had made new friends or even whether I was coping with the educational demands of the higher B stream. None of my teachers picked up on my disguised unhappiness either and it was just assumed that as I wasn't complaining, and outwardly appeared to be content, all was well in my life.

Everybody thinks everything is okay in Nolwen's little world, I thought, as I lay in bed, unable to sleep the night before school. *Nobody knows how sad I am, how scared I am to go to school or even how desolate and lonely I feel. Nobody cares about me at all.* I was too tough to cry.

I returned to school with the slimmest of hopes that there might be yet another new girl moving in from a different area, perhaps with a spotty face and the skinniest of legs. *If so, perhaps she can become the boys' latest victim*, I thought, *and they will leave me alone.* Unfortunately, this was not to be the case, and I had no option but to sit on my own again.

There was one particular boy in class 4B who I really did not like at all. His name was Rhys and, reminiscent of Janice in my old junior school, he established himself as the leader of a group of bully boys. Rhys was ginger-haired, freckled and very well built for his age. He was also, like the other boys, almost a foot taller than me. He revelled in belittling me in front of his mates, who thought him very amusing, and he invented my very first nickname, which for some strange and unfathomable reason was "Frankie Gosling". At first, I could not understand why this was the name Rhys had chosen. After some deliberation, I decided that his rationale must have been that I resembled a newborn gosling – not the most attractive of creatures. *Nolwen, you must be really ugly*, I thought, and then, *Ah! The word "Frankie" must be short for Frankenstein. Frankenstein was lonely, miserable and an outcast, and so am I.*

Just as the bed-wetting song had degraded my self-esteem in my earlier years, the nickname "Frankie Gosling" had the same effect in my teenage years. I had considered myself to look okay and imagined that I would be popular in my new school, but the horrible Frankie Gosling nickname prompted me to reconsider my personality at length and to take a closer look at my face in the shower room's mirror. The thin, straggly blonde hair and the black thick-rimmed glasses, worn over eyes that sadly looked back at me, did nothing to allay my fears and I concluded that Rhys was right: I was ugly. Every morning, after washing my face (I still did not clean my teeth), I pulled faces at myself in the mirror, took my glasses on and off, and yanked my hair up over my head or pushed it behind my ears to see if I could make myself look any prettier. Nothing worked. *You have inherited Grandma's chubby face, Mam's thin lips and Dad's stubby nose, and there is nothing you can do to change those features*, I concluded unhappily.

I then considered make-up and new glasses, but we weren't allowed to wear make-up at school and, although many of the girls discreetly wore mascara, I could not afford this kind of extravagance. There was also no hope whatsoever of my parents splashing out on some new non-NHS spectacles for the foreseeable future. Every time I saw my reflection in the mirror, I walked away with my eyes downcast and feeling miserable, but I consoled myself with the fact that although I would remain ugly, there were changes that could be made as far as my personality was concerned.

There is only one option, I thought. *I must become more aggressive and start sticking up for myself. I can be a "Smart Alec" with my retorts when Steffan irritates me, so why not verbally abuse the boys at school in the same way as they abuse me? I am going to make every effort to become less of an introvert and retaliate in the best way possible to the torments of the bully boys, especially those of their ringleader, Rhys.*

This was the first of many personality changes I consciously made during my life.

Chapter Nine

1971

*Anguish, Low Self-Esteem and Personality Change
Number One*

The verbal bullying continued and, to the further amusement of Rhys's gang, I started to defend myself with scathing criticism of the way they behaved. I called them the worst possible names I could possibly conjure up and pulled the most grotesque of faces at them. I never swore, though – and to be fair, neither did they.

Despite my new defence strategy, I did my best to avoid trouble, but the bully boys were more often than not hanging around the bus stop, waiting for me when I finished school. They had no reason to rush home, so no matter how much I dawdled to avoid them, they were waiting for me. Usually as I walked out of the school gates, I was able to see them ahead and keep my distance. One day, I heaved a sigh of relief as there was no sign of them on my route, but as I passed a little newspaper shop – where, unbeknown to me, they had dropped in to buy some cigarettes – they suddenly leapt out of the doorway and blocked my path. With the element of surprise on their side, I stood there, feeling helpless and stunned, temporarily unable to bring to mind any of the contemptuous adjectives I was now used to using. They didn't touch me, but were verbally abusive. When they moved away, I walked on. From a distance, I turned my head back towards them and let loose with, 'You load of stupid morons! You hog-nosed yellow-bellied skunks!' and heard them laughing in my wake.

Unfortunately, my reaction that day proved to be so appealing to their warped sense of humour that it encouraged them to regularly hide and jump out behind me, while jeering or yelling out my horrible Frankie Gosling nickname. With hindsight, I suspected that they were just bored and I provided them with the entertainment they craved when they had nothing better to do. I was not convinced that any of my verbal reprisals did any good and inwardly I still felt emotionally damaged and very upset, but my retaliations had allowed me to rid myself of some pent-up fury and gain just a little bit of their respect for my pluck. Rhys was later to learn, though, just as Janice had at my junior school, that when I was pushed to the limits of my endurance, I was very capable of transforming myself, quite readily, into an incensed and raging beast.

**

For the next few weeks, not only did I dread hearing the Frankie Gosling derogatory taunts, but was constantly tense and primed for the surprise ambushes that the boys deemed to be very funny. My nerves were continually on edge and I struggled to sleep properly at night. Some luck was on my side, however, as one Saturday morning in June, my mother opened a letter addressed to us, which she had collected from the caravan park office. It was from Porthgranog Council.

'Nolwen, Steffan,' she shouted excitedly. 'We have been allocated a brand-new council house in a place called North Cornell. It's not far from here and you will be able to walk to school. We can move in two weeks' time.'

'Hey, that's great,' I called back, inwardly celebrating the fact that I would no longer need to stand at the bus stop and could avoid the school thugs by finding a new route home.

Over the following two weeks, my mother was allowed to visit our new property to measure up for carpets and curtains while I was at school. My mother always lived within her means and worked out that she could not afford fitted carpets for the house, so ordered squares of edged carpet for the lounge and for her and my father's bedroom. She bought a carpet runner for the stairs and chose linoleum, which was much cheaper than carpet, for the kitchen, the hallway and for Steffan's and my bedrooms. She had enough money left for some cheap curtains and a bath mat. All were in place before a hired removals van, driven by one of my father's brothers, arrived with our furniture and the remainder of our possessions from Trehywel. We moved in before the end of the school term, after selling our caravan for twenty pounds to the Delfrynmawr Caravan Park owner.

Meanwhile, I managed to limit the bullying to a degree by continuing to stay in the library during class breaks, where, if it did take place, it was witnessed by girls in my class who felt sorry for me and told the boys off. Also, by being able to avoid the bus stop when I walked home, I could minimise the opportunities for an ambush.

'Where were you last night, Frankie?' Rhys asked one afternoon in class. 'We waited for you at the bus stop. Has your gypsy caravan moved to another site?'

'There is nothing wrong with gypsies or their caravans,' I retorted. 'If you weren't such an ignorant blockhead, you would understand their culture and why they choose to live in caravans. And to answer your snoopy question, I will have you know that my family has moved into a huge brand-spanking-new house in North Cornell.' I elaborated on this further and boasted, 'And my father will be able to pick me up in his new car from school, so I won't be waiting at the bus stop anymore.'

I added the additional lie about my father and his car with two objectives. Firstly, I hoped that I would go up in Rhys's estimation by giving him the impression that my family's fortunes had changed and we had gone up in the world, and secondly, to dissuade him and the other boys from following me on my walk home.

'Oooh! Bully for you,' Rhys said scornfully after hearing my explanation. He walked off with his usual swagger, but, to my satisfaction, did look slightly contemplative. It wasn't long before Rhys was to receive more than a few lies and reciprocal name-calling from me.

My revenge took place a little while later, when I was asked by our RE teacher, along with some other pupils, if we would give up our next Saturday morning to help a well-known local animal charity. I agreed without hesitation. All the volunteers were issued with T-shirts to wear on the day, which, to my delight, we could keep. These had the name of the charity printed on them and underneath the name was a picture of a flop-eared rabbit. We were also provided with official money collection tins similarly identified. Our teacher advised us to stand outside various shops in Porthgranog town centre and to do our best to raise lots of money by smiling at all the passers-by and rattling our tins. *I think I've done really well*, I thought on the day. *Lots of people have stopped to chat about the charity and donated generously.* Although I had no idea how much money I had actually collected, my tin felt extremely heavy.

We had been advised to hand our collection tins into school during the second lesson of the following day. My first lesson, though, was geography with a teacher called Mr Edwards. Ten minutes into the lesson, Mr Edwards' lecture was interrupted by a knock on the classroom door and the voice of a school receptionist.

'I am sorry to bother you, Mr Edwards,' the receptionist said, 'but could you pop up to see the head urgently please?'

Mr Edwards left the room after cautioning his class

to behave and advising us to re-read a section in our textbooks. As soon as he had left, many of the pupils began to chatter and wander around the classroom. I remained in my seat with my head bowed over my book. The charity collection tin sat on my desk and I fiddled with the carrying cord subconsciously while deeply engrossed in my reading. My studies were disturbed when Rhys and his gang began to throw paper, which they had rolled up into balls, at the back of my head and started chanting, 'Frankie, Frankie Gosling, Frankie is a boffin…'

I told them to shut up and leave me alone, but they persisted in provoking me.

'Frankie, Frankie Gosling, get your beak out of your book and fly back to where you came from,' Rhys chanted, flapping his arms and strutting around doing a chicken dance.

This did look funny and the other children, despite our teacher's cautioning to behave, began to laugh at the impersonation. Encouraged by the laughter, which Rhys perceived to be support for his mockery, he came a little closer to me and did a repeat performance. I bit my top lip and feigned nonchalance, but the strutting and harsh words continued. I began to seethe with rage inwardly, but this emotion was not yet apparent to my classmates or Rhys. I became more and more aggravated and my fingers tightened around the cord of the charity box. I clenched my fist and held the cord so tightly it almost cut into my fingers. Suddenly, enough was enough and I leapt up from my chair. With the cord of the collection tin still in my hand, I stretched out my right arm and swung the heavy tin as if it were a discus. It flew high in the air, right across the room in the direction of Rhys.

Mr Edwards walked back into the classroom just as the missile ended its flight and reached its target. It smashed into Rhys, hitting him fairly and squarely on his chest just below his left shoulder. He let out a high-pitched groan. The tin then landed noisily on the floor. Rhys, with one hand on his sore chest, picked up the tin and submissively carried it over to my desk and placed it carefully in front of me.

Silence descended on the classroom. I looked very sheepish and Mr Edwards, glancing at me, rightly concluded that it had been me who had thrown the tin. With a stern but confused expression written across his face, he turned to me and asked, 'Nolwen, what on earth has come over you? Why did you throw that collection tin at Rhys?'

Not wanting to face any more ridicule by telling him the story of Frankie Gosling in front of the whole class, I declined to answer him. He counselled me on the use of violence and dismissed me from class. I picked up my tin and books and left the room. Later that day, I meekly handed over a very dented but still heavy collection tin to the RE teacher.

Sometime later, I found out that some of the girls in the class, including Diana who had loaned me her books when I was ill, briefed Mr Edwards on everything they knew about my being bullied. Mr Edwards arranged detention for all the boys who had been involved in causing me so much distress. He also arranged for a school counsellor to present a lecture to all pupils on the consequences of bullying, which included the devastating and long-lasting effect it can have on the victims. This had a transformative effect on Rhys and his friends and they ignored me from then on. I reciprocated with relief, but still considered myself to be ugly and a person that no one liked. I remained inwardly tormented by a lack of self-worth and low self-esteem all through the summer holidays, but took satisfaction from knowing that at least some benefit had come from what was to be the first of many self-contrived personality changes.

Mr Edwards must have decreed that more needed to be done to resolve my problems than just a counselling session and admonishments for the bully boys, so after the holidays he discreetly engineered a protective friendship for me with Diana and some other girls in my class. I went back to school the next term, this time in a navy uniform and with the comfort of Ffion sitting next to me. Ffion had been true to her word when she moved into my class and became a good friend. Having friends and someone to sit next to made an incredible difference to my school life, as I was no longer treated as an outsider and was, at last, fully accepted.

Chapter Ten

1971- 1973
Growing Up

My home life and family's lifestyle also improved significantly over the next year. While we didn't have the car I had boasted to Rhys about, we now lived in a proper house, which, although small, had separate bedrooms and proper beds for Steffan and I. My father still sometimes complained about breathlessness at work, but this didn't seem to unduly concern him and he was content with his job and his new home. What we didn't know was that his work colleagues had decided to take over all of the high-level work that involved climbing ladders, leaving my father to work comfortably at ground level. As for my mother, I have fond memories of her being perfectly happy during this period of our lives. She encouraged Steffan and me to have friends around and would cheerfully dish out sandwiches and Rich Tea biscuits to everybody.

My sixteenth birthday arrived and I was growing up. I remember that day in September very well. My father, treating me like a lady of leisure, brought me my breakfast in bed and my mother thoughtfully bought me my very first album. It was by Neil Sedaka and I was awakened in the morning by a very loud rendition of the song "Happy Birthday Sweet Sixteen" being played on my father's radiogram.

'Happy birthday, Nolwen!' my parents and Steffan said to me when I eventually climbed out of bed and joined them downstairs. My father had bought me a huge box of chocolates – my very first. He later checked inside the box to find that I had eaten almost half of the chocolates in one sitting. Irritated, he advised me that ladies receiving a box of chocolates would normally eat just a few and leave the rest for another day. I thought back to his guidance about my walking around ensuring my toes pointed forward as a little girl. The eating of chocolates was another lesson from him on etiquette for ladies that I always remembered.

I opened all my birthday cards and, later that day, my mother took me to Cardiff on the local bus to buy me my very first handbag and a pair of gloves. I think these gifts had probably been my father's idea. Wanting the very best for his daughter, it was important to him that, despite our status in life, I should grow up to be elegant and ladylike. Mam and I had a lovely day out together. If my mother was happy, then the whole family was happy too.

Some weeks later, my mother managed to get a job in Porthgranog Woolworths, which pleased her further. As I had reached the age of sixteen, she arranged for me to join her in the store on Saturdays and during the school holidays. Porthgranog Woolworths was much larger than the store in Trehywel and was extremely busy, particularly during the summer holidays when the miners from the valleys took their holidays locally to be close to the sea.

My mother and I initially worked together in the toy department. She was my mentor and although we worked congenially together as a team for a few weeks until I knew the ropes, it soon became apparent to her that I was turning into a young woman who, on the surface, knew her own mind and didn't always want to conform to instructions or respect her opinions. This was the time that our mother-and-daughter relationship began to slowly deteriorate. Unbeknown to her, my experiences with Rhys and his gang had taught me how to stand up for myself and I had learnt the art of rebellion.

Initially, I was my mother's trainee, which meant I had to conform with her directions for a while. I think this gave her a sense of authority over me. For a while, I accepted her guidance and respected her knowledge and experience, but then started to do the job in my own way. I began to voice my non-acceptance of her instructions. I challenged her views and dared to tell her that I did not respect the way she spoke very negatively about colleagues who she didn't see eye to eye with. I noticed that whenever something untoward happened in the store, my mother, with no evidence to substantiate her logic, would conclude that the guilty parties were those people she disliked the most and would try unsuccessfully to convince me that she was right. I can only assume that she acted in this way to impress me with her powers of perception and raise her standing in my eyes, just as she had tried and succeeded in doing when she had criticised other mothers and Auntie May in my younger years.

During one particularly busy week in the Christmas season, it was rumoured that the store takings weren't adding up as expected. My mother deduced that there was a guilty party involved and that that party was a member of the back-office staff who didn't meet with her approval.

'It has to be Mrs Ashman, Nolwen,' she said, trying to persuade me that her unfounded suspicions were correct. 'She empties all the tills twice daily and has access to all the safes and even our wages,' she added conspiratorially.

Having always trusted my mother's opinions and taken her words at face value, I found myself believing this story and, for a while, whenever I saw Mrs Ashman, I watched her suspiciously. However, the more I pondered about it, the less convinced I became.

'You might be wrong, Mam,' I told her, with my new-found stronger personality coming to the fore. 'Anyway, you should not go round accusing people of doing things when you have no proof.'

'Don't you lecture me,' she retaliated nastily. 'You might be sixteen, but I am still your mother and I don't need lessons from you on what's right and wrong.'

I walked away from her resolutely, convincing myself that I was right. Fortunately for her, I did not repeat her suppositions to anyone, as if these had reached the ears of management, she might have needed to face some grave consequences.

It was at this point that I really began to question my mother's integrity and direction. My relationship with her became steadily worse, especially as I was outwardly showing signs of developing a mind of my own and becoming more involved with other teenage pursuits, including an interest in boys. She knew that she was losing control of her daughter, even though this was irrational, and she could not bear the thought of "her Nolwen" changing from a child into a woman. Her reasons were either selfish or unjustifiable, and her disciplinary methodology did more harm than good.

Despite my strengthened personality. I knew I had to manage the situation I found myself in. I began to live in fear of upsetting my mother and, in the interests of a peaceful existence, I learnt to prepare in advance how and when I was going to talk to her if I needed to broach a subject I knew she would disagree with or disapprove of. Her objections usually came from a place of over-possessiveness or were completely illogical.

It was not too long after the Woolworths argument when it was my father's turn to experience the recent changes in my character and to realise that I was growing up and would soon be less complaisant and less dependent on both him and my mother. I realised that my father, unlike my mother, had embraced this inevitable change when, one evening during dinner, following the usual order from him to eat my greens, I placed my knife and fork quietly but resolutely across my plate next to my vegetables and said, 'No, Dad, I am not eating them.'

He looked at me over the top of his glasses with an expression of amused resignation and thought about his response, 'Well! There's not much I can do about that then, is there, Nolwen?'

Steffan looked at me in astonishment and I heaved a sigh of relief having got away with such disobedience. Taking advantage of my father's good humour, when it came time to eating our chosen Saturday night cakes after dinner – mine, a meringue with cream; Steffan's, a chocolate éclair; my mother's, a lemon tart; and my father's, an apple turnover – I waited for him to respond in his usual manner when I asked politely if I could have *my* cake.

As I expected, my father admonished, 'It's not *your* cake, Nolwen. Just ask if you can have *a* cake.'

I pointed to his apple turnover and said, 'Well, I'll have that one there then.'

This time, everybody laughed at my impertinence.

***

At sixteen, I was still way behind my school friends when it came to fashion and the on-trend clothes I needed to help me really fit in and join in the socialising outside of school. I therefore needed to formulate a plan. *The first item I need*, I thought to myself, *is a new coat so that I don't have to wear my school gabardine everywhere. That coat really does nothing to help my kudos with the girls and certainly not my popularity with the boys.*

By the New Year, having saved up all my Woolworth's wages, I managed to buy myself a green plastic shiny coat, which was very "à la mode". It took all the money I had at the time, but I justified the cost by telling myself that it didn't really matter how shabby my clothes were underneath it – during the winter, at least – as nobody would see them. *I've got my navy-blue school uniform for school, a Woolworth's shop overall for Saturdays and, as I only go out on Sundays occasionally, a new coat will suffice for now,* I decided.

The new coat did the trick temporarily. My friends were impressed with my style choice and I found myself welcome to hang out with them on Sundays. The problem came some weeks later, when, after I had managed to supplement the coat with some Wrangler jeans, brogues and a long cardigan to wear over my rabbit charity T-shirt, I started to meet these friends in what my father thought to be inappropriate places for a young lady.

I was out socialising with these friends one Sunday evening. It was well before dark, but my father came up with the unlikely excuse that he was concerned about my homework, so decided that he was going to search the local area to locate his daughter and bring her home. He found me with a gang of friends hanging around a local chip shop and off-licence. To my embarrassment, he beckoned me towards him.

'I don't consider it seemly, Nolwen, for ladies to hang around in the streets or in front of chip shops,' he said. 'I don't want to ever find you there again.'

Unlike with the vegetable incident, he didn't relent and for a while, I only met up with friends at school or in our homes. Although I failed to acknowledge my mother's attitude to my growing up, I had to admit that my father's mentoring, as usual, was quite correct.

I thought it would be some time before I had the opportunity to show off my new clothes again following the chip shop incident. However, I was lucky as, a few weeks later, my parents were made aware, while chatting to a neighbour, of a group of Pentecostal church members who had set up and ran a Friday-night club for youngsters in a local village. The neighbour, aware that we were new to the area, told my parents that his daughter, Glynnis, went to the club regularly and suggested that I could go along, too.

'I am more than willing to drive Nolwen and Glynnis there and back,' our neighbour said. 'It's somewhere safe, where youngsters can enjoy themselves instead of roaming the streets with nothing to do.'

My father agreed with him and persuaded my mother that it would be a good place for me to spend time out of school with other people my age. As I knew Glynnis from the school choir, which I had recently joined, and was still under-confident when it came to doing anything out of the ordinary on my own, I approached her and asked about the club.

'Come along, Nolwen,' she said kindly. 'I go every week and I think you will enjoy it, especially as you, like me, enjoy singing. We do a lot of that in the club and there are loads of different musical instruments available that people can borrow and learn to play.'

I went to the Friday-night club with Glynnis most weeks after that. We enjoyed cups of coffee or glasses of Coke, food snacks, singing in groups and playing games of table tennis. The Pentecostal church also organised a week's holiday in the Welsh seaside resort of Tenby every Easter. The holiday accommodation was in the basement of a chapel in the centre of the town. Just off the chapel vestry were two sleeping areas, one for the girls and one for the boys. There was also some toilet and washing facilities and a small basic kitchen, where some lady volunteers cooked our meals. As it was free, with my parent's permission, I packed a small bag and caught the coach to Tenby with Glynnis. The club organisers took guitars and other musical instruments, so that we could provide outdoor evening concerts on the promenade for the benefit of other holidaymakers and tourists. The songs were sung either in Welsh or English and were chosen for the religious message they imparted – not that we minded. Leaflets were also handed out by our adult organisers, advising the holidaymakers of Pentecostal values and beliefs.

The church members had good intentions and, to be fair, provided somewhere to go for children on Friday evenings and gave many youngsters a holiday that they perhaps would never have had otherwise. They were, I believe, intent on converting us all into devout Christians and I felt, at times, that there was a tendency by some of the organisers to try and brainwash us. For a while, in my teenage years, I can remember feeling absolutely convinced that as I had been "saved" and had repented my sins under the guidance of the chapel members, I had undoubtedly reserved my place in heaven. I was sure that many of those around me, including my mother, who was a true believer in God, had not been "saved" and would therefore not properly qualify for this reward. I believed that my mother and father were destined for hell when they left our world. My beliefs, though, were short-lived and, with Glynnis on side, I decided that disco-dancing, pop-singing, sneaking odd drinks of alcohol and, in Glynnis's case, smoking cigarettes were far preferable to praying and speaking in tongues. Our teenage ordinary pleasures, thought at the time to be sinful, meant we were categorised by the Pentecostal church members as being unreformable backsliders. We rebelled and only ever went on the one holiday in Tenby. We gave up the Friday club not long after and our religious beliefs fell by the wayside.

***

At the end of the next school term, I asked my parents if I could join other members of my school and attend a county youth choir and orchestra training course, which would last for a week and be held in a local campus just outside Porthgranog. The course would conclude with a classical concert for the public, which would take place in the town hall in Swansea.

These courses were popular with teenagers as, in addition to the training courses, the social life in the evenings was brilliant with discos and other events. I had to be selective with the detail I passed on to my mother about the course, as I was well aware that if she heard anything she didn't want to hear, my chances of attending would be low. While I could appraise her of the accommodation arrangements, the training and the concert, I dared not mention that these courses were also open to university students and there was a likelihood that some of the tenors and base singers would be men of age eighteen or more. As it was, with the limited information I gave to her and the encouragement of my father, she agreed reluctantly that I could attend.

I could not contain my excitement and, along with some of the other school music students, looked forward to the course for weeks. All the girls were thrilled at the prospect of meeting new boys and as there was no uniform to wear, we splashed out on some new clothes and other essential items such as mascara and lipstick.

By the time of the course, my father had purchased a small, second-hand Austin A40 car and he dropped me off with another friend, Bethan, at the campus gates. I thanked him for the lift, waved goodbye and Bethan and I walked through the entrance gates, arm in arm, chattering enthusiastically about the week ahead.

Halfway through the course, my parents, accompanied by my Grandmother Jones, who was visiting our home with a view to coming to the concert, decided to pay me a surprise visit at the campus. They registered their arrival at reception and asked if the lessons could be interrupted so that they could see me. Their visit was untimely as I had decided, fuelled by the encouragement and enthusiasm of Bethan and others, to skip a scheduled training session in order to spend some time in our dormitory, playing records, dancing around and acting a little silly.

Once I was located by the reception staff who, seemingly unconcerned about finding me in my dormitory as they had come across truancy many times before, led me to join my parents and my grandmother, who were sitting and waiting for me in the campus coffee bar. To my alarm, as soon as I entered the room, the staff told my parents where I had been found and what I had been doing.

My face reddened and my body tensed, as I knew I had been caught out. However, the expression on my parents' faces seemed neutral, so I dropped my shoulders and relaxed. My grandmother smiled pleasantly as she was so pleased to see me and we enjoyed a happy couple of hours together. A few days later, though, I received an extremely severe reprimand in the form of a letter from my mother. Her words were damning about my misconduct during their visit and she said that she had been particularly annoyed because Grandma Jones had been with them. The strong words in her letter cut me to the bone. I read, to my dismay, how she was utterly ashamed of me and how I needed to think about the disgraceful situation I had created.

I was troubled, hurt and very upset by the letter's content. It was on my mind throughout the remainder of the course and I was unable to enjoy the concert. I read the letter time and time again and pondered over its content before falling asleep in my bed every night until the end of the course. *Was my behaviour really that bad?* I questioned. Surely we were only having a bit of fun.

Should I really feel this ashamed of myself? I thought guiltily.

I have no idea whether my father knew about the letter, but there was no further mention of it when I, very warily, returned home at the end of the week, braced for further rebuke. I suspect my mother later regretted writing it, but, at the time, it had clearly allowed her to exercise a satisfying, if inappropriate level of power over me. I didn't have many pleasures in my life at sixteen and to unnecessarily cut short the one pleasure I had been looking forward to for months was mean. Once again, I questioned her unreasonableness, but this time, taking things a step further, I made up my mind that I needed to break free.

***

It was one sunny Sunday afternoon, when having sat our examinations, Bethan, Diana, Glynnis and me were idling our time away in a park, while waiting for some other friends to join us, that we started talking about our future career plans.

'I've decided to join the army!' Diana exclaimed.

Glynnis, Bethan and I looked over at her, then at each other in shock. Diana was a reserved, studious girl, who did not seem to be an army type at all.

'I have decided to train as a nurse,' Glynnis revealed.

Continuing the future career theme, Bethan advised us that she might continue her studies and go to university. I told my friends, as I lay on the green grass pulling at clover leaves, that I was unsure what I wanted to do but knew I was ready to leave home. I explained that the thought of another year or so in school before being able to have my independence from my mother had slowly become daunting. The girls nodded their heads, understanding my predicament, and proffered some ideas. It was only after a suggestion from Diana that I should consider joining the military that I considered my future seriously.

When I arrived home, I scanned some advertisements in a local newsletter and sent off for some military service brochures. The first to arrive was a glossy brochure from the Army Recruitment Centre in Cardiff. I looked at the front cover, where a young army recruit was portrayed standing at attention on a parade square. I hated the green uniform and peaked hat she was wearing, so dismissed any idea of joining the army within seconds and without reading any of the literature.

Two days later, a brochure arrived from the Royal Air

Force Recruitment Centre in Swansea. I glanced over the pictures and then read the detail with interest.

A few days after that, I showed it to Bethan who, within minutes, also became interested in a career in the WRAF and asked if she could take the brochure away with her to read. That night, my imagination, which often still ran away with me, went into overdrive and I pictured myself and Bethan sitting together in an aircraft control tower with our headphones on our heads, guiding jet fighters into land.

Bethan dropped around to my house the next day and although similarly excited, she had her feet more firmly on the ground than me and said she wanted to make enquiries about the different trades available, training times, the location of RAF stations, units or camps, as they were sometimes called, and the opportunity for overseas postings. Within twenty-four hours, armed with some additional information that Bethan had obtained, we both abandoned any ideas about studying for our A levels and decided to enlist. I was very relieved that Bethan was going to accompany me, as I was still a follower as opposed to a leader, and was very dependent on others to support and guide me in new situations or on unfamiliar journeys.

Although I had quite firmly made up my mind about the WRAF, there was one obstacle ahead of me – my mother. I would not have reached the age of eighteen by the time I was ready to embark on my chosen career, so needed the consent of my parents to join up. *Ah!* I thought. *I wonder what Mam will make of me leaving home and losing control of her eldest child.*

I decided to leave the RAF brochure lying around the house for a few days in the hope that my father would take an interest in it. This he did, and after expressing some reservations about my leaving home at such a young age, he opted to present my case to my mother, and later accompanied me to the RAF Recruitment Centre in Swansea. There, we discussed all the trade options available, I sat a short examination and completed some preparatory formalities. We returned home and after some long conversations with my mother, supported by the mothers of Diana and Bethan, who were very enthusiastic and proud about their daughters forthcoming independence and future careers, her only option was to join in the excitement and give me her blessing.

Within weeks, I was enlisted into the WRAF. What I didn't envisage was how the negative emotions – including loneliness, low self-esteem, guilt, abandonment and, last but far from least, diffidence and anxiety – I had experienced so much of in my young life were bound to influence my future and undoubtedly affect my personality and ability to survive in my chosen career.

What I did know was that I would miss my father and Steffan terribly. Steffan had managed to escape much of my mother's proprietorial nature, but some years later, he reached the same conclusions as me and followed in my footsteps. After three years in university, he also joined the RAF, where he enjoyed a wonderfully successful career.

Chapter Eleven

1973
Directional Dyslexia and Fear of Failure

Stepping onto the train at Porthgranog Railway Station on the 22nd of November 1973, destined for my WRAF basic training in Lincolnshire, was the moment that changed the course of my life. I didn't know it at the time, but I was setting off on an extraordinary journey that would lead me back and forth, through undulating periods of emotional instability, uncertainty, trepidation and aspiration, all interspersed with changes to my character, achievement and success, to a final intriguing destination of surreal reminiscence.

My parents and Steffan waved me off at the station. I was travelling to Lincolnshire alone, as although Bethan had also enlisted and would be at the same RAF station as me, she had chosen a different trade and her start date had been a few weeks earlier than mine. She reassured me before leaving home that she would look out for my arrival and would make sure she was around to give me all the usual hand-holding I needed. I was still very nervous when I boarded the train as I was alone and this was the very first train journey I had ever made. The train took me to Paddington Station where my father, knowing I had no sense of direction and was not familiar with the underground system, advised me to take a taxi to King's Cross from where I would board a second train to the station at Lincoln. I was expected to arrive at my destination at 2pm.

I kept glancing at the little Timex watch my father had bought me as a farewell gift, hoping my two trains remained on time. I kept a close eye on my suitcase, which Grandma Jones had given to me, and which sat on the rack at the end of the carriage. I wore my one and only green shiny coat, having handed the gabardine school coat into a charity shop. Beneath the green coat, I had – at my mother's insistence – donned a plain woolly pullover, which matched a plaid skirt, and had added some sensible court shoes. I carried my birthday handbag and gloves. With Bethan's guidance before she had left home, I had bought myself a striking pair of silver non-NHS spectacles and had my blonde straggly long hair cut into a neat short style, which, according to her, really suited me. All in all, I felt that I would give a good impression of myself when I arrived at my very first RAF station. My confidence was boosted a little more when I reminisced about Glynnis and Diana, who, while saying their goodbyes to me the night before I set off on my adventure, had told me that they could not believe my transformation when they saw my haircut and glasses.

'You look great, Nolwen,' Glynnis had said. 'You are lovely and slim, and I can hardly believe the difference those two changes have made to your appearance. You'll have all the airmen queueing up to take you out.'

Perhaps I will, I thought happily as the train sped through a long tunnel, soon taking me across the border from Wales into England for only the second time in my life. I came back to earth quickly, though, when I reminded myself that my first objective was to get to Lincoln without getting lost. And before considering relationships with airmen, I should probably do my best to fit in with the other girls on my flight. "Flight" was the group name used to identify me and my fellow recruits, I had read.

During the journey, I comforted myself by remembering that Bethan would still be at the basic training camp when I arrived and would give me the low-down on what to expect. I had only heard from her once since she had left home and presumed that this was because she had very little time to write letters. From her one letter, I only had a rough idea about what to expect during the six-week WRAF basic training course, otherwise known as "Square Bashing". I guessed that Bethan – knowing that although I had toughened myself up in recent times, I was still under-confident when away from family and friends – hadn't wanted to worry me with too much detail. She needn't have been overly concerned, though, as despite my insecurities and inner reservations, I had already decided that no matter what I was to be confronted with over the next six weeks, I had no intention of giving up and going home. I was too proud to fail.

I arrived at Paddington Station, summoned a taxi and was dropped off at King's Cross Station. I looked in awe at the impressive buildings I passed on my journey across London and was surprised at the number of people and volume of traffic on the streets of the huge, frightening city. Overwhelmed by it all, I was relieved to set off on the second leg of my travels from King's Cross. My second train chuntered all too quickly into platform one at Lincoln Station. I was met there by two Corporals (Cpls) in their meticulously presented uniforms, my name was ticked off on a check-sheet and I was directed to board an RAF grey military coach, along with some other groups of very excitable but clearly apprehensive young girls.

I arrived at my training unit a couple of hours later. There were about sixty girls, including me, allocated to "B" Flight and, after being given a short lecture on ranks (mine was ACW, short for Aircraftwoman), our unique service numbers, which contained a letter followed by seven digits, a training programme and a meal in the mess dining room, we were accommodated in four dormitories on two floors of a barrack block. The barrack dormitories had plain curtains on all the windows and polished wooden floors, and all the doorknobs, metal window catches and handles were made of brass. The floors and brass furniture shone like mirrors because of repeated polishing by previous recruits. Although they were warm and light, the rooms were stark and sparsely furnished with only a bed, wardrobe and dressing table allocated to each person. There was a small communal table and a few chairs at one end of each room. We were briefed that all personal possessions had to be stored away each morning and that nothing, not even a single framed photograph, was allowed to be left on display. We were informed that lights off and bedtime was at 10.45pm, followed by a warning that all recruits would be bed-checked each night for compliance with this rule by the duty Senior Non-Commissioned Officer (SNCO).

***

The first half day of training was all-consuming and after climbing into my bed that night, although exhausted, I lay awake for some time reflecting on my situation. Signing on the dotted line to serve queen and country and arriving at my first unit was just the start of a huge step change in my life. I had six weeks of intense and autocratic training to complete and as I was a young woman, or rather a "new recruit", already damaged by ridicule, abandonment, guilt and shame, who carried repressed emotions such as diffidence, anxiety and feelings of low self-esteem, the professional ladder, precariously balanced against an uneven wall, seemed likely to be more difficult for me to climb than for most of the other new recruits. We all missed home; we were all strangers to life in the services; and we were all apprehensive, but from observing just on that first day the way my fellow recruits quickly reacted and adapted to the pressures and demands of military life compared to me, I considered myself to be at high risk of failure. I decided, even before prompting, that I needed to make more of an effort than the other girls to convince our flight SNCOs and Junior Non-Commissioned Officers (JNCOs) that I was worthy of retention. Outside of my emotional issues, which I hoped I could conceal, I knew that the biggest encumbrance to my early career was the possibility of getting repeatedly lost and not properly knowing my left and right.

As I tossed and turned in my unfamiliar bed, way after midnight, on that first night, I started to really worry about how I was going to ensure I did not get lost getting myself from A to B on the camp and potentially arrive late at whatever training session was next on my schedule. I was also concerned about how I was going to be able to find my way to the B Flight table in the mess dining room after visiting the food servery to select my meals. The mess I had dined in the previous evening was enormous and there were hundreds of recruits who, from a distance, all looked the same to me in their uniforms. We all sat at identical tables, but not always in the same place, which I knew would make things worse for me. Thinking about my first visit to the mess made me cringe. I relived the experience, now in a cold sweat beneath the stiffly starched white bed sheets. I thought about how I had picked up my meal, glanced slowly around at the vast and noisy room, and then wandered aimlessly around it with my tray, desperately hoping that, just by chance, I would come across my fellow recruits. My sweating became more profuse and I fidgeted in my bed as I recalled what had happened next.

I had been embarrassingly rescued by a tall fit-looking, bemused male corporal who had rightly concluded that I was lost. He was smartly dressed in his uniform and wore shoes that shone like mirrors. He asked me which flight I belonged to.

'I think it's B Flight,' I had said nervously.

'I think it's B Flight, what?' the corporal had asked, pointing to the two stripes on his arm.

'I think it's B Flight, Corporal,' I replied formally.

'That's better, ACW Whatever-your-name-is, but you are going to have to buck your ideas up if you want to pass the orienteering phase of your training course,' he said sarcastically. 'You are clearly incapable of navigating yourself around the mess, never mind the Lincolnshire countryside.'

I had looked at him cluelessly, but was relieved when he shook his head with a supercilious look, tutted and led me to the correct table.

I need a plan to ensure that I don't keep getting lost in the mess, I thought to myself. *I don't want that corporal, even though he was rather handsome, to catch me out again.*

I worried about the problem for a while, but it was soon overshadowed when the penny dropped about something else he had said. I had clearly got an orienteering exercise ahead of me at some point. This knowledge kept me awake for even longer and concerned me much more than finding my way around the mess.

Eventually, I put my worries behind me and, thinking about my longer-term future, fell into a happier imaginary world. At this point, I did my best to deliberately avoid falling asleep, relishing the period before I dropped off because it felt like a luxurious private space for my own pleasant thoughts, and for as long as that period lasted, I felt comfortable and content, protectively cocooned in my own bed and my own imaginary world. *The sooner you fall asleep, Nolwen, the sooner tomorrow will arrive with all of its challenges,* I told myself.

I replicated my "not falling asleep quickly" philosophy every night for the next six weeks in an attempt to put off my training and the start of the next day for as long as possible, even though I was exhausted.

***

In the very early hours of the next day, I woke up and quickly remembered where I was. Not wanting to disturb the other girls who were sleeping peacefully around me, I got out of bed quietly and risked switching on my bedside light. From my dressing table drawer, I took out my copy of the training programme for the following week and checked it over. I didn't want any surprises as I had decided that sound preparation was the key to success.

Nearly every day was scheduled to be almost a repetition of the previous day, but with training periods in a different order and with different timings. I noted that all the recruits would be on duty on Saturday mornings, but on Saturday afternoons would be free to relax or go shopping in the nearest town. Saturday nights looked to be the highlight of the week as I read that all our flights would be bussed to the nearby men's RAF Basic Training Unit, where a disco would be held and there would be the opportunity for the WRAF new recruits to socialise with their counterparts in the RAF. Sundays were indicated as also being free, but it was suggested that they should generally be reserved for personal tasks such as the writing of letters to family, clothes washing, ironing and personal administration. I decided that, in my case, it might be beneficial to also use Sundays for extra preparation for my lessons for the following week. It turned out that Sunday was the only day we were not woken up by the duty NCO, who would normally switch on all the dormitory lights and yell at us to get up at an ungodly hour.

The room around me remained quiet as I continued reading, with some girls gently snoring as they slept. I sat on my bed examining the training programme and worriedly contemplating what my first full day had in store. Physical education, lectures on military responsibilities and visits to the camp clothing store to be measured up for our uniforms appeared on the pages. These were activities I had expected and they held no real fear for me. I balked, though, at the thought of other training sessions, which I assumed would involve close individual scrutiny, marching around or the need to respond instantly to verbally shouted orders. I had never been a quick responder or thinker.

Training sessions on "military drill" were my worst fear, but none of these appeared on the programme for the next few days. Unfortunately, for me, this skill was something I needed to be able to cope with effortlessly if I was to participate in the B Flight passing out parade, which would signify my successful inauguration into the WRAF.

The thought of drill training was so bad that I was relieved to see lots of sessions on the programme given over to dental checks or the receiving of vaccinations, which were mandatory for all service personnel, as these, in my eyes, were preferable to anything that might be associated with drill. The root cause of my fear of drill and marching in general was, of course, my undiagnosed directional dyslexia. I knew that I had rhythm and could swing my arms and probably walk in step, but I had no automatic left/right reflex or sense of direction. I also knew that this generally unrecognised impairment had to be overcome; I was, after all, in the military and drill was essential for the performance of our duties through practice and prescribed movements. I got back into bed with that thought in my head and fell asleep for the second time that night. Unfortunately, my non-sense of direction and left/right issues proved to be totally inexplicable and embarrassing and plagued me throughout the rest of my training.

***

I need not have worried too much about finding my way around the camp the next day, as before the crack of dawn, despite not having been fully kitted out with uniforms or having had any drill training, B Flight was rounded up and formed into three ranks under the guidance of one of our two flight JNCOs. These JNCOs were called Cpl Badcloth and Cpl Pimpleton. That morning, it was the turn of Cpl Badcloth to lead us, as one body of people, to the mess for our breakfast.

Once we had settled ourselves into a band of disorderly and unruly fledgling airwomen, Cpl Badcloth brought us to attention. We responded by just slightly stiffening our bodies and holding ourselves in a semi-upright position.

Reasonably satisfied with this response, Cpl Badcloth then shouted loudly, 'Flight, right turn!'

I wasn't the only person to turn left instead of right that day and all of us who got it wrong quickly swivelled round to face the direction the majority of the recruits had taken, then stood still in line with everyone else.

The next order clearly articulated was, 'Flight, by the left, quick march!' Our unlikely band marched off in three columns, chatting and laughing, while simultaneously trying to align our feet with the "left, right, left, right, left, right" footstep guidance from Cpl Badcloth.

'Shut up!' Cpl Badcloth yelled at us. 'I said, shut *up*!' she repeated, heavily emphasising the word "up". Losing her patience and after only a few yards of marching, we heard her shout the command, 'Flight, halt.'

Some of the girls in the flight stopped abruptly while others took their time, which led to cartoon-like consequences.

After giving us a stern dressing-down about talking in the ranks and failing to concentrate, Cpl Badcloth set off once more with her disorderly band in the direction of the mess where we were to take breakfast. Fortunately, for me, I wasn't in the front row as I was far too short to be what was called a "marker" – responsible for not only listening to orders on direction, but also for guiding the way for the whole flight. All I had to do was follow the person in front of me to get myself safely to my destination. Cpl Badcloth had not been happy with our undisciplined performance, so we were lucky to get any breakfast at all that morning.

We soon found out that the formation into three ranks and marching under the instruction of either Cpl Badcloth or Cpl Pimpleton was to be the norm for moving around the camp. This took a lot of pressure off me as I did not need to find my own way to get anywhere. It also meant that I could never be late for my lessons. We became more and more proficient at marching as the days passed. Snowy conditions a few days later set our standards back a little, but this was no excuse for poor marching, so we soldiered on accompanied by numerous reprimands.

***

That first full day had been a steep learning curve for all of B Flight and it wasn't many days later that the full reality of what we had all signed up for became fully clear. Our working day started at about 5.45am and finished after dinner at about 7pm. In addition to working these long days, our Monday evenings, known as "Bull nights", were taken up with the thorough cleaning of our dormitories and barrack block communal areas, in preparation for an inspection the next day. The remaining evenings allowed for plenty of chatter between the recruits within each dormitory as we worked together washing and pressing our uniforms, and polishing – or "bulling up", as it was called – our two pairs of black, lace-up leather shoes. One pair of these shoes was retained purely for our passing out parade, which would signal the end of our basic training. Special attention had to be given to these shoes and to our parade uniforms, known as our "Number Ones". In the case of our parade shoes, these would only pass inspection if they shone like mirrors. Our uniforms had to be perfectly pressed and in pristine condition. Once a week, all RAF-issued items of clothing that hadn't been worn during that day were uniformly folded and laid out by the recruits on their beds, where they were checked by our corporals as being present and in a good state. All recruits were required to stand at attention at the end of their beds during any of the room or uniform inspections.

There was another chore which every recruit was required to carry out outside of the working day. Every morning, we were ordered to strip our beds and, by following a dormitory example, had to fold and stack our bed sheets, blankets and bedspreads into the exact shape, form and size of what was called a "bed pack". These bed packs resembled a thick, block-shaped sandwich, which had been sectioned to show its filling. Using the appropriate colour blankets to represent the bread and filling and the white sheets to represent the butter, our stacks were produced as per the example. If bed packs were not perfectly constructed in size and form, their elements would be tossed around the dormitory by the inspection staff.

One evening, I set a new daily routine for myself. I decided that at the sound of my alarm clock, which I would set for fifteen minutes before anyone else's, I would switch on my little bedside light, strip my bed and quietly build up my bed pack. I would then creep out of the dormitory and arrive in the ablution area before the other girls. This routine would give me a head start on my fellow recruits and was intended to ensure that I had a quarter of an hour in reserve to cater for any hiccups I might encounter with the rest of my pre-breakfast duties. This strategy worked and kept my anxiety levels down, which rocketed whenever there were time constraints or deadlines to meet.

I also came up with a mess dining-room plan. I managed to ensure that I didn't get lost in the mess by following Wendy, a recruit who I always marched next to, to the food servery. Choosing the same meal as her, following her to the drinks station, then selecting the same drink meant that I didn't stray far from my unsuspecting guide. I then stuck to her like glue as she made her way effortlessly back to our table. Communal grace was said before we were allowed to eat our meal, so I always took the opportunity to thank the Almighty, whom I had previously renounced after my holiday in Tenby, that Wendy, like me, did not like fish!

The new recruits were all strangers and everyone in each dormitory, just like me, made efforts to make friends and bond with each other as quickly as possible. Although we shared the communal areas with all members of our flight, it wasn't easy to make friends from other dormitories as there was just not enough spare time in the day or evenings to wander around the barrack block and socialise. A passing "hello" or "goodnight" had to suffice.

If I have little opportunity to meet the rest of the girls in my own flight, I thought worriedly, *I doubt I will see much of Bethan in her "F" Flight over the next few weeks.* As it happened, I didn't see her until the Christmas break when we both returned home.

Chapter Twelve

1973
Directional Dyslexia, Poor Eyesight and Fear of Failure

It was a week after our arrival, when all the recruits had been issued with their full quota of working dress uniforms, shoes, hats, gloves and, to my disbelief, gabardine coats that the dreaded word "Drill" appeared on my training programme. The working dress uniforms, unlike our "Number Ones", were made of a rough, hairy fabric and consisted of jacket, skirt and an optional pair of trousers, which were given the nickname of "Hairy Marys". The gabardine coat, although air force blue in colour, resembled my school uniform coat, but it was belted and did not have a hood. The shoes were flat and comfortable, and ideal for marching with their studded soles. Sadly, our flight was one of the first to miss out on being issued with the smart, thick woollen double-breasted greatcoats I had been attracted to when I saw them modelled by airwomen on recruitment posters. *I would have felt a lot warmer in one of those*, I thought, as I stood shivering in my gabardine coat, my head bent forward against the icy cold wind on a parade square, waiting to be taught drill for the very first time.

Drill was normally the first lesson of the day. It was either held on the outdoor official parade square or in a huge, virtually empty, cold military hangar, which had a few windows and a concrete floor. Drill was always under the direction of either Cpl Badcloth or Cpl Pimpleton, who were qualified drill instructors. The format was almost the same each day, but with more advanced manoeuvres introduced as the date for the flight's passing out parade drew nearer.

Our performance was watched over by our flight commander, a young recently commissioned officer called Flying Officer Hart. She was accompanied by our Flight SNCO, Sergeant (Sgt) Fairclough. Both sat in the hangar on a couple of plastic chairs, warm in their greatcoats at one end of the square hangar. They had a personal stake in B Flight's progress in drill as Flying Officer Hart would be the parade commander on the day of our passing out parade, with Sgt Fairclough supporting her as our flight commander. For the most part, though, it was our two corporals who gave us our instructions and made every effort to mould us into fully fledged airwomen. Cpl Badcloth was a strict disciplinarian, whose professional and fair approach gained her the respect of the new recruits. Cpl Pimpleton, on the other hand, was "just a strict disciplinarian" – one of those JNCOs who gained compliance, but without the respect of her subordinates.

It was Corporal Pimpleton's turn to take charge of our very first drill lesson and I managed to make a complete fool of her and myself within minutes. It quickly became evident that if anyone was going to let Flying Officer Hart and Sgt Fairclough down during the passing out parade, it was going to be me. The flight was brought to attention and we set off with our studded shoes clicking heavily in unison on the concrete floor around the hangar, following the yelled-out command, 'Flight, by the left, quick march.'

By this time, I was used to being marched around camp and, although tense, I swung my arms, looked at the head of the person in front of me and was perfectly in step with everyone else. The problem came when the command, 'Flight, left turn', was given. This order on the move was new to me and differed to the "left wheel" command used to gently guide a whole flight around junctions or obstacles when we were marched on roads around camp. The command "left turn" when on the move demanded that the recruit adjusted her step and turned her whole body smartly in the direction ordered as an instant reaction and in time with the other recruits. The inevitable happened to me and instead of turning left, I turned right. I took a few more marching steps, felt like an idiot when I realised there was no one in front of me, shuffled, stopped, went red in the face, turned and ran off quickly to find my lost place in the three ranks of airwomen marching smartly away from me.

I pushed and shuffled my way into the group and then into step with the others as quickly as I could, but, needless to say, the disruption meant that the whole flight had to be halted by Cpl Pimpleton, who admonished me for lack of concentration. I think she thought my error would be a one-off occurrence, but she was very wrong.

It happened three times more during our first drill session and then regularly over the next few days, by which time, the three NCOs and Flying Officer Hart had quietly run out of patience and Cpl Pimpleton had used up all her derogatory admonishments with no positive effect.

You are running out of chances, Nolwen, I thought one night, as I got into bed and considered the words of Sgt Fairclough who, witnessing Cpl Pimpleton's continued frustration, had taken me aside and given me a warning. I then mused over the training programme for the next day, wishing that for once there would be no drill. Suddenly, I remembered my question to my father just after I had become lost in the open-air market at Trehywel on how to determine my left from my right. I thought of his words and instinctively lifted the hand I used to hold my pen. *That's your right, Nolwen*, I thought and finally dropped off to sleep.

I survived all the remaining drill training sessions without embarrassing myself again. I did this by simply clenching my right hand as tightly as possible while I marched and continually, and without fail, reciting the words "This is your right, this is your right, this is your right, this is your right" in my head as I marched along. I was thus always primed to turn in whatever direction was required of me with no hesitation or mistake. Of course, neither my fellow recruits or corporals knew how ACW Jones had suddenly become so alert and obedient during her drill lessons.

Despite becoming a star on the parade square, I was unable to keep my general lack of confidence under wraps and those in charge of B Flight soon became aware of it. To receive our weekly wages, we were all required to stand in line, wait for our names to be called out, then individually march up to our flight commander's desk, salute her (this action was often referred to as "paying a compliment") and sign for our pay, which was then handed to us in little brown packets. My hand would shake visibly as I reached out for my pay packet. I was sure Flying Officer Hart had noticed my discomfort, but to my relief she was kind enough to say nothing. If I had had a choice, I would have opted to receive no pay at all as opposed to going through this ordeal every week.

Cpl Pimpleton, however, showed no such sympathy or discretion when she noticed my uneasiness and openly reprimanded me by shouting out loudly, 'ACW Jones! There is no need to shake,' whenever she became aware of my discomfort.

'I am sorry, Corporal, but I can't help it,' I would reply in a timid voice as I stood to attention at her words, my body trembling even more under her scrutiny.

Cpl Badcloth's rebukes were a little more considered, but even she questioned my nervousness. One morning, when she inspected the neatly folded items of uniform that were placed on my bed, she noticed that some of my PE kit was still damp after washing.

'Do you think it's a good idea to sleep in a damp bed, ACW Jones?' she asked.

My immediate reaction was to say that, until recently, I had been quite used to sleeping in a damp bed and that it didn't matter, but instead replied subserviently, 'No, Corporal.'

Cpl Badcloth removed the damp items from my bed and commented on my hands, which shook visibly as I reached out to take the offending items off her. 'Why are your hands trembling, ACW Jones?' she asked.

'I don't know, Corporal,' I answered. 'I think it's nervousness, because I want to get everything just right and am afraid of failure.'

Seemingly either impressed or at least satisfied with my honest explanation, she nodded her head and walked away saying nothing further.

***

Although I was convinced that Cpl Pimpleton had concerns about my suitability for the WRAF, I hoped that I had impressed Sgt Fairclough and Flying Officer Hart sufficiently enough for them to disregard any reported or observed disproportionate reservations from this corporal. I hoped that they would take into account some of my positive attributes in their end-of-course review, particularly as I had done well during their classroom lectures and had, after all, rectified my left/right issue on the parade square. However, I thought my new career was well and truly stymied, due to an incident late one night in the dormitory after lights out.

I was lying in bed and as usual was doing my best to stay awake to prolong the one and only part of the day when I was alone with my thoughts and in relative safety from the military world surrounding me. I started to sniff and felt a wetness running onto my upper lip. As I didn't have a cold, I guessed that I was having a nosebleed. Against regulations, I had no option but to sit on the side of the bed, put my little bedside light on and reach into my top drawer of my dressing table for a tissue. Sure enough, the tissue was soon soaked in blood. I sat there, pinching and dabbing at my nose, when our dormitory door opened and in walked the duty SNCO, flashing her torch over all the beds to ensure that all the recruits were present and correct. She approached my bed and before she could say anything, I offered, 'I am sorry I am out of bed, but I'm having a nosebleed.'

'You're having a nosebleed, what?' she replied, prompting me to add the obligatory rank at the end of my explanation.

'I'm sorry, but I can't see your rank,' I said straightforwardly.

The SNCO shone her torch onto her left epaulette. 'You're having a nosebleed, what?' she prompted again.

'I still can't see,' I explained once more.

'Why can't you see?' she said, shining her torch even closer to her shoulder and rank badge, but this time with an irritated tone to her voice.

'Because I haven't got my glasses on!' I replied.

I genuinely hadn't meant to be facetious; I had thought about guessing her rank, which could have been sergeant or flight sergeant, but decided honesty was the best policy. The SNCO turned on her heels and stomped out of the room.

My nosebleed eventually stopped, but I laid awake for another hour or so, worriedly contemplating how I would explain my unintentional flippant answer to the duty SNCO, which would surely appear in her report and be brought to the attention of my flight commander the following day.

That, I thought, *is probably the final nail in my coffin and will probably ruin any chance I have of completing my training course.*

I can only presume that despite her outward appearance of annoyance and frustration, the duty SNCO had had a sense of humour as I heard nothing more about the incident. The event, though, brought to the fore that, like my Grandad Jones, I obviously suffered from very poor eyesight. This affliction plagued me for the rest of my life. It was never fully corrected, despite wearing glasses.

***

Our basic training continued with little variation week on week. We were approaching Christmas and the weather was extremely cold, with snow on the ground for days on end. However, this did not deter our corporals from marching us around camp or from ensuring that we kept our barrack blocks spotlessly clean, despite us being unable to avoid placing dirty footprints from the slushy snow on the highly polished floors whenever we entered our accommodation blocks. Fortunately, our drill practice was often held in the huge hangar, which, although cold, was at least dry.

One morning, B Flight stood at ease in the hangar, waiting for the arrival of our flight commander. We were brought to attention on her arrival, but then ordered to stand at ease again as she had an announcement to make that apparently concerned us all.

'Good morning, B Flight,' she said in what to me sounded like a posh but kindly voice. 'I have some news that some of you might find very welcome.' She paused for effect and then continued from a pre-prepared script with, 'Due to the government's need to reduce electricity consumption and conserve coal stocks associated with potential miners' strikes, the Christmas and New Year break for all recruits will be extended by seven days. This means that, exceptionally, your basic training will be reduced from six weeks to five.' She stopped speaking, as despite now being highly disciplined, the recruits could not suppress their delight, albeit reservedly. 'We will shortly issue an amended training programme, but I must caution you, B Flight,' she added, 'we now have a limited period in which to ensure that your proficiency in drill is up to the high standards required for your passing out parade. Sgt Fairclough and I must be entirely confident that you will not let us down and that you will all perform flawlessly on the day.'

With that, we were brought to attention and our drill training continued in earnest.

I could not believe my luck. *This news is the best Christmas present I've ever had, even better than the sack of presents from Meg and Ifan*, I thought, thinking back to my time in the caravan with my family. These thoughts impaired my concentration and I forgot to clench my right hand as I marched around the hangar.

At the second command of, 'Flight, right turn,' I turned left and this time deservedly experienced the wrath of my flight commander as well as Cpl Pimpleton.

Chapter Thirteen

1973–1974
Success

After receiving the news that our basic training was to be cut short, B Flight did indeed receive extra drill sessions until the Christmas break, but I focused on my right hand throughout and made no further mistakes. Additionally, on checking over the revised training programme, I noticed, to my great joy and relief, that the orienteering exercise I had been dreading had been cancelled. I needed nothing more to encourage a spring in my step as I marched with the rest of my flight to our last evening meal in the mess before our Christmas break. This last meal was a full Christmas dinner, carefully prepared for us by the RAF cooks. It was a wonderful and very welcome surprise.

After dinner, all the recruits, even those from different flights to ours, rushed off excitedly to pack their suitcases in readiness for the extended Christmas break. Everyone in my dormitory talked feverishly about their Christmas plans and many, like me, were too elated to fall asleep after lights out.

The next morning after breakfast, we exchanged seasonal greetings and reassured each other that we would return in the New Year despite our mixed thoughts on the difficult few weeks we had endured together. We were then transported by a convoy of RAF coaches to the local railway station. I arrived home many hours later, exhausted from the journey and from the pressures of the training I had received. My family, including our boxer dog, were delighted to see me. My mother was a little more reserved than everyone else, but we enjoyed a very happy Christmas together.

Over the next few days, I caught up on lost sleep and was spoiled by my father bringing me breakfast in bed most mornings. My mother cheered up and there were no arguments or grumbles. *She's not so bad, after all*, I thought to myself, as I chatted to her one morning about my training.

The following weekend, I managed to meet up with Bethan and we exchanged our WRAF basic training experiences over a coffee, both appreciating why we had not managed a get-together in Lincolnshire. Our service lives went their different ways after that point, although we kept in touch with the occasional letter and phone call.

I reluctantly returned to camp in January 1974, but still with a determination to succeed. I completed the remainder of my WRAF basic training and the B Flight passing out parade was scheduled to go ahead a week later. The morning of the parade, which was due to start at 11am, dawned bright and clear and there was no sign of the frequent icy wind or snow that I had become used to. The majority of the recruits were excited because the day of the parade had finally arrived, but I was extremely nervous.

The station car park filled up as families and close friends arrived to watch the spectacle. They made their way towards some chairs that had been set out opposite the podium where the reviewing officer, our station commander, was expected to stand in his ceremonial dress to assess the standard of B Flight's drill and our degree of discipline efficiency. A small military band positioned themselves in their usual spot and began playing some arrival music.

At the sound of Flying Officer Hart's first command, our band of airwomen set off in perfect unison. Tunes like "Those Magnificent Men in Their Flying Machines" and "The Royal Air Force March" were played as the parade progressed. The music that resounded around the square made the hair on the back of my neck stand on end as I marched with enthusiasm and pride, replicating the movements of the airwomen in front of me and by my side. Although there were a few shouted commands as we moved around the square, there was no "left, right, left, right" guidance, as, by the day of the parade, we were all expected to march with musical rhythm and in step, while keeping to the well-practised parade format.

At one point, the reviewing officer walked along the ranks to inspect our uniforms and every now and again stopped to offer comment. When he stopped in front of me, I brought myself to attention, but my body visibly shook. He appeared not to notice my discomfort and, to my relief, only imparted some words with a smile.

'Well done, Airwoman, and good luck in your military career,' he said and moved on.

Thanks to my hand-clenching and the determined concentration of all the recruits, the parade was completed without a single hitch and we were applauded by the reviewing officer and all of the visitors when it came to an end. I was disappointed that my parents, due to the costs involved, had not been able to attend the parade like the parents of my fellow recruits and had missed such a great opportunity to tell me how proud they were, but I understood their reasoning. I also knew that even if they had managed to make the journey, although they would have been secretly pleased with their daughter's achievement, neither of them would have been able to put this emotion into words. All my young life, I had sought praise, the odd compliment or approval, but they were never forthcoming.

After the parade, I said my goodbyes to my friends, politely thanked my instructors and paid the appropriate compliment to my flight commander with a smart salute. Of course, no one knew how I had had to find a tactic to hide a medical condition that had hindered my training progress so severely. As the years passed, I kept my own counsel about having to tightly clench my fist and utter the words, "This is your right. This is your right," quietly under my breath to enable me to form part of a parade whenever the occasion called for it.

Later that afternoon, I set off for Wales once again, but I was thrilled to be wearing my smart "Number One" uniform this time. My father, slowly taking in the sight of his daughter so smartly dressed when she arrived home, couldn't have been prouder and, despite not conveying this in words, insisted on my visiting friends and family in uniform so that he could show me off over the following few days.

I was delighted that my basic training and square bashing were now over. Sadly, and as shocking as it sounds, it was fair to say that I had hated almost every minute of it! I knew, though, without any doubt, that actual service life would be completely different to the military experience I had endured to date.

***

I had one weekend at home before making another journey, this time to start my RAF Telecommunications trade training. Initially, this was a nine-week course, but was later followed up with more specialist training as I climbed the promotion ladder.

The trade training didn't start that well, as I arrived with a particularly bad cold and was told to report to the medical centre for two days. I worried about falling behind on my training, but was assured that the first few days were for induction purposes only and that I would soon catch up. The training unit covered a vast area so my next worry was how to navigate myself to the medical centre and back again. I tried to appear as if I knew where I was going and walked with a sense of purpose. I knew, though, that I must have been walking around in circles as I passed buildings I was sure I had come across previously. Many of the buildings looked the same, which didn't help me. To my alarm, I was then reprimanded by a commissioned officer for not paying him the expected compliment as he passed me in the distance.

'Airwoman,' he shouted. 'It's no good pretending you can't see me.'

His rebuke was justified as I had caught sight of him across a car park, but had kept my eyes downcast as I was unable to confidently determine his rank from a distance, and there is nothing more embarrassing than saluting a person who doesn't warrant this respect. I looked up after hearing him call out to me as if I had been taken by surprise, apologised and, knowing exactly what was expected of me, saluted smartly.

I eventually found my way to the medical centre. The reprimand episode re-emphasised that my eyesight, despite wearing spectacles, was poor and likely to be the cause of embarrassment in the future. The only way I could limit the risk was to either hang back and follow the example of others walking in the vicinity or, to get from A to B, ensure that I rode a bike, carried an open umbrella or carried lots of packages, thereby keeping my right hand fully occupied. I had no option but to rely on these strategies throughout my service career.

At the end of my confinement in the medical centre, one of the medics was luckily also heading back to my barrack block, so I walked back with her, followed her example when she saluted and was able to return to my block with my head held up high.

My trade training was a breeze compared to my basic training and I found my classroom lectures easy. There was no drill instruction or parades, just the usual marching from lessons to the mess for meals or to and from our accommodation blocks. There were the obligatory Monday "bull" nights, but these were less demanding than they had been previously. Although I would willingly have boycotted it, unfortunately I still had to be paid each week and was therefore still required to put myself through the usual process of standing in line, marching up to the issuing officer, collecting my pay, followed by a smart "about turn" before returning to my original place in line.

My trade training continued over the next couple of months with only two further events worthy of recall. The first was when I arrived back at my barrack block from the medical centre after recovering from yet another cold. Although dormitories were a thing of the past, the furniture in my four-man room was identical to that of my basic training unit. I searched in my handbag for my wardrobe and dressing table keys only to find them missing. I panicked as I was due to resume my lessons thirty minutes later. I tried the door to my wardrobe where the course notes I needed for my lessons were stored on the top shelf, only to find it locked, as I expected. I sat on my bed with my head in my hands, knowing I was not going to give a good impression of myself if I was late.

'Please, God,' I whispered. 'Help me to find my keys.'

My hand spontaneously and inexplicably shot out in front of me, then my fingers gripped the handle of the top drawer of my dressing table and yanked the drawer open. There, sitting on top of my best gloves, was my bunch of keys. Some kind soul had obviously seen them lying around and locked my wardrobe, then thoughtfully placed my keys in the drawer. I thanked God, feeling guilty about having renounced Him after my Pentecostal disaffection. I set off for my lesson with my notes on time and with an umbrella in my right saluting hand – luckily for me, the weather had changed for the worst and had become wet and windy.

The second and most important event at that time, and the one that had as much influence on my life as joining the WRAF, was the evening I met someone called Greg. The social life during our trade training was superb and I was out one evening with a couple of friends, two of whom had been accommodated with me in the B Flight dormitory at my previous unit. One of my friends was going out with an airman, who was, that evening, accompanied by another good-looking, blue-eyed, blond-haired seventeen-year-old recruit, and both joined us at our table. We all went to the NAAFI club disco later that night. Afterwards, the good-looking airman asked if he could walk me back to my barrack block – which was surprising to me, considering my Frankie Gosling days. I had presumed he was out of my league. I said yes and later agreed to meet up with him the following evening. After joining the WRAF, this was the second-best decision I ever made in my life.

I passed my course examinations with flying colours and a few days before leaving my unit, along with the other trainees in my class, I was given a proforma that allowed me to provide the RAF Personnel Management Centre with three "first permanent posting" preferences. Greg's technical training was to last for a further eighteen months, so, to be able to continue our relationship, I chose three RAF units closest to our training unit. There were no guarantees but, as fate would have it, I was posted to a station in Gloucestershire, which was only about a two-hour drive away and allowed us to spend time together most weekends. Later, Greg's first permanent posting brought him forty-five minutes away from my first permanent unit, so we were clearly meant to stay together.

Chapter Fourteen

1974–1978
Achievement, Guilt, Loneliness and Personality Change Number Two

Having finished my trade training, I was promoted to the rank of leading aircraftwoman (LACW) and I arrived alone at my first permanent RAF station. I reported to the WRAF administrative office and was shown to a four-man room. No one was in the room at the time, but it was equipped with very recognisable furniture. A round table with matching chairs was positioned in the centre and there were four wardrobes, four dressing tables, four beds and four bedside lamps. This time, though, the room had posters on the walls and signs of being occupied.

I settled myself in, then sat on my allocated bed as I was not due to arrive at my workplace until the following day. Very suddenly, I was overcome by a strong sense of loneliness. It was reminiscent of the time I had spent with Auntie May and Uncle Gwyn, when I had missed my parents terribly. This feeling stayed with me until the remaining room occupants arrived in from work and was to reoccur whenever I arrived alone at a new RAF station throughout my military career.

I stayed awake long after my new roommates that first night, feeling very unsettled as, once again, I found myself to be in an unfamiliar environment with a new job to face in the morning. My thoughts were productive, though, and I made a conscious decision that as I had now arrived at my first permanent unit, I should change my personality – outwardly, at least – for the second time in my life. When I was being bullied by Rhys and his gang of friends, my efforts to appear more confident and less of an introvert ultimately led to victory. *Perhaps now is the time to build on those efforts and make another similar change*, I thought.

As I lay contemplating in the dark, it seemed to me that if I wished to be respected and progress as a true professional in my chosen career, my character should not be identified as it was during training, as being diffident and anxious, even if that was the real and true Nolwen. If I wanted to move up through the ranks, I needed, at the very least, to be perceived by my seniors and colleagues as being determined, confident and ambitious, I decided. *Perhaps I need to become a little more guileful too*, I thought to myself.

Before I dropped off to sleep, I admit that I considered the kind of devious tactics my mother had resorted to when she had been determined to get us a new house, and when she had manipulated my trusting old headmaster into moving me up a grade to further my education. *Similar tactics might prove to be very useful if I want to get promoted quickly*, I concluded.

***

After my first night of apprehensive thoughts, it didn't take me long to settle into my new unit. The girls in my room were nice and Greg visited me as regularly as he could. Apart from annual Battle of Britain and Remembrance Day parades, there was no marching and "bull nights" were few and far between. To my relief, my salary was paid automatically into my bank, which took away the necessity to grin and bear the agony of collecting my pay each week with the usual accompanying regime. I still carried an umbrella or some packages on my way to and from work to avoid reprimands for inappropriate saluting.

My place of work was a small, unsophisticated elementary communications centre, run by elderly Warrant Officer (WO) Doddery, who spent most of his day staring out of his office window, and a very pleasant, laid-back SNCO, who was as soft and gentle as his unusual name, Sgt Bunny. The centre itself consisted of two rooms, one equipped like an office but with two hatches cut out of the walls. One hatch was used for the delivery of handwritten messages, which had to be typed up error-free on a teleprinter and then appropriately transmitted. The other one was used for the handing over of received messages to "runners", who delivered them to departments in the rest of our building. The second room was usually noisy as it contained a small number of teleprinters and some additional items of telecommunications equipment. Operationally, there were five corporals and a mix of airmen and airwomen.

As was usual for new arrivals, I was mentored by a more senior operator. My mentor was Senior Aircraftman (SAC) Dick Morton, who was short and overweight, but very experienced and had served in the RAF for just over twenty years. He was conversant with his role in the communications centre but was cocky. I didn't like him at all, so very quickly my premeditated personality change number two, which included deviousness, came into play and I realised that it was important to "use" Dick and his arrogant willingness to share his knowledge to my advantage.

Our communications centre occasionally processed correspondence for a small government office at Worcester. When querying with Dick why this was the case, I pronounced the town as "War-chester" instead of "Wuster." Dick corrected my pronunciation unkindly, pompously and with no discretion. A couple of airwomen in the vicinity laughed at his comments. *He needs to be brought down a peg or two*, I thought malevolently. For the time being, though, I tolerated his method of tuition until I was schooled enough to warrant promotion to the rank of senior aircraftwoman (SACW).

The evening of my promotion, I went to the NAAFI club to celebrate. As I walked in, Dick – who, unlike everyone else, had not made the effort to change out of his uniform – was sitting with some of our colleagues at a long table. He was eating a bowl of greasy chips with tomato sauce and shouted some mildly derogative comment about my unsuitability for promotion. His military beret sat at my end of his table. I picked it up with no hesitation, rolled it into a sausage shape and flung it at him. It hit his face and then landed, to the amusement of everyone, in his chips. This wasn't a violent attack, as the beret was soft, and the act was deemed funny, but I had undoubtedly seen red and my words to Dick that followed were intentionally wounding.

'You pompous little git!' I shouted. 'Twenty years in the RAF and still an SAC. Watch this space!' The tenacity of my first personality change, which had come into effect during the Rhys and his bully gang era, had clearly been maintained and was very apparent that night.

***

After achieving my promotion to SACW and while I was in the confines of my familiar working environment, armed with the objective of personality change number two, I gave an impression of being confident and self-assured. Furthermore, not satisfied with my current rank and its low salary, I was determined to gain further promotion if only to be able to avenge Dick and be true to my harsh words after throwing his beret at him.

One afternoon, a small opportunity to earn some professional admiration transpired. When it was my turn to "make the crew brew", I knocked on WO Doddery's office door and announced my arrival with a pleasant and composed, 'Good morning, sir,' then walked in and placed the grey-haired, elderly WO's huge teacup, with the word "Boss" printed on it, onto his desk. He was sucking the end of a pen and as he stared out of the window, it was clear to me that he was pondering over a page of written text on a sheet of paper in front of him.

'Ah! SACW Jones,' he said as he drew the cup towards his lips. 'Thank you. A cuppa is just what I need.'

I saw an opening to impress him and took a few seconds to formulate a plan. 'Are you struggling with something, sir?' I asked tentatively, referring to his document with my forefinger.

'Yes, I can't see the wood for the trees with this draft report,' he replied.

'Well, if it's not confidential, sir,' I said, with some hesitation, 'and you don't think me rude, I could review it for you if you like. There's nothing better than a fresh set of eyes on written text,' I added manipulatively.

He picked up the sheet of paper and handed it over as I selected a spare unchewed pen from a pot on his desk. I sat on a chair at the opposite side of his room, reviewed and amended his work, making a conscious effort not to be patronising when I handed it back to him with a quick, 'There you are, sir. I hope that helps.'

WO Doddery read my amendments and was delighted with the changes. From that day on, he regularly used me as his personal scribe. In addition to this new-found responsibility, I was careful never to put a foot wrong operationally and wittingly kept on the good side of my subservient easy-going sergeant. These somewhat devious tactics resulted in accelerated promotion to the special acting rank of corporal within two years. I was very pleased with myself when the promotion was formalised and couldn't wait to tell Greg and my parents about my "high-flyer" news and then flaunt my two new stripes around my unit, especially in front of Dick Morton, my old mentor.

It was not long after that my easy-going Sgt Bunny was posted to another unit and was replaced by a totally different character. Sgt Cross was a small, ambitious Irishman who rushed about our communications centre as if his pants were continually on fire. His role was the same as that of his predecessor, but he seemed unable to cope with his responsibilities in a calm or steady manner and was always openly under excessive pressure. He was also terrified of losing out on promotion because of any telecommunications procedural errors made in his department. To cover his back, he added an additional "check and sign off" layer for all the centre's transactions. The responsibility for that extra layer, at WO Doddery's suggestion, was allocated to me. Awkwardly at first, as I was newly promoted compared to the other corporals in the centre, I found myself responsible for checking, correcting and reporting to Sgt Cross, sometimes unavoidably negatively, on the operational standards of my resentful peers, as well as for the writing and reviewing of my WO's correspondence. Seeing the advantages, I began to savour the accolade of both activities and gratefully accepted the applause in my annual performance reports, despite, for obvious reasons, being the envy of, and losing my popularity with, the rest of the team.

Having been selected for the "check off and sign" role, I became, like SAC Dick Morton, self-opinionated, but, in my case, I was also ambitious and had no intention of either being complacent or just satisfied with my recent success. I had already established that the route to a successful career in my chosen telecommunications branch clearly demanded not only sound trade knowledge and the ability to hide my inner weaknesses, but the skills to influence, manipulate and "manage" the opinions and expectations of my seniors. I therefore made the decision to look after my own interests, even if this was at the expense of others, and to continue to strengthen my personality to suit the behests of my seniors.

Sgt Cross's nature was such that in the interests of my own career advancement, I was obliged to abstain from counter commenting when he unfairly discredited his subordinates to WO Doddery. I am also ashamed to say that I continued to ingratiate myself with this SNCO until I received my next posting notice. Deep down, I was never comfortable with my approach, but in the interests of a promising career and in line with my personality change number two, I did not change it. I had my WO totally wrapped around my little finger due to his need for my writing skills and I also very quickly and craftily established that Sgt Cross needed my trade skills to keep him safe operationally.

I thought my future promotion prospects were very much on track until I overheard a surprising conversation about me between WO Doddery and Sgt Cross one afternoon. Unbeknown to them, at the time of the conversation, I was sitting in a training room adjacent to my WO's office where the wall between us had ears. WO Doddery was being very complimentary about his "favourite corporal", but Sgt Cross, possibly jealous about the professional relationship between me and his boss, was being subversively disloyal to me and dishonest. *My goodness, what a backstabber!* I thought to myself as I strained to catch everything he had to say.

'She undermines my authority and operates and acts above her station,' I heard Sgt Cross tell my WO. I was furious, as I had shown him a loyalty that was often misplaced and only acted above my station because of the "check and sign off" position he had put me in. I instantly yearned to retaliate, but had to bide my time.

Sometime later, Sgt Cross was so overwrought and overwhelmed with his responsibilities that he finally snapped and, before my very eyes, unjustifiably threw a wooden ruler in the direction of an airwoman called LACW Heather Plant in a fit of temper. She had inadvertently used an incorrect teleprinter to transmit a message to another RAF station and should have received the new arrival training she had been waiting for, as opposed to being openly ridiculed. Ashamed of his impulsive action, my sergeant privately asked me to keep the incident to myself. I promised that I would, but did not use my family's truth word – "honest" – at the end of my sentence. Knowing that he regularly lost his temper and remembering his disloyal comments about me, I forwent my allegiance and reported his unacceptable behaviour "in the strictest of confidence" to WO Doddery. The SNCO received an informal warning and was apparently referred to the station medical officer for some anxiety medication and anger management counselling. When he returned to duty some weeks later a changed man, he must have guessed that it had been me who had betrayed his trust.

Although I knew I had done the right thing in reporting Sgt Cross, as violence in the workplace could not be condoned even in the services, I admitted to myself that I shouldn't have made a promise that I couldn't keep and that my motives were wrong. These were more in the interests of increasing my good standing with WO Doddery and in retaliation for my sergeant's disloyalty than they were for the injustice shown to LACW Plant. I received a posting notice not long after Sgt Cross's return to work.

Chapter Fifteen

1978
Loneliness and Low Self-Esteem

My second permanent posting, this time holding the full rank of corporal instead of "special acting", was to another small RAF station, set in the heart of the Wiltshire countryside. The location meant that Greg and I were able to continue our courtship and meet up once a month.

Even though I was now a JNCO with just over four years' experience in the military, I was still very ill at ease at the thought of a new challenge in an unfamiliar environment. On the day of my arrival, I walked, fortunately in civilian clothes, which meant no umbrella, bike or packages were required to avoid saluting officers, through the camp gates and reported to the WRAF administration office.

As a corporal, I was automatically allocated a single room, which contained the usual furniture but no companions, and as soon as I shut my door, I was once again overwhelmed by the now familiar sense of loneliness. This time, I not only felt lonely, but was troubled when I considered my departure from my previous unit. Although there had been the usual goodbyes and good luck wishes, I guessed that these had been insincere. I knew that I had left under a cloud. I was aware, deep down, that apart from WO Doddery who "wouldn't be able to see the wood for the trees without me", I would not be missed. Perhaps it was a feeling of justifiable low self-esteem, as, after all, I had been selfish, manipulative, devious and conceited throughout my time at my first unit. *I am not proud of myself*, I thought, as I equated my emotions to the "Janice and brick" incident.

By the end of the following morning, which was a Friday, I had, despite my eyesight issues and navigational fears, almost completed the routine formal arrival process on my unit, to include reporting into the supply squadron where, to my delight, I managed to obtain a station bicycle.

'There's not much call for the ladies' bikes,' the storeman advised me. 'Most of the ladies work within a short distance from their accommodation block and are happy to walk around the camp. You can keep this on loan for as long as you like providing you sign for it.'

He handed me a supply loan card with my details neatly printed on it. I readily signed for one lady's bicycle in the appropriate space, tried the bike for size, thanked him and, after asking for directions to the station communications centre, rode away with a restored feeling of confidence. The storeman had no idea how much he had helped me that day. While riding my bike, I could avoid saluting appropriately or inappropriately.

I arrived at my place of work, another communications

centre that looked almost identical to that of my previous unit. There, I briefly met the SNCO in charge, who was the bearer of good news. I was to be a shiftworker and as my shift was currently off duty, I was not required to report to work until the following Monday.

That Saturday, my parents decided to pay me a visit. I had visited them on numerous occasions since finishing my training, but they now wanted an insight into my military life and my unit was near enough to home for them to carry out the journey there and back in one day. They arrived early in the morning and I obtained special permission for them both to be able to look around my barrack block and to have lunch with me in the mess. They were very impressed!

My father had made me a set of pine cupboards and a shelf unit, which he had managed to get into his little car. While in my room, he placed the shelf unit on top of the cupboards, explaining that it could house a small black-and-white portable television if we purchased one together later that day. I was delighted with the furniture, which complemented the standard military-issue wardrobe and dressing table and made my room cosy and unique. Above the unit, I hung a large handcrafted wooden key, which was decorated with ribbons and had: "Congratulations on your eighteenth birthday, Nolwen. Love from Mam and Dad", painted on it, together with my address written in marker pen. Unable to afford the shop-bought silver paper-coated plastic keys, with their ribbons and gift packaging, my father had made the key himself and had sent it unwrapped through the post when I was at my previous training unit. It had amazingly arrived intact on my eighteenth birthday, but I had not at the time been allowed to place it on the wall. I knew I would keep it forever. When I thanked him for the furniture, I looked into his eyes and thought fondly about how kind and thoughtful he was, and how he was so popular with his colleagues and people like Meg, his old landlady, and her husband, Ifan.

We spent the rest of the day looking around the facilities on camp, which included a visit to the NAAFI shop, where I bought my first little portable black-and-white television on a hire purchase agreement. We then explored the local area. We finished our day together with tea and sticky buns in the NAAFI café, where I decided to tell them about my boyfriend, Greg.

My parents set off on their return journey to Wales just before dark. It was fortunate that they visited when they did, as it was not long before my father was obliged to sell his car, as he didn't have enough money to insure it.

When my parents had gone, I comfortably lazed on the bed in my room, admiring my new furniture and vaguely listening to a programme on my new television. I reflected on the lovely day we had enjoyed together, but couldn't help remembering a few negative comments from my mother, which suggested that instead of being proud of me, she was perhaps a little jealous of my achievements, lifestyle and my independence. *Perhaps you were too boastful, Nolwen*, I considered reproachfully as I thought over the day.

Surprisingly, my mother had had few questions and little to say when I had mentioned my boyfriend, Greg, but I knew that her curiosity would eventually get the better of her and an interrogation would be forthcoming when we were on home ground. Although she had pretended indifference and tried to disguise it, her discomfort that I now had a boyfriend had been evident in her facial expressions. I foresaw that she would envisage what Greg was like and have plenty of premeditated questions ready for me when I next went home. My mother, like me, spent a lot of time daydreaming if she had time on her hands and jumping to conclusions. I warned myself that I would need to be conservative with my answers to her questions.

I remembered Greg telling me that his parents lived in a bungalow, his dad drove a BMW 3 Series car and his mother was a great cook. *Mam will have mixed feelings if I reveal all of that to her*, I decided. *On the one hand, these things will give her something to boast to Auntie May about, but on the other hand, she will not be able to contain her jealousy.* I cautioned myself to prepare well.

Sunday was a quiet day for everyone as there was little to do on camp, so I spent most of the day alone and in my room. Being alone was not always good for me, as it would inevitably lead to daydreaming or unhealthy soul-searching. When I glanced around my room and saw my cherished furniture and my father's home-made "key of the door", my mind again drifted to thoughts of my parents and their different characteristics. Then, examining my own disposition, I concluded that my superficial adoption of personality change number two had indeed facilitated a change in the perception of me by my seniors and colleagues, but I had probably got carried away. I had become, to some extent, my mother's daughter. I had copied her example, some of her traits and her constitution to disguise the person I really was. Of course, this conscious change had worked well to camouflage my diffidence and my anxieties, and had allowed me to achieve the results I coveted, but at what cost to the real me? Just as in my bed-wetting and Frankie Gosling years, my self-esteem – this time, because of my own doing – reached a new low.

That night, as I lay in bed, I revisited the time I had spent on my unit in Gloucestershire. Although I was pleased with the performance reports I had received and the consequential promotions, I was not proud or gratified by my *"modus operandi"*. *I don't think people like me and I don't think I like myself.* I pondered for a while longer and concluded that personality change number two had not done me any true favours and it was time for an upgrade to change number three. I dropped off into an uneasy and restless sleep.

Chapter Sixteen

1978-1982
Poor Eyesight, Directional Dyslexia and
Personality Change Number Three

The following morning heralded my first day on shift, but I awoke feeling unrefreshed with brain fog and a heavy heart, as well as feeling apprehensive and anxious about the day ahead. I had a new personality to formulate, a new unit to navigate and a new workplace in which to establish myself. The two stripes on my arm gave me certain powers and some privileges, but they could not prevail over my self-contempt, my disguised inner insecurities or combat my orientation issues. *Pull yourself together, Nolwen,* I ordered. *Today is a new day with a new job and an opportunity to meet new people who don't know you. It can be a fresh start.*

I looked around my room before I left it and thought once again about my father, who had always been my guiding light. His qualities were those that would see me through to a successful career. He should be my role model, not my mother.

I put aside defining personality change number three for the day, skipped breakfast as I had done since my arrival, as I didn't have the confidence to join others I did not know in the mess. I unlocked my bike, asked a passing airman to confirm my directions and arrived at my new workplace a short time later. I was introduced by my SNCO to my new WO, who welcomed me with an air of superiority. This suggested that this WO expected subservience and would, unlike WO Doddery, be more than capable of "seeing the wood for the trees" in any capacity. This introduction was followed by another to my work colleagues. My mentor for the next few weeks was a very professional, well-thought-of and experienced WRAF JNCO called Cpl Joan Winters.

Joan was a lovely person whose immediate smile put me at ease. She patiently briefed me on my operational surroundings and then, for a month or so, generously taught me all I needed to know about my new job. My position, like my previous one, was in a very elementary communications centre with no complexities, so I quickly reached the level of efficiency I was used to. I soon realised, though, in a genuinely grateful way, that I could learn a lot more from Joan than her operational expertise. She was a very respected team leader, with superb supervisory and interpersonal skills and, most importantly, she was clearly liked. *I really must try and follow her example*, I decided one day as we worked together. I was pleased that an ideal opportunity to do this came about the very next morning.

Joan held a briefing for her team most mornings and the next day we received notification that the centre had been tasked with supporting a mobile telecommunications squadron who were "on exercise in the field". I watched my mentor intently and listened to what she had to say as she gathered up her subordinates for the brief. She ensured that everyone had been introduced to me, then, with a welcoming smile and with open recognition of my seniority compared to the rest of her audience, she asked everyone to take a seat close to her. She began her brief by firstly asking how everyone was feeling, then pleasantly chatted congenially to one or two individuals.

After a few minutes, the tone of her voice changed, the atmosphere in the room transformed and all the voices except hers became silent. Joan immediately commanded everyone's attention.

'Okay, everyone,' she said. 'Time to focus and listen in, please.'

The team, including myself, were in no doubt that Cpl Winters had switched from being familiar and genial in an instant to a professional and earnest JNCO who had serious matters to impart. Her demeanour commanded respect. The mood in the room changed and all attention was fixated on the face and words of this highly regarded leader. Joan began her brief, gave us the facts about the task ahead and never forgot to respect my rank as senior to those around me as she spoke. She warned that there was a longer than normal working spell ahead of us and that we would be tasked with some procedures that we were not used to. At the end of the briefing, she asked for volunteers to carry out some mundane and unpopular tasks. Willing arms shot up to please her and I was surprised to see the number of people who offered her support. She then invited questions, checked for understanding and advised everyone to approach her at any time during the exercise if they became unsure of process or made any mistakes.

'I would sooner know about any insecurities or errors before they escalate,' she warned. 'I don't mind how often you ask for help or if you ask the same questions repeatedly,' she added, encouragingly.

She then picked out one airman and ordered him to collect all the exercise joining instructions from the safe in our WO's office, adding humorously, 'Hurry along, Jim. There's a good troop!'

He nodded enthusiastically followed by a, 'Yes, Corporal,' and moved off with a wide grin spreading across his young, pale face as he considered her instruction and the funny endearment. Joan thanked everyone for their attention, which signalled that, for the time being, the formalities were over.

By listening to and watching Joan leading and motivating her team by encouragement and example, I soon concluded that to help with personality change number three, I could learn a lot from her and that there was much more to being a successful JNCO than just being clever at the job. My previous role had restricted me to operations and although my personal qualities had been assessed, albeit with bias, neither WO Doddery nor Sgt Cross had seen fit to introduce supervisory skills into my portfolio.

I therefore had to concede that my performance reports in this category must have been completely fabricated, meaning that I had probably been promoted before my time and was not truly worthy of my current rank.

Night shifts in my second communications centre were usually quiet once the midnight routines were completed, so, during one particular night shift, instead of reading a book, I decided to work on some notes for devising personality change number three. Instead of impulsively choosing a new Nolwen, I wanted to be sure who and what she wanted to be this time. I resolved to adopt the new personality progressively, so irrationally decided to turn the whole change exercise into a structured personal development plan with notes and to-do lists.

That night, I drew up a list of the Nolwen characteristics I wished to delete from my previous personalities, followed by a list of those I aimed to develop over time or retain, such as popularity, trust, leadership and honesty. I had learnt many of these natural gifts from my father and was now learning them again from Joan's example. I pondered over the first word on my second list: popularity. I made this my number one priority with a start date of tomorrow. I had longed to be liked all my life and even though I had enjoyed the success and accepted the preferential treatment from my superiors at my last unit, I knew this was at the expense of popularity. I was determined that this wouldn't happen to me again. I wanted to be liked as soon as possible.

I followed my development plan and seemed to be doing well with my progressive personality change number three, and soon felt happier and better about myself. I developed a proper definitive relationship with my seniors and with my subordinates. I also became aware of the boundaries associated with rank, what was expected of me as a corporal and the levels I was allowed to reach without overstepping the mark, thereby being seen to undermine authority. I was not comfortable with my character being curbed by others in this way, but I put my reservations aside as I certainly did not want to disturb the status quo.

Outside of my private methodology to change my personality, I learned another new skill from Joan, which was to look out for positive or negative body language and the facial expressions of others. These, she advised, would invite me to respond or react accordingly. I took on her advice and noted one facial expression in particular that I gave some careful thought. *Whenever I walk into Joan's office, she always looks up and smiles and I automatically smile back. You are never the person to smile first, Nolwen*, I thought critically. *How often have you heard the expression "Smile, it might never happen" in and around your workplace?* I suddenly recognised that I seldom felt the need to smile, even though I was sure that the expression on my face did not necessarily reflect my inner emotions. I placed the words "smile first" on my development list and endeavoured to do so more often in the future without looking like the proverbial grinning Cheshire Cat. This newly found facial expression smoothed my way for many future challenges and boosted my own mood.

I made the most of Cpl Winters' mentoring throughout most of my second posting in a positive way and not just as a conduit to promotion. With my new interpersonal skills slowly being ticked off my list, a station bike to get me around camp and more work experience, I eventually settled in well at my second unit. Later in the year, I applied and was accepted for a new non-shiftworking role. I was still ambitious and this was a more high-profile job. However, despite the achievement, I was still intent on keeping my feet firmly on the ground and continuing with my personal development plan.

Joan Winters was posted away some time later and I regretted not thanking her for setting such a good example and for coaching me, often inadvertently, in the art of building and inspiring teams. I was too ashamed of myself and far too proud to openly admit to my previous shortfalls.

***

My final aspiration, during my second posting, was not WRAF-related but reaffirmed my problems with my still undiagnosed directional dyslexia and poor eyesight. Despite not being able to afford a car, I decided to learn to drive and booked myself some lessons with a very patient instructor.

The day of my test arrived. I was anxious and my hands sweated profusely when I got behind the wheel. The examiner didn't help matters as his face was stern and unsmiling, and his instructions were very firm. All seemed to be going well until I was instructed to turn left at a junction. The examiner tutted and then pointed out irritably that, contrary to his command, I had turned right. We continued with the test, but this error demanded a change to the scheduled test route and meant that we were late returning to base. Once the car came to a standstill and I switched off the engine, the annoyed examiner advised me that I had failed the test. He clarified that I had failed it for various reasons and added that he had been baffled as to why I had not followed his directions. I shrugged my shoulders, apologised but gave him no explanation. I knew it was because I had had a lapse in concentration and had forgotten to focus on my writing hand when I unclenched my fist to switch on the windscreen wipers.

Fortunately, the same route was taken for my second test, which I took some months later. This time, I followed the examiner's directions correctly. The only issue that day was when I was asked to read a car number plate at a distance. I had previously tested myself on this and had been successful. However, on that day, I felt sure we were too far away as I could not tell whether one of the letters was an "E" or an "F." I chose to mumble "E" and was asked to repeat what I had read. I changed my mind and opted the next time for the letter "F". I was either lucky with my second guess or the instructor, who was as old as WO Doddery, could not read the number plate from that distance either. Either way, he put a tick in the check box of his examination report and I passed with flying colours. My father, who had previously told me that I would never pass a driving test, had been proved wrong and I think he was privately delighted that I had passed, although he didn't say too much about it.

Chapter Seventeen

1978
Home Visits

In the autumn of 1978, I received a letter from my mother, telling me that my father had had to finish work as he was just too breathless to paint and had been taken into hospital with chest pains. She explained that he had been discharged having been diagnosed with a faulty mitral valve in his heart, probably as a consequence of catching rheumatic fever as a child.

'He is now on a waiting list for a major heart operation, but as long as he avoids stress and takes things easy,' she explained in her letter, 'there is no immediate cause for alarm. He has been advised by the consultant that although he must stop painting, he can apply for jobs that are less physically demanding,' she said.

On hearing this news, I was concerned, not only about my father's health but his state of mind. I knew that non-physical jobs were difficult to find for people like him, with no academic qualifications, and this would worry him at a time when he should be avoiding stress. If my father was worried, then so was I. I decided to visit my parents more often and to send some money home regularly to help them out.

My visits home at that time, even with the best of intentions, were not great. My father was in the house every day, waiting for his heart operation and feeling bored, ineffectual and incompetent, having tried unsuccessfully to obtain numerous non-physical jobs. He was very aware that money was extremely tight, which worried him further. My mother unhelpfully gave up her Woolworths' job, seemingly to look after my father. Being a daydreamer, she justified her action by telling us that when she had been employed at the store, she had joined a small syndicate of workers who paid into a premium bond scheme. She had convinced herself that a big win was imminent, so she didn't really need to work. This false hope and the regular funds she received from me – that allowed her to continue paying into the scheme – plus an easy life at home initially kept her satisfied. However, when the big win did not materialise as quickly as she expected, her mood changed and she took things out on me and my father. Fortunately for Steffan, he was away at university and on a government grant, so was, for the most part, immune not only to my mother's dissatisfaction but my parents' financial pressures and my father's worsening state of mind.

There was one visit in particular that I remember well. I had arrived home for a weekend a few weeks before Christmas and had taken the train and then a bus to get home, as my father was unable to meet me from the train station having sold his car. Once I had settled in with a cup of tea, I noticed that whenever I instinctively smiled at them, my father smiled back but my mother did not. The phrase "Smile, Nolwen. It might never happen" came into my head again, but I refrained from repeating this expression to my mother as I had a good reason to keep her sweet. I had decided to walk on eggshells for the duration of my stay, as I wanted to tell her a little more about Greg and even suggest that I bring him home to meet her and my father. For this, I needed her to be in a good mood and it was essential that I chose my timing carefully and my words wisely.

As we sat together that evening, I assessed my mother's frame of mind and after hearing that my Uncle Gwyn and Auntie May were visiting the following weekend, I reticently broached the subject of Greg to my parents once again. I described him and proudly told them about his role in the RAF as a radar technician. Then, watching for my mother's reaction as Joan had taught me, I mentioned the bungalow where he had lived with his parents and the BMW 3 Series car his father drove.

'Oh! He seems nice,' my mother said, followed by, 'it sounds as if he comes from a good family who've got a bit of cash.' She then glanced at my father for his agreement.

He nodded, but, like me, suspected my mother's opinion would change as time went on. For the time being, I was relieved to have judged her mood correctly. The detail about Greg and his "posh" family was just what she wanted to hear in time for her forthcoming sister's visit. I deliberately missed out Greg's mother's cooking credentials, deciding that these would not offer much in the way of an appropriate qualification for her to boast about.

The rest of the weekend passed uneventfully, although at one point my bag was packed in readiness for a premature return to my camp after an argument with my mother – fortunately, not about Greg. It was about a government scheme course that my mother had been offered as a consequence of her being on employment benefit for several weeks. My mother had been able to choose a suitable course for herself, but was now considering rejecting it at the very last minute. I made the mistake of trying to encourage her to accept a new challenge – advice that she resented from her protégé. My father, ever the peacekeeper, persuaded me to unpack my bags, forget the argument and stay until the Sunday evening. As it happened, my mother had little choice but to attend the training course. Later, she told us all that she had done very well during her lessons, but had decided that she was too under-confident to take dictation and would stick to retail jobs. In my view, she had lost out on a good opportunity to better herself at a time when a good salary was needed, but I kept this opinion to myself. She eventually found another part-time retail job in a small family-run grocery store on the same estate as our house.

I left home on the Sunday evening, bound for the train station after a weekend of mixed emotions. I said my goodbyes to my parents as they stood at their front door, watching my departure and holding on to my dog, who was determined to follow her co-owner. My father looked at me fondly and smiled.

My mother, with a stern expression, said, 'Goodbye, Nolwen.' Then, as though it was an afterthought, she added, 'Perhaps you could bring your boyfriend home to meet us next time you come.'

I smiled at them both appreciatively, guessing my father had intervened in some way and persuaded my mother to invite Greg to our house.

I returned to my unit looking forward to resuming the challenges of my second posting. Working a normal nine-to-five day, five days a week meant it was much easier for me to see Greg at weekends. Having finished his training, he had been posted to an operational flying unit in Oxfordshire. Both our units provided temporary accommodation for visitors, so we met up at either his RAF station or mine every weekend. However, having received the permission I needed from my mother to introduce Greg to my family, it was soon an appropriate time for us to change our usual weekend routine and visit the homes of our mutual parents.

I enjoyed my visits to Greg's home in Yorkshire, although my lack of self-confidence was such that I was quite reserved when in the company of his family. His mother and father never gave me permission to call them by their first names, which presented me with rather a dilemma. Being extremely polite and not wanting to assume we were all on first-name terms, yet not wanting to formally refer to them as Mr or Mrs Hall became a problem for me. I found I had no choice but to ensure I never got into a conversation that warranted my referring to them by their names, and never positioned myself at a distance that would force me to call out to them using their names. I found this very awkward and my discomfort lasted for months, but we all laughed about it later, when it became obvious that they had expected nothing other than first names and had never considered that permission was a prerequisite to use them. I became especially fond of Greg's mother over the years and she inoffensively taught me many valuable lessons in life.

The visits to Porthgranog were a little different to those in Yorkshire. Sometimes they went well and sometimes they did not. Everything was dependant on my mother's mood. The first visit involved a firm handshake and smiles between Greg and my father. My mother, more due to social anxiety than anything, did not approach him physically, but put on her superior "posh" voice and asked him if he wanted a cup of tea after his journey.

Greg, taking the initiative, turned to her and said, 'Hello, Annie, I'm pleased to meet you.'

I immediately bristled, as did my mother! He had not been given permission to use her first name. The visits over the next few months continued with their ups and downs, but my mother seemed to warm to Greg. Despite this, though, she always prompted my father to get up in the middle of the night to check that there was only one person in his daughter's bed.

Chapter Eighteen

1979-1980
Mixed Emotions

Although I visited my parents quite often, we continued to exchange letters as we had done since I first joined the WRAF as they didn't have a telephone. My letters were usually upbeat, but my mother's, full of complaints, were often depressing and my father's, always one to hide his feelings, were neutral. One morning, I received a letter from my mother that contained no moans and groans, but some good and some upsetting bad news. The bad news was that Kim, my boxer dog, had passed away in her sleep the night before my mother wrote the letter, but, to compensate, the good news was that my father had received a date for his heart operation, which was to be a few months later in the August of 1979. I was very sad to hear about Kim, especially as I hadn't had the opportunity to say goodbye to her. Although pleased that my father now had a date for his operation, which I knew would bring him some relief, thoughts of the risks involved worried me as I folded up the letter.

Life continued to be hard for my parents while they waited for my father's operation. As for me, my work life and the time I spent with Greg became more and more enjoyable. We couldn't wait to spend our weekends together and we were so happy and head over heels in love that we decided we would like to get married. Due to an imminent posting for Greg and my father's forthcoming operation, we plumped for a date in the spring that year.

Knowing how old-fashioned and conventional my parents were, and how my mother detested the thought of her daughter growing up and becoming more independent, I did not want to announce our plans by letter. I therefore insisted that Greg and I drove to South Wales and persuaded him to go through the ritual of asking my father for his daughter's hand in marriage. This he did; firstly assuring him that he would always look after his daughter and then, predicting that my father's next concern would be the cost of the wedding, assuring him that it would not be a great big affair and that we were saving hard to pay for it. My father shook Greg's hand warmly and agreed to the marriage.

The next step was to tell my mother the good news. *Thank goodness I am not pregnant*, I thought, as I prepared Greg and myself for a difficult conversation. Ultimately, my mother had no choice but to accept our news, as she found it difficult to intimidate Greg in the same way as she did me. She voiced some reservations, then gave in to the persuasions of my father and my future husband.

Our weekend visits to Wales before the wedding were difficult, with my mother being particularly controlling about our plans. My father, although poorly, desperately struggled to maintain law and order between his now very independent daughter and her headstrong mother. Greg, being a straight-speaking Yorkshireman, complicated things further as he found it impossible to mince his words when my mother voiced her opinions. This resulted in me being the "piggy in the middle" of the arguments, which caused me a lot of distress. In the end, we all agreed to disagree and everything came together with the arrival of the big day.

Despite some nerves and foolish erroneous thoughts that I was not the prettiest of brides, the wedding went ahead in the spring as planned. The day dawned bright and sunny, and I was delightfully happy. There were only a couple of minor hiccups, the first being that my father was so nervous during the reception that he forgot to toast the bride and groom and skipped his speech, and the second, more an observation by the guests than a hiccup was that my mother was unable to bring herself to congratulate or embrace Greg or myself after the wedding. Her discomfort was probably because she had never been tactile and didn't know how to be so, as opposed to reasons of unacceptance. Although I was in the limelight that day, a situation I hated more than any other, I managed to enjoy a wonderful day with the help of my two lovely bridesmaid cousins, Mary and Julie.

Despite my pre-wedding insecurities, I was congratulated by friends and relatives and complimented on my choice of a long, white wedding gown studded with white pearls, which fitted my slim body perfectly. I was welcomed into the Hall family with open arms and lots of embraces as photographs were taken outside of the church. My father kissed me very fondly on the cheek, but kissing and cuddling was just one step too far for Annie – the mother of the bride!

After the wedding and short honeymoon, Greg and I drove to my family home to pick up all our wedding presents with the intention of staying the night and musing over the wedding and our photographs with my parents. We had been allocated a married quarter at his unit and were looking forward to living together as husband and wife. My mother inexplicably refused to let us stay overnight. I don't think she could bear the thought of her Nolwen and Greg in bed together under her roof. It took her a few years to get over that very strange and unusual phobia.

The following few months flew by and my next visit to South Wales was at the time of my father's heart operation. I took seven days' leave. Steffan joined my mother and I, and we sat together in the waiting area of the huge University Hospital of Wales in Cardiff for the duration of the long operation. Everything went well, but, strangely, my only real memory of that time, other than sitting in the waiting area, is the day after the procedure when it was mine and Steffan's turn to visit my father.

We donned our protective gowns and paper shoes and walked into the intensive care ward. I found it upsetting to see my father in his bed, surrounded by machinery, wires, tubes and stands holding plastic bottles. He lay flat on his back with his arms each side of his body and flapped his hands, indicating that his now grown-up children should each walk to the left and right of his bed. I walked to his right and held his hand. I am not sure if Steffan did the same on the other side of the bed, but that moment felt as special for me as the time he had put his arm around me in the cinema on our one and only family holiday together. This time, I hoped it was him being comforted and not the other way round. Unusually for me, I cried when we left the ward due to a mixture of sadness at seeing him in such a critical state and relief that he had pulled through his operation. I don't think my mother or Steffan noticed my emotional state as we walked away from the hospital.

I visited my father every day of my week's leave and I thought him very brave. He complained of nothing, even though the surgery must have caused him a lot of pain and discomfort. He had to return to hospital a few weeks later due to a post-operative problem that needed investigating, so I returned to my parent's home once more. My mother was in a strange mood, but accompanied me to the hospital the next day. However, when we arrived at the ward entrance, she stopped in her tracks and said, icily, 'I am not going in, Nolwen. You can go and see your father yourself.'

Bewildered, I asked her for a reason. She explained acrimoniously that on the previous day, she had gone to the hospital intending to visit my father. On opening the ward door, she had seen his former landlady Meg's daughter, Sue, sitting at his bedside. Sue had called in to bring my father some fruit. My mother, feeling jealous and suspicious, had turned on her heels and left the hospital without going into the ward. My mother always liked to play psychological games with her victims when she had a bee in her bonnet and had left my father wondering why on earth his wife hadn't visited him. I glared at her and went into the ward alone. I explained to my poor father as he lay in his bed what the problem was.

'Mam visited you yesterday, but when she arrived at the ward doors, she saw Meg and Ifan's daughter, Sue, sitting by your bed. You were deep in conversation apparently, so she left feeling very disgruntled. Her jealousy has been festering in her brain ever since,' I added sardonically.

'But I haven't done anything wrong, Nolwen,' my father declared.

The expression of profound sadness and despair on the face of the man I loved so much, especially as he was unwell, cut into me deeply. I said my goodbyes and reassured my father that I would speak to my mother about Sue and that things would be okay. I think, though, that the thought of this conversation worried him even more, as he knew that it was near impossible for his daughter and her mother to have a calm and civilised discussion about anything contentious. Just as she had when she'd decided for herself who the innocent thief was in Woolworths, she went down in my estimation. I could not understand her reasoning or logic. It was at this point that I began to see my mother for the person she really was. She cared more for her insecurities than my father's well-being. Our relationship deteriorated.

My mother and father patched things up and my father returned home from hospital. It took him many months to fully recover from his surgery and he became increasingly frustrated by his inability to change his situation job-wise. As for my mother, juggling her finances to pay the household bills, no big premium bond win, and the certain knowledge that her children had unbridled themselves from her charge fuelled her discontentment. To make matters worse, she had reached menopausal age, the effects of which inflamed her already argumentative and unpredictable nature.

I arrived home one weekend evening on another visit to find a fist-sized hole in our lounge door, which was the result of my mother throwing a poker in a fit of unjustifiable rage because things weren't going her way for some unexplained reason. The poker had impaled itself into the plywood of the door's frontage. Fortunately, my father did not retaliate and was not provoked into attempting to restrain his wife as he had done at Trehywel when I had been a small child. He did though, refuse to repair the hole.

'I'm leaving it as it is so that Nolwen, Steffan and your sister May can see it when they next come here,' he told her. 'They will then understand what I have to put up with.' Whenever anyone commented on the hole, he deferred the explanation to my mother. She always put a humorous spin on it, but I did not think it funny.

Not satisfied with just throwing items when things did not go her way, my mother, knowing how important the value of decorum was to my father, got into the habit of annoying him by wandering around the house in her dressing gown and some old slippers until late in the morning. If this did not get her desired reaction, she would open the front door and shout at him like the proverbial fishwife from the doorstep, hoping to embarrass him into submission, while at the same time entertaining the neighbours. Due to financial hardship, my mother's emotional state and being under each other's feet day after day, it took some time for my parents' relationship to change for the better.

Chapter Nineteen

1980–1982
Happiness

Six months after his heart surgery, my father successfully completed some rehabilitation training and learned how to manufacture and assemble printed circuit boards. The assembly skill required attention to detail, which was second nature to him, and dexterity, which was an ingrained talent he had inherited from his own father as a young boy. Social Services or the equivalent of that service at the time, then found him an appropriate job, working for a huge telecommunications company in Hertfordshire. This involved relocating to a prearranged council-owned maisonette in that county. Just as my mother had supported my father when he wanted to move his family to South Wales, she saw the advantages of this opportunity and they accepted the proposal on offer to them. After settling in, my mother obtained a part-time job in a local supermarket, her menopausal symptoms miraculously cleared, my father's spirits soared and the tide turned on their lives. They had never been happier. When my parents were happy, so was I.

The two years between February 1980 and February 1982 were the happiest years of our lives as a family. Steffan graduated from university and started his own RAF career, I was happily married, my father recovered well from his heart operation and my parents liked their new home in Hertfordshire. Both were working and although they were not earning large amounts of money, they managed to buy, albeit taking advantage of available hire purchase agreements, some new furniture for their maisonette and a brand-new scooter for my father. He used the scooter for local journeys around town and to get him back and forth from his work. They replaced their very old and battered lounge sofa and chairs, and the old radiogram that had been used to play the Neil Sedaka album on my sixteenth birthday with a new sofa suite and wall unit. Realisation dawned that their children had flown the nest and that 1980 was the start of a new era. I even think they rekindled the romance of their youth after a week's holiday in Brighton. This romance had sadly been consigned to oblivion due to many years of hardship and, in my mother's case, her dissatisfaction with life.

My happiness extended into my working environment, too. Well into my second tour of duty, I had remodelled and upgraded my character with my personality change number three and had learnt much professionally. I had retained my determination to succeed in my chosen career, but was pleased that this determination would be in accordance with my development plan and not through manipulation or at the expense of others. Importantly to me, I was confident that I was liked, respected and popular with the team.

My relationship with my superiors was well balanced, too, in that I delivered excellent results operationally while exercising self-control to ensure that I did not cross over the boundaries associated with my rank by being too outspoken. I was pleased with my performance reports, which were excellent, but this time, the good scores were for the right reasons. Additionally, I made every effort to ensure that my underlying diffidence and anxieties were never apparent in my familiar work environment. When on duty, it was my self-confidence that was ostensible to others, even though, actually, this was a pretence.

Generally, the average posting at RAF units lasted for about three years and I knew I was overdue a move. I worried about the new location, but I was lucky and found myself posted to an underground telecommunications centre at an RAF station close to Bath. Greg had been posted to another operational unit in Wiltshire some months previously, where we now lived in our second married quarter, so the close locations of our stations fortunately continued to work well for us.

After thanking everyone for their farewell gifts and cards, I said some fond goodbyes to my colleagues in the small communications centre in the heart of Wiltshire and to my trusty bike, which had served me well. Before leaving, I re-checked my personal development plan and was satisfied that I had made good progress. I concluded, though, that after formally arriving at my third permanent unit, I would need to set myself three further objectives, which I decided could be undertaken in any order. I wanted to become good at my new job, endear myself to those of my seniors who were going to be responsible for completing my performance reports, and continue in my efforts to gain the respect and popularity of my peers and other colleagues.

CHAPTER TWENTY

1982-1988
Fear and Resolve

I had held the full rank of corporal for over five years when I moved to my new station. Fortunately, I managed to replace my bicycle with a car and established that, when practical, I would use this for driving around the camp. Whenever this was not possible, I knew that my former worries about rank recognition with my poor eyesight would return and I would have to walk around carrying an open umbrella or packages, or alternatively be continually alert for danger and/or embarrassment.

My posting this time was to a signals unit, which was completely different in many respects to the small communications centres I had been used to. What I didn't know at the time was that I was about to experience the most terrifying ordeal I had ever endured in my life.

On my arrival, I was advised that I would be a shiftworker once more and that I was due to start work the following day. Meanwhile, I was invited to take a tour around the unit accompanied by a SNCO whose duties included inductions and familiarisation training. The location of my workplace was very unusual and alien to me, in that it consisted of numerous offices, workshops, storerooms and huge open-plan operational areas, all with no windows, set deep into the chambers of an old underground quarry. The signals complex consisted of different sections where each required different skillsets, ranging from network management to teleprinting, wireless operations and the noisy processing of reams and reams of five-unit ticker tape. I was impressed by the complexity, but knew instantly that this time I had a lot more to learn about telecommunications. I hoped that my inner shortcomings, especially my anxiety and under-confidence, which I had been at great pains to hide at my previous units, would not surface with a vengeance. There were also many more people spread across numerous work areas, on different shifts and of differing ranks, who would need to become the focus of my "popularity" objective.

The very next day, I was to find out that one of the least popular and most mundane duties for non-technical corporals on shift, male or female, was the task of "paper-burning". Recycling was not normal practice in those days, so the task demanded the piling of a dozen or more large brown paper sacks, which were full of waste teleprinter paper, forms and ticker tape, onto a sack trolley. This was then wheeled out of the brightly lit, carpeted, functionally furnished operational area into the stark, roughhewn but dimly lit quarry tunnels. I was asked if I would mind performing this duty by one of my sergeants before I was allocated a mentor to guide me through the more important operational aspects of my role. Thinking this sergeant might be responsible for my performance reports and knowing that, as the "newbie", I needed to give an impression of positive amenability, I readily agreed.

There was a set routine for the task, which was explained to me by a colleague. I was to wheel the solidly built trolley, with its sacks, out of my office environment and along a well-maintained concrete path into the main deep quarry area of the complex. I was assured that this was very easy to find and was usually clear of quarry stones or rubble. On reaching a very sturdy steel-plated airlock, which had airtight doors to the entrance at one side and an exit on the other, I was required to open the entrance door and load the sacks of wastepaper into the airlock, leaving the trolley behind. I should then join the sacks inside, close the entrance door and, once that door was secure, release the lock on the exit door, proceed through it with the sacks and lock that door from the other side.

I asked for these instructions to be repeated, nodded my head to show that I understood and waited for further guidance. I was told that I then needed to carry the sacks one by one from outside of the airlock to an easily located incinerator for burning.

'Usually there is a maintenance worker stoking up the incinerator and waiting for the arrival of the waste, which he is then responsible for burning. You must hang around to witness that all the paper is burned,' my colleague advised.

I was told that there was no requirement to wear overalls or protective equipment so, dressed in my uniform skirt and jacket, with medium-height block heeled shoes on my feet and, as was usual for me, some make-up and varnished nails, I set off on my first mission of the day. All I carried apart from the paper sacks was my handbag, in which I had placed a paperback book to help pass the time, a small bottle of fruit juice and a KitKat chocolate bar. I exited the signals unit and trundled my way along the dimly lit concrete path, through tunnels and a couple of high quarry chambers, pulling the sack trolley behind me. I stopped at the halfway point and listened as I was surprised to hear a distant rumble. I had been told that the quarries were normally silent and a bit spooky, so this surprised me. I heard nothing more, so moved on. Just before opening the door to the airlock, which I found easily, I heard the noise again, but this time it was louder and closer. I paused but concluded that there was probably some maintenance work going on which I wasn't aware of. I conducted the procedure of releasing the entrance door as I had been briefed, loading the sacks into the airlock, while making sure there would be enough room for me to stand next to them, and switched the internal light on. I parked the trolley close to the entrance, stepped inside, then locked the door behind me. It was a bit of a struggle to squeeze past the sacks to release the lever that opened the exit door, but I managed it. After scrambling my way through, I opened the door and glanced towards the incinerator. I cursed as the maintenance worker had not arrived, meaning the task would take longer than I had hoped.

Before I had a chance to unload any of the paper sacks, there was a huge boom and a horrendous crashing and cracking noise. The air outside the airlock filled with clouds of dust, as rock, stones and bricks started to hurtle down from the roof above and land on the ground. Some, as far as I was aware, also fell onto the airlock roof. I instinctively slammed the exit door which became jammed and stood next to the paper sacks, stunned and unable to move. This reaction was followed by an overwhelming sense of terror. To make matters worse and even more petrifying, the airlock light flickered and then went out. I was plunged into absolute and total darkness. I remembered trembling and shaking in fear of my inspecting corporals during my WRAF training years, but that was nothing compared to the fear I felt in that dark moment. As soon as my brain began to commute what was happening around me, I was primed for danger and my heart raced so fast that my body did not only tremble and shake, but convulsed. This fear was followed by an unexpected sense of relief as I suddenly realised that I was safe inside what amounted to be an armour-plated small cabin that had another door!

"Pull yourself together, Nolwen," I said out loud, but to no one except myself. "Try the other door; you will be able to get out. Just try! Just try! Try!" I yelled, as some driving force compelled me to take a few steps and feel my way past the sacks in complete darkness, my hands stretched out in front of me. I very quickly reached the door I had entered through only a few minutes previously. With fingers that shook uncontrollably, I felt along what I hoped was the centre of the door until I located the door circular release lever. With relief, I grabbed it with two hands and turned it. It clicked and I pushed the heavy door open, but it clanked against some kind of heavy object and would not budge any further, despite my frantic shoving and pushing. No light appeared through the small gap I had created between the door and its frame.

'Let me out! Let me out!' I shouted repeatedly, with panic clear in my voice as I realised that I was surrounded by fallen rocks and stones. I stopped shouting and listened while still shaking uncontrollably, but heard nothing except the sounds of gravel and small stones sliding and dropping onto a solid surface. Defeated, my body slowly slid down the wall of the airlock and I sank into a crouching position on the floor.

While on the floor, I thought of turning to God once more but decided that as I hadn't reassumed the doctrines of the Pentecostal ministers following the "lost keys" miracle I had encountered during my trade training, I needed a different strategy. I decided that it might be more productive to control my breathing, stop panicking and consider my predicament. *You are not injured or completely entombed. You can move about and you can breathe, Nolwen*, I reasoned. *Keep yourself calm. Sit and just wait.*

I tried not to consider what could or might happen next, as the minute I did so, negative thoughts flooded my mind and overrode any of my efforts to be positive. "Don't think about those things, Nolwen. Think positively," I repeated time and time again out loud. I knew that I could not bear the thought of my body being trapped and immobile under rubble and that if I let my mind drift in that direction, I would be overwhelmed by panic attacks.

I searched around the floor until my hands touched upon my handbag. I picked it up and cuddled it close to my chest. It felt familiar, soft and squashy like a comforting teddy bear or doll. After a while, I thought about its contents and remembered that it contained a small compact make-up mirror with an integral light. I searched the bag frantically and located it. As soon as I clicked open the lid, the little light shone onto the mirror and was the most welcome glimmer of light I had ever experienced. It felt like a glint of warm sunshine appearing out of a dark and gloomy cloudy sky. I was delirious with relief. I shone it around my surroundings and my fear subsided instantly. Once I was reassured by this small and, at the time, very precious object, I closed the lid and extinguished the light. The very fact that I had the light and could turn it on or off whenever I needed to was the saving grace and consolation that kept me sane and my mind positively constructive about my prospects of survival.

I felt around in my handbag, which seemed to be my only friend and link to the outside world, once again and pulled out my bottle of juice and the KitKat and placed them on the floor besides me. I then searched for anything else inside the bag that might prove useful, but finding nothing, I put everything back for later. My next thought – to keep my mind occupied more than anything else – was to feel my way through a few of the paper sacks, searching for anything that might be useful. I wasn't sure what I was looking for as I knew that these sacks were never used for household waste. I gave up after three sacks, having only found a large plastic bag that I decided I would keep in case I became desperate for a comfort break!

I made myself a kind of armchair out of the sacks, sat down comfortably, had a little to drink and one half of my KitKat, then convinced myself that the rockfall was probably localised and that I had everything I needed to survive for a few hours. I chatted to my father in the darkness, asking for his reassurance that I would be okay, and talked to Greg about the new house we were in the process of buying, which was in a lovely village in the heart of the Wiltshire countryside and which I determined we would still be moving into. I also daydreamed intermittently about my rescue and the reception I would receive from my colleagues and Greg. When negative thoughts entered my mind about whether my latest work colleagues liked me enough to persevere with their searches for me, I quickly pushed these aside. Periodically, I switched my mirror light on and scanned my surroundings to ward off panic attacks when I sensed their onset or whenever I became despondent. I switched it off quickly to save the battery.

Five hours later, having finished my drink and eaten the rest of my KitKat, I heard some chipping and the scraping of shovels against hard stone and gravel. I listened intently and then, to my great relief, I caught the sound of men's voices calling out my name. Finally, I saw the flashing of torch lights through the gap I had left between the door and door frame. The station fire crew had arrived, supported by a team from the local town fire brigade and some airmen from my shift. Both fire crews regularly carried out fire and rescue training in the quarry area where I was located and knew the tunnels and chambers well.

Once they had cleared a way through what was indeed a localised rockfall, they found me easily. One of the crew dragged the door open, reached his hand out to me and pulled me up from my armchair made of sacks. I had never been so relieved to feel the warmth and firmness of someone else's hand or see a group of human beings in my life. The crew had expected the worst as they presumed that I had been buried under the rubble, but were surprised and delighted to find me scared but protected and safe inside the airlock. Although they were covered in dirt, dust, scratches and scrapes by the time they reached me, I was completely unscathed and walked back along the path they had cleared to my working area, looking calm and collected and as smart in my WRAF uniform, heels, make-up and nail varnish as I had been when I had left earlier in the day! I put my sanity down to one piece of good luck, having found my precious compact mirror and light. Without that, I think I would have succumbed to hopelessness and sheer terror.

Greg, who was fraught with worry, was waiting impatiently at the entrance to the quarry area when I returned to the communications centre. He had been away from home on a short detachment to another RAF station, but was contacted via a chain of station duty officers and advised about the rockfall and my not-fully established predicament. Fortunately for us both, he was flown back to his home base within a very short time and arrived at my unit an hour or so later. His face lit up when he saw me walking through the entrance safe and well and he wrapped his arms around me comfortingly.

We were led to the unit canteen, which was cleared of all other diners, where I was met by the station medical officer and given a large and very welcome mug of hot sweet tea and a sandwich. I was checked over and advised to go home with Greg and rest for a few days. I didn't pull through the unfortunate incident completely unscathed, though, as I struggled to fall asleep in a dark bedroom for weeks on end. Where previously I had savoured my pre-sleep time, delaying the arrival of the day ahead, I now experienced feelings of unease before falling into an agitated and restless sleep. I would also wake up suddenly and repeatedly and shoot up into a rigid sitting position. If the room was dark, I would then experience a panic attack, which was more severe if Greg was away working and I had no company. After a few weeks of following some prescribed self-help techniques, I recovered but suffered with mild claustrophobia for many years.

It took just over a month for the repair work to be carried out in the quarries, each side of the airlock, and when this was complete, it took a team of corporals to transport and witness the burning of what had become a huge backlog of paper sacks filled with wastepaper. I was not part of that team and was excused paper-burning responsibility for the rest of my tour of duty.

***

Some six months later, when my military life had very much returned to normal, I ascertained that I had achieved two out of three of my latest development plan objectives in that I had become not only very competent at the job, but was liked, respected and accepted as an integral part of a shiftworking team, which was otherwise known as a "watch". I had also, with the support of various mentors, managed to conceal my under-confidence and anxieties, because for a while there was always someone to lean on for help and advice. The objective that remained outstanding was to fully endear myself to those of my seniors, who were going to be responsible for completing my performance reports and pave my way for promotion.

Soon, my naturally ambitious nature, combined with a need for the greater respect that came from being a SNCO by both senior and junior ranks, drove me to strive in earnest for another promotion, this time from corporal to sergeant.

Greg was a technician. This meant that his service contract was different to mine in that provided his performance reports were "acceptable", he would receive guaranteed promotion to SNCO level within set timescales. Promotion in my trade was far more difficult to achieve and was dependant not only on "higher than acceptable" performance reports, but these had to be consistent over an unspecified period. Unless I wanted to be another Dick Morton and complete twenty-plus years' service in my current rank, my reports had to be continuously very highly scored and supplemented with narratives that would normally be associated with the description of superhumans or God. The term "one blip and you are out" might be an exaggeration, but it wasn't too far from the reality.

Additionally, the boundaries of rank I had recognised and learned to cope with in my previous posting were overly apparent now that I was desperate for promotion. The often-restricted freedom to speak without fear of repercussion that I felt, encouraged a set behaviour. I compared this to what, in my mind, was the brainwashing of my Pentecostal days, in that the beliefs and examples set by the higher ranks filtered down to the lower ones. I recognised that – for the time being, at least – I needed to continue with my objective number three: "endearing myself to my superiors". I felt obliged to cautiously plan conversations with my superiors in advance and to say only what I thought they wanted to hear, just as I did with my mother. Nevertheless, I persevered and my prospects for promotion looked good.

I detected a risk to my professional advancement sometime later when a new SNCO called Sergeant Joe Payne arrived on our watch. For the most part, my relationship with my seniors had gone well, but Sgt Payne and I, quite simply, did not get on, and after questioning myself as to whether I was the problem or whether it was him, the strengths of my personality changes came to the fore and I concluded that it was him and that he was nothing less than an idiot. He reminded me of Cpl Pimpleton, who had been my JNCO during my WRAF basic training. She had been a strict disciplinarian who commanded no respect. Sgt Payne had the same approach. I knew that despite my self-devised personality changes, if who I was didn't fit with the expectations of Sgt Payne, my career prospects could be thwarted. *It only takes one to ruin my career path*, I thought.

Instead of complying with my development plan by putting on my Cheshire Cat smile and making every effort to win him around, I decided to opt for an easier solution. Helped again by my newly strengthened character, I manipulated myself a move onto a different watch and, lo and behold, my new shift commander was to be WO Doddery, who had, to my great surprise, just been posted into my unit. We were reintroduced and he welcomed me with open arms.

Within days, I resumed the duties of his scribe, continued with my development objectives and was confident that my desired career progression was well and truly secured. I mentally noted, though, that WO Doddery also had some new objectives to achieve. The first was to get used to having no office windows to stare out of and the second was to get to know the new me.

I thoroughly enjoyed being an intrinsic part of my new large shiftworking team, where a group of people, almost like a family, performed interdependent tasks that, with the guidance of their superiors, resulted in the accomplishment of a common mission. We all looked after each other and everyone made a point of regularly checking on my welfare since the collapsed tunnel incident. My new watch, like the previous one, performed like clockwork and I enjoyed working with those who played their part in delivering nothing but the best operational expertise for the following few years. The shift consisted of a mix of characters across all rank levels from LAC(W) through to WO, who all balanced a strong professional work ethic with a measured amount of comradeship, banter and wit.

Despite enjoying my work and my career optimism, I started to become more and more conscious of the clear difference in mindset, culture and professional behaviour between the technicians (like Greg) and operators who worked alongside me. While I accepted that there was a difference in skillsets and capabilities between the two parties, there was a compartmental inequality that was, in my view, totally unnecessary and something that baffled Greg and privately infuriated me. The root cause in my mind was not the operational/technical inter-relationship itself, where I found that people complimented each other with support, reliance and a mutual respect, but the attitude of a few small-minded operational personnel who, because of the difficult "no guarantee" path to promotion, instilled within their subordinates a behaviour of compliance with needless unwritten rules of etiquette. This, in my eyes, was reminiscent of the attitude of two of my teachers at school and rankled me. I disliked unfairness.

To attempt to change the culture of those who were answerable to me as a JNCO would not, at that time, have done my personal career path any good, but I resolved that once I achieved SNCO status and headed up my own department, I would adopt a technician culture within it. I think the driving force behind this was the injustice I had experienced at school with what I considered to be my unfair class allocation and the unjust accusation from my teacher following the "brick" incident. After all, I reasoned, if technicians enjoyed the freedom to flex the rules, use first-name terms, respectfully challenge authority, use their own initiative and avoid petty discipline, while ensuring they did not overstep the "mark", why should these liberties pertain only to them and not to me and my colleagues? I could not understand why the operational "mark" was built up so high that it was impossible to even attempt to step over it without a fall. In my eyes, the cultural difference did not make sense as we were all in the same RAF and the technicians philosophy lent itself well to even better, happier and genuinely dedicated teams than those I currently worked with. I placed my "change team culture" objective onto my personal development plan to address when the time was right.

CHAPTER TWENTY-ONE

1982–1984
Shock and Denial

Meanwhile, my parents were still enjoying their comfortable, happy lives together in Hertfordshire, but my mother confessed to me in a letter one day that my father's health seemed to be deteriorating once again and that he became breathless when climbing the stairs to their first-floor maisonette. Following an appointment with his doctor, who advised my father that he could not hear his replacement heart valve working correctly through his stethoscope, my mother explained that he had been referred to a consultant.

A little later, she wrote to me again saying that the consultant had confirmed the doctor's diagnosis and my father was placed on a waiting list for a second major heart operation. If he was dreading the prospect of this, he didn't say so, which was typical of his brave character. This time, as his job was not strenuous, he continued to work until a few days before the operation, which took place some three months later. Steffan and I returned home to support my parents through the surgery and his hospitalisation period and were relieved when he pulled through the invasive procedure successfully with better prospects of long-term success, due to more modern techniques and an improved artificial heart valve. Steffan and I returned to our respective RAF units, content in the knowledge that my father was doing well and that he would not encounter financial worries while he recovered, as he had been granted a generous period of paid sick leave.

It was only one year after my father's second operation that the station duty officer knocked on the door of our married quarter early one Sunday afternoon. Greg answered the door and invited her into our lounge, where I was contentedly reading a book. The female officer was immaculately dressed in her "Number One" uniform and asked if she could sit down. I knew instantly from her demeanour that she was the bearer of bad news and I was also aware that it was standard procedure in the RAF for duty officers to personally deliver any bad news to families out of normal working hours. She advised me, with compassion, that my father had died in the early hours of that morning. I perceived with a sad heart that my parents' second chance at romantic bliss had clearly come to an abrupt and very sad end.

Greg and I quickly gathered some clothes and essential items together and immediately drove to Hertfordshire to comfort my mother. With a fuzzy head throughout the journey, I was unable to take in the news I had received. I just could not come to terms with the reason for our journey. When we arrived at my parents' home and I walked through the front door, I found my mother sitting with Granny Lane, who had managed to get to our destination before we did. My granny got up from her chair, put her hand on my arm and said how very sorry she was.

'I know you are, Granny,' I replied, calling on all my character strength to fight back my tears. Even in those awful circumstances, my mother and I could not embrace.

I learned a little later that my father had been rushed into hospital late the previous evening due to a ruptured aneurysm, which I understood had led to a severe brain haemorrhage. He had been taking a prescribed anticoagulant drug, which was intended to protect him from serious complications after his heart surgery, but in his case, the drug had seemingly negated his chance of survival after a bleed on the brain because his blood would not clot. In those days, the dosage of anticoagulant drug levels after heart valve replacement surgery was not monitored as regularly as it was in later years. I was totally bereft and devastated.

Steffan must have gone through the same traumatic experience as I did when he was told the same sad news by his station duty officer. After joining us in Hertfordshire, he and Greg took the lead in organising my father's funeral. This took place a week later and was simple, yet sedate and fitting. The atmosphere on the day was composed. For some strange reason, I suffered a mental blockage for some hours after the occasion and was unable to remember any of the service. It was only when I woke up in the middle of the night, after what had been a very unhappy day for me, that my lost memories came flooding back. These included gently touching my father's coffin and mentally saying my very own personal and private goodbye as we slowly walked up the aisle of the church. Greg thought that I had behaved a little strangely before the service, too, asking him the same questions repeatedly about the funeral arrangements. He put this down to my sadness and shock and said nothing to me about it at the time.

Steffan was at a critical stage in his RAF training, so, after the funeral, he returned to work while Greg and I remained on compassionate leave with my mother for a little while longer. My parents had been new to the area and she had no family in the vicinity, which made it difficult for me to leave her, but we had to return to duty eventually. My mother had now been widowed for the second time and at a relatively young age. She was not only bereaved but lived alone and I worried about her constantly. As was usual for me when I was worried, I scorned sleep. For some nights after my father's death, I pondered over my mother's situation with dark thoughts, gloomily contemplating and relating the aftermath of the loss of her husband to an imaginary aftermath of the loss of mine and wondering about our respective coping mechanisms. I concluded that I had no concept of how I would cope if I lost Greg and therefore had no idea how I could even begin to console my mother.

My mother had always been tough. This, combined with her prayers, were the key factors that saw her through an extremely difficult time. Generously, my father's former colleagues had collected a considerable amount of money, which was given to my family as a gesture of their sympathy, and we used this money to get a telephone installed in her maisonette as a matter of priority. The telephone enabled Steffan and me to speak with her most evenings, which gave her some comfort. I also continued to write letters, primarily just so the postman would call. She was also fortunate in that she had grown close to the residents of the flat below hers, where a Mrs Fellows, also a widow, who was well into her eighties, lived with her single disabled son, John. Every morning at around 10am and every afternoon at around 3pm, Mrs Fellows would bang repeatedly on her ceiling with a long-handled broom. This was the signal for my mother to join them for a coffee and a chat. Without this kindness, the telephone calls and my letters, I am not sure how my mother would have survived.

As for me, immediately after the initial period of shock and denial, my grief was clear to those closest to me and to my colleagues, but soon my life appeared to return to normality. In actual fact, that grief was closeted deep inside me, where it joined my hidden diffidence and other anxieties. When it did rear its ugly head, it rekindled the feelings of abandonment I had experienced as a child when my father had left home for South Wales and the loneliness I felt whenever I arrived at a new unfamiliar unit. Fortified by the resilience I had learned as a teenager, I opted, in the longer term, to grieve in private.

A year or so later, my mother returned to live near her sister, Auntie May, in Trehywel in West Wales where she gratefully received the support of relatives and old friends. She eventually found a part-time job in a small greengrocer shop, too, which at least kept her occupied for a few days each week. Many years later, she showed me a letter she had written and given to my father in the happiest period of their lives, the day before his second heart operation. That letter expressed her love for him and contained words and phrases that conveyed nothing but affection and tenderness. It finished with her reassurance that she was looking forward to spending the rest of her life with him and would be at his bedside when he woke up. I had no idea that my mother could feel such strong, positive emotions of love or proclaim this kind of beautiful sentiment in a letter.

Chapter Twenty-Two

1988
Terror

Although I had now completed around fifteen years' service and was enjoying my third permanent posting, I was lucky enough to have never worked on the front line or experienced any kind of tactical combat or armed conflict at close quarters. One reason for this was that I was classified as being "non-combatant" and wasn't expected to undertake any weapon training or carry a weapon. Being non-combatant was the norm for airwomen who enlisted into the WRAF in the 1970s. I believe it was for this very reason that we were paid less than our male counterparts.

Life was very different in the military in those days in that there was a line drawn between airwomen and airmen when it came to physical activities or what was then considered to be traditionally masculine or feminine undertakings. Although we were not weak and feeble by any stretch of the imagination, we were cosseted to a certain extent. These disparities changed over time and as I progressed in my chosen career. However, by the early eighties, they had only, to my personal relief, been reformed minimally. Although I had thought myself a bit of a tomboy in my childhood years, this changed during my teenage years and I became a "girlie girl". By the time I reached adulthood, influenced by my father's counsel and reprimands, I matured into the elegant lady he had envisioned and had no desire to moderate my comportment with the passage of time!

As a female, the WRAF literature I had read prior to my recruitment did not promote tactical operations, hazardous working environments or dramatic adventures. Given this literature, as well as being non-combatant and not a technician or a mechanic, I did not expect to experience any of these things. However, as it happens, although I never experienced working on the front line, I was to chance upon a dangerous incident albeit to a relatively minor degree compared to some military operations. This took place towards the end of my third posting.

With the collapsed tunnel incident long forgotten by my colleagues and put to the back of my own mind, I never considered that I would encounter a second dramatic adventure that was as memorable as the first. "Adventure" is the only term appropriate to describe my experience, even though, to me, it was terrifying and not something I would care to repeat.

I was still a non-combatant member of the WRAF when I was sent on a short detachment from my underground unit to Northern Ireland in June 1988, not long after I read that three members of the RAF had been killed and four others wounded by the Provisional IRA in the Netherlands. I said my goodbyes to Greg, my mother and my fellow watch-workers and packed sufficient uniform and personal effects to last me for the next couple of months.

I arrived at my station in Northern Ireland and, after completing the usual unit arrival procedures, I placed all my luggage in my allocated single room in the WRAF barrack block. I looked around at the bare walls and sparse furnishings and, once again, I was overcome with the sense of loneliness I had come to expect when arriving at a new, unfamiliar place. I knew, though, that this would pass when I reported in for work or found company in the communal lounge. The communications centre I was allocated to was small and basic, like those of my first two permanent postings, so although I was anxious initially, it did not take long for me to familiarise myself with my duties. My barrack block was occupied by about twenty members of the WRAF who I quickly bonded with.

In those days, there were lots of rules and regulations associated with personal security in Northern Ireland that applied to me, even though I was a female who never carried a weapon and was never part of any security patrols or similar activities. I also feared for my own safety and therefore rarely strayed outside of the camp confines, especially at night. On the odd occasion I did venture out, I was very aware that in those difficult times, at the very least I needed to apply caution and some common sense by wearing civilian clothes, socialising in authorised and specified locations, and not becoming isolated from the groups of people I was keeping company with.

On one particular evening, I had been persuaded, against my better judgment, to dig out some party clothes and join a group of service friends who had planned a leaving get-together for a JNCO who I knew pretty well. An approved venue was chosen and we set off in four unmarked civilian vehicles for our destination. Sometime after the farewell speech and gift presentation, and towards the end of a pleasant and fun-filled evening, I went into the ladies' restroom. What I saw when I opened the door took me aback for a few seconds. Standing in front of me was a very panic-stricken young lady, who I presumed was a civilian as I didn't recognise her. She was coughing and clutching at her throat. As I approached her, she delved into her handbag and pulled out a packet of minty sweets, which she shook rigorously and pointed to her mouth. It was plainly obvious that she had swallowed a sweet and was now choking to death. Fortunately for me and for her, basic first-aid training was regularly taught to WRAF recruits and again on arriving at new units, so I was able to react instantly. I encouraged her to bend forwards and hit her firmly with the heel of my hand between her shoulder blades. To my relief, the offending sweet popped straight out of her mouth and landed on the floor in front of us. The lady, who I found out was called Maggie, let out a huge cough, a relieved sigh and then began to breathe normally, but it took some time for her to control her frantic emotions. I comforted and reassured her for a few minutes, then, once she had composed herself, I went into the building's restaurant kitchen, which was nearer than the bar, to obtain a glass of water for her. She was very grateful for my help and, once fully recovered, quickly left the restroom to join her friends. I followed her out a few minutes later, pleased that she was okay and feeling rather proud of myself!

I made my way back to find my own friends, only to find our table empty. I looked around the bar, wondering if I had lost my way and was in the wrong room, but saw my jacket hanging with some others on a clothes peg. I grabbed it and pushed my way through the crowd of people congregating around the bar and rushed out through the front door of the building, hoping to catch up with at least one member of our party or spot a car with its engine running, waiting for my arrival. The car park spaces where our cars had been parked previously were empty and there was no one I recognised in sight. I realised with a serious sense of concern that everyone had left without me and I had no way of calling them back to collect me. I presumed that each group had assumed I had left with another one.

I sat on a bench set in the pub garden and contemplated my position. I could not be sure whether anyone I had come out with would notice my absence that night, as the cars might arrive on our camp at separate times and everyone would go their different ways and to their own rooms. *Ugh, you are in a bit of a predicament now, Nolwen, and someone is going to get into big trouble if it is found out that you have been left behind*, I said to myself, feeling a mix of fear and dread overwhelm my thoughts.

Worry and concern for my safety then transcended over me, but I sat upright on the bench and made an effort to pull myself together. I had two options, I concluded. The first was to go back into the pub and make a call to the station guardroom and ask the duty SNCO, who would not be pleased with me, for assistance. *That's the correct course of action but it's bound to get someone into trouble,* I mused. *Alternatively, I can get myself back to camp safely and discreetly and no one will be any the wiser.* I stupidly chose to do the latter and decided to call a taxi. To protect my military identity, I also decided that I would ask to be dropped off close to a park, a mile or so from my camp, and walk from there.

I made my way back into the pub and found a public payphone in a corridor just off the bar. There were numerous taxi numbers pinned up on the wall and after unsuccessfully ringing two of them to find they were busy, my fortunes changed with the third. I was advised that a car would be with me in fifteen minutes. I returned to my bench seat in the garden and, while I waited, I pondered about how I was going to direct the driver to an appropriate drop-off point, as I was not familiar with the street names in the camp area.

I was picked up fifteen minutes later and I explained to the driver, who was elderly, pleasant and kindly looking, that I wanted to be dropped off outside an apartment block that overlooked the main public park in Ballymill, but that I would direct him as he got nearer to my bogus home. Some five miles later, after driving down a busy road closely following another car, he slowed as both cars approached a roundabout. My driver was busy checking right for a break in the traffic before proceeding, when the car in front of him stopped abruptly and he crashed into the back of it. The car bonnet crumpled and blocked my view, and my seatbelt tightened across the front of my body, holding me in place. The impact had not been severe enough to trigger the airbag and no one involved was hurt. *Just your luck, Nolwen*, I cursed silently, as I waited to see what was going to happen next. There was a bit of a kerfuffle and some note-taking, then a radio call to the taxi office by the driver, who was told to wait indefinitely for assistance. The driver of the other car involved, whose car had suffered minimal damage, offered to give me a lift to my destination, but I felt uneasy when he looked at me and declined with thanks.

My driver explained that I wasn't far from home and could easily make my way there on foot.

'You will be safe enough if you stick to the well-lit roads that run through that residential area over there,' he said, pointing to his right. 'You can't get lost. Just take that road with the yellow skip parked in the lay-by,' he explained, pointing again with a shaky, knobbly finger, 'then turn right at the community centre and follow your nose until you reach the park.'

I set off, tottering at times in my high heels, but with a conscious sense of purpose, hopefully giving the impression to any onlookers that I knew exactly where I was going. I slung my handbag over my shoulder and kept my right hand firmly clenched, repeating, "This is my right, this is my right, this is my right," under my breath as I walked at a good steady pace. *Concentrate, Nolwen, you really cannot risk getting lost in this unfamiliar area even though it looks safe enough*, I warned myself.

Having passed the yellow skip and making a point of turning right at the community centre as directed, I then followed a long straight road, which was lined intermittently on both sides by parked cars in front of terraced properties with gardens. It was now close to midnight and there were not many downstairs lights on, but the homes were clearly occupied, which was reassuring.

Suddenly, the hair on my neck and scalp stood on end, and my heart rate and breathing speed increased, as I heard a rustling and turned round. I remembered that there had been branches from a young willow tree hanging over a garden wall and into the path on the opposite side of the road and suspected that the branches had blown in a breeze, but when I turned back to look, I noted that the night was silent and there was no breeze at all. I did not want to stop walking, so a little further down the road, I glanced over my shoulder very briefly as I made my way towards the end of the terraced houses. I caught sight of what I thought was a heavily built, tall man quietly passing under a streetlight on the opposite side of the road. I turned again a little while later, but the walker had made little progress and was still some way behind me. I quickened my pace as best as I could while trying to appear nonchalant, but at the same time reasoning that unless someone was walking a dog – and I had heard no familiar clip-clip of dog toenails on the flagged path – it was unusual and disconcerting that any man would choose to walk seemingly without purpose, behind and at the same pace as a small woman in heels.

I reminded myself that I was in Northern Ireland in troubled times, in a situation I shouldn't have been in, and that I had received clear warnings that not everyone was a friend or approved of my military presence. I hypothesised, perhaps irrationally because I was unnerved, that someone who was opposed to the British military could have, despite our security precautions, followed us to the pub or, alternatively and by chance, joined us in the pub and suspected who we were, despite our civilian clothes and guarded conversations. My isolation from the group and my vulnerability had probably been observed. It was quite feasible that the foe had followed my taxi and then engineered the car crash or been in control of the driver. My heart raced; I began to sweat. I was probably wrong, but I needed a self-preservation plan.

After deciding against knocking on the door of a stranger's home, risk being turned away and forced back into the path of my stealthy follower, I formulated a different but quick and very simple course of action just before I reached the end of a terrace house on the street, which had a light on in an upstairs room. I fumbled in my handbag and deliberately made a point of jangling my bunch of keys loudly, as if I was preparing to walk into my own home. I walked through the open gate of the last terraced house and across the gravel of the garden, making my way round to the back of the premises as if I intended to enter it by a back door. I couldn't believe how fortunate I was, as there was a robust-looking shed in the garden and, when I tried the door, it was unlocked. I jangled my keys loudly once again, then stepped inside the shed and deliberately slammed the door behind me, hoping my furtive and hopefully slow-witted assailant would conclude that I had entered my own home and wasn't whoever he thought I might have been.

I attempted to peer nervously through a small dusty window set in the side of the shed, but realising that the security light had illuminated the garden when my presence was sensed, I quickly ducked down and crouched in silence, listening keenly for footsteps on the gravel. Once the security light switched itself off, I repeatedly but surreptitiously peeked out through the window whenever I could pluck up the courage to do so and saw nothing. Even though I heaved a sigh of relief and considered that I was now in relative safety, I could not help but re-examine my ordeal, and considered that I could still be in danger if that man's scheme had not been thwarted and he was intent on discovering where I was hiding. The reality of my situation fully hit home and I remained very afraid.

Eventually, I quietly sat down on the floor and, after an hour or so, I decided that if the man who was following me was intent on establishing my identity and doing me harm, my plan had worked and he had given up. It was true that he might have just been a local resident taking a stroll, but, either way, I had no intention of leaving my current lodgings until daylight hours. Besides, I then realised, it would have proved impossible for me to walk through the security checkpoint at the camp gates in the hours of darkness, alone and dressed in party clothes, without triggering a full investigation with associated repercussions. I knew that I would be lucky to get away with just a few curious stares even in the morning.

I wrapped my arms around my knees, knowing there was no chance of sleep, but appreciating that the weather was warm at least. I prepared myself for a long night of self-recrimination and, to some extent, thoughts of third-party blame for the predicament I had found myself in, but then remembered I had saved someone's life that night in the pub and at least had something to be proud of.

Although I walked through the station gates the next morning with no questions asked, I made the correct and sensible decision the following day to report the incident to our security officer. I really had no option but to do this. Afterwards, though, I questioned my logic repeatedly and struggled with a feeling of guilt for letting my friends down. One of my "party-goer" colleagues was disciplined and I received an informal warning, but luckily neither of us suffered any long-term consequences in relation to our careers and, unlike after my paper-burning incident, I experienced no psychological after-effects.

Chapter Twenty-Three

1988
A Welcome Surprise

After my father's death, I supported my mother in the best way I possibly could over the next few years by telephoning, continuing to write letters to her and, outside of my time in Northern Ireland, visiting her in West Wales from my home in Wiltshire once a month. I was still a shiftworker, meaning I often had time off in the middle of the week, so could avoid the heavy weekend commuter traffic and make the seven-hour round trip quite easily. I decided never to tell her about my paper-burning or Northern Ireland adventures. We spoke about my father often, trying to focus on the happy times we had spent with him, as opposed to the tough times when he had been poorly and out of work. My mother was clearly made of sterner stuff than I was and seemed, to my relief, with the support of family and friends, to be coping well. I never, though, dismissed from my mind that she had been bereaved and would always go through some very difficult periods of sadness, especially when she was alone. I respected her fortitude.

Something that I became aware of whenever I visited her after my father's death was how amiable and agreeable she had become. It was as if she had undergone a personality change, similar to those I had undertaken in the past, except I suspected that hers had not resulted from her own conscious decision. Her normally aggressive and controlling nature was somehow subdued. I supposed she had had the spirit knocked out of her due to the death of my father. This, in some ways, was sad, but, in others, it had turned her into a much nicer person. Her financial circumstances had not changed a great deal, in that she had a part-time retail job and received a widow's pension. My father had never taken out a life insurance policy, apparently because he had feared the medical examinations required would affect his job prospects. Additionally, and for some unfathomable reason, he had not paid into his company "Death in Service" scheme, so she received no additional benefits moneywise. With only herself to spend her money on, though, she seemed very satisfied with her lot, although any occasional small premium bond win she received was always very welcome. For the next decade or more, apart from normal minor disagreements, we really enjoyed each other's company and I appreciated having her as a friend whenever Greg was away on detachments or longer-term duties. We all stayed connected with Steffan, who was still in the RAF and was, by the time I returned from Northern Ireland, married with three children. He and his family lived a good distance away in Norfolk and he led a busy life.

Greg decided to make a rather dramatic career change and, with my blessing, moved into the RAF aircrew world. After a long period of training, he was often away from home on his flying duties. I missed him a lot, but absence definitely made our hearts grow fonder, and we always looked forward to being together and spending time in what was our very first proper home in the lovely village of Bromingford, close to Bath. Living in married quarters had its advantages, but there were many restrictions when it came to "putting your own mark on the place" and this didn't suit us as we grew older. Greg enjoyed DIY and was pleased to knock down the odd wall or two in response to ideas that generally came from me. This type of renovation work would have definitely been frowned upon by any RAF estate manager!

Workwise, I was still doing well and I resumed my secondary duty as assistant to WO Doddery with his writing dilemmas. My performance reports were excellent and no serious notice was taken of the small adverse comment about the "adventure" that appeared in my Northern Ireland detachment report. I had apparently redeemed myself by taking the correct reporting action and putting my first-aid skills to good use.

A short while later, during a training course I had been instructed to attend, I received an offer of promotion to sergeant. I was delighted, but, this time, the promotion notification did not go to my head and I had no desire to inappropriately flaunt the three stripes on my arm. I was reservedly proud of my achievement and grateful of the offer as the rank of sergeant was equivalent to becoming a manager in civilian terms. The rank was also significant in that it automatically commanded greater respect, not only from subordinates but from seniors alike.

Unfortunately, I found out that my promotion was conditional on my accepting a posting to a unit in Lincolnshire. The posting news was a blow as the amount of quality time Greg and I had to spend together was already limited with his irregular flying hours and detachments. I was close to turning my promotion down, but was persuaded differently by one of the very respected training course instructors, who had seen my career grow from strength to strength over the years.

'Nolwen,' he said, 'you have worked extremely hard for this promotion. Accept it and see how it works out. You may well regret it if you don't and it won't get offered to you again for some considerable time.'

I considered his words and added under my breath, "Yes, I only need another Sgt Payne to become my SNCO and any second chance of promotion could be well and truly scuppered." I discussed the situation with Greg and, a few days later, I accepted my new rank.

The following week, I undertook an almost five-hour drive across country, which would have taken nearer to four hours if I had not deviated inadvertently from my route several times. I reported in as normal, carried out the arrival process and moved into a small suite of rooms in the sergeants' mess at my new RAF station.

As it happened, I was the first female to ever live in single accommodation in my new unit's mess, which came as a bit of a shock to the existing residents, who were very set in their ways and enjoyed their own male company. Many of the residents were married men, who, like me, had received postings away from their "owned" family homes and had not wished to uproot their families and move back into married quarters. Others were single men either coming to the end of their military service or youngsters who had received early promotion. The first hurdle I had to get over was obtaining my first meal in the mess, which, fortunately, was very small with only about eight tables, so no risk – or little risk – of my getting lost. I walked in and all heads turned towards me. Glancing around, I had a very quick decision to make and posed a question to myself. *Nolwen, do you sit on that table in the corner on your own or do you choose a spare chair on another table and ask if you can join the men sitting around it?* With my development-plan Cheshire Cat smile on my face, I bravely chose the second option and was, to my surprise, greeted warmly.

For the remainder of my posting, or "tour" as it was often referred to, I respected the privacy of the male SNCOs by keeping away from their communal television room where I knew they relaxed as men like to do when not in female company. This relaxation included their TV sports programmes, expletives, occasionally smelly feet and the odd can of beer. In return, they were on hand for any "fix it" tasks, which included the building up of a bike I purchased the following weekend, any problems with my car and all my room maintenance. The mess chefs and dining room staff treated me like royalty, especially an old, near-retirement chappie called William, who had served hundreds of meals to male SNCOs in his time in his one and only mess, but who had never previously waited on a female. With his soft spot for me, extra special cakes and puddings prepared for me by the kitchen cooks, and my fellow residents at my beck and call, I was killed with kindness, overindulged and spoiled rotten.

My first role as a WRAF SNCO included responsibility for the station telephone exchange, another small communications centre, and a small team of JNCOs and airmen and airwomen. True to my development plan, I adopted a democratic management style and encouraged a "technician" type culture. What I found, though, was that my predecessor had been very "old-school" and set in his ways, so his old habits were well ingrained into my team and the traditional boundaries of rank were well embedded. It was many weeks before my juniors in rank became relaxed enough, even in private, to call me Nolwen instead of an abbreviated form of sergeant. Personally, I was lucky in that there were no operations personnel in my workplace who were senior to me, so my immediate superior was a chief technician called Glen Cluff. Glen was the best boss I ever worked for in both my military and civilian careers. He was a good mentor for democratic leadership, who trusted me to professionally deliver my work objectives and assignments. I had no intention of letting him down.

I left Lincolnshire a year later – in many ways, sadly – gratefully accepting the first opportunity I had to return to my former underground unit near Bath, this time as a SNCO. Meanwhile, I was pleased to be able to rejoin Greg in our family home on a full-time basis. I left my unit with my car jam-packed full of gifts from my work colleagues, the sergeants' mess manager and his staff, and from the mess members. *Way hey, Nolwen!* I thought, with some self-satisfaction as I waved goodbye to a group of colleagues and friends. *Everyone must have liked me!*

CHAPTER TWENTY-FOUR

1989–1998
Success and Achievement

The next few years flew by really quickly and what I didn't yet know was that my military career would come to an abrupt end sooner than I expected. However, I was pleased to return to my old unit, despite the working environment being noisy and having no natural daylight. Although I was a shiftworker, my second tour in the underground complex was, this time, as an SNCO, so paper-burning was not one of my responsibilities and I stayed away from the quarry area. Previously, as a corporal serving on the same unit, I had regularly deputised for my sergeants, so I had little to learn in my new role. Not much had changed except WO Doddery had retired and, although not on my shift, I was delighted to hear that FS Joan Winters, my former mentor, had taken up a newly created post. *It's a small telecommunications world, Nolwen*, I reminded myself. As fellow SNCOs, Joan and I often socialised together, and I found the right opportunity to tell her just how much I had appreciated her guidance earlier in my career, when I was struggling to gain the support of those who worked for me.

One year later, I was given the opportunity to apply for a nine-to-five, five-day-a-week role at the same unit, responsible for my own team. The role was in demand and the competition for selection was considerable. My performance reports as a sergeant had been excellent and I had the required skills, both of which stood me in good stead. However, as it happened, my being selected for the post came down to the recommendation of the very respected sergeant I was hoping to replace. He had no reservations that I was the right person to take over his role and made his views perfectly clear to the selection board. I was offered the job. I owe an awful lot to that man's intervention, as the experience I gained from that particular role provided me with the foundation, skills and credentials that I needed to achieve a successful career in similar fields later in my life.

My role was the equivalent to an operations manager role in civilian terms. I chose the best-calibre JNCOs and junior ranks for my team, trusting that they would support me in my endeavours to become one of the most respected and remembered WRAF operational managers of the time. Clearly, I still felt the need to prove myself and give my self-esteem a boost. The completion of performance reports was now, as an SNCO, one of my responsibilities and I rewarded my team with fair and justifiable narratives and scores. I secretly hoped, though, that they were just as motivated to work well for me personally, as they were for their own career ends.

There was no room for error in my new job, which was at the heart of operations. I had a stickler of a boss who demanded nothing but perfection, but as I was never in the limelight as such, my confidence held up and I took the role in my stride. Once again, I introduced the "technician" culture to my team and, for some time, enjoyed the most satisfying and successful job of my entire working life. I reached what I considered to be the pinnacle of my WRAF career and was proud to receive an Air Officer Commanding Commendation in the New Year Honours List 1992. Despite this, I was still not ready to discard my development plan or dismiss any thoughts of a personality change number four.

In 1994, the WRAF formally merged with the RAF, marking a full integration of women into the RAF. This meant that women could now be employed in tactical combat and armed conflict roles. Although I recognised this to be a huge and positive step forward for many women, I made the personal decision to retain my non-combatant status for as long as possible. However, this option was lost to me in 1996, when, once again, I was offered promotion on the understanding that my non-combatant status would change. I accepted the promotion, this time to the rank of Flight Sergeant (FS), along with a new post on the same RAF station, but in a different "joint service" department. With much regret, though, I was obliged to say goodbye to the wonderful department I had enjoyed working in more than any other in my military career.

By the time I held my new rank, I was still very much a "girlie girl", with my father's old-fashioned codes of behaviour for ladies deeply entrenched in my very being. Although my under-confidence had been obscured for some time, it was still dormant and capable of resurrection in new or unfamiliar environments and situations. I worried about this shortfall becoming apparent to others or affecting my performance in an alien combat role, especially given the expectations of my rank. When I accepted my promotion, I laid awake the night before my prerequisite weapon training, concerned that my poor eyesight was not conducive to the distant-target weapon training involved and that my directional, left/right issues might be exposed. Once again, though, I pushed these reservations aside and, along with the men and other women on my course, qualified as required and became a combatant member of the RAF.

I was never completely at ease with my change of combatant status and my transition from the WRAF to the RAF. For the first time in almost twenty-five years, tentative thoughts of a career change entered my mind. I was in my early forties and was carrying out an enjoyable telecommunications auditor's role as a Flight Sergeant, but was aware that to stand every chance of a second successful career, 1998 was probably the right time for another step change in my life.

My mind was made up, when, one morning, I was sent for by my immediate superior who was, most unusually, a Royal Navy officer. Although this officer was aware of the role I carried out, in my mind, he didn't know me, had never taken any interest in my job and had no understanding of the role's demands and complexities. I thought he was petty and demanded respect whenever he entered my office but demonstrated no attempts to earn it. With what I thought was a total disregard for my SNCO status, time served and military value, he issued me with the worst performance review of my entire career. There was an opportunity for redress, but I declined this as a matter of principle and, unusually for me, felt no real incentive to fight for justice.

The following day, I made, at what turned out to be the right point in my career, the third best decision of my life, which was followed by very positive consequences. I handed the officer my letter of resignation with no self-recrimination, bitterness or regret. I was ambitious and keen to move on.

CHAPTER TWENTY-FIVE

1998
A Surprise Encounter

I left the RAF in early 1998 after taking some retirement leave and attending various resettlement training courses. This was to be the second huge step change in my life, the first being to join the WRAF as a seventeen-year-old in the winter of 1973. I had left the military after many years of loyal service with no respect for my last boss, but with wonderfully fond memories of many people, especially those who had formed part of my own teams. I had been transported through training courses, experience, mentoring and my own conscious personality changes from a young, naïve and ineffectual dreamer with no sense of self, to an ambitious, strong and motivated realist, whose latest hunger for success, despite repressed anxieties, ignited yet another inner determination to flourish and triumph.

I applied for only two positions immediately after leaving the RAF. My application for the first role had instigated two interviews, one informal and one formal. These were followed by a presentation to a large group of managers about myself, my proficiencies and my strategic approach to the advertised position. Despite my years in the military, I still hated to be in the spotlight or under personal scrutiny, so I felt uncomfortable, sure that my suppressed anxieties must have been apparent. I had expected the same process with the second role, but I was wrong. It was a much simpler and more straightforward procedure with just one informal interview by a person called John, who, if I were to be successful, would be my future director. I felt as if I had struck a chord with this man and hoped that he would choose me to work for him. To my delight, I subsequently received two job offers. I declined the first, but accepted the role to work for John.

My new dream role was an operations manager position for a local medium-sized telecommunications company called Manage and Integrate Networks Simply Ltd (MINS). I started my civilian career a month later.

My first day involved an induction process with human resources (HR), followed by a "Welcome to the Business" interview with my director and an invitation to join one of his weekly project review meetings later in the afternoon. Having arrived one hour early to ensure I had time to spare in case I lost my way, I was obliged to wait in the company's reception area until the first member of the HR department arrived for work. I sat all alone and became bored with reading the business magazines set out on the coffee table in front of my seat, so started to look around at my new surroundings. I noticed a framed photographic montage on the wall opposite me, which I presumed held photographs of the business executives. I left my seat and went over to see if I was right, which, as it happened, I was. I took in all the images, but was most interested to see the picture of the chief executive officer (CEO). I thought it might be important to be able to recognise him in the future, so I made a note of his name and committed his image to memory. I returned to my seat and, ten minutes later, and to my surprise, a side door opened in the reception area and the person who walked through that door was the very CEO I had seen in the montage. Without thinking it through, I stood up, made my way over to him and asked if he was the person I thought he was, explaining about my interest in the photographs.

'Excuse me, good morning!' I said, with my Cheshire Cat face on. 'I think I have identified you from your photograph on the wall over there. Are you Mr Burnley, the MINS chief executive officer?' He was, initially, a little taken aback by my approaching him, but then smiled warmly back at me, perhaps impressed by my powers of observation.

He replied with a particularly bad stammer. 'I am, you are reh... reh... reh... right. Who... who... who... who are you?' he asked.

Summoning up as much courage as possible, I introduced myself and explained that it was my first day of work for his company and what my role was expected to be.

He offered his hand, which I shook, noticing the warmth and strength of his handshake. 'Oh, ger... ger... good,' he said. 'Wer... wer... wer... welcome to MINS. I am aware of the... uh... uh... network you mer... mer... mer... mention. Will... will... will you be working for my director of oper... oper... oper... operations, John Twer... Twer... Twer... Twerton?'

I nodded and smiled again. 'Yes, I will,' I replied. 'I am hoping to meet with him shortly.'

'Oh well, ger... ger... ger... good luck with everything. I hope all go... go... go... goes well for you.'

'Thank you, Mr Burnley,' I replied politely.

Before taking his leave, he added, 'Mike, please call me Mike if we mer... mer... mer... meet again, which I am sure we... uh... uh... will.'

I thanked him, said I hoped so and we said our goodbyes. What I didn't know at the time was how this chance encounter would bring me both pleasure and pain some years later.

It wasn't long after my surprise meeting with the CEO that a lady from the HR department came to find me. We completed my induction and I was escorted to meet the gentleman who had informally interviewed me previously and was now my new boss, John Twerton. After a cup of coffee and a general chat, John gave me the rundown on what he expected of me as his operations manager. I was then, apart from our weekly project review meetings, left almost entirely to my own devices.

Chapter Twenty-Six

1998–2008
Anxiety, Achievement and Self-Acceptance

I had never worked so hard in the WRAF as I did in my first six months with MINS. This was not due to pressure from above, but to my own determination to succeed. The driving forces for me were to receive admiration from Greg and genuine appreciation from my seniors and, to a greater degree, obtain self-satisfaction and my own sense of achievement.

The role itself came with pros and cons. On the positive side and importantly for me, I did not have to take part in parades, so not knowing my left from my right was not particularly concerning. There were no risks associated with incorrect rank recognition due to my poor eyesight and I did not have to ride a bike or unnecessarily carry an umbrella or a package to avoid embarrassment. Additionally, I felt as if a great weight had been lifted off my shoulders once I had discarded my rank badges and uniform, and switched to civilian clothes. This meant I could be Nolwen, just Nolwen, with no outward signs of my ranking in the business. Apart from my immediate colleagues, few people working for MINS knew my true status and, within reason, there were no constraints on what I said or how I said it. I was pleased that people were interested in me and what I could do, not what I looked like or how I presented myself. There were few clear boundaries or lines I was afraid to step over. I felt free. Free to be myself.

Right from day one, another pro for me was that I no longer needed to care about performance reports. Gone were the days when I would feel apprehensive about listening to report narratives, which could be critical or complimentary, or read forms that might contain good or bad scores. I had been advised during my induction that no performance measurement systems existed in MINS at the time. I was never formally appraised while employed as a civilian; instead, I was "inspired" to perform well by gaining the respect and appreciation of my superiors, and I was incentivised to change roles as and when the previous role or project was completed successfully. I found that advancement followed success for the business and not from one person's personal opinion of another.

On the negative side was the pressure I put myself under to please my director, combined with the fact that I allowed myself quite readily to be persuaded by flattery into taking on extra responsibilities. These were often beyond my capabilities unless I drove myself above and beyond the norm, which, of course, I did.

While adjusting as best as I could to the demands and

cultural differences between my old and new very different careers, I proceeded with the support of a new team to deliver the operational responsibilities of my contracted role with no outwardly visible qualms.

Six months later, I attended my very first civilian business review. It was a routine but important review of the service my team had provided so far. I was inwardly nervous and apprehensive when I walked into the large, light and airy boardroom. Numerous executives sat around a highly polished table, which was positioned in the centre of the room. After a brief introduction, I was invited to sit down and, along with everyone else present, I listened intently to the words of John, my director, about my department. It soon became apparent, to my amazement and delight, that in the preceding six months my team had done exceptionally well. We had met all our deadlines, reached all internal performance targets, met our prescribed service level agreements and the business had paid no penalties to our customer. This was unheard of in MINS history of network management and I experienced a great feeling of pride and team achievement.

After the review, I joined John in the MINS canteen for a coffee. By this time, I knew him well enough to be able to talk to him freely about any business concerns. I knew he was pleased with the business review, but, nevertheless, probably because of my repressed diffidence, I prompted him to counsel me about any shortfalls or weaknesses he was aware of in me as a manager.

'In all honesty, Nolwen, there is nothing for you to worry about. With your exceptional personal skills, you have a promising future here with MINS. If you really want to further your business knowledge, though, you could perhaps make yourself more aware of the differences between running a business for profit and being a member of the military, where I guess budgets were of no concern to you.'

I thanked him and, as was my propensity, resolved to visit my local library and conduct some research on the management of businesses and limited companies as soon as I could.

I conducted some research in my local library the following day and was pleased to find lots of guidance on financial management. When I returned home armed with armfuls of literature, I dug out my old development plan. I glanced through the lists of development needs, behavioural change additions and deletions, and considered adding the topics of finance and budgets, and some more personality improvements I had identified for myself. However, with John's words, "exceptional personal skills", rolling around in my head, I did nothing. Even if he had just used the adjective "good" before "personal", I would have been happy. The word "exceptional" was beyond my expectations.

Instead of making the changes, I placed the plan on the kitchen table, made myself a cup of coffee, picked it up again and after a second quick scan of the carefully written lists, promptly tore it up into tiny pieces and tossed the whole lot into the bin. I swiped my two hands together twice with a sense of satisfaction and muttered under my breath, 'Well, that's the end of that.'

I knew at that moment that although I was going to better my knowledge on business finance, there was never going to be a "personality change number four" and that I no longer needed a project-management style plan with priorities and start/finish dates to change who I was.

Having torn up my development plan and effectuated three conscious, self-devised personality changes, although it had taken until my mid-life to achieve, I was assured that I had finally found myself. There were some negative emotions from my childhood that I still had to contend with, but my character was fully formulated and, more importantly, it was me, Nolwen, who was satisfied with the outcome and the person I had become.

I then took some time out to think about the "creature" I had been and why I had felt such a desperate need to change my make-up and persona. I didn't find the complete answer, but settled on just a few main reasons. I had been conflicted by the different parenting skills and examples set by my mother and father, had often felt unliked, had been the subject of ridicule, which damaged my self-esteem, and had had my hopes and aspirations dashed when I thought I was deserving of support and reward. Additionally, I was, of course, a daydreamer who had always imagined who and what I would become. I supposed my dreams had finally come true and it was time to enjoy their fruition.

You cannot be everything to everybody. You are who you are now, Nolwen. Just be yourself and enjoy the challenges ahead of you.

I remained in the same role for the next two years, but following what was to be my last business review with the same great results as the first, I received a telephone call from my director, John, asking me if I would like to consider a new job opportunity. Unbeknown to me, following my first ever business review, I had apparently impressed so many people that I had been placed on a company "People of Potential" register and my business performance was being privately monitored by some executives. John explained to me that it had been agreed by himself, these executives and his managing director that I should be asked to consider a new "business improvement" role. This was to put the skills and expertise I had recently demonstrated to better use by auditing some of MINS' failing internal departments. It was thought that I should use my relationship skills to work with the relevant department managers, to re-engineer working practices and to implement changes to procedures and computer systems to improve performance. I would subsequently be required to refine any failing integration processes between departments internally and with customers.

After a discussion with Greg and with little hesitation, I accepted the new role. This came with some additional benefits – to include a better company car and a salary increase – and I would no longer report into John, but to our managing director, Phil Buckley. I promoted a member of my old team into the position I vacated and once more said my goodbyes to a wonderful group of people who had supported me well.

The problem that faced me in my new role was the company bureaucracy. In the RAF, if a superior required a job to be done, an individual was given responsibility for that job and the power to achieve the task either alone or with the unconditional support of others. Nothing was allowed to unnecessarily impede progress. As a MINS employee, before anyone could begin to implement change of any kind, they were obliged to formally present the aims and concept of the task to all interested parties, then produce and achieve multi-party sign-off on numerous documents. Only once these presentations had been given and the documents had been reviewed and agreed on would the tasked individual be allowed, despite the edict of senior executives, to proceed with the actual implementation of the task.

Another downside was locating, tasking and getting results from those people who did not work directly for the person endeavouring to instigate change, but who were responsible for playing their part in the change implementation. In the RAF, everyone was industrious, willing to please and worked "for the greater good". However, in MINS, there were some people who liked to bury their heads in the sand, keep a low profile and avoid any extra work, especially if this involved exceeding the scope of their normal employment. Then, there were those who were supposedly "living in the fast lane", but were, in reality, flitting from one meeting to another, at different locations, where they had a lot to say, but were adept at coming away with no assigned tasks or actions.

Given these hurdles, there was no doubt in my mind that the road ahead was to be challenging, but it was one I relished and enjoyed for some time. On saying this, however, there was one particular task I despised and never became accustomed to. This task was carrying out presentations to large audiences. Presentations were typically intended to inform all concerned about ideas and initiatives, persuade third parties to agree with any changes, then inspire and motivate the people involved to support and work with me to achieve results. They were considered imperative and I had no choice but to do them.

I was always required to give my presentations in the enormous MINS lecture and conference room, which, with its high-quality acoustics, was equipped with top-notch AV equipment and an intelligent lighting system. At the push of a button and at the very moment I spoke, the conference room main lights would dim and I would be left fully illuminated and standing alone on a huge stage, with just my laptop and a huge projection screen for company. For a person who hated being in the limelight, this was a pretty daunting experience and I had to call on all my inner strengths and resolve to stay in control and present myself as being confident and professional.

The night before each presentation, just as I had done as a WRAF recruit, I laid awake, worrying about the challenges facing me the following day. Even though I knew my subject, I felt nauseous, feared failure and slept for only a few hours. On the morning of each presentation, just as I had done during my service basic training when I built my bed pack before my roommates had risen from their beds, I prepared early and proactively set myself up in the lecture and conference room hours before I needed to. Before starting, I was always nervous, restless and tense, but reassured myself by thoughts of my father, who would have been proud of his elegant and immaculately dressed daughter, who walked gracefully onto a stage with her toes pointing forward and no signs of a slouch. The second the conference room lights went down and I began to speak, I forced myself to slip into my own private world as if I was alone and just rehearsing in a room with no audience.

'Good morning, everybody. My name is Nolwen...' I always began, appearing self-assured and totally in control. I just hoped my trembling hands, which spoke to my listeners in support of my words, would not give away my inner anxiety.

CHAPTER TWENTY-SEVEN

2008
A Reacquaintance

My audience in the MINS lecture and conference room almost always included company and customer executives, but at my last presentation while working for Phil Buckley, there was a surprise in store. Before the main lights dimmed, I noticed and recognised Mike Burnley, the CEO with a stammer who I had met briefly in the MINS reception area, on my very first day with the company. He was sitting in the front row of the conference room. I couldn't really understand why he was there, but dismissed this thought as I launched into the presentation I had meticulously prepared for during the previous week.

A week later, I received a telephone call from Mike Burnley's personal assistant (PA), Philippa Giles, which turned out to be not only a catalyst for my next – very unusual and emotionally rewarding – role within MINS, but, by sheer coincidence, led to a relationship with Mike that was to leave its mark on my private life.

Mike was known to be a very clever, astute, calm and personable executive, who had succeeded in business despite his severe speech impediment. His career progression had been difficult at times, so when he joined MINS as a director of operations almost fifteen years earlier and found he was entitled to use the services of a PA, he had recruited Philippa to fulfil this role. Philippa had remained his personal assistant and events manager when he progressed from director to managing director, and then again when he became the CEO of MINS.

By his own admission, Mike depended on Philippa to a large degree and could not have retained credibility in his very senior executive role without her. Philippa took on the role of his "speaker", aiming to alleviate any embarrassment and to limit the hindrance of Mike's stammering when he wished to express himself quickly during meetings or events. Mike and Philippa were extremely close professionally and Philippa knew her boss's needs intimately. She could very quickly, easily and diplomatically jump to his aid by reading the room or closely monitoring his facial expressions and hand movements. They would spend much of their working day, jointly understanding and transcribing all of Mike's articulate, visionary, smart and compelling written work – which not only included his business strategic documents, but his day-to-day notes and agendas for meetings – into formats that Philippa could verbalise on his behalf. What Philippa did not wish to do was to stand on stage and pitch or present Mike's pre-prepared speeches, lectures and talks to large audiences.

Over the previous few years, I had presented many times and even though I was inwardly riddled with anxiety, I had learnt through experience and practice how to connect with my audience, grab their attention and, with some charm and a Cheshire Cat smile, persuade my listeners that my subject was of interest and of value to them. I had endeavoured to develop pitch qualities and traits that I hoped separated me from other more mediocre speakers. I was later to learn that, apparently, news of my distinctive pitching technique and engaging presentation methodology had reached the ears of Philippa. Seeing an opportunity to assist Mike, she had encouraged him to attend one of my presentations. He had sat in the front row, not out of particular interest for the project I was selling to interested parties, but with the sole intention of assessing my ability to become his personal presentations manager. He told me sometime later that as soon as the conference room lights had dimmed and I was illuminated and primed to speak, he remembered my face and connected the presenter with the comparatively reserved new employee who had boldly introduced herself to the most important man in the MINS enterprise almost ten years earlier.

I received a job offer within days and, after some sleepless nights, decided that no one with ambition or common sense ever turned down a position offered to them by a CEO. I put aside my anxieties and accepted the offered role, which came with a promise that I would be allowed to engineer any operational role and job title I wished within the business once I tired of it. I knew from my business improvement projects that there was a need for a MINS director of service delivery, which would allow me to make the most of all my experience and skillsets. While handing over my job acceptance paperwork, I discussed these thoughts with Mike, who was very supportive of my idea, but emphasised that, for the time being, he needed my skills as a presenter. I committed my future inspirations to memory, but then focused on the immediate challenges of my latest position.

Over the next month, it was not only Mike who depended on Philippa. I needed to understand and take advice from her on his preferred method of working and how to read and respond to his discreet signals. She and I became close friends, and she confided in me that Mike had experimented with various devices and therapy to help him to communicate verbally, but nothing had really worked well enough to remove the problem. I found myself able to talk to her about my directional dyslexia, my personal anxieties and my diffidence with public speaking, but explained how these latter emotions flowed away the second the conference room lights dimmed. I also explained how difficult it would be for Greg and me to spend quality time together if Mike needed me to accompany him on long-distance business trips. This concern applied more if these journeys involved numerous overnight stopovers. She understood my anxieties and reluctance to spend too much time away from home, but, for the time being, we kept these conversations out of Mike's earshot.

My work life was relatively easy outside of the presentations themselves, particularly because Mike prepared all of his slides himself. I knew instinctively that it wasn't good enough to just stand on the stage and read words from a script or slide, so we reviewed and edited the slides together. This meant that I was not only familiar with the subject we were presenting, but that I understood the points he wished to emphasise or linger on, and his main objectives. I kept myself otherwise occupied by assisting Philippa with much of her administration and event management, and by getting to fully understand her working partnership with Mike.

Mike and I agreed our stage tactics and it was decided that the format would always be the same, in that after setting myself up with the usual equipment, I would introduce us both and Mike would retreat to a seat behind a desk at the corner of the stage. I would explain to the audience about Mike's speech impediment and then would routinely express a wish to be able to present our slides on his behalf without interruption, giving assurances that questions would be invited at the end. Mike would take a note of all posed questions and, during a comfort break, would type them up and then send the questions and his answers to me electronically, whereupon I would verbally communicate the content to our listeners. I would finally express our thanks to everyone who had listened. As usual, at the end of our presentation, the conference room's main lights would be undimmed, signalling our time to exit the stage.

The night before our first presentation, I went through the usual pre-performance anxieties, but everything went according to plan on the day. After heaving a sigh of relief at the end, then exchanging a smile of satisfaction and mutual thanks, Mike and I gathered up our material and equipment and happily left the stage together. This presentation with my CEO really brought it home to me what a superb strategic mind he had, and how tenacious and modestly intelligent he was. He had no intention of being beaten or losing credibility due to his disability.

Mike and I worked amiably well as a team over the coming months and, most importantly, I knew that he had every confidence in me as his presentations manager. It was also a bonus that Mike was willing to drive when we were required to present at the premises of customers, so I did not have to navigate myself from one place to another. I would have been terrified if he had relied on me to chauffeur him from place to place. As this was not the case, my still undiagnosed directional dyslexia remained a secret between Philippa and myself. The other advantage was that I did not have to painstakingly originate any of our presentation content or prepare myself for the anxious period of potentially very awkward questions. I did, though, have to concentrate when walking around some of the huge, luxurious hotels we stayed at, in order to locate my bedroom and the restaurants – where we would eat together most evenings.

Mike and I had a bit of a break from our presentations in the run-up to Christmas that year and I was reminded that it was customary practice to hold our MINS annual concert just before the festive break. Philippa always organised this on Mike's behalf and it routinely took place in the lecture and conference room. Tickets were charged for and all proceeds were donated to local charities. The aim was to invite everyone employed in the business or, in some cases, our customers to perform on stage and entertain their colleagues. This wasn't a karaoke type event, so the response list was shortlisted with the final invitation only being extended to professional or semi-professional performers. This particular year, Philippa advised me that lots of volunteers had come forward, including solo instrumental musicians, two pop groups, a juggler, a Pam Ayres lookalike who planned to read some of her poems, a magician and even a stand-up comedian. She added, with a mischievous smile on her face, that there would also be a mystery guest singer who would perform two solos, but then refused to provide me with any further details. I presumed she had managed to engage the services of a well-known celebrity. It was this charity concert that led to a second relationship with my new boss, which both negatively and positively connected with my private life and surprisingly rekindled some emotions I had not felt since my youth. A week before the concert, Mike invited me to dinner at his home.

Chapter Twenty-Eight

2008–2009
Rekindled Emotions

Mike's invitation to dinner at his home was – he said, a little evasively – to give me the opportunity to get to know him better. I was a little uneasy about the engagement as sometimes my social skills failed me, but I bought myself a new conservative black knee-length dress and matched this with a glossy silver clutch bag and, after much deliberation, some high-heeled shoes to complement my outfit. Following the directions Philippa had given to me, I reached Mike's "residence" on time and, for once, without getting lost. His home was a beautiful, thatched cottage, which had been sensitively extended and was set in a huge garden in a small village just a few miles south of our offices. I arrived at his front door armed with a couple of bottles of wine and knocked hesitantly.

After knocking again, this time a little more forcefully, I heard the door latch lift and then the door squeak on its old hinges as it swung open. I was greeted warmly and invited in by a very charming, handsome gentleman, who smiled at me pleasantly and introduced himself as Joe, Mike's partner. I think I might have blushed a little when realisation dawned on me that Mike must have been gay. I kicked myself for being so presumptuous when I had accepted the invitation. Mike and Joe later explained to me that their relationship was an open secret, but wasn't something they wished to be talked about freely within the business. I gave them my word and kept my promise as conscientiously as I had done many years ago with the tramp and my father's boots.

We had a lovely dinner together with just the three of us being waited on by Mike's wonderful housekeeper, Jane, who had cooked a superb four-course dinner and who joined us at the end of the meal for coffee and petit fours. We all sat together in a cosy dining room warmed by the flames of a log fire in the huge inglenook fireplace and chatted amiably. Joe and I understood Mike's difficulty with communicating very well and both patiently waited for him to find his words during dinner without pre-emption or butting in. He seemed to be just as comfortable and relaxed in my presence as he was with Joe's, and we learned a lot about each other that night. Mike disclosed to me that he had two passions, cycling and singing and that he was actually a classically trained tenor. I then discovered that Mike was, in fact, Philippa's mystery guest singer at the forthcoming charity concert.

Mike and Joe were interested in getting to know me, so I selectively ran through the highlights of my family life in

West and South Wales, leaving out that we had lived in a tiny caravan for a while, and some of our other family hardships. I knew Mike was aware of my WRAF career, so I touched on this briefly for Joe's sake. As we spoke about Mike's singing, I told them about my childhood passion for music and about my *eisteddfod* competitions and fondly reminisced about my school and county youth choirs. By the time we reached dessert, the wine had been flowing well and we found ourselves talking a little more about the forthcoming charity concert. Before I knew it, supported by Dutch courage, I found myself succumbing to Mike's persuasive charms and I made my second promise of the night. I agreed to follow Mike's singing performance at the concert with a solo of my own. Fortunately, I had added a condition with some laughter that the conference room main lights would have to be dimmed so that I could enter my own private world and pretend I was singing alone at home in my bathroom.

The next day, I was horrified at what I had committed myself to doing and worried about my foolish bravado for days afterwards. Agreeing to sing at the concert was the second promise I had made to Mike and I reminded myself that I never went back on a promise. Philippa took no time in organising the production, printing and distribution of the concert programme, which was sent out with my name boldly printed just beneath the mystery guest performer. It advertised the title of the song I had sung many times at school – the well-known aria "Where'er You Walk" from *Semele*, composed by George Frideric Handel.

Reminiscent of my WRAF days, I did my best to avoid falling asleep the night before the concert, relishing the period before I dropped off, as this was the time before I made a complete fool of myself by singing a solo as a follow-on performance to the professional voice of my CEO.

The evening of the concert came and the conference room was jam-packed with employees and privileged customers. I was still on duty as a presenter and made the opening speech on Mike's behalf from the centre of the stage, apparently looking attractive and elegant in my long sparkly evening dress and high heels. I attempted fruitlessly to override an enthusiastic reception from the crowd, who all recognised me, with an explanation about the local charities who would benefit from the concert proceeds and then, once the room grew silent, explained the format of the show.

People who were performing sat in the front row and got up from their chairs when it was their turn to show off their talents. Every performer was met with unrestrained rounds of applause and supportive cheers as they mounted the stairs to reach the stage. This applied especially to Mike, when it was revealed that he was the mystery guest. Excitement filled the air as everyone prepared for the thrill of being entertained by known colleagues, no matter what their status or position.

Mike was introduced to the stage by Philippa as I, by that time, was a nervous wreck. The concert continued wonderfully, especially so, when the time came for the audience's CEO to sing his two classical pieces consecutively. After a few bars of his first song, it became very obvious to me why Mike took so much pleasure from his music. He was able to sing beautifully with no signs of a stammer whatsoever and was, for a short period of time, free to express himself with no inhibitions or embarrassment.

Once the enthusiastic applause had died down following my boss's performance, it was my turn and I stepped onto the very familiar stage. The lights dimmed; I paused, took a deep breath and forced myself to take control of my emotions. I waited for my intro and began to sing my solo. The words of the first verse of "Where'er You Walk" left my lips, as my eyes gently closed and a frown creased my brow with emotion and concentration on my pitch, tone and volume. I hadn't heard myself sing solo in front of an audience for over thirty years, but I knew from singing around my home in recent times that my voice had changed and developed in tone over the years. The pure, velvety sound that bounced and reverberated around the room with its wonderful acoustics surprised me more than it did anyone else in the audience. It was all very surreal; I felt as if the mellow voice being projected so powerfully and from deep inside me wasn't mine, but belonged to someone else. I experienced an indescribable sense of silence in the room, which swathed the richness of a beautiful contralto voice that I barely recognised, and I was moved to tears. These tears flowed slowly and gently down over my cheeks as the music, the words and the sound of what eventually registered as being my own voice evoked a strange bittersweet sensation of sadness versus pride. I did not feel the need to hold the tears back.

I returned to my seat next to Mike in the front row of the conference room. My hands were trembling and my legs were shaking uncontrollably with the relief that I was now off the stage. Bizarrely, while I knew where I was, why I was there and who I was with, once I returned to my seat, I was unable to remember any applause or anything Mike might have said when I sat down next to him. I was not even able to recall the lights being undimmed or walking down the stage steps. I was also unable to recollect all the aspects of my performance, but what I did know was that I was euphoric and satisfyingly pleased with myself.

My memories returned in full later that night when I awoke in my bed from a deep sleep. I was then able to revisit my performance in full and analyse the emotions I had felt during and after it. I concluded that the sadness was probably linked to my childhood memories of singing and of a wasted talent. This contrasted with a merited feeling of reward by being able to release so openly, through my voice, some private and deeply personal feelings of triumph over so many adversities. I knew then that I had given a wonderful performance, which had been applauded exuberantly by my colleagues and the rest of the audience. I heaved a sigh of relief, though, when I assured myself that I would definitely not be coerced into singing again at the next Christmas charity event.

A month or so later, when I thought the events of the concert had long been forgotten, and after many apprehensive pre-presentation sleepless nights for me, Mike, Philippa and I were in his office contemplating some issues with the wording on his slides. We seemed to be going around in circles and not getting anywhere fast, so decided to take a well-earned coffee break. This gave Mike the opportunity to raise the subject of his passion for singing and something that he had apparently been mulling over since the evening of the charity concert. He was quite excitable, which meant his stammer became more pronounced, but we waited patiently for him to get his words out. He reminded me about the concert and told me how he and many others had been moved during the rendition of the aria I had chosen to sing.

I had a premonition about what Mike was about to say and thoughts of the next concert jumped into my mind. I attempted to explain what an ordeal it had been for me before the performance, but he interrupted my few words of intended resistance and went on to tell me a little about his passion for music and where this passion had led him. He explained that he usually sang accompanied by Joe playing the piano and they were often supported by a small in-house orchestra. They performed semi-professionally at music festivals, community events and organised live shows, which brought them both much pleasure. He pulled at my heart strings further, by saying that this pleasure was particularly relevant to him as, for a brief but welcome time, he was released from the embarrassment and hampering chains of his speech impediment. He then went on to advise me that, unfortunately, their repertoire was becoming limited and a little stale. *Oh no*, I thought, as my heart began to pound. *I really think I know what Mike's going to say next!*

I was absolutely right, because Mike then went on to explain that he had an idea about how he and Joe could refresh their portfolio and revitalise their performances. Just as he was with his business customers, when Mike had an idea, he became very persuasive and determined. He managed his pre-planned discussion well and, intending to not over-alarm me, gently eased his conversation on to the subject of voice training. I was made aware that he took regular training himself to continue to refine his vocal and breathing techniques and, more importantly, to boost his self-confidence.

Seeking to enthuse me further, he explained that his tutor, John, made a point of identifying appropriate musical pieces for Joe and Mike's portfolio, which were so expressive that the lyrics and melodies quickly dissolved the singer's fear by fomenting strong emotions. Mike then announced that he and Joe were free to choose two or three preferred pieces from the portfolio to sing on the day of a forthcoming event. Cutting to the chase, he then let me know that his tutor had agreed to give me an audition. He walked out of the room and left me to ponder my new predicament.

Needless to say, the following week, Joe and Mike accompanied me to the prearranged audition. At first reluctantly, I sang "Where'er You Walk" once again and had to admit that, after a few bars, I fully enjoyed every second of the experience with only the tutor, John, Mike and Joe for an audience. John expressed no reservations about Mike's idea and, after encouraging me to sing alone and then listening to both of us singing together, he agreed to source some new material. Their plans unfolded before my very eyes and before I had any opportunity to protest, "our" tutor stated that he would choose some contralto solo music for me and a selection of duet arrangements that he thought Mike and I could rehearse under his guidance and sing together. He assured us that this new material and changed format would, without doubt, be the boost the couple needed to enable them to re-captivate, enthral and entice new crowds and followers to attend their shows. I left the audition feeling very ill at ease, but with Mike and Joe chatting excitedly about their musical future, I just put on a forced Cheshire Cat smile and said nothing.

Not wanting to appear negative, I agreed to give the lessons a try before fully committing myself to the concerts and shows, but I inevitably became drawn into Mike and Joe's inexorable enthusiasm. I very quickly found myself enticed into a position of no going back and eventuated into singing with them at festivals, recitals and other gigs for almost six months. Unbeknown to the couple, sleepless nights and the very troubled agitated state that preceded each and every concert took their toll on my well-being. That period of my life became as painful for me as my WRAF drill, marching and parade days had been. Despite the undisputable success of our trio and our popular performances, our tutor could not work miracles for me. Unlike Mike and Joe, despite his perseverance, I never learnt to handle my nerves and cope with my anxieties until I heard the opening bars of the music. This worked well for the audience and for Mike and Joe, but didn't feel fruitful enough for me to counterbalance my distress and anguish.

Chapter Twenty-Nine

2008–2018
Fond Memories

Meanwhile, outside of work and my concerts, Greg and I were still very much in love. At this mid-life period of our lives, we particularly cherished any time off we could spend together and were determined to take advantage of any opportunities that came our way and to make the most of our free time and annual leave. We had already visited most countries in Europe over the years, but made the decision that we would travel the rest of the world before reaching the age of sixty.

Our first long-haul holiday was a three-week tour of China. In those days, this was an unusual travel destination for British tourists and proved to be a fascinating experience. Greg and I were not only interested in seeing the most famous highlights of every country we visited, but were keen to get a taste of real life, to engage with local people and to gain an understanding of the different cultures in the foreign lands we chose to visit. Because of this appetency, we selected travel companies who specialised in the countries we travelled to, were ethical and not inappropriately intrusive to local people. We chose tour operators who offered small group tours, which gave us the best opportunity to see and experience the best and sometimes the worst of our destinations. We climbed the Great Wall of China and saw amazing sights, such as the famous Terracotta Warriors, interspersed with visits to Chinese hospitals, schools and factories. We were also though, sometimes confronted with children begging, and had upsetting glimpses of physically impaired people struggling to survive on the streets, which we had to come to terms with. Undeterred, we resolved to continue with this kind of travel to broaden our minds, marvel at the scope of our world and create lifetime memories.

It wasn't difficult to find countries that paralleled the attractions and peculiarities of China, so over the following ten years, we visited India with its Taj Mahal and funeral pyres of Varanasi, Brazil with its world-famous Christ the Redeemer and favelas in Rio, South Africa with its famous Table Mountain, wonderful safari holiday resorts and contrasting deprived, over-populated settlements, followed by trips to Mexico and Central America to name just a few others. One destination that enthralled us and almost surpassed China in our memories was Peru. Here, memorable highlights included the magnificent Machu Picchu, the floating homes on the reed islands of Lake Titicaca and a three-night tour into the Amazon jungle. The indigenous Uros families who lived on the self-made reed islands of Lake Titicaca warmly welcomed Greg and I as we arrived with our tour guide on a locally sourced fishing boat. We had armed ourselves with colouring books, crayons and balloons for the children, who, we were told, rarely had access to such items. Our jungle experience was equally memorable; our accommodation was in wooden huts on stilts with no walls, so as to allow us to fully appreciate the unique sounds of the jungle as we lay in our beds. Animal-loving patrols kept us safe from unwelcome visitors, which did not include the most dangerous of large animals. These, to my relief, kept themselves to themselves in the more remote areas of the jungle. Nevertheless, I felt the need to sleep under my firmly tucked-in mosquito net, fully clothed and with my boots next to me to ensure that they did not become a temporary home for curious snakes or scary insects.

We sometimes chose cruises, which allowed us to see multiple destinations in one trip. Although these were enjoyable, the ports they called in generally did not offer the in-depth cultural and real-life experiences of land tours that we were most interested in.

Another activity during this period, which I was somewhat involved with, but which kept Greg fully occupied in his free time, was the unexpected but exciting opportunity to build our own home close to Chittington, our local town. We were the successful bidders at an auction and, at the drop of a hammer, we purchased an old derelict Wesleyan chapel. The chapel was positioned on a third of an acre of land in a small hamlet, set in the heart of the Wiltshire countryside. Working with my ideas and layout preferences, Greg designed our home and project-managed its construction, which was undertaken by a local building company. The result was an impressive, uniquely designed, cottage-style stone home with a modern interior and with striking features for a new house, such as original beams and inglenook fireplaces. Once the house was built, every free minute of our time was taken up with turning it into a comfortable home.

Our global travels were totally disparate from my fondly remembered but single family holiday in Blackpool and the house was an unbelievably far cry from the caravan I had lived in with my family during my teenage years. However, I never forgot my roots, always appreciated my good fortune and spent many hours reflecting on the evolutionary personal goals and step changes in my life that had enabled Greg and, especially, me to reach a level of prosperousness that bore no resemblance to the level of underprivilege in my youth. My only regret was that my father was not around to witness my success and to see that his daydreaming daughter, with her lack of capacity to concentrate on a board game, or complete the simplest of errands in a timely manner, had achieved so much in her professional and private life.

CHAPTER THIRTY

2009
Directional Dyslexia

Although I led a very busy life with my presentations for Mike, my work with Philippa and our concerts, I still did my best to visit my mother in Trehywel regularly, as she was showing signs of discontentment with her life, but with my commitments, travels and having to work every weekday, I could not easily manage the monthly visits she had become used to. Steffan lived in Norfolk and, with a demanding career of his own and three children, could only manage the long, slow, cross-country journey to West Wales once or twice a year, although he kept in touch with us all by telephone. After one particularly busy month, I was exhausted but forced myself to drive to Trehywel, mainly because I wanted to explain to my mother how difficult the demands of my work were and how I was finding it harder and harder to visit her every month, especially as I was forced to make the four-hour journey on a Friday night when traffic levels were at their worst and when I was most tired.

The journey had taken five hours due to traffic jams by the time I eventually reached the quieter country roads of West Wales. I breathed a sigh of relief as I pulled up outside my mother's small bungalow. Even before I had emerged from the car, the front door opened and my mother stood there, eyes bright and smiling.

'Nolwen!' she said. 'Just in time. The kettle has just boiled.'

As my mother cooked a typical meal of sausages, tinned vegetables and potatoes, I filled her in on some light-hearted news about me and Greg. She was obviously so happy to see me that I felt a twinge of guilt about what I had come to discuss. Fatigued by the journey, I decided to leave it until the morning. That night, before dropping off to sleep, I pondered over the dilemma that faced me the following day. I knew my mother wouldn't take my news of fewer visits well, despite having lots of family and friends to support her without my father. I started to consider my choice of words and a preamble, but my eyelids closed and I drifted off into a deep but disturbed sleep.

The morning came too soon. After delaying the conversation until after our porridge breakfast and a linger around the kitchen table with our coffees, I eventually plucked up the courage to broach the predicament I found myself in. Getting the gist of what I was about to say after a few sentences, my mother bristled and immediately adopted a defensive pose, pre-empting that a discussion was about to take place that she did not want to take part in. Despite this, I forged ahead and explained the demands of my work to her, followed by the story of how I had been coerced into the musical "extra duties". Her disgruntlement was plain to see and I felt pressurised into offering her a solution to the problem.

As such, an option to soften the blow popped into my head and, in desperation, I voiced an idea that would take some of the travelling strain off me and hopefully appease my mother's distress. The idea was quite simple; my mother should occasionally visit me instead of the other way round. The only flaw in my plan, which I glossed over, was that her journey would involve taking a local bus to her nearest large town, changing service there and boarding a coach directly to our local town, where Greg or I would meet her. Reassuringly, I added that although the journey was a little complicated, it wasn't that difficult and, to my relief, she reluctantly agreed to attempt it. We enjoyed the rest of our weekend together.

Later on, my mother, in her late sixties, undertook her solo maiden voyage from Trehywel to Chittington over an Easter bank holiday. She carried a small suitcase and her handbag, and she was warmly dressed. As expected in those days, she had no mobile phone. Her outward journey went well; she arrived on time and Greg met her at the bus station terminus, and they made a note of the exact pick-up point for her return trip. When he arrived home, Greg handed my mother over to me, discreetly explaining that from that point on, she was my responsibility for the duration of her stay. Apparently, she had irritated him by complaining bitterly, not only about his driving, but about a talkative passenger on the bus who had taken a seat beside her, and about the weight of her suitcase. This moaning and groaning had lasted for the duration of the short car trip from the bus stop to our house.

Following her rather long but uneventful journey, I did my best to ensure that my mother enjoyed a pleasant few days with us. She was especially pleased that I took her shopping and focused totally on helping her to replenish her wardrobe, as Trehywel had little to offer in the way of department stores. Her purchases meant she had to borrow an additional small suitcase from me for her return journey, but despite her complaints to Greg about the weight of her luggage on the way to our house, she had no concerns about carrying this additional suitcase home. During her visit, I noticed that her usual argumentative and controlling nature, which had been somewhat subdued since my father's death, had resurfaced and her old fighting spirit was back with a vengeance. Our relationship became occasionally strained and I have to admit that I wasn't overly sorry when her five-day trip came to an end.

My mother only made the journey once. This was not because Greg had annoyed her with his so-called aggressive driving or because of her fellow passengers, or the weight of her luggage, but because her first return journey home proved to be more problematic than any of us had envisaged.

On the morning of her departure for West Wales, I could tell she was uneasy, but I reassured her that everything would be fine.

'You don't need to worry about anything, Mam,' I said as we got into my car. 'You have all of your belongings and your bus ticket, and I have checked on your connecting Trehywel bus. It will not leave until your first coach arrives at the terminus. In other words, it will wait for you. Everything will be okay.'

As I pulled into the bus terminus at Chittington, I noticed that there was a coach already waiting at the pick-up point that Greg and my mother had identified, so I hurriedly parked my car and assisted her with her luggage.

'Bye, Mam,' I called out as she climbed the steps of the bus. 'Safe journey. Call me as soon as you arrive home.' I then handed up her luggage.

'Bye, Nolwen,' she replied quickly, preoccupied with thoughts of her journey.

I waited at the bus stop until my mother, having presented her ticket and placed her suitcases on the luggage rack, had chosen a seat at the front of the bus, presumably where she could keep a close eye on her belongings. As usual, there had been no embrace, but I managed a smile when she reached her seat by the window. This wasn't returned, but she waved, and I knew that she had enjoyed her stay. I waved enthusiastically until the bus pulled away and watched it disappear towards her destination.

Three hours later, our house telephone rang and I recognised my mother's voice.

'Hello, Nolwen, it's me,' she said.

'Oh hello, Mam!' I replied brightly. 'I presume you've arrived home in one piece?'

'Well, no, actually I haven't,' she stated hesitantly, followed by a pause.

'Why not? Where are you?' I enquired worriedly.

'I'm at Chittington.'

'Why on earth are you back at Chittington?' I questioned with disbelief.

'I've been to Heathrow and back!' she announced.

Feeling astonished and keen to know what had happened, I gathered up my car keys and quickly made my way to the Chittington bus terminus to collect my mother. It was on that day that I realised my directional dyslexia must have, without doubt, been inherited from her. I had witnessed her getting lost and looking blankly around shops, car parks and cafes when she was unable to locate me after only a short distraction or route deviation, but I had not fully connected our disorders. Although the journey destination error had been my fault to some extent – for not checking the displayed sign at the front of the bus – we had, in my defence, been in a hurry. The error was in fact due to the late arrival of the correct bus and, of course, the fault of the bus driver, who had unbelievably checked my mother's ticket when she boarded. Incredibly, though, my mother had not realised that she was being driven in the opposite direction to Wales, had not missed the Severn

Bridge or any of the well sign-posted M4 junctions to Newport, Cardiff or Swansea. She assured me that she had not slept a wink during the journey and only realised "that Nolwen had put her on the wrong bus" when she spotted the Concorde Aircraft Model through the bus window, which stood in the centre of the roundabout connecting the M4 motorway to the Heathrow flight terminals.

Acknowledging his lady passenger's distress, the negligent bus driver advised her to remain on his bus and explained that after a quick turnaround, it would shortly return to Chittington. His parting words to her when she arrived back at my hometown were, 'Sorry, love, perhaps you could try again tomorrow!'

CHAPTER THIRTY-ONE

Guilt

Following on from my mother's Heathrow adventure, which led to her declaring a refusal to attempt the journey again, I made my mind up to properly rethink my work-life balance. There were four constituents I needed to address: one – my mother was becoming increasingly unhappy in West Wales and, despite my heavy commitments, I felt obliged to visit her more often; two – Mike had plans to expand the business into new locations, which would involve more time away for me at a time when Greg and I wanted to be together and enjoy our own travels; three – I was anxious about our concerts and had over-committed to them; and finally but most predominantly, number four – the apprehension I suffered before every presentation. The latter had become unbearable. All in all, I became as fundamentally unhappy in my current job as I had been in my first six weeks of basic training in the WRAF.

Out of the four constituents that affected my work-life balance, I reasoned that it was completely in my power to eliminate three of them by having a serious conversation with Mike. However, I determined that this elimination process came with two separate dilemmas. The first related to my role as a presenter and the potential new locations my CEO had mentioned. On the one hand, Mike relied on me and, although inwardly anxious, I gained a great deal of personal satisfaction by acting as his voice and flawlessly conveying his thoughts to his listeners. On the other hand, I wanted to spend more time with Greg. The second dilemma related to our concerts and my singing. Although I loved to please Mike and Joe with my contribution to their new portfolio, and I enjoyed the personal sense of reward and pride when we delighted our audiences, the pre-performance stress and anxieties were having an adverse effect on my health. I knew in my heart that I needed to address my concerns with Mike as soon as possible.

My best intentions were derailed, however, when Philippa called me with some "good" news. Our trio, having entered a talent competition, had been given an opportunity to perform on one of the main stages at Glastonbury the following summer. She reminded me that this performance would be a few weeks before we were due to perform at the famous Symphony Hall in Birmingham with its renowned, wonderful acoustics. I thanked her for the call, feigned delight and replaced the receiver resignedly as I knew that the time was not right to let Mike and Joe down.

Having delayed one strategy to eliminate three of the main factors that affected my work-life balance, I focused my efforts, a little impulsively and rather selfishly, on the remaining element: my mother's increasing unhappiness in Wales and my unwillingness to visit her once every month. I don't remember making many regrettable decisions in my life, but the one I made about this particular problem certainly sat in this category.

It had been well over twenty years since my father's death and I became more and more aware that my mother's old, argumentative character had returned. She was showing repeated signs of discontentment with her life. On the first evening of what was to be my last but one visit to her home in Trehywel, she told me of her latest grievances. She had, not for the first time, fallen out with her sister, May, and Grandma Jones over something and nothing, and was becoming so disgruntled with her part-time job that she had threatened to resign on numerous occasions.

She explained that her gripe was with the greengrocer who owned the shop where she worked. Ostensibly, the guilty party was miserly and, to save money, kept his premises too cold for her even in the warmer months. I privately rationalised the situation and concluded that it was more likely that the poor man's fruit and vegetables needed to be kept cool, and that he preferred to keep the front door open to encourage footfall. My mother, now well into retirement age, told him in no uncertain terms that her extremities were frozen for most of the day and that she wanted the heat turned up and the door closed. I was sure a compromise could have been reached, but my mother had now regressed back to her former stubborn self and I judged the odds of a satisfactory conclusion were likely to be low.

Setting aside the downsides associated with my mother's job and her quarrels with Auntie May and Grandma Jones, which I knew would eventually resolve themselves, she was, with the benefit of hindsight, fundamentally content and happy in Trehywel and just thrived on complaining. She had a part-time job that got her out of the house for a few days each week, a comfortable rented bungalow that she liked, and friends and family to keep her company. However, because I was so fatigued with my lifestyle, I chose to take her unwarranted complaints at face value and, without thinking things through properly, used those complaints as an excuse to put my interests before hers. I instigated a conversation I was later to regret and which left me with a lingering, long-forgotten feeling of guilt.

'Mam,' I said tentatively as we watched the television together in her small but cosy lounge. 'I have an idea that might help us both. Can you remember that, some years ago, we agreed that I should submit your details for inclusion on mine and Greg's local council's housing list? If you recall, we did this with a view to giving you the option to move nearer to us as you got older so that I could look after you.'

My mother frowned, thought for a while and then nodded. 'Yes, I remember, Nolwen, but why are you mentioning this now?'

After reminding her about her greengrocer issues and

family quarrels, I explained once again about the demands of my work and how I was finding it harder and harder to visit her regularly. 'Perhaps now is a good time to give some thought to moving to Chittington,' I suggested.

The room fell silent and, as I expected and fully understood, my mother didn't initially warm to my idea. Although she seemed to enjoy complaining, what she was never interested in, especially as she got older, was a solution to her issues. She had a well-used phrase after expressing any dissatisfaction and being offered a solution, which was, "Well, I'll leave it for now," and she would then forcefully and frustratingly shut the conversation down. After ruling out the move idea with the "leave it for now" phrase, she did agree that I should verify her position on the housing list, which I did when I returned home. On checking, I found that her position was now very near to the top.

***

Some months later, Granny Lane, the singer who had shown no interest in my hobby as a child and was now an old lady in her nineties, died. My mother and her mother were not particularly close and she showed no outward signs of sorrow at her loss. Sadly, this death was shortly followed by the passing away of Greg's father and then Grandma Jones.

Greg was away working over the period of Grandma Jones's death, so I travelled to Trehywel for the last time and paid my respects to this wonderful lady at her funeral alone. For some unexplained reason, my mother didn't wish to attend. Once the funerals had taken place and noting that my mother was still on bad terms with Auntie May, I decided that the time might be right to re-broach the subject of leaving West Wales and moving to Chittington. I supported my case by reminding her that if she joined us in Wiltshire, she would be much closer to me and I could look after her for the rest of her life.

With no hesitation this time, my fate was sealed and my mother agreed that she would indeed like to move closer to her daughter. I dropped into the Chittington council offices as soon as I could and, as luck would have it, there was a one-bedroom flat a couple of minutes' walk away from our town centre, which had become available and was ready for immediate occupation. My mother had two weeks in which to make a firm decision on whether to accept the flat or not. I picked up the keys and Greg and I looked around the flat, agreeing that with a bit of cosmetic work, it would suit my mother's needs perfectly.

On hearing the news and our views, my mother, putting aside memories of her earlier Heathrow traumatic experience, decided to make the journey to Chittington to look at the flat. She stayed with us for three days and, in that time, she signed the necessary paperwork, chose a new kitchen, some carpets and curtains, and assured me that she was very enthusiastic about the flat itself and the relocation.

Once my mother returned to Trehywel, she organised a removals company to pack up her belongings and, with the assistance of friends, prepared herself for yet another house move. Meanwhile, I completed all of the formalities and engaged the services of a decorator, kitchen installer and plumber. I later ordered the carpets and curtains she had chosen, supervised everything and, within a month, my mother had moved into a very compact but cosy, bright new flat, where her cupboards had already been stocked up with provisions by me and her furniture put in place.

It was, though, only one day after the move-in date that my mother's enthusiastic mood changed to one of dissatisfaction. Instead of inviting her to lunch with Greg and myself, thinking she would be busy settling herself into her new home, I delivered her a plated meal for the microwave. This did not go down well and I was admonished for my thoughtless behaviour. My spirits dropped and I fought back tears as I had worked conscientiously to ensure her move had gone without a hitch. I even questioned my new-found personality, but quickly moved on. I hoped the incident was a one-off and that we could put it behind us and enjoy our new lives as friends, as well as mother and daughter. Things didn't go entirely to plan, though. My mother, it seemed, had reverted to the mother I recognised from my childhood.

I had been genuinely very excited at the prospect of having my mother living just a few miles away from my home and I hoped we could resume the relationship we had experienced during the first few years after my father had died. We had got along well during that period and I saw no reason why this couldn't be the case now we both lived in Wiltshire. I explained that I would spend as much time as possible with her, but that she would also need to try and make a new life for herself. She agreed this at the time but, as it turned out, was incapable of doing it. Instead, as the weeks passed, she became more and more demanding, and because she lived alone in a new environment and her under-confidence drove her towards introversion, I felt a constant need to support her and spend time with her. I therefore dropped in to see her most evenings and every other Saturday morning.

My evening visits were seldom pleasant as my mother would routinely switch the television off on my arrival and then insist, as if I were a child of six years old, that I sit down beside her. I was forced to listen to her reasons for being so dissatisfied with her life in Chittington and how her unhappy situation was my fault. She unequivocally blamed me for the decision we had both made and was unrelenting in her endeavours to get me to understand her predicament. She had nothing positive to say, nothing about how convenient her flat was for the town centre and all its conveniences, nothing about how nice it was for her to be able to spend more time with her daughter, nothing about how lovely I had made her flat, or how not having a garden to care for made her life much easier. Her life was miserable, so she ensured mine was, too.

There was no escape route for me during the evenings at my mother's home. Surrounded by silence, I was forced to endure her strong, opinionated views on her current situation and I usually left earlier than I had planned, feeling in low spirits and riddled with guilt. The latter, of course, was her objective. Just as she had in previous years with my father, she enjoyed playing psychological games. The evening visits became so unbearable that I decided to forego them and restrict the time we spent together to Saturdays when, at least, I concluded there would be the diversions of shops and cafes to distract her from her misery.

Giving up all my Saturdays with Greg meant that, at least when I arrived at my mother's door, she normally had her coat on and was ready to go out and I was released from her lectures. I could switch off to her moans and groans while we shopped, which alleviated tensions to a degree, but when we sat together for lunch, instead of enjoying the experience, she would often make every attempt to provoke an argument evocative of her early married life with my father. Now, though, it was Nolwen's turn to be blamed and punished.

***

Our new routine was disrupted one particular Saturday, as when I knocked on her door feeling as apprehensive as usual and hoping her mood was good, she opened it and moved back to let me in. She did not have her coat on, so I became very tense. There were no pleasantries. She just blurted out bluntly, 'Oh, it's you.'

I had little choice but to step inside and walk with her through to her lounge.

'Right, Nolwen…' (My mother often started her conversations with the word "Right", which was her launch word for the ticking off or lecture to follow.) 'Sit down,' she commanded.

I duly obeyed after a timid protest that my time was valuable and that we should go out as we usually did and enjoy our time together.

'Now, listen to me,' she ordered, indicating that I had no choice in the matter, and launched into her complaint of the day. Seemingly forgetting that we had visited her flat together before accepting the keys and signing the contracts, a barrage of complaints and blame was to follow. 'I should never have moved here, Nolwen. You did not point out to me how small the flat is. You never asked me to consider whether I wanted a garden. You didn't explain how far away you and Greg live from here… you… you…' she continued, blaming me for her woes. The main objective of her argument then manifested itself. 'I don't want to come and live with you,' she declared, meaning the opposite, 'but I do want to be able to just pop into your house for a coffee and a nice chat whenever I want to.'

Mam, you and I rarely have a coffee and a nice chat these days, I thought to myself. I then stiffened at the idea of my mother being able to "pop in" to give me a lecture whenever she felt like it and I openly cringed at the thought of her throwaway comment about moving into my home.

In an attempt to diffuse the situation, I replied to her reasonably, 'Mam, I only live ten minutes away from here by car. It's not far away at all. I do pick you up and take you to my house sometimes, but that means double the journey time for me, so it's much easier if I come here. We can also do our shopping and treat ourselves to lunch out in town, whereas there are no services close to our house.'

This reasoned explanation was not what my mother wanted to hear, so the conversation developed as I pre-empted into an argument that was repeated over the following three Saturdays. My mother's cryptic objective was now very clear. She wanted to vacate her flat and move in with me and Greg.

I shuddered at the thought of co-location and knowing that there was no point in discussing my mother's intention with Greg, I determined, there and then, that my mother was never going to move in with us. I also realised very quickly that although I had made my decision, she would never let up on her game plan and would do everything she could to grind me down until she had her own way. Having lost her evening visits, my mother's Saturday visits were now also in jeopardy.

She's her own worst enemy, I thought to myself, as she finally donned her coat and we set off into town.

My mother, intent on instigating arguments, succeeded in turning our social visits into hours of misery for many weeks afterwards. Eventually, her determination to voice her bones of contention became intermittent, but the likelihood of reoccurrence meant that I was always on edge before knocking on her door. My body stiffened and I was uneasy until I saw that she was ready to go out and had her coat on. I was always hopeful that she just might be in a good mood when I arrived, but could never be sure of this. If I sensed that she was happy, I relaxed and, with relief, would often dedicate the entire day to being with her as a "secret reward for good behaviour", but at the expense of spending less time with Greg. These good days were usually a one-off, though, and by the following week, no lessons were learned. Her mood would change and we would be back at square one. No matter how badly my previous visit had gone, though, I always put this aside and went back for what would likely be yet more criticism and blame.

At one point, worrying about our relationship and my mother's state of mind, I came up with a couple of ideas that I thought might help us both. I set up a very informal interview for her with a lovely, kind and easy-going friend of mine who ran a small charity shop in the town centre. I thought a few hours in her favoured retail environment would give Mam the opportunity to meet people and get her out of the flat, but she would not entertain this opportunity. I then suggested that Greg and I could help to pay for her to move back to West Wales and find her another home there if that was her preference, but my mother once again demonstrated that she was only interested in her own solutions and firmly rejected this offer, too. I was at a total loss as to what more I could do. Moving my mother in with Greg and I just wasn't necessary and it wasn't an option. I therefore had no alternative but to live miserably with the status quo for the next few years.

Chapter Thirty-Two

2009–2011
Honesty and Relief

During our performances at Glastonbury, despite the fantastic efforts of the music acousticians and organisers, and rapturous applause from the huge audience afterwards, I personally thought that my voice lost its quality without echoes around walls and the usual reverberations. With no walls and ceilings in place to contain the sound, my chosen solo piece particularly seemed to just fly away with the breeze. This disappointingly meant that, for once, I lost out on the pleasure that drove me to keep singing, which was the sound of my rich contralto tones reflecting back to my own ears, allowing me to immerse myself totally into the beauty of the music.

Singing both solo and duets with Mike in the Symphony Hall in Birmingham, though, with its purpose-built reverberation chamber enhancing the wonderful acoustics, was a completely unique experience and very special. As usual, I suffered tremendously with my pre-performance nerves, both before falling asleep the previous night and then during the day of the event. Despite singing a couple of classical pieces with Mike, accompanied by Joe on the piano first, when it was my turn to sing my favourite solo "Where'er You Walk", I was still in a high state of anxiety. Without Mike by my side, and despite his reassurances, my fear was almost overwhelming, but I walked proudly and outwardly confidently onto the stage. Even though I was aware that Greg was in the audience, I switched off my thoughts of him and my surroundings and immersed myself into the music, luxuriating in the sound of my own voice.

The Nolwen, Mike and Joe trio celebrated its successful performances at Glastonbury and the Symphony Hall with a Sunday lunch with Greg at a local pub. I knew that the time was now right to have the serious conversation with Mike that I had put off some time ago. Greg was supportive of this decision and, although he was very proud of my career achievements and my singing performances, he knew that my success in both activities came at the great expense of sleepless nights, stress, sickness and anguish, all of which were slowly but surely taking their toll on my health. We had, at an earlier point, discussed the options available to me, remembering Mike's promise that once I tired of presenting, I could engineer any operational role and associated job title I wished for myself in the business. Greg and I were realistic, though, and agreed that the latter would undoubtedly involve more travelling, given Mike's latest strategy to expand the business. We had both previously agreed that it would be favourable if I resigned and embarked on a third less-demanding, short-term career, which could, in time, lead me nicely into retirement. Greg left the decision on the future of our trio to me, but during that lunch together, I decided to kill two birds with one gently tossed stone.

I was very reassured by Greg's presence when I tentatively broached the subject, not only of my resignation, but of the future of our musical trio. I was well aware that my boss could be very persuasive and my nature was such that I could, albeit regretfully, be cajoled into succumbing to his charms. With Greg at my side, I reasoned that Mike would be less assertive and would respect that husband and wife had jointly made a difficult decision. I had already postponed what I knew would be an unwelcome conversation once and, this time, I was determined to think of myself and Greg. Despite any feelings of guilt, I wanted to complete the task with the honesty and openness my father had instilled in his young daughter many years ago.

I needn't have been so overly worried about Mike's reaction as, to my relief, once I had fully explained about my high-functioning anxiety, my directional dyslexia and associated reluctance to travel, he related this to the tribulations of his own speech impairment and was gracious enough to express an understanding of my dilemma. Both he and Joe were most surprised that I had managed to hide my conditions from them both for so long and expressed a genuine sorrow, not only because it was time to say goodbye, but because I had suffered so silently. I cheered them up by describing the moving emotions that overcame my anxieties when I sang and although I could not extend this joy to Mike's presentations, explained that it had been a privilege to be a locum for his voice.

As expected, Mike had not forgotten his promise of an alternative operations role in MINS for me and, putting his business hat on, attempted unsuccessfully to incentivise me into accepting a director role. I declined this with appreciation. I completed four more pre-organised presentations for Mike in 2009, after which he generously arranged three months' gardening leave to give me the time to source a new opportunity and we agreed on a voluntary redundancy package.

Meanwhile, I applied for three new roles and – probably due to the very complimentary outline of my skills in the carefully written reference letter from Mike – subsequently received three job offers. I accepted a local position, with no travelling involved, for a specialist footwear company. The contact from the recruiter came as a complete surprise as I had never worked in retail, but I was to find out that it was a "back office" position for a very successful start-up company where the managing director needed the assistance of a team of executives to help him take the business forward. In support of existing staff, he was in the process of recruiting new department heads. My role included responsibilities for customer services, logistics, project management of IT solutions and the operational integration of all three. I was also expected to manage a team of about thirty people.

The environment I initially worked in could not have been more different to the luxurious offices and high-tech conference and meeting rooms I had become used to in my previous role. I found myself working out of some redundant farm buildings with an adjacent barn as a warehouse for boots and shoes. The IT and telephone systems were good, but needed refinement and future proofing, and I needed to recruit a larger team. Despite all of this, the business was doing very well financially and its future was bright, but when looking around my working environment, I did, at times, wonder what on earth I had let myself into.

The objectives of the role were easy but very time-consuming, and I worked long hours to put an operational foundation into place. Professionally, I was pleased to be back on home ground and positioned to use the knowledge and experience from my earlier years with MINS and the RAF to deliver what was required of me. A bonus was that I only needed "the buy in" of my MD, the support of my team and the goodwill of my fellow heads of department to instigate change. I did not miss the hindrance of presentations or documented plans, and was pleased to find out that these were replaced by informal chats and agreements over a coffee.

After assisting with the relocation of the company to new, more suitable premises, contracting out some of the IT infrastructure and putting in place the operational processes and procedures to enable the business to achieve its objectives, I relaxed into what was effectively a familiar operations manager role with no anxiety or stress. Throughout the first year or so, though, I had been just as determined to achieve success as I had been when I climbed aboard the train from Porthgranog to Lincoln, having signed up to join the WRAF at the tender age of seventeen. Failure was no more of an option for me in the retail sector than it had been as a new recruit, the only difference being that, during the last stage of my working life, I was armed with the benefits of three personality changes, my development plan and the accoutrements of experience and expertise.

I felt no need to conduct any self-examination while working for this company and there were no sleepless nights, although I guessed aspects of my inner nature remained dormant. I cautioned myself that although the way I carefully considered the needs and expectations of other people and how I treated them had vastly improved, and this had a positive effect on the way I felt about myself, not all the recurring negative traits I attributed to my past, such as guilt and anxiety, were behind me.

Fulfilling the head of service delivery role for this footwear company contributed to what was to be a gentle, satisfying downhill path into retirement. In my final few days before saying goodbye to my professional life, I found myself reminiscing once again about how I had been transported through training courses, experience, mentoring and my own conscious personality changes from a young, naïve and ineffectual dreamer, with no sense of self, to an ambitious, strong and motivated realist, who could head up so many departments.

I could not, though, have achieved what I did without the support of wonderful and unforgettable teams of people. I hoped that some of the team who supported me in my final role had learned from my example, taken advantage of my teachings and would succeed in the opportunities I engineered for them before I resigned and moved into the next and third step change of my life: retirement.

Chapter Thirty-Three

My Mother

Despite being able to spend more time with my mother during my retirement, she was still very dissatisfied with her lot and became even more demanding. Things came to a head when I was driving home one evening after visiting a poorly friend who lived in Liverpool. I was just ten miles from home and was feeling the usual fatigue after a long journey, when my mobile phone rang. The mobile was on hands-free, so I accepted the call.

The female caller was a nurse from the Royal United Hospital in Bath, who explained that she had been given my number by my mother. I was immediately alarmed at her words and, with a pounding heart, quickly pulled into a nearby lay-by. The nurse advised me that my mother had contacted the emergency services earlier in the day, had subsequently been taken to the hospital by an ambulance and been fully examined by staff at A & E. The nurse then confirmed that they had found no reason to admit her and that she was ready to go home. I thanked her and added that I would drive straight to the hospital and expected to be there within the hour.

When I arrived at the A & E department, feeling both tired and concerned, a staff nurse met me at the entrance and said, 'Ah, you must be Nolwen. Your mum is ready to go home. She is fine and, well, uh, to be honest, shouldn't be here at all.' She shrugged her shoulders, held out the palms of her hands questionably, expressing her exasperation, and added, 'There really is nothing wrong with her.' She then walked away.

I breathed a deep sigh of relief, apologised to the quickly retreating nurse and went in search of my mother. I found her in the A & E waiting room, where she sat with other members of the public, some of whom were suffering with obvious minor injuries. She was wearing her dressing gown and slippers and looked very sheepish when I approached her. Not wanting to delay our exit, I led her straight to my car. Once inside it, I asked her gently what had happened.

'I felt unwell, Nolwen, so I dialled 999.' At that point, she shut the conversation down and refused to say any more.

For the sake of a peaceful life, I didn't broach the subject with her again and hoped the episode was a one-off. I did, though, conclude that "enough was enough" later that evening and decided it was time for a brotherly/sisterly chat.

The next day, I contacted Steffan, who, although he could avoid it to a certain degree, was as aware of my mother's impossibly displeasing and illogical nature as I was. I told him about her frame of mind and the hospital incident.

Fortunately, he was sympathetic to my case and, to my relief, agreed to give my problem some thought.

A short time later, Steffan rang me to outline a possible solution to my frustrations and my mother's dissatisfaction with life. Coincidentally, he was also considering his own work-life balance, explaining that he was struggling with the demands of his profession and could do with "Grandma's" help to look after his three children. His solution was a three-way win, whereby, if my mother agreed, she could move to Norfolk and spend more time with her grandchildren, he could commit more time to his work, and I would be relieved of the stresses and strains of being my mother's only companion.

We then did something she would never allow us to do, which was to collaborate on Steffan's idea without her knowledge or input. We both knew that we would have to tread carefully, repeatedly reminding each other that our joint plan may not work out as our mother rarely warmed to solutions that were not of her own making. For the time being, I left everything in Steffan's capable hands, knowing that he had an easier relationship with my mother than I did. Feeling mutually apprehensive, we kept our fingers crossed for a good outcome.

When I next saw my mother, she said nothing about Steffan's idea at first, but had a knowing, almost pompous expression on her face, which I read to be a perverse satisfaction at having a secret that she presumed I was not party to. Steffan had clearly had a conversation with her about his idea. She could not contain herself for long, though, and two hours later, over a coffee, once she had established that I was not going to be forthcoming with questions about her tormenting demeanour, she announced her decision to move to Norfolk.

Over the next couple of weeks, with lifted spirits, my mother spoke excitedly about the new bungalow Steffan had miraculously managed to secure for her. She told me that it was a two-bedroom bungalow with a garden, which was in walking distance of his home so she could pop in whenever she liked (I wasn't sure the "popping in whenever she liked" was part of Steffan's plan, but said nothing). She showed no consideration for my feelings and expressed few regrets about leaving me. I responded by neither supporting nor protesting about her decision, as although I wanted her to move away, I did not want to be blamed for persuading her to make a decision that might prove to be wrong in the fullness of time. I had already made that mistake once and I was not about to repeat it.

Steffan led a busy life, so I once again dealt with all the formalities of the relocation. When everything was in place, I drove my mother to her new home in Norfolk. She chatted amiably throughout the journey and was clearly excited about the new life ahead of her. When we arrived, I found her bungalow key under the doormat where Steffan had left it and settled my mother in. The bungalow was perfect for her. There was a mini supermarket next door and Steffan's home was only a few steps away, so very convenient for "popping in and out"!

Once Steffan finished work for the day, he joined us at the new bungalow, which signalled the right time for me to leave and head back to Wiltshire. I said my goodbyes, smiled at them both, then glanced over at my mam. Tears welled in my eyes as I walked away. For a brief moment, I was sorry to leave her and knew that, despite everything, the reason for that was that I loved her.

Over the next few weeks, it was clear that my mother was settling in well and seemed to be fulfilled by the intermittent responsibility for – and, doubtless, attempts to "control" – her grandchildren. The problem came some years later when they eventually flew the nest and Steffan's need for her services inevitably diminished.

Chapter Thirty-Four

2011–2018
Contentment

The best thing about retirement was, for me, the rarity of waking up to an alarm clock. I had never been a morning person, probably due to many nights of lost sleep because of stress. In my past, I had deliberately postponed sleep, preferring to luxuriate in a space for my private thoughts and enjoying that secure feeling of being cocooned in my own bed. There, I had been in my own private world where I was out of trouble, until I was forced to meet the new day and face the challenges it presented.

Greg had retired from the RAF on the same day as I finished my working life, and once my mother had relocated to Norfolk – meaning Steffan took away the burden I had borne for over six years – our immediate priority was to finish our world travels. We planned to continue with our explorations for as long as we were young enough to put up with the inconveniences of long-haul travel and had the energy to continue with our small group specialist tours. Many of these, although fantastically rewarding, were often strenuous and tiring due to their unusual itineraries. Within two years of retirement, we had visited most of the Far East, Australia, New Zealand and the USA, and as a follow-up to our previously enjoyed destinations of Peru and Brazil, we ticked off most of the other South American countries.

We then decided to take a break from distant lands and confine our holidays to Europe, as we had done in our youth. France, being so accessible and with much to offer, was our clear favourite. Pre-empting this plan, and needing a hobby in retirement, I had started to learn the French language as soon as I retired. Although I put as much effort into this as I did with everything else, my neuroplasticity must have decreased over the years, as it was only after almost ten years of private tuition that I finally became a French speaker and, even then, my lack of understanding and forgotten vocabulary would often let me down mid-conversation.

Meanwhile, my mother continued to live close to my brother in Norfolk and, despite the long cross-country journey, I visited her as often as possible. Whenever I telephoned her, she complained about having a garden that took a lot of looking after and about the limited services available in her village. However, certainly for the first few years, while she was needed for the supervision of Steffan's teenage children and her youngest grandchild's school runs, she seemed to enjoy a renewed sense of purpose. She kept her days full by helping my brother with his housework, which gave her the freedom to drop into his home whenever she liked. I was genuinely pleased for her, but also relieved for myself, because, as always, if my mother was happy, then so was I.

For the most part, my visits and telephone calls went well, until my mother's discontentment began to manifest itself again and she decided that it would be a really good idea if Nolwen and Greg moved to Norfolk to join the rest of the family. As was usual, once my mother had an idea, it dominated her mind and, despite the opinions of any third parties involved, she would relentlessly pursue compliance. Greg and I were happy in the home we had built together and had no intentions of moving to Norfolk. However, deterred by the thought of renewed constant arguments, I opted not to dismiss her idea and employed her own well-used phrase, "Well, I'll leave it for now," followed by a promise to think about moving, which, being an honest person, I did, but only very briefly.

***

Life was good for Greg and I during the "middle" period of our retirement. Outside of our travels, we enjoyed cooking, which we shared, often preferring to make delicious foreign meals from scratch at weekends as opposed to the traditional British Sunday lunch or similar. I enjoyed reading and Greg, being a keen cyclist, took advantage of the wonderful local countryside and any fair weather, whatever the season. He rode too far for my liking, so I kept myself fit by using an indoor cross trainer, which meant that I had no excuse to avoid exercise, even on a rainy day. We both loved the sunshine, so outside of our foreign travels, we took advantage of this by settling ourselves outside our local pub on the banks of the Kennet and Avon Canal, so that we could watch the narrowboats go by, or by visiting Bath, where we frequently searched out a well-positioned table to people-watch over a cocktail or two. We also had numerous favourite restaurants in the city where we regularly dined with our closest friends, Anne, John and their daughter, Lizzie, who we had known since living in our second RAF married quarter, where they had been neighbours. They now owned a house close to the wonderful Abbey Church of St Peter and St Paul.

Cardiff was another city I regularly visited by train. There, I would meet up with old school friends and make the most of the brilliant shopping – another hobby I finally had time for and adored. On one occasion, while browsing in a clothes shop, I heard someone call out my name.

'Nolwen! Oh my goodness! Nolwen Jones!' the voice exclaimed, using my maiden name. 'It is you, isn't it?'

I turned around and, to my amazement, I immediately recognised the face of Heather Plant, the former LACW who had had the ruler thrown at her by the overly stressed Sgt Cross during the days of my first permanent RAF posting. I tensed slightly, remembering my behaviour in those days, but Heather didn't seem perturbed about meeting up with her old corporal after such a long time.

She suggested we exchange contact details, with a view to meeting up for a catch-up on our lives at some point in the future. As it turned out, we did this numerous times and she became one of my closest friends.

Heather was a straightforward speaker and during one memorable chat over coffee, which followed a shopping spree and an enjoyable lunch out together in our favourite Welsh city, we started to reminisce about "the good old WRAF days". During this conversation, although Heather attempted to soften what she had to say with her laughter, she revealed her opinion of me in those early days, which was rather critical.

What pleased me, though, was that after her criticism, she added, 'You are a completely different person now, Nolwen. You are so much more approachable, thoughtful and kind. You were very stern and intimidating in those days, but now you are happy and I've noticed how much you smile, particularly when we first meet up.'

I blushed and apologised for my old character and for not defending her as much as I should have done from the wrath of Sgt Cross. We embraced with laughter and appreciation for our new-found friendship. I didn't mention to her, knowing that she would have thought me crazy, that I had written a personal development plan all those years ago and had worked my way through it almost until my retirement. It was reaffirmed to me on that day in Cardiff that this plan had, indeed, served its purpose and, combined with my conscious personality changes, had shaped and created the new me.

***

Having finished our long-haul travels, I found that I had even more free time on my hands, so I endeavoured to visit Norfolk more often. It was lovely to spend time with Steffan and his three children, two of whom had plans to go to university and would be leaving home and escaping – what they humorously described as – the overly protective care of their grandmother.

My mother sometimes gave me a reprieve from her endeavours to persuade Greg and I to move to Norfolk and, when she did, we managed to enjoy pleasant quality time together. We went shopping, focusing on clothes and shoes for her, as she had little dress sense and preferred to rely on me for ideas and suggestions. Then, of course, we participated in a cup of tea and a cake once our shopping bags were full. My mother still had her sweet tooth and there was still no such thing as "just a cake" – it had to be a "big cake". This period was another time in my life when I was fond of my mother and enjoyed her company.

In addition to learning French, our holidays, trips to Cardiff, Bath and Norfolk, and my reading, I decided that I had room in my life for another hobby. I decided to search out some local choirs. My preference was to find a choir that focused on classical music and I soon came across "The Chittington and Welford Classical Voice Choir". The choir was led by a well-known musical director whose mission, according to their website, was to inspire people with his choice of emotional choral music, which suited my needs perfectly. The website advertised regular performances in prestigious venues mainly in Gloucestershire and Wiltshire, which with my aversion to travel worked well for me. It also stated that I would be required to audition; this was a little unnerving, but I was sure I could pluck up the courage to sing a few well-practised pieces from our trio portfolio. Nevertheless, I hoped the auditioning audience would be small.

After finding out all the details about the rehearsal schedule, I decided to attend a couple of the choir group's "Sing Together" workshops before auditioning. The workshops gave me a chance to meet some of the members, who I found to be encouraging, welcoming and friendly. I auditioned, confirmed that I would be able to attend the weekly rehearsals, made it clear that I would be unlikely to volunteer for solo work and was delighted to receive a letter of acceptance from the musical director a few days later.

I soon attended the first of many rehearsals for a concert to be held in Bath some weeks later and really enjoyed singing selected movements from Mozart's C Minor Mass with the choir's alto voices. It was wonderful to release the emotions associated with the music through my own voice without stress or anxiety, and I was unable to hold back the tears whenever I heard Susan Jones, the choir's soprano soloist, singing, "The Kyrie Eleison". I couldn't explain, even to myself, how beautiful music affected me in such an emotional way.

Some people find it difficult to adjust to retirement, but Greg and I saw it as a reward for years of hard work and separation. It was great to escape the daily grind, even though, for the most part, we had both enjoyed our professional careers. Neither of us really missed the sense of purpose that came with our jobs or the structured days.

Personally, I also felt, for the third time in my life, a sense of freedom. I was, for the most part, relaxed and totally fulfilled with my new, busy lifestyle. Outside of rarely setting my alarm clock, the next best thing about retirement for me was spending as much time as possible with my wonderful, supportive and loving husband, Greg.

CHAPTER THIRTY-FIVE

2018–2020
Transient Global Amnesia and Bereavement

Retirement, as wonderful as it was, did not mean that all the inherent negative emotions deeply ingrained inside my soul disappeared and there would no longer be times of anxiety. I had finished work and had stopped singing solo with the trio, which helped tremendously, but my mother's discontentment, even though this was less prevalent than it had been, still triggered feelings of stress and guilt from time to time and, of course, as is the case for everyone, my life in general had its ups and downs.

Early one Saturday morning, after returning from the local supermarket, Greg received a telephone call from the residential home where his mum, Jean, now lived. I could tell from the tone of his voice that the caller was the bearer of bad news. Jean had unexpectedly passed away peacefully in her sleep just before breakfast time. We were both shocked as we had visited her the previous weekend and, although we had thought her frail, she was doing well for her age.

Greg and his sister organised a very fitting funeral for her and we all consoled ourselves with the knowledge that until her husband had died, she had led a lovely life, had not suffered in old age and had passed away peacefully in her sleep. I wrote what I hoped was a very fitting eulogy in her praise and as a term of my endearment. Remembering that Jean did not like to see me dressed in black, I wore a dress she had previously admired to the funeral service. I was extremely fond of my mother-in-law and we had never once had a cross word. I often reflected on the many valuable lessons in life that she had inoffensively taught me over the years.

Strangely, after her funeral, I lost all memories of the service and could not even remember the celebrant reading my carefully prepared eulogy words. I also repeatedly asked Greg the same questions time and time again about the format of the day. The same weird episode of forgetfulness had also happened after my father's funeral and when I sang solo during the MINS charity concert. We were both aware that something untoward was happening with my mind, but as I functioned normally in every other respect, we put the experience down to stress or grief, as we had done after my father's funeral and the concert. My lost memories returned the following morning as soon as I woke up.

***

Jean and my mother had been born in the same year, but my mother was still fit and well and was fortunate enough to be still living independently in her Norfolk bungalow. Her discontentment started to re-emerge with a vengeance, though, and became even worse when her youngest grandchild left school, started a training course at a local college and was no longer in need of my mother's care. To make matters worse, my brother employed a cleaner, which meant that my mother's services in his home were no longer required. My brother's family always made her welcome when she visited them, but she had lost her *raison d'être* and was becoming progressively unhappy. Her emotional state had a negligible effect on Steffan, whereas I was more sensitive to her moods, which, of course, my mother knew and took advantage of. She began, once again, to play psychological games intended to elicit feelings of guilt in me. Claiming loneliness, she again repeatedly raised her need for Greg and I to move to Norfolk, and told me how abandoned she felt whenever I went on holiday.

As was usual for me, I felt obliged to seek out some alternative solutions to help with her loneliness. I contacted her local authority's social services department, who, following an assessment of my mother's needs and circumstances, authorised some daily care for her and free attendance for up to three days a week at a local day centre for the elderly, and they also put me in touch with the manager of the local Befriending Team. As luck would have it, the manager of the scheme lived in the same village as my mother and Steffan, and she kindly volunteered to be my mother's befriender herself. Lucy was a lovely lady, who was very skilled in the handling of people, especially the elderly. Even my mother could not fail to warm to her and the relationship between the two of them developed positively. Steffan was always busy professionally, so Lucy became my confidant whenever I was concerned about my mother's welfare and would step in as an adjudicator when required.

'Nolwen,' she once said to me. 'The problem with your mam is that she doesn't know how to be happy in the moment, but, be reassured, when she reminisces about her past life, she has only positive thoughts and memories. She is also alone and without your father is insecure. The only way she feels she can deal with this is to retain control of you and Steffan, but you have your own lives to live,' she added.

I thought over her words and realised that she had put things into perspective and was right. Unlike Steffan, I still allowed my mother to get under my skin and found it difficult to disregard her demands.

My mother agreed to attend the day centre once a week, which she seemed to enjoy. Lucy popped in to see her whenever she could manage it and Steffan was at home most weekends and would invite her for dinner or call in to see her for a chat. I telephoned her religiously every evening and she called me whenever she felt the need to talk. I never quite knew what to expect when I picked up the telephone. Sometimes she was pleasant; other times, her voice sounded curt and her tone was cold. Bearing in mind her age, I did my best not to be provoked into an argument and would attempt to reason with her. When she tired of listening, the call would end abruptly, as she slammed her handset into its base station. Steffan's answer to her moods was to either ignore her for a week or so and get on with his life, or reprimand her with a few well-chosen words. Despite my new-found personality, I was unable to take either approach when it came to my mother, so to purge myself of guilt, I would, without exception, tentatively make the next daily telephone call to make amends. My mother deviously knew this would happen, of course, and could therefore confidently instigate a quarrel whenever she felt like it – secure in the knowledge that I would relent and call again.

***

A year or so later, my mother, having given up her endeavours to persuade me to move to Norfolk and relinquish my holidays, sought out a different tactic to improve her lifestyle. She did what she had once done when she lived close to Greg and I and called the emergency services unnecessarily. She was taken to hospital, checked over and discharged with only some painkiller medication for a claimed severe headache. It was Steffan's turn to face the nursing team and apologise for my mother's actions. I would have liked to discuss the reasons for her 999 call to establish whether she had been poorly or was struggling with a troubled mind, but knew that this would be futile and only lead to further arguments or a shutdown of the conversation. She repeated her call for inappropriate assistance again a couple of weeks later, but this time received a scolding from Steffan and it didn't happen again. Her actions achieved one objective, though, in that her son and daughter were left with a persistent worry about their mother's potential reluctance to call for help in what could be a genuine emergency.

My mother's next visit to hospital was of genuine need and was at the insistence of her doctor. This time, she was diagnosed with an infection that had genuinely made her poorly. Steffan was working abroad for a few days and I was in France on holiday at the time. After an overnight stay, receiving some medication and being pronounced well enough to go home, my mother, as persistent as ever, came up with another plan to move into the home of one of her offspring. She refused to leave the hospital and insisted that she had no desire to return to her bungalow. I was subsequently contacted, not by the hospital team, but by a social services adult care duty officer, who advised me that she had had no option but to place my mother into a care home on a temporary basis. Once there, my mother had a change of heart about where she should live and made her own very firm decision that she liked the care home and had every intention of staying put. It seemed to us all that no one, not even her allocated social services case manager, could change her mind.

Needless to say, on my return from France, after a chat with Steffan and being, as ever, the dutiful daughter, I drove to Norfolk to visit my mother in her new place of residence. It was true; she was adamant that she did not wish to live alone any longer. I drove her to her bungalow to have a confirmatory last look around and to collect all the personal belongings she wanted or needed. As usual, Steffan was very committed with his work, so I willingly took over all the administration needed to formalise my mother's relocation. This included changing her residency from temporary to permanent, and putting all her furniture and personal belongings into storage, just in case she should change her mind about returning to independent living.

Six months later, her furniture was donated, at her request, to a local charity and her remaining personal belongings given to Steffan for safe keeping. I sensibly arranged a third-party bank mandate, which was properly authorised by my sound-minded mother, to enable me to deal with all her financial needs. Sometime later, she accused me of "controlling her spending" and "putting her into a home", but I ignored these comments and continued to look after her from a distance, more out of duty than love.

I think my mother was one of the most troublesome residents her care home had ever assumed responsibility for and I received many phone calls asking for advice on how to manage her non-medical needs and wants. Despite this, the carers were wonderfully patient and some even managed to bring the very best out of her character. One particularly kind carer regularly set up FaceTime calls and at the end of each call, she encouraged my mother to blow her daughter a farewell kiss. This was a first for my mother, but she had little choice except to follow her carer's instructions. I, of course, responded in kind.

***

It was just before the Covid pandemic that my mother, following bouts of different infections and hospital admissions, succumbed to asymptomatic leukaemia, which had lain dormant in her body for many years. Steffan and I were advised by her doctor that she did not need to be hospitalised, but that the end of her life was imminent. I made my final journey to see her and, while driving, hoped and prayed to the God I had renounced in my teenage years that she would be in a good mood when I reached the care home and that I would have fond memories of our last few hours together. When standing by her bedside, I asked her if she knew who I was.

Without any hesitation, she said, 'You are Nolwen Mary Jones.'

The use of my maiden name made me smile. 'I am, Mam,' I replied happily, pleased that her mind was still in good working order. 'You are absolutely right!'

We had a lovely couple of hours together, chatting about old times, our dogs, our caravan, our holiday and my father, until my mother became very tired. I then made what I think was yet another good decision in my life, which was to contentedly leave her while she was so congenial and we were on good terms. I decided that I did not want to risk any unpleasantries that may lead to my final memories of my mother being resentful or guilt-ridden. I never returned to her care home nor saw her in person again. Steffan continued to visit her over the next few days and set up FaceTime calls so that she could see me and hear both of us talking to her while she rested. At the end of the last call before she died, I blew her a kiss and she raised her hand to her lips and returned the gesture.

With some relief, I did not suffer any memory loss after my mother's funeral, but I was pensive both during the service and after it. I privately examined my feelings and contemplated the relationship I had had with her since my early childhood, her influence, her parenting skills and how her character had shaped me. Probably because of the sensible decision I had made, and the carer's thoughtfulness in encouraging my mother to blow kisses, my memories of our relationship became reasoned, balanced and without bitterness. When I blew her my final kiss, as well as my love, I think I subconsciously blew her my forgiveness.

***

My life returned to normal after my mother's funeral, although I was overcome by an emotion from time to time that dropped over me like a thick, black cloak, which I could not identify and had never previously experienced. I could be enjoying a meal with Greg, out walking or lazing on a beach in the sunshine with a cocktail in my hand, when I would be seized by what I could only describe as a deep feeling of sorrow or pining. The emotion was so strong that I felt near to tears, although these never came. It usually lasted for about ten minutes and I experienced an intense sense of relief when it passed. I did not understand the feeling. The minute it lifted, I returned to my normal self.

One morning, the strange emotion lasted for a few hours and I wondered whether I would ever shake it off. It eventually passed on its own and never returned. It was weeks later that I realised the probable cause was bereavement.

Once I had fully come to terms with my mother's death, the bereavement period had passed and following a chat with my friend, Heather, I felt very much at peace with myself. Over the years, I had changed my character by incorporating within it the best teachings of my father and eliminating the worst parenting skills and influences of my mother. With the benefit of mentoring, strict perseverance with my own personally instigated development plan and personality changes, I had developed into a completely different Nolwen from the little girl who had suffered in her young life from the negative emotions of shame, loneliness, embarrassment, anguish, diffidence, guilt and low self-esteem. It had taken a long time to rid myself of the strongest adverse feeling on that list, but with the passing of my mother, I was completely absolved of guilt.

CHAPTER THIRTY-SIX

2020
Diagnoses and Covid-19

Outside of my yet undiagnosed directional dyslexia, which could not be resolved by any kind of development plan, and which Greg assisted me with by drawing maps, demonstrating proposed routes with reference to images on Google Earth or by shepherding me around, I was suffering, albeit only occasionally, with a health curiosity I needed to fathom. This was the matter of my lost memories. I had experienced these lost memories after singing my first solo at the MINS charity concert and following the funerals of Jean and my father. I experienced one short episode later during my retirement when I became separated from Greg during one of our holidays abroad. He insisted I make an appointment to see my doctor, which I did, and this was followed by a referral to a consultant physician, who, after numerous tests, diagnosed a disorder called transient global amnesia (TGA), a rare medical condition where the patient suffers from sudden episodes of memory loss.

The consultant explained that during a TGA, it is not possible to form new memories and it is difficult to recall recent ones. He also explained that an episode was typically triggered by a stressful or upsetting event, and that memory function returned to a normal state within a few hours. Surprisingly, he advised me that procedural memory remained unaffected, so automatic tasks like driving a car could be performed with no problems during an episode. His very words were, 'Nolwen, you could fly a rocket to the moon when you are experiencing a TGA with no adverse consequences.' I didn't confuse matters by explaining that, at the best of times, I could get lost on my way to the shops, never mind attempting to navigate my way to the moon. He advised me not to worry about the condition, as in accordance with its title, the problem was always transient and there was a possibility I would never suffer from another episode.

Taking advantage of the appointment, I then explained about my continually getting lost and not knowing my left from my right. Within seconds, he made a second diagnosis, which was that I suffered from directional dyslexia and again suggested it was nothing to worry about. Although I had always known that something was wrong, I was pleased to find out that this was a recognised condition and that I wasn't the only person in the world to suffer from it. Greg and I were also relieved to receive the TGA diagnosis and to be in a position to recognise the signs of the condition in the future without becoming overly concerned. As it happened, there were far more concerning issues on the horizon, which put directional dyslexia and TGA episodes into perspective.

***

On the 3rd of March 2020, Greg and I went into Chittington with friends to celebrate his sixty-fourth birthday. Not long after, on the 23rd of March, Prime Minister Boris Johnson announced the UK nationwide lockdown to curb the widening outbreak of what was to be the Covid-19 pandemic. We knew this would, without a doubt, result in a blip to our retirement plans, but, like everyone else in Britain, we didn't at the time fully realise how serious the situation was and how long the problem would last. We very much appreciated that being retired and in good health, we were better off than many people, particularly key workers and those people with underlying health problems, living alone or those already in hospital with illnesses of some kind.

Like most people, we took our prime minister's advice seriously and apart from essential visits to the supermarket, we stayed at home. By May of the same year, the restrictions were relaxed a little, but Greg and I remained very conscientious and abided by the rules, still only venturing outdoors individually for shopping that couldn't be delivered, taking some outdoor recreation and avoiding close contact with other people. I escaped confinement indoors by walking in the local area, while Greg chose a short cycle ride once or twice a week, but he always rode alone.

On the 20th of May, Greg had an extremely uncomfortable and sleepless night. He was feverish and had a sore throat. He suggested that I move into the guest room to avoid catching what he thought was the onset of a cold. The following day, he seemed to be a little better, but his symptoms became worse later in the evening and during the night, with the return of the fever and the start of what was to become a bad cough. Over the next few days, his condition deteriorated; his coughing was relentless; he had no energy, lost his appetite and sense of taste and smell, which indicated that he had most certainly contracted Covid. We tried to establish how and when he had become infected by the virus and concluded that it must have been either when he accepted the home delivery groceries or perhaps when he had helped a fellow cyclist in trouble. He had kept his distance from the cyclist and the delivery man, but the shopping or hardware he had touched had possibly been contaminated and perhaps he had not properly sanitised his hands. We came up with no conclusive answers and just hoped his condition would improve.

It was almost a week later that Greg's health deteriorated rapidly. In the morning, he was short of breath, still had the symptoms of a bad cold and was exhausted. By the evening, he was incredibly ill, his chest was tight and he was wheezing and gasping for his next breath. We made the decision to call for an ambulance, which arrived thirty minutes later.

The paramedics had been briefed on Greg's symptoms

and, expecting to have to convey him to hospital and provide him with breathing support on the way, were appropriately but alarmingly dressed in full white gowns with hoods covering their heads. They also wore medical-grade masks, visors and gloves. Their names, which I will never forget, were written on paper covered in plastic and were secured firmly to their chests. Communication between the medics and their patient was difficult as their voices were muffled by their protective equipment. They also found it difficult to hear Greg through their hoods when he desperately attempted to tell them how he felt. The team did not come into our house, but, after asking Greg to walk up and down our garden path to enable them to assess the severity of his symptoms, they helped him into the ambulance.

I was not permitted to join him and shouted through the emergency vehicle doors, 'I am not allowed to come with you, Greg, but I will ring the hospital soon. Try not to worry. You just need assistance with your breathing. I love you!'

He waved at me feebly. I could not force a smile and wondered whether I would ever see him again.

After the ambulance had left, I went indoors and sat down in my lounge. I felt helpless and shocked at the surreal events I had just witnessed and remained contemplatively and silently immobile for at least half an hour with only my thoughts as company. Realising that I needed to share my feelings and verbalise the evening's events, if only to allow the experience to sink in, I called my neighbours, Steffan and some friends in turn. Outside of imparting comforting and reassuring words, and assuring me of regular telephone contact, they were all frustrated at not being able to do much more. My immediate neighbours, who were wonderful, insisted on coming to my front door. They comforted me as much as they could through gestures and words from a distance, which provided the next best thing to physical embrace and sympathetic cuddles. The couple regularly rang my doorbell for an update during the days that followed.

Unable to contain my impatience, I rang the hospital two hours after the ambulance had left. I could barely hear the words of the specialist ICU nurse who spoke to me, because of her PPE and the sounds of medical equipment situated close to her. She confirmed that Greg was in intensive care and I established that he had been put on a ventilator to assist with his breathing and was sedated.

'Your husband is reasonably comfortable,' she advised kindly.

I was, to a certain extent, relieved at her words, which allowed my thoughts to quickly turn to myself and the situation I now found myself in. I would have to isolate, of course, but apart from being physically alone, that was not such a problem. The real concern for me at that moment was whether I had also contracted Covid and might soon find myself too ill to enquire about Greg's progress or take care of our affairs. The nurse gave me her best advice, which was to try and get a good night's rest and call again the following morning. I called the same number again at 4am the next day.

Each time I called the ICU, I became increasingly aware of how exhausted and harried the nursing team and the doctors were, but I had no choice but to keep in contact with them. Even though they told me that they would call if Greg's condition worsened, I could not contain myself for much longer than a day. I usually telephoned in the early hours of the morning when I hoped the pressures in the ward might be a little less and this seemed to be the case. I was assured that once Greg improved, although I wouldn't be able to visit him, the staff would arrange for me to communicate with him by telephone. This sounded positive and gave me some hope, but, nevertheless, I decided that it might be worthwhile to pray to the God of my youth and ask him to keep Covid from my door and for his assistance with my husband's recovery.

God did not perform any miracles for Greg, whose situation worsened over the next few days, but I did not develop Covid. This was, perhaps, because my Maker, having listened to my prayers, had decided that as I was not a true believer, only a compromise on my requests was in order. I found out that God had let me down even more when, during my usual call to the hospital in the early hours of the eighteenth day since Greg's admission, the doctor I spoke to compassionately advised me that they now feared the worst. Greg was unconscious and it was unlikely that he would make it through the day. Four hours later, the doctor called me to say that despite the best efforts of the medical teams, he was very sorry, but Greg, after contracting acute respiratory distress syndrome had suffered septic shock and kidney and cardiac failure and had sadly passed away.

I was stunned, shocked and numb. I could not believe that the phone call I had just received had actually taken place. I then reprimanded myself for not asking the doctor any questions. I had not enquired as to whether Greg had been at peace or in pain or discomfort. I did not ask if he had regained consciousness or whether he had been alone. I hadn't asked if he had spoken or left me a message. Nothing. I had asked nothing. I was angry with myself, then angry with Greg for leaving me. I released a gut-wrenching sound, which I later described to others as a horrifying howl. I was not yet ready to share my grief and curled up into the foetal position on my bed. I sobbed and howled successively until I eventually fell silent.

Sometime later, my doorbell rang and I dragged myself to the front door. My neighbours, Roy and Jill, stood in front of me as they had regularly done every few hours, every day for the last three weeks. I stepped back into my hall, knowing that on seeing my grief-stricken face, they would conclude that Greg had died and would be unable to restrain themselves from gathering me up in their arms. I sat myself down on my hall floor, confirmed their worst thoughts and then waited while Roy gathered up a couple of chairs from his garden shed, which he placed on my garden path. They sat with me for the next hour in silence.

I slowly organised my thoughts while we sat together, appreciating their silent company and thoughtfulness. I do not know what I would have done without this couple in that hour of tremendous need and grief. At Jill's prompting, I went inside and made myself a cup of tea. The couple left the outside of my house for a few minutes to do the same. When they returned, we sat at my doorway for another thirty minutes, gratefully sipping away our hot soothing drinks while I gathered up enough strength to tell them about the heartbreaking telephone call I had received. Eventually, I stood up, realising that there were other people in Greg's life and mine who needed to be given the sad news. I assured my neighbours that, for the time being at least, I would be okay and then began the arduous task of informing our closest friends and family that Greg had died. It was far from easy.

Death during normal times is difficult to cope with, but during the first wave of Covid, it was even more so. Despite living alone, I was spared from true isolation by the love and support of my friends, neighbours and my family, even if that was either from a distance at the doorstep or by telephone. I pulled myself together and dealt with the immediate formalities, including the organisation of the funeral. Everything was done by telephone or electronically, and anything I couldn't cope with, was picked up by my closest friends. In normal circumstances, I presumed that many of Greg's former RAF colleagues would have attended his funeral, but as it was, the service was small, strange and surreal with the requisite social distancing and limited number of people paying their respects. Somehow, I endured it and, after experiencing my fifth TGA, attempted to prepare myself for another difficult period of bereavement.

Chapter Thirty-Seven

2020–2021
Coping

I had encountered some difficult times in my life, but the year after Greg's passing was the worst and some of the distressing emotions of my youth returned. I went through the usual stages of bereavement, but, like everyone else, the experience was particular to me and each stage had its own peculiarities. At first, I buried my head in the sand and just survived. Thoughts of Greg and how I was going to manage without him rolled round and round in my head, especially at night when I lay in bed. The thoughts were so wild, I was convinced that one day I would become insane. In the past, I had relished the period before I dropped off to sleep because it felt luxuriously like a space for my private thoughts, in which I had prepared myself for the challenges of the day ahead. Now, I laid awake for most of the night, unable to control my mind or suppress my feelings of grief, and when the morning eventually arrived, I was totally apathetic and unresponsive, not only to the sound of birdsong or the sunlight streaming through my shutters, but, sometimes, even my doorbell.

Even when I dragged myself out of bed, cleaned my teeth and splashed my face with water, I had no enthusiasm to get myself dressed, let alone do my hair or put on some make-up. If I had been a smoker, I would have survived on coffee and cigarettes – as it was, the coffee sufficed. I had no appetite for food and certainly no appetite for life. The pain of living was unbearable and I considered taking my own life, looking for the ways and means to kill myself on the internet. Fortunately, I dismissed the idea of jumping off a tall building or motorway bridge, lying on rail tracks or cutting my wrists, as I was compassionate enough to consider the effects of my actions on any third parties involved, family and friends. I contemplated taking an overdose but, on researching this, realised that unless I really knew what I was doing, knew what drugs to use and could persuade pharmacists to supply me with sufficient volumes of medication, I was more likely to end up with severe stomach pain and sickness. Furthermore, I concluded that if found before I died, I would be hospitalised and would add to the burden of the already stretched hospital teams who were still fighting to keep Covid patients alive.

In reality, it wasn't the rationality of my logic that saved me, but fortitude salvaged from my first self-devised personality change and the concern of my friends and neighbours. People persevered with ringing my doorbell and I was encouraged to go for walks with my immediate neighbours and some ladies who lived close by, their intention being to give me a reason to face the day. Friends telephoned me regularly and Steffan, who couldn't make the long journey from Norfolk to Wiltshire due to the Covid restrictions, rang me every morning to encourage me to get out of bed. He then rang later in the day to ensure that I had progressed from my "coffee breakfast" and had showered and got myself dressed.

Although I had previously overcome most of the destructive emotions I had endured during my younger years, the feelings of loneliness and abandonment that I had felt whenever either of my parents weren't with me in my youth, and when I arrived alone at a new RAF station, now enveloped me for many hours of each day. The only reprieve from these feelings was the distractions my friends and neighbours created.

From time to time, I relived the same angry frustration I had felt when I threw the charity collection tin at Rhys in my classroom that day so long ago. I threw items around my home, smashing them on walls or the floor as I attempted to rid myself of pent-up fury, especially if I caught sight of any of Greg's possessions, which I knew I would have to dispose of at some point. Every time I entered his man cave, where I had been used to seeing him, I had visions of him sitting in his chair. I heard his voice calling me and even heard him moving around our house or working in our garden, only to suffer from a dreadful sinking feeling in my heart afterwards when I realised it was all in my imagination. I was in an agonisingly emotional mess.

***

As the Covid rules relaxed, our closest family friends, Anne and John and their daughter, Lizzie, who had telephoned me religiously every evening since the funeral, were finally able to call in and spend some time with me. We weren't allowed to hug, of course, but it was comforting to have their physical presence in my home. My friends could tell from the dust-coated furniture, the lack of food in my fridge and the state of my appearance that I was not doing well, and Anne insisted that I contact my doctor. She took on my mother's old bossy character and, despite my protests that I didn't think a doctor could help me, she relentlessly persisted with her suggestion for weeks.

Ground down by Anne's perseverance, I eventually contacted my doctor, who listened sympathetically to my story and assured me that the signs and patterns of behaviour that I described to her were perfectly normal in bereavement, but that I needed some professional help. She referred me to a superb, incredibly supportive bereavement counsellor, whose name was Donna. Donna had, before the Covid lockdown, held twice weekly counselling sessions in my local town, but was now offering group therapy via Zoom or one-to-one consultations using FaceTime. As I wasn't ready to share my experiences and emotions with groups of people, I chose the latter and found our calls to be cathartic and helpful. With Donna's support, I eventually felt able to move forward with some necessary practical tasks.

Although I had dealt with some of the more immediate notifications and formalities before my husband's funeral, the time came when I had no choice but to begin the chore of taking over all of the household bills, managing my budget and taking charge of our financial and other private affairs. Greg had previously taken responsibility for all of these things, which meant I faced a steep learning curve, at a time when I was emotionally least able to cope with new challenges. To make matters worse, I was obliged to circumnavigate the limitations and restrictions in place due to the Covid pandemic.

Even though I was computer-literate, I frustratingly lacked some of the skills I needed to fully utilise the internet and other technologies to achieve my aims, and I struggled daily with hardware issues or software process failures. To make matters worse, most people in the service industries worked from home, so it was no longer possible for me to just drop into banks or building societies or attend appointments at the local solicitor's office for practical advice and assistance. I had no choice but to confront the situation I found myself in, formulate a plan and do my best to get on with that plan from the confines of my home.

With little enthusiasm, I began the process of identifying everything I needed to do. I opted to call upon some long-forgotten project-management experience and drew up a simple spreadsheet, which at least put everything into perspective. The volume of tasks and hurdles ahead of me was daunting, not helped by sporadic bouts of transient global amnesia and the same deep, recurring feelings of sadness and pining I had experienced after my mother's death. However, cognisant that keeping myself occupied was preferable to sitting alone and dwelling on negative thoughts about my future, I set about putting my life in some kind of order.

Each and every day over the next year followed the same daily pattern. I got myself up, throwing on the first item of clothing that came to hand, dragged a comb through my normally well-styled hair, had a coffee breakfast and then settled myself in front of my laptop, where I attempted to address the tasks listed on my spreadsheet. These proved to be more complicated than I first thought, but I battled away at them alone, often feeling frustrated when they proved to be beyond my technical capabilities.

As soon as the postman dropped the mail through the letterbox and I heard it fall onto the doormat, following an adrenalin surge, I stopped whatever I was doing, picked it all up and thumbed through it with mixed emotions and hope. There was the hope that it consisted of only junk mail, meaning I could heave a sigh of relief as that demanded minimum attention and could be thrown in the bin; hope that none of the formally addressed white envelopes contained correspondence that demanded IT skills I didn't possess; and, finally, hope that some of the envelopes contained some impatiently awaited information that would enable me to close down one or two of my outstanding spreadsheet tasks.

Evening time was the most difficult for me, as it was at that time of the day that Greg had routinely vacated his man cave to cook dinner, while I committed myself to thirty minutes of exercise on my cross trainer, which was set up in a spare bedroom. I had no more incentive to do this exercise now than I had to eat my own hastily produced unimaginative evening meals alone. As a couple, we had religiously spent the remainder of our evenings together, convivially reading, watching TV or chatting about the events of the day. I now found that I was unable to concentrate on my books and my mind constantly wandered off from the programme I had chosen to watch from one of the terrestrial channels on TV. I didn't know how to access any of the alternative Sky or streaming services from the baffling selection of remote controllers that sat redundantly on my side table. Greg had always been the person to use those.

I went to bed at about 10pm every evening. I tossed and turned, agitated by exhaustion, yet unable to part company from foreboding thoughts of my future and interminable worries over the undiminishing tasks on my spreadsheet. Eventually – exhausted, harassed and overwrought – I would descend into a fitful sleep, only to find myself tormented by dreams that were also stressful. The dreams were not specifically about the labours of my spreadsheet targets, but they transposed those labours into different exhausting, bizarre, illusory crusades, such as frantically searching in vain for treasured possessions or lost items, or desperately crawling along dark, narrow tunnels in a futile attempt to reach a light that never became closer, or I would run incessantly for a bus I never caught.

After these dreams, I woke up feeling completely drained and fatigued, which added to the exasperations of my days. However, the compulsion to progress with at least some of my objectives during the day ahead overrode my exhaustion and forced me to rouse myself, get showered, dressed and then face the next daily challenge, which was often to, once again, open the daily post.

By the spring of 2021, I had somehow muddled through with all but one of my spreadsheet tasks. As far as the financial and administrative world was concerned, Greg had never existed.

Chapter Thirty-Eight

2021–2022
Humour in Everything

Without Greg's calming influence and support, I experienced renewed high anxiety levels with other new-found responsibilities over the forthcoming months. Greg may have tolerated my lacking IT skills, but he would have turned in his grave at my approach to home maintenance. Never wanting to take advantage of the time and kindness shown by my friends and neighbours, I often made futile attempts to carry out repairs myself instead of seeking help, which resulted in either damage, a bodged job or an augmentation of the original problem. Greg had been a patient, capable perfectionist whereas I was the complete opposite and, through incompetence, impatience and frustration, I made holes in walls that weren't meant to be there, blew fuses, pulled machinery apart that couldn't be put back together, burst water pipes and once carelessly sucked up some ill-placed nuts, bolts and washers, which I had removed with my best endeavours to clean out a blockage in my vacuum cleaner.

For the sake of my health and safety and the value of my property, I put an advertisement in the local newspaper for an odd job man. Greg had often given me well-meaning advice about being able to do things for myself and I could remember his words clearly: "You'll be sorry when I'm gone if you don't learn a bit of DIY or if you don't familiarise yourself with the equipment around the house." I had always responded with a rhetorical: "It won't be a problem; I will just get a 'new man' in!"

True to my words, I did what I had humorously threatened and the "new man" who responded to my advert was a chap called Paul. Paul was a trusty well-known handyman who lived locally and was only a phone call away. His first job was to teach me how to effortlessly use my TV and identify the correct remote controllers for the variety of equipment connected to it. With the arrival of spring 2022, Paul set himself the task of attending to my overgrown and unkempt garden, another job that had been Greg's responsibility and not mine.

Setting aside the sudden spurt of weeds, dead plants and grass as high as my birdbath in my garden, spring 2022 brought some glimmers of light for a better future. Following the successful programme of Covid-19 vaccinations, all the legal domestic Covid measures in England were lifted. With the suspension of all the isolation rules and new freedoms, I had no excuse now but to address the one remaining task on my spreadsheet. This task was the disposal of Greg's ashes.

***

I hadn't previously been able to part with the ashes, which stood in an urn on the floor in the corner of the man cave. I had sometimes shouted at the urn in moments of frustration with IT and household appliance failures, cursing my husband for leaving me, but, at other times, I had taken comfort from its presence and chatted to it amiably. Little had amused me in the two years since Greg had so tragically passed away and I had no expectations that the day I chose to say my final goodbye would turn out to be a memorably funny day and one that brought some all-important laughter back into my unhappy life. Someone once told me that there is humour in everything, even in life's darkest moments. That person was so very right.

Greg wasn't a religious man and wouldn't have wanted a fuss, so my plan was to scatter his ashes along a short length of one of his old cycling routes with my best friend, Anne, for company and then return the urn as a donation to the funeral home afterwards. I chose a pleasant sunny afternoon and picked Anne up from her home as she didn't drive. I drove to the spot where I had chosen to start our pilgrimage, with Anne, silently and solemnly sitting in the seat next to me, holding on to Greg's urn on her lap. Once we arrived at our destination, we exited the car and made our way along the track until I was ready to start the scattering. Anne unscrewed the lid off the urn and compassionately gave me the container. I smiled at her gratefully as I gently tipped it upside down and let all the ashes slowly drift away into the breeze as we strolled along. Our final goodbye only took a matter of minutes, a quiet time in which we respected each other's private thoughts. Once the urn was empty, I linked my arm with Anne's and we made our way back to the car.

When we arrived at our parking space, we realised that, at some point, Anne must have dropped the urn lid as, after a frantic search, we couldn't find it anywhere. We retraced our steps and an hour later, having located it lying in some short grass in the middle of the track, we returned to my car and set off for the funeral home with the urn intact. On the way, I couldn't resist ignoring the advice of my satnav, feeling sure that I knew the way back into Chittington better than it did and inevitably took a wrong turn on the outskirts of the town. This error resulted in us arriving in the centre just ten minutes before the funeral home closed for the day.

Car-parking spaces on the main high street were in short supply, so I parked in a very small space in between a huge oak tree on Anne's side of the car and a white transit van on mine. To be able to get out of the vehicle, I was obliged to park so close to the oak tree that Anne couldn't have exited the car on her side even if she had wanted to. This caused neither of us any concern as Anne didn't need to leave the vehicle and accompany me. I hurriedly set off with Greg's urn discreetly disguised in a supermarket plastic bag.

On my way back from the funeral home, after getting myself briefly lost in some side streets, and as I walked towards the car, I heard the sound of a car alarm going off and stopped in my tracks. I recognised the familiar noise and my face paled as the realisation dawned that I had, from force of habit, locked the car with Anne inside it. Eventually, her movement had triggered the alarm and as I approached closer, I saw passers-by stopping and curiously staring at the car, and some people were even peering in at my passenger through the front windscreen. Anne, forgetting the sobriety of our day, was furious when I unlocked the car and got in beside her.

'Where the "beep" have you been, Nolwen?' she demanded. (Anne didn't often swear.) 'Why on earth have you taken so long?' she scolded, which conjured up memories of my father telling me off after the outdoor market incident during my childhood, when I had taken too long on his errand due to my lack of sense of direction. 'The car alarm has been going off,' Anne continued to explain angrily, 'and all the people walking along the street have been stopping to gawk at me through the car window. Some have even been tapping on the windscreen, despite my waving and shooing them away. I've felt a right blithering idiot sitting here, helpless, and unable to get out of the car,' she added, with a scowl on her face.

Unusually for Anne, she remained hopping mad for the next few minutes. I, returning to the character of my former self, quickly saw the funny side of her situation and started to laugh unrestrainedly. My laugh was so infectious that after a few seconds of annoyed disbelief, Anne was unable to maintain her hostile admonitory stance and we laughed and laughed together uncontrollably until our stomachs ached. Anne hadn't been nimble enough to crawl over to the driver's side of the vehicle to get out and hadn't thought about trying to open her car door from the inside, which would have reset the alarm. Additionally, as she wasn't a driver, she was unfamiliar with the controls inside the vehicle. In her attempts to switch off the alarm, she had pressed every button, disengaged every switch and moved every lever she could possibly reach. Needless to say, we set off on our journey home to the onlookers' further amusement with the car lights on, windscreen wipers working at full speed and the tailgate fully open! Greg would have been pleased to know that a day that had started on such a solemn note had ended in fits of laughter, all because his wife had, as usual, lost her way and her trusty friend had been unable to keep hold of his urn lid.

Having completed my last bereavement task, I slowly began to consider my future. Although I was now free to travel abroad, I was not inclined to visit France without Greg, but the new freedom of travel after Covid did give me the welcome opportunity to visit Steffan in Norfolk occasionally and for him to visit me. I was also finally allowed to join in social activities with groups of friends and, to my unaccustomed delight, I received notification from the musical director of the Chittington and Welford Classical Voice Choir that rehearsals had recommenced for a forthcoming performance of Dvořák's "Stabat Mater" at the Royal Theatre in Bath. I jumped at the invitation to join in and found that rehearsing the music allowed me to shut myself off from the real world, albeit for a short period of time, and fully engross myself in the rhythms and harmonies of the music.

Additionally, Donna's bereavement counselling sessions resumed in a local community centre in Chittington, which, as I was now more confident in my ability to vocalise my experiences of bereavement, I decided to attend. I found comfort in listening and talking to people who had also lost wives, husbands or partners, and I became firm friends with some of the attendees outside of the formal gatherings. We met for a coffee and a chat at each other's homes and spoke together about the challenges of our lives and the future that lay ahead of us, providing mutual support.

When I did spend time at home alone, although my old culinary hobby was still apathetic, I resumed my enjoyment of books and was appreciative of being able to change channels and enjoy watching a variety of TV programmes, all thanks to the patient efforts of my "new man".

Chapter Thirty-Nine

2022–2026
Boris

Despite the positive turning point in my life after the scattering of Greg's ashes, and the Laurel and Hardy-like comedy show that took place in my car on the same day, there were certain times during my bereavement when the old cloak of loneliness I had experienced as a child again descended over my body and lowered my spirits. This cloak sadly wrapped itself around my shoulders at times when, under normal circumstances, I would have felt happy. It swathed my soul whenever the sun shined and the weather was warm enough to go for a walk or sit outside a café or bar to enjoy a view or to people-watch. These pastimes had, during our retirement, become a large part of Greg's and my recreational lives together, but when I attempted to do them alone, I found the experiences disheartening and difficult to enjoy. The feeling of loneliness and melancholy was even more prevalent whenever I returned to my silent empty house. At first, I avoided the summery weather and remained indoors, and I left a radio playing to welcome me home whenever I left the house, but I was soon to find a much better solution to my sentimental over-emotional dilemmas by actuating the love and attentions of a stranger. His name was Boris.

Purely by chance, I came across Boris at a converted community centre located in a town a few miles away from Chittington. Following some research, I found out that the centre had been redeveloped and then formally established to provide temporary shelter, care and rehabilitation for its residents with the goal of finding more suitable accommodation and placements elsewhere in the longer term. The organisation was part of a charitable trust and was called "The Welford Dog Rehoming Centre". It was run by a team of professionals that included a part-time vet, two managers and two administrators, and was supported by almost thirty volunteers who were fully trained canine carers.

A week later, I telephoned the centre and made an appointment to visit one Saturday afternoon after a choir rehearsal. By the afternoon of my visit, the weather had changed to become miserable, cold and gloomy, but my mood was buoyant and I was quite excited as I wandered around the various-sized dog enclosures, which were located in the grounds of the old Welford Community Centre. Each of the enclosures contained a kennel for shelter and either a couple of dogs or one dog on its own.

Within a short time, I was determined to adopt and provide a loving home for at least one of the abandoned animals. After much deliberation, I chose what could only be described as a golden retriever/spaniel cross-breed with a scruffy soft blond-coloured coat, deep sorrowful brown eyes and long ears, who was the size of a springer spaniel. The carer who introduced me to Boris had given him his name on account of the straw-coloured unruly mass of fluffy fur that stuck out in all directions on the top of his rather large head. She explained that he was very friendly but had been with them for a while, because, at already nine years old, nobody really wanted him. After answering a series of questions about my personal circumstances, I explained that as I was close to seventy, Boris's age suited my probable lifespan and my capabilities perfectly. After accepting some advisory leaflets and agreeing to a home visit by one of the adoption support volunteers, it was agreed that I could pick Boris up a week later.

Boris and I got on extremely well. He was wonderful company and, although not fully trained, his mature years meant he was calm, loved a cuddle and was usually compliant and well behaved. We did have a temporary battle about which "seat" Boris should take in *my* house, but he won by a narrow margin and took the largest, softest armchair in the front row opposite my TV. The other seat, which had been Greg's favourite, was now mine.

Boris was rather greedy and would do absolutely anything for a dog biscuit, even if this meant standing on his head or attempting to do a sideways roly-poly. He was also very funny and his antics brought laughter back into a house that had been sad and unhappy for, what seemed to be, a very long time. There was one antic in particular that regularly reduced me to tears of laughter and which had many of my visitors in hysterics. This involved Boris's favourite bin trick. Boris took a liking to the bin that sat in my bathroom, as he had once found a boiled sweet paper in it. It was a small round bin, made of plastic, with a convenient hole in the lid for rubbish to be easily popped through. The lid was detachable and could be taken off with minimum effort for convenient emptying of the bin's contents. Boris, recognising the squeak of the bathroom door whenever it opened, and hoping the bin might just possibly contain something edible, would rush past me into the bathroom and promptly push his large head through the hole in the lid, attempting to retrieve anything in reach that might be of interest. Unfortunately, when he tried to pull his head out, the detachable lid came with it and then sat comfortably on his head like an old-fashioned motorcycle rider's crash helmet. With his graceless and gawky demeanour, he would then parade around the house, unable to get the lid off, and resigned himself to being a bumbling and clumsy clown, seemingly oblivious to the amusing spectacle he presented.

Apart from being a greedy dog who liked to wear a crash helmet, Boris was a wonderful companion and helped me through the next few years of my life. Having responsibility for him began to take away the last remaining negative emotions of loneliness and grief that I still experienced at specific times. We went out for regular walks, rain or shine, and on sunny days, we sat together outdoors and people-watched. Passers-by could not resist stopping and taking the opportunity to chat and shake a paw with Boris, while I, being just his aide, smiled politely and patted his large, scruffy head. At home, he was a good listener and unwittingly helped with my decision-making and eased my frustrations. Most importantly, he relied on me, he needed me and he gave me a lovely reason to return home.

At first, my grief had been unbearable, but over the years, with Donna's help, Boris's faithful companionship, my odd job man and the tremendous support of Steffan, my friends and my neighbours, the pain eased and I learned to live without my beloved husband. Greg had been my first love and I never fully came to terms with his death, but I had finally adjusted to a different life. Boris and I grew old together until, at the ripe old age of thirteen, when I had just celebrated my seventy-first birthday, he glanced up at me from his favourite seat and, with a heavy sigh, closed his eyes and passed away peacefully. At this point, I made the decision to prepare for the next stage in my life.

Chapter Forty

2026–2033
Michael and Molly

It took some time of contemplation and decision-making before I made some positive moves to enable the last step change in my life. With no Boris to keep me company, and never having been a person who enjoyed her own company, I attempted firstly to find an alternative companion of the opposite sex. However, this companionship wasn't easy to find and Boris had set a high bar. I no longer participated in the bereavement counselling sessions, so the only real opportunity to meet eligible gentlemen was at my choir rehearsals. I was fussy, though; the choice of eligible men was limited and my preferences and needs had evolved over time. After two liaisons, which went well until there was physical contact – my body stiffened unresponsively and I felt inclined to reject the proffered overtures – I resigned myself, at least for a while, to staying single.

As my twilight years approached, and with no companionship at home to stimulate conversation, my mind grew lazy and I became aware that my memory was beginning to fail me. Before Boris had died, I had left him tied up outside my local newsagents on two occasions and had come home without him. He hadn't made a sound as I walked past him with my mind on other things, but must have just looked on, wondering when he would be collected. I had also fed him his evening meal twice (not that he minded) on more than one occasion. I noticed that I repeatedly left lights on, doors unlocked and cupboard doors and drawers open, and I began to forget some of the French vocabulary I had taken great pains to learn over my retirement years. I also made mistakes with appointment dates and other timings. I wasn't overly worried about my forgetfulness, putting most of it down to lack of concentration, as even as a child, I had often been told off for daydreaming and repeatedly advised to focus on the task in hand by my father. I guessed that little had changed. Eventually, though, after reading an article in the newspaper about dementia and the importance of early diagnosis, I decided to make an appointment with my doctor who gave me a memory test.

The first question asked of me was, 'Do you know what year it is?'

Unbelievably, even to me, as I realised my mistake as soon as I had said it, I replied, 'Yes, it's 1926.'

My doctor looked up from his test sheet with shock and amazement written all over his face. I quickly rescued the situation and admitted my mistake, advising him that he need not call in the "men with white coats" just yet, as I had just been nervous and the year was actually 2026.

He gave me the benefit of the doubt and we moved on. I made a few more errors in the test, which I was unable to talk my way out of, so it was agreed that I should have a CT and MRI scan and be referred to Wiltshire's Memory Assessment Service. I was ultimately prescribed some medication to help with, what was diagnosed as, a rare brain disorder similar to dementia, which, fortunately for me, was still in its mild stage. The condition was known as zibendrer disease and I was advised to enrol for some cognitive stimulation therapy.

The therapy revealed that I was an interesting case and, after being reassured that experimental treatments to better slow the progress of the disease were advancing well, I was asked if I would be willing to participate in some medical trials. The trials were scheduled to begin in four to five years' time and my participation was offered on the basis that my health progressed in line with expectations. I signed up to participate without hesitation. A day or so later, I was requested to write a detailed resume of my life and to provide a description of my personality, which I completed quickly with the help of my therapist. She advised that this document would be held on record and would be referred to during and after the trials.

The diagnosis, although not life-changing at the time, prompted me to seriously consider my future. I concluded that I would have only limited support in old age as I had no relatives living close by and most of my friends and neighbours were of a similar age to me. I concluded that the best solution would be to research the availability and suitability of residential care homes and then sell my house. At the time, I was relatively young, enjoyed independent living and was very mobile, but I knew that I needed to consider the potential risk of further memory loss and the possibility of being unable to care for myself in the future. I didn't rush into anything and it took almost another year of research before I eventually decided upon the best solution to cater for my future needs.

Having identified two assisted living apartments for sale in my local area, both of which suited my needs, and while I still had mobility and my faculties, I resolved to act swiftly to register my interest and I put my house on the market. Both apartments I had chosen were located in retirement villages not far from my home and were future-proofed with co-located care homes advertising nursing and dementia care.

The house-selling process, as I anticipated, was problematic and I lost out on one of the village options due to an unresolvable break in the property chain. Fortunately, the second was still available when contracts were exchanged and before the completions. I gave my friends, neighbours and my odd job man "first dibs" on furniture and other items, such as Greg's tools, which could not be taken to my new home for practical reasons. Other items were collected by a local animal charity. With the help of Anne and John's daughter, Lizzie, I packed up all my clothes and treasured personal possessions and then set off on a short but exciting journey, which was the preface to the final step change in my life.

I suffered what was to be my last TGA episode on the day of the house move. It began when I took a final look around the house Greg and I had designed and built together some twenty years previously. As usual, the lost memories came flooding back during the night when I awoke to find myself in my new apartment. I reran the events of the previous day, which included handing over my house keys to my solicitor, the journey by car to the retirement village, and the introductory tour of my new home and meeting its residents. Reflecting on the positive times in my childhood, my time in the WRAF and MINS, Greg and our wonderful holidays together, I soon drifted back into a deep, relaxing sleep with no regrets about my latest decision.

***

I enjoyed living semi-independently, with even my previously latent anxiety confined to ancient history. I lived in my own apartment for the next three years, but never relishing too much of my own company, I spent most of my days and evenings in the easily accessible communal areas of the village's main residential hall – if I had no guests or planned "away days" to meet up with friends. This gave me the opportunity to meet new people and to join in the organised events and activities. In the main hall, there was a coffee lounge, a bar/bistro and a wonderful restaurant where I could, if I wished, join other residents for the three main meals of the day. Outside of the hall, there were beautifully landscaped grounds, with comfortable seats and picnic tables, where I could sit with good company and listen to the birdsong, while daydreaming and taking advantage of the sunny days I had learned to love again.

It was during my first, rather hesitant visit to the communal restaurant that I met a set of elderly twins called Michael and Molly. The restaurant was nowhere near the size of the airmen's mess where I had become so disorientated during my WRAF basic training, but was still large and noisy with the clattering of crockery, cutlery and voices. A lady called Natalie, who I soon found out was one of the loveliest carers in the retirement village, spotted my discomfort as I stood at the restaurant entrance and led me into the room. She then introduced me to the couple, who sat together around a table normally intended for four. The table was situated in the corner of the restaurant, next to a large window overlooking the gardens, and I knew that it would be easy for me to find if I chose to sit there again. Michael and Molly warmed to my Cheshire Cat smile, which had laid dormant in recent years, and were both kind and welcoming and had no objections to my joining them. From that day on, I sat with these lovely twins for my lunch and evening meal most days and, following their insistent invitations, joined them whenever they sat in the gardens, popped into the communal bar/bistro or participated in organised games.

Molly and Michael, more often just referred to as "the twins", were real characters and were very popular with the care home staff and the residents. While Michael, a former doctor, was reserved and clever, Molly was a natural comedienne, whose sense of fun had not diminished with age. She spent much of her day tormenting her twin brother or teasing the staff and other residents and usually managed to rope me into her shenanigans. As time passed, and I also became conjoined with Molly and Michael, the "twins" label was lost and, for the second time in my life, I became part of what was then known around the village as "The Trio". This time, though, there were no musical performances but lots of fun and laughter.

As time went by, I noticed that there were some ungrateful and miserable residents who were often rude or impolite to the people they needed and relied on most – the cooks, the cleaners, the servers and the care assistants. I referred to them as "the complainers". Not wanting to be one of their number and remembering the lessons of the personal development plan I had composed in my youth, I made, what did not always come naturally to me after Greg's death, a conscious effort to be as equally nice to them as I was to all of the other residents, as I had not lost that old established yearning to be liked.

My efforts to be nice were successful, except for the day when I was forced to defend myself after being called "an intruder" by one of the complainers, who accused me of sitting in what he termed "his" lounge chair. For the most part, I forgot all about the incident, but I had his card marked. It later turned out that he apparently respected my requital and decided that he rather liked me!

In addition to enjoying Molly and Michael's company most days, I learnt to enjoy the pleasant communal atmosphere of the village as a whole. The meals in the restaurant were first class. Lots of people sat together chatting convivially in the bar/bistro most evenings, although seldom beyond 9pm when sleep beckoned. And of course, all the daily organised activities brought everyone together. Even the complainers who, after being subjected to Molly's good-humoured chastisements, relented and joined everyone to participate in the bingo sessions and quiz nights. The carers worked very hard, often in difficult circumstances, and despite sometimes having to manage the more "difficult" personalities, they were always kind and thoughtful. I grew particularly fond of Natalie, who had first introduced me to the twins and who seemed to endear herself to "The Trio". Whenever she had some spare time, Natalie would join us for a chat and was interested to hear about "the old times" and our backgrounds and life histories.

***

Over time, Michael, Molly and I became very close – or, to be more specific, Michael and I did. Michael often dropped an arm across my shoulders as he leaned over the back of my chair to invite me to join him and his sister, who sometimes settled themselves in another part of the main hall or the garden. Unlike the two liaisons I had shunned before I moved into the village, I did not flinch at Michael's touch and found his contact warm and comforting. His arm around me, albeit briefly, felt strong and protective and his masculinity appealingly sent a shiver of forgotten pleasure down my spine. As Michael grew braver, as well as kissing his twin sister before retiring for the night, he also put his hands on my shoulders and dropped a kiss onto my cheek. This brought an approving smirk and knowing expression to Molly's face, which she shared only with me. Michael and I began to spend more time alone together and I noticed that Molly was often too busy having her hair styled, listening to her radio in her room or participating in a crochet and knitting class to "play gooseberry"!

Michael and I couldn't really leave the village and go on "dates", so instead, we became more acquainted by visiting the village bar/bistro, where we often chatted amiably over an evening meal. Unexpectedly but appreciatively, we were, on our arrival, always shown to a table set for two, which was tucked away in a discreet low-lit corner of the room. We suspected with amusement that the table's position was engineered by Natalie and Molly, with the support of the bistro manager, as these tables were normally set for four or more and situated in the centre of the room.

It soon became apparent that, coincidentally, Michael and I had more in common than we had first thought. I was aware that he had been a doctor before he retired, but was delighted to establish that he had been a military physician and had served for almost thirty years in the Royal Army Medical Corps, both in the field and in military hospitals, which gave us lots to talk about. He also shared my love of music and modestly told me that before his hands had become partially crippled by arthritis, he had played both the violin and clarinet in a national youth orchestra as a teenager and later in the BBC Philharmonic Orchestra on a part-time basis, as and when his career allowed. Although I spoke to him at length about my years in the WRAF and my time in MINS, I divulged only that I had competed as a singer in many Welsh *eisteddfods* as a child and had won a few silver cups. I did not want to bring sadness into our conversations by revealing how my lack of self-confidence and anxieties had resulted in such wasted talent.

I found Michael to be charming and his personality engaging and personable. We were too old to fall in love, but we did fall into a deep pool of fondness. I found him to be physically attractive enough to enjoy his arm around my shoulders when he wished to speak to me and I appreciated his brotherly goodnight kiss. I also left my hand in place when he covered it with his, as we sat at our discreet bistro table or alone at a picnic table in the village grounds on a bright, sunny summer's day.

***

More often than not, Michael would knock at my apartment door mid-morning to let me know his and Molly's plans for the day and where we could meet up. Not being a morning person, I never joined them for breakfast, but ate some kindly delivered croissants and fruit in my apartment at leisure once I had roused myself from my bed.

One morning, in the middle of December, Michael knocked at my door as usual, but, to his surprise, no one answered. He peered through my windows, but I was nowhere in sight and there was no reply to his call through my letterbox. Michael made his way back to the main hall as fast as his arthritic hips would allow and, after searching around for me to no avail, he reported my strange disappearance to the village manager. Half an hour later, a carer found me wondering around in the garden, with no coat on and my hair and clothes damp from the drizzle that had set in for the day.

'What are you doing out here, Nolwen?' the carer asked softly as he approached me slowly.

It seemed as though his words brought me back to the present, but I still felt confused and didn't recognise who he was at first.

'I am looking for my boxer dogs, but they are nowhere to be found.' The carer nodded knowingly, put his arm around my shoulders and we walked back into the warmth of the main hall together, where I gratefully accepted a cup of hot tea.

Over the next few weeks, my carers and Michael and Molly noticed that I wasn't myself. I kept leaving things behind on chairs I had vacated and often forgot our agreed rendezvous points and even the events of the day. Items weren't where they should be in my apartment, which was often left unlocked, and lights regularly shone from the windows when I wasn't at home. After finding my shower running one afternoon, Natalie sat next to me in my apartment and asked if we could have a chat.

'Nolwen,' she said kindly. 'I think you probably know that you are becoming very forgetful these days. Would you consider leaving your apartment now and moving into Goldfinch Wing in the main residential home, where I and the other carers can take better care of you?'

I thought carefully about her words and asked, 'Did I leave my shower running today?'

'Yes,' Natalie replied, 'I am afraid you did and not for the first time.'

'Then I think I had better move into the main residential home with Molly and Michael,' I replied.

The following week, Natalie reminded me that some years previously I had agreed to participate in some medical trials and enquired whether I would still like to get involved in them. I agreed without hesitation and a few days later was prescribed some special trial drugs, which we hoped would stem the decline of my memory significantly. At the same time, with the help of willing carers and Lizzie, who came to see me from time to time without her parents, who, like me, had moved into a residential home, I sifted through my treasured possessions and put aside a huge stack of photo albums, which I was determined to take with me when I moved. Together, we made the necessary decisions on which of the other items I would have space for in my new single room accommodation and which items I would have to leave behind. Lizzie assured me that the possessions I had discarded would be passed onto my brother, Steffan, and his family where they would be stored away safely. I was relieved to leave my apartment, as deep down I knew that I could no longer cope with only limited daily care.

***

I was very happy living in the Goldfinch Wing of the main residential care home and discreetly enjoyed some more "mature" tender moments with Michael. Molly kept me amused and I spent most of my days relaxing in a comfy lounge chair, either daydreaming or taking an interest in the conversations between fellow residents, including the small group of complainers. When alone in my room, I usually kept myself occupied by watching the television or leafing through the stack of photo albums I kept in my room cupboard. The photographs brought back many fond memories. Meanwhile, my trial drugs worked well, although at times, I was very aware that my memory on some days in my daily life was far better than others.

It seemed like a couple of years later when Natalie came and sat down next to me on my bed, before tucking me up for the night. She compassionately explained that the next morning, I would be moving into Swallow Wing, which was the secure wing of the home, because I had resumed my garden wanderings, even during the night, and the care home feared that they were unable to keep me safe. She also explained that despite my medication, I was experiencing many days when I became very muddled and there were some days when I had no memory at all. Natalie added kindly that she would continue to be my carer in the new wing and promised that she would either accompany me back to Goldfinch Wing to visit my friends, or ensure that Molly and Michael were able to drop in to see me whenever I was well.

I can recall that Natalie and the other carers referred to my new home as "Swallow Wing", which, I thought at the time, was a rather nice name. I can't remember much of my time there, but I think I was reasonably content in my new surroundings. On saying that, I can recollect complaining on one Saturday afternoon that Molly and Michael hadn't come to see me for many months and that I felt rather cross about that. I also recall that one of the patient and hard-working carers tried to convince me that the twins had visited me the day before, but I refused to believe her. Furthermore, I can also recollect that, one morning, I woke up in what I thought was a different room to mine and was convinced that I had moved rooms for a second time during the night. I remember feeling confused until I was reassured by someone, who I think might have been a doctor, that I was safe and sound in what was, without doubt, my own room.

Convinced that I had received no visits from my friends for a long time, I attempted to continue my memoir, filling in my daily diary and reading my books to offset this disappointment, but I struggled. I recollect that I consoled myself with thoughts of Natalie popping in, so that we could reminisce over my photo albums. I am told we did this every day, yet when I cast my mind back, I feel sure we only looked at them on Mondays. When I really force my brain to work harder and concentrate fully, I have a vague memory of my favourite carer telling me that she enjoyed looking at my pictures on what she referred to as my "good days", but I am baffled as to what she meant by "good days". I am sure she explained everything about them to me, but, I must admit, I can't remember what she said. I have become very forgetful these days.

If I fight really hard to focus my mind, just as my father advised me to do when I was a child, I can visualise Natalie coming into my room on one particular bright and sunny day, grabbing some albums from my cupboard and settling herself down on a chair beside my bed. The last clear memory I have before drinking my mid-morning cup of tea with her on that day is that our chatter was interrupted by a tap on the door and, to my delight and surprise, who should walk in but my dear friends, Molly and Michael.

Part Two

CHAPTER FORTY-ONE

2033
Natalie

My name is Natalie Roberts and I work in Nolwen's Village Residential Care Home. I have worked in the health and social care environment for fifteen years and have successfully completed various training courses on the awareness of dementia and general dementia care. I became Nolwen's principal carer when she moved from her village apartment to the co-located village care home and I decided that I would like to complete her life story, as this is something Nolwen is now sadly unable to do for herself.

To give you some background information, in addition to some assisted living apartments where people live semi-independently with limited care in the village, there is also a co-located residential care home. There are two wings attached to the main communal hall: Goldfinch Wing, which is a dual care and nursing home, and Swallow Wing, which offers comfortable, safe and secure specialist dementia care.

Nolwen had moved into a village apartment after being diagnosed with a very rare brain condition. Her illness was called zibendrer disease. Her symptoms were similar to mild dementia and these had apparently prompted her to consider her future in old age. However, after some years, it was noticed that the disease was progressing and that Nolwen had started to become more forgetful and confused. When I thought the time was right, I gently suggested to her that she might like to consider leaving her apartment and moving into Goldfinch Wing, where I explained that carers, including myself, would be on hand to take better care of her. Nolwen, aware that her memory was failing her, agreed immediately to the move.

Personally, I was confident that the relocation held no fears for Nolwen, as she had spent most of her days in the main residential home anyway and it had become a familiar space. Additionally, she had become very friendly with a set of twins called Molly and Michael, who also lived in the home. Nolwen had often visited Molly in her ensuite room, which was spacious and bright, and had a large feature window with views over the gardens, so she knew exactly what to expect.

Just before the move took place, the village manager advised me that he had it on record that Nolwen had agreed to taking part in some medical trials some years ago when she was first diagnosed with her brain disorder. We sought advice from her doctor, who agreed the time was right for her to begin the trials, and once it was established that Nolwen still wished to participate, the medical trials research team was contacted. The team provided me with the necessary support and guidance I needed and gave the permission for the trials to begin. It was explained to Nolwen that any prescribed standard medication for sufferers of her disease would be replaced by trial drugs and that I had been tasked with monitoring her closely and maintaining records of her daily life.

Nolwen was delighted to hear that "her favourite carer, Natalie" was the person nominated to look after her on a one-to-one basis and that it would be me who was responsible for maintaining records of her daily activities and state of mind for the research team. Surprisingly unconcerned, Nolwen asked me if Michael, as her confidant, could join us whenever I was making up my notes about her condition. She advised me that being a retired military doctor, and her friend, he was interested in understanding the effects of the trial medication and yearned to learn more about his friend's life history. After consulting with the research team, we all readily agreed to her request, seeing Michael's support as being helpful and comforting. This all took place at the beginning of September 2031.

I was pleased to see that Nolwen was very comfortable and content when she first left her apartment and moved into Goldfinch Wing. Her trial drugs seemed to work as expected and she was well enough to enjoy many organised activities and the daily company of her close friends, Michael and Molly. Spurred on by mischievous Molly, she maintained her sense of humour and spent most of her days relaxing in a comfy lounge chair, either daydreaming or listening to the chatter of her carers and fellow residents.

However, after about two years of "quality" time,

various carers noticed that Nolwen's memory had deteriorated and I observed that there were days where her confusion was becoming steadily worse. In time, her condition became so bad that, with the agreement of her doctor, we decided that we were unable to provide her with the care she needed in Goldfinch Wing. Following that decision, I sat next to Nolwen on her bed one evening and explained gently that as she had managed to evade the carers, had successfully vacated the residential home a couple of times in the middle of the night and had also been aggressive with one of the residents who she sat next to in the communal lounge, it was in her own interests to move over to Swallow Wing. Nolwen couldn't remember her garden wanderings, but admitted that she had shouted at a resident and explained that the guilty party was a tall, well-built man who had towered over her, had been teasing her and had, for some unfathomable and unlikely reason, which I never really got to the bottom of, called her "Frankie Gosling". None of the carers at the time had a clue what a "Frankie Gosling" was and were surprised at the untypical strength of character demonstrated by Nolwen that day. All I could do was to promise her that I would tick the nasty man off.

Just as Nolwen had readily agreed to move out of her assisted living apartment, she trusted my judgement and nodded her head, agreeing that the move was a good idea. I assured her that I would still look after her and that when she was well enough, I would bring her back to Goldfinch Wing to visit Michael and Molly, or they would visit her in Swallow Wing. I informed the medical trials research team, Nolwen's doctor and my manager of our decision and I was requested to keep the research team informed about Nolwen's progress and to continue maintaining my daily records.

***

It wasn't long after moving Nolwen into Swallow Wing that I noted her state of mind had become very changeable. I became aware that she had entered a memory cycle of what I termed "good days", "muddled days" and "forgotten days". Nolwen's good and muddled days tended to come in fours, followed by a single completely forgotten day. She was still able to enjoy her life to a degree, as on every good day, she either spent time with Molly and Michael in Goldfinch Wing or, alternatively, the twins accompanied me to visit her. During her muddled days, though, she lived in her own confused world and engaged in some strange activities and on her "forgotten days" spent her time mainly in her bed, oblivious to her surroundings. Bizarrely, on her good days, she could recollect some of the strange activities she carried out during her muddled days and support these memories, often with sound reasoning. With some gentle probing and careful listening, Michael and I were usually able to piece together what lay behind these strange actions, disorganised thoughts, presumed delusions and her emotional reactions.

I soon understood that when she curiously chatted to a friend called Ninan, who sometimes sat next to her, she was, in fact, chatting to an imaginary friend of the same name, who had kept her company during some of her lonely childhood days. If she stood at a window, waving goodbye when there was no one to wave to, she explained that in her mind, on the muddled day, she had been waving to her father, who she had felt sure was abandoning her to find a new job, then followed this with the true story of how and why her family had moved from one area of Wales to another.

Sometimes Nolwen pulled her bedding off her bed and ran her hands over her mattress, while saying, 'I am a good girl,' or she laid out some diligently folded garments including her underwear, skirts and sweaters on the top of the mattress and then piled up her bedding in a rough stack on her room floor. On a good day, after some pondering, she evaded an explanation about the "good girl" words, but explained that when she felt muddled, she must have been reliving her WRAF basic training days and had been preparing for daily inspections. Michael was able to corroborate this story based on his own military career and explained to me that military uniform was often inspected and that the pile of sheets and blankets Nolwen had placed in a rough square shape on the floor of her bedroom was an attempt to build a military bed pack, a skill she had clearly lost touch with long before her zibendrer disease days.

Neither of us had any idea that Nolwen spoke French until, during one of her muddled days, she slipped from English to French quite readily, baffling the carers, who had no idea what on earth she was talking about.

When, during her good days, Michael and I were, as

usual, attempting to find the underlying cause of Nolwen's strange actions and activities, we usually found her mind to be sharp and her memory reliable. She was able to respond easily and clearly to my daily memory tests and vividly remembered events and the circumstances that had shaped her life and character. She was always keen to share her recollections with the two of us over a cup of tea or coffee. We were both particularly surprised to hear about her directional dyslexia, which I had never heard of and which we thought might have been made worse by her condition, as she was becoming more and more disorientated in what had been very familiar surroundings. Her revelation led to tales of her getting lost throughout her life and her escapades on the parade square when she had first joined the WRAF. From a photograph of Nolwen in her uniform, which showed her rank, I knew that she had somehow overcome this disorder and had been successful in her chosen career.

Nolwen also briefly told us about the death of her husband and parents and, more interestingly, her mother-in-law. She tried to explain how she had suffered what she referred to as a TGA where she had lost all memories of that lady's funeral until many hours later when the memories came flooding back. Once I had established from her doctor's records that Nolwen had indeed suffered from transient global amnesia (TGA) and I understood the symptoms, I added this disorder and her directional dyslexia to my medical trial records.

Eventually, the cycle of good and muddled days changed, and the muddled days began to take over. Nolwen became unable to explain to Michael and me about her actions and thoughts during the latter, so all I could do was to make a record of the conversations she held with imaginary people and note her mood. I could determine this from her musical preferences, which would range from a strange chant about "Nolwen being a pig" to rather loud renderings of a range of joyful classical pieces.

I was totally baffled by Nolwen's familiarity with such a wide range of classical music, so I typed her name into my computer search engine, which brought up a connection with a Mr Mike Burnley and a Mr Joseph Smythe. To my surprise, I found out that Nolwen had been the contralto singer in a musical trio that had performed in some of the UK's best venues and which had been the subject of great reviews. Nolwen had never disclosed anything about a singing career, but I established that she had given up singing due to under-confidence and anxiety. I presumed the "Nolwen being a pig" chant was connected to bullying at school.

I never contradicted Nolwen's divagations or verbal rationale when her disease assumed control of her actions, but joined in her meanderings, as if I was there understanding or enjoying the moment with her. Additionally, instead of dissuading her from her efforts to resolve any of her occasional imaginary problems, particularly when she seemed to be frantically searching for something or somewhere in vain, I supported her as if her objectives were real. I found this approach reduced her anxiety and it kept her calm. I always assured her that I was there to help her with her search and that the item or place she was looking for would soon be found. This approach brought her immediate relief.

For the most part, Nolwen's days in Swallow Wing seemed to be happy and she always smiled broadly, almost like the proverbial Cheshire Cat, when she caught sight of me (although she was very irritable whenever she mislaid her spectacles, declaring that she was completely blind without them). If she appeared anxious or sad, I drew her out of these moods by sitting next to her and leafing through the mountain of photograph albums she stored in her locker. All the photographs were captioned with place names and dates, which established that Nolwen and her husband had been very happily married and had travelled the world together just before and during her retirement.

Through the course of my monitoring and recording, I concluded that Nolwen had not only tolerated impaired eyesight, TGA episodes and directional dyslexia, but had also either lived with, or subsequently defeated, many negative and – at the time – stigmatised emotions, which had possibly been spawned during a turbulent childhood or her adolescent years. These emotions included sorrow, loneliness, abandonment, low self-esteem, guilt and anxiety. I wondered if Nolwen could have been spared her emotional turmoil if she had received positive reassurance from her parents and teachers. I felt sure though, that this turmoil must have been balanced later in her life by her happiness with her husband, her successes in the WRAF and her singing achievements. Some of these emotions re-emerged to an extent as her illness progressed and I recorded them. I wondered whether there was any connection between her TGA episodes and her memory loss in old age. I also noted from other carer's records in Swallow Wing that they had to ensure that a low light was left on in Nolwen's bedroom and that her door was kept ajar every night. Nolwen had become terrified of the dark and confinement. I added "fear" to my list of her emotions, but never established what had triggered this.

Something else I noted was that Nolwen spent a lot of time in what seemed like a contented dreamlike state and that she appeared to have the ability to switch quite readily from one personality to another, which was baffling.

Although not professionally qualified to conclude formally, I judged that, overall, Nolwen had fared better on the trial medication than without it. As the dosage was increased, her good days had been extended, her forgotten days were reduced and she had been able, for some time, to make sense of her muddled days. The latter meant that I could support her with what previously I would have ignored as being nonsensical delusional activities. Of course, alongside these cycles, there were, on occasions, the traditional symptoms of zibendrer disease, such as disruptions to her sleeping patterns, a short attention span and difficulties with reading, writing or getting herself dressed, but Nolwen was fortunate in that the trial medication had clearly been successful in staving off some of these symptoms for a good length of time.

Apart from the term "Frankie Gosling", there was only one other niggling piece of Nolwen's life jigsaw, which she spoke about often during the later days of her illness, but which neither Michael or myself understood, and that was what her relationship had been with, or how she had come to meet, former Prime Minister Boris Johnson, who apparently was a motorcycle enthusiast.

In the autumn of 2033, just after Nolwen's seventy-seventh birthday, I had been sitting listening to her slowly weakening chatter when we were interrupted by a tap on the door. We stopped talking and I got up from my chair as Nolwen's friends, Molly and Michael, walked cautiously and quietly into the room. Nolwen was lying down comfortably with her arms each side of her now frail body, but looked up at them happily as they made their way nearer to her. She flapped her hands, indicating that the twins should each walk to the left and right side of her bed. Michael walked to her right and held her hand; Molly did the same on the opposite side of the bed. That moment was very special to all of us and I smiled reassuringly at Nolwen from the corner of the room. After shifting her gaze from the twins towards me, she returned my smile and nodded her head gently, which I read to be a sign of her appreciation and contentment.

'They are here!' she said. 'They must still like me!'

That day was the last of Nolwen's "good days".

Nolwen passed away peacefully in her sleep some months later and I filed my records and report with the medical trials research team.

ABOUT THE AUTHOR

Nolwen Jones was born in a remote seaside town. At the age of seventeen, she joined the WRAF and completed 23 years' service. She later worked for a large corporate company where she wrote many business documents, but now has the time to write books for pure enjoyment and for the pleasure they bring to others. Happily married, she has travelled the world with her husband. Though they have lived contentedly in Gloucestershire for many years, her heart will always lie in the country of her birth, Wales.

This book is printed on paper from sustainable sources managed under the Forest Stewardship Council (FSC) scheme.

It has been printed in the UK to reduce transportation miles and their impact upon the environment.

For every new title that Troubador publishes, we plant a tree to offset CO_2, partnering with the More Trees scheme.

For more about how Troubador offsets its environmental impact, see www.troubador.co.uk/sustainability-and-community